Me and Caesar

The Lost* Chronicle

*Also, perhaps accurate

John Hoffman

ACKNOWLEDGEMENTS

Many of these pages are about family of one kind or another and building
relationships. To Mary Jo, Mike, Mom, Dad and everyone else who
encouraged me to keep pushing Caesar along and provided such invaluable
thoughts and help, there's an old Latin expression that seems just right:
"No one learns except by friendship." To all of you.

Special thanks to Mike Mikottis for the stellar cover art.

John Hoffman

The First Scroll

MISSION

As he stood there in line trying to choose between the fava bean salad or the roast vulture plate – fava bean or roast vulture, fava or vulture; both options seemed to Paul like too much to eat, even after nothing to eat for so long; fava vulture – at just this moment of decision for Paul, there was, in a suite of upper-middle management offices five floors above, an "Approved" stamp about to fall upon a work order of arguably alarming distinctiveness.

Priority: Urgent.
Send designated employee immediately. Assignment will offer significant hazards – note, however, employee is currently rated as *Remarkably Expendable.*

Special Orders:
1. Unusual nature of assignment can be expected to measurably diminish lifespan and/or net number of functioning limbs of

designated employee. Strictly as a precautionary measure therefore, Assistant Accountant recommends eliminating all anticipated future payroll costs for this assigned individual. Savings from any freed-up costs are to be used to offset expenses of Garment Rack Replacement program in executive foyer. (Let's try to buy one with big enough hat hooks this time.)

2. Resistance not a concern. Recurring appearance of several terms in designated employee's personnel records – e.g. "visible but muffled palpitations," "notably imperceptible" and "mumbled something during a fidget" – offer assurance that he will not protest assignment. He is sufficiently pliable. Still, must not be told of dangers he will face from persons of supreme authority, nor who selected him specifically for task.

3. If in some way he completes task safely, may be offered up to 15 minutes extra comp time, or surplus promotional company beverage coasters (set of four) from the shipment that was over-ordered. At discretion of Shift Supervisor.

Assignment No: 15-753-JC
Authorized by: Claudius Lucius Trebonius

———

Three of his co-workers, meantime, had stepped in front of Paul. This circumstance occurred not so much because Paul had paused at the item board to look at his choices or even out of the common brutishness of human society. This likely owed more to Paul's generally unobtruding spirit and his modest build, which, in social settings, often caused a somewhat pronounced sense of absence to envelop him. He simply went not noticed.

No offense by his co-workers probably was intended, and he took none. These things just tended to happen. Indeed such incidents often served as small but meaningful occasions of relief for Paul, as they helped him to achieve his steadfast and lifelong ambition: Not being involved.

Yet he was about ready to move now.

Paul had decided against both the lunch specials. Maybe just a little pita pocket or some soup instead. For one thing, the lunch specials cost a lot, which would leave no money for dinner, to help out his addled mother or much else. They really were usually too filling anyway, regardless of how bare the stomach's been feeling for the past couple days. And any second he could be directed to dart off again to only-the-immortal-gods-knew-where. Yes, something little. Going smaller suited Paul. It probably made more sense, he thought.

This occasion was to be the last, for a very long time, in which Paul would make a decision for himself of any kind of consequence.

Unearthing the
Lost Chronicle of Rome

A note from the editors of
The *Told-You-So* History Series

It is almost one hundred years ago.
Europe and portions of North America are enjoying a rather satisfying summer: An okay amount of humidity, about the right number of pool party invites, some well thought-of footwear sales, the suitable level of typhus. The season, in sum, feels pleasant and relaxed.

It is amid these easygoing conditions that an astonishing discovery grips the world's imagination.

Enjoying the first swallow of its morning coffee in a late August, the public snapped opened up its early edition newspapers. Banner headlines proclaimed the revelation in tall, broad font: Three buried calfskin scrolls, just pulled out of the earth by a startled road crew. They allegedly contained an unthinkable historical find. Nothing less than the only direct account to one of the most consequential moments in the story of humanity.

It was said the three scrolls had been buried away 2,000 years earlier. They offered a firsthand telling of the upheaval around the assassination of Julius Caesar, tumults that convulsed an empire and indeed shaped who we are today. They presented something curious, too. They purportedly told the unexpected saga of an ill-fated lone citizen who found himself increasingly thrust into the middle of the most infamous conspiracy ever.

So astounding was the news that the international reaction would soon come to be known as The Grand Collective Spit Take of 1921.

A typical headline (Sydney *Morning Herald)*:

Dig Surrenders Sensational Caesar Secrets!

As the subhead noted: "Revelations about great figures of history thrill experts, story of reluctant outsider who accidentally played key role mystifies them".

The scrolls – which you entered into moments ago and will return to shortly – were quickly dubbed The Lost Chronicle of Rome.

Controversy erupted almost from the start. Scrutinizing them, scholars acknowledged that the incidents they told were remarkably consistent with the Roman histories of the era. They seemed even to offer a sort of insider's tell-all memoir, a private look behind very public lives. As one researcher noted, the scrolls revealed the leaders of the era to be "strangely familiar to us in modern times – an admixture of bombast, swagger, impulsiveness and inability." Nor could any specialist point to evidence of fraud or fakery related to the documents.

But the unusual circumstances surrounding the find raised questions. Rudimentary dating techniques of the time suggested that the scrolls had been left undisturbed for thousands of years. Yet they had been discovered in the ground just outside Bayonne, New Jersey. Further, they had been found wedged inside an old olive jar.

Authorities became increasingly doubtful. After the first thrills of excitement, consensus in the academic world congealed quickly. Complex hoax, some declared. Or the enigmatic invention of a feverish mind.

The original documents are unfortunately no longer available for contemporary analysis. The scrolls were destroyed at a symposium dinner in 1937, after a distractible senior professor of anthropology confused the soda siphon and the tableside flambé torch. Nor can experts today examine the alleged site of the discovery; it is occupied at present by the driveway apron of a Budgetway Inn & Suites, just off Interstate 78.

Within a short time, the scrolls had been largely forgotten. Today, they are virtually unknown.

Yet what is the truth about these singular documents?

As we approach the hundredth anniversary of this compelling

find, we present the first ever full English-language rendition of The Lost Chronicle of Rome. (We hope you purchased the Centennial Commemorative Edition with simulated classical binding and attached fabric bookmark, well worth the extra $9.95.) While initial plans to retain the International Society of Classical Linguists for this project proved prohibitive, we know you will find the translation here more than serviceable, and we acknowledge with gratitude the many volunteer graduate students who responded to our Oodle posting to make this volume possible.

It is to you now to decide the reliability of this extraordinary account of the past. You now are the judge.

So please, strap on a sturdy pair of hiking shoes, cinch up your pants and prepare to go back again two thousand years. Prepare to go back to a world where, as one of Shakespeare's masterworks shows, the characters of history clash and "bestride the narrow world like a Colossus."

We again send you centuries in the past to rejoin the first scroll of The Lost Chronicle of Rome –

"It must be further understood that the citizenry regard him not only as a brilliant military tactician and fearless leader but also as their intimate and personal guardian ... Yet while the common populace might believe his ability is illimitable and his wisdom unbounded, in the Senate he confronts a potent and cunning force of opposition. We would do wrong to underestimate the wiles of any of these dangerously skillful rulers of Rome, on either side of the divide."

- Anonymous envoy of Parthia
(From an intercepted diplomatic pouch)

STRUGGLE

E ven as his eyes began to convulse, his ribs clenching and fingertips stinging with numbness, his body ceding to a force greater than his own great powers, even at this instant Gaius Julius Caesar bit resolutely for air and, as he had uncounted times over measureless years, he called upon all his spirit to free himself from the hard decree that the Fates had set against him, and by doing so, struggled not only to release himself but to blazon to the brutish world that he would not be vanquished: Not this day.

In short, it was, for Julius Caesar, turning into a typical morning trying to dress himself.

Caesar released as much of a breath as one in his condition can. He closed his eyes, took a moment to let his heart rate return to normal and reminded himself that there had to be other people in Rome who also have a little trouble putting these things on. But oh how Caesar hated togas.

The song: He thought of the song again.

Caesar had to wriggle for some minutes before his toga began to loosen its hold on him – he could never figure out exactly how he ended up affixing the thing too snuggly – and as he squirmed he called to mind the words of the toga-tying song. He would try the toga-tying song one more time; maybe that would do the trick. It was, he knew, his last, best hope.

He started over.

Soon a noise similar to singing could be heard, interrupted from time to time by ruminating grunts.

"Pretend your hand is Mrs. Fox, who's running back to your socks."

If you looked very closely, you could see Caesar's lips move a little as he tried to remember all the words to the toga-tying song. His ears waggled faintly when he struck "hand" and "Fox", and his tongue pricked out as he focused harder on where to put the folds and loops flopping off his hands.

"Then through the hole, the white mouse goes [Back to G7 chord]. And right behind: The cat's nose."

But again Caesar began to feel the accustomed tightening around his body. Again he had to stop himself and attempt to relax. The truth is, no matter what anyone might say, nothing can make putting on a toga very easy, Caesar felt, and even a song written to help does not really help that much.

After he ran through the toga-tying song three more times – after all the imagined mice and vixens and armadillos and handsome Praetorians and everyone else should have been slid effortlessly through their hiding places and doorways – he stared down mournfully at himself. He had at least not again put himself into bodily peril. But it still would not do.

Instead of presenting a stern yet lustrous figure of masculine authority (which is what he planned for today when he hopped out of bed), Gaius Julius Caesar, if he were honest about it, would have to acknowledge candidly that he might be giving off more the appearance of a hastily organized linen closet.

He could blame it all on being preoccupied over the big events coming up. But it always seemed to end up this way. Putting on a toga truly is one of the harder things to do, Caesar always thought. Probably harder than propping up puppet kings, holding the pillage to a reasonable level, spelling, and finding the right diet to keep the weight off – all those combined. The average man who goes around in basic garb every day has no idea.

Despite common perception, wearing a toga is not like just throwing a bed sheet over your shoulder. The material has to be scrunched up at specified points, with tabs and eyelets being created and all kinds of other complicated requirements.

It was at just such trying moments that Caesar might feel a solemn intonation welling inside. He lifted his head and blinked with deliberation three or four times.

"O to be thusly Caesar," Caesar began to intone, solemnly. "Lesser stationed men might call upon the aid of an attendant to help dress their persons of a morning and with their common needs. But history herself calls upon only Caesar to be seen to serve Caesar's own selfsame self. Caesar can ask for no assist, for Caesar stands alone atop the world."

His range of motion considerably restricted, he hopped around in a circle, glancing about. No one else seemed to be in the room; he made a mental note to use that line again someday, so it could be recorded for posterity. He imagined he would enunciate the line slower next time, too, and if his arms weren't strapped down losing all feeling, as they were now, would add an insouciantly flourishing gesture.

He began trying to release the spooling of apparel clamped to his body. Yes, in reality, the toga-tying song never seemed to work out quite right, despite what his wife Calpurnia had promised when she wrote it for him. He was always puzzled by the time he got to the third loop, near the right nipple. Is that supposed to invite in the sparrow or chase out The Gaul? And which fold is supposed to be The Gaul anyway? He reluctantly admitted to himself that hope had been lost, and he called out, at full volume, for his house servant.

Caesar's servant, in fact, had secreted himself earlier in the morning behind a nearby armoire, waiting for this moment.

"Sire." Nimbus spoke flatly, as he came around the armoire, acting like he'd been down the hall the whole time. "Do we need another undoing?"

Caesar glared. This particular house-slave was admittedly well stocked with competence. He knew his job well. But the man's imperturbable air could on occasion be unnerving.

"You look like you just had an ice cream," Caesar said as accusingly as possible.

"No, sire."

"You sure that isn't fudge on your left upper lip?" Caesar squinted, knowing full well there was no lip fudge but wanting to distract attention from the fact that his fingers had begun again going numb, and, further, that he couldn't predict where his right foot had ended up. "Or maybe a candy sprinkle?"

Nimbus had already started to wend around and up and down the Caesarian presence, detaching fabric from his master, unwinching, jimmying, and deslotting wherever he found a loose space or fissure. It was a puzzle, but this wasn't the worst he had seen. The week before last, while attempting to put on a formal vestment, Caesar had closed off a major artery and nearly passed out – the reason for Nimbus positioning himself silently in the room since then waiting for the shout for help.

"Anyway, got a really important day today, you know," Caesar let out, in an effort at indifference. "The big pre-war festival party I'm putting on, the big speech after. Public speaking, waving, nodding graciously, and so forth."

From outside came the cacophony of a city that's enjoying a day off work: The peal of drunk laughter and of spontaneous street fairs and fights punctured deep into Caesar's private residences. Most the people of Rome could not tell you the first thing about the ancient purpose of this particular holiday. The people were provided, after all, so many of them, jubilees and commemorations and celebrations, one after another.

If memory served the populace, this one was called the sacred Lupercal Festival, or the Lupercalia, or some such. It didn't matter. The point was that it meant getting potted all day instead of having to punch a time clock.

"And I've got one surprise hidden up my slee—" Caesar glanced at his garmenting and decided against giving full voice to the metaphor – "er, well, that is, there's that one surprise I'm not even telling Mark Antony about. Let's just say, it's a pretty big deal."

He smiled. In general, Julius Caesar did not give himself over to introspection. Most every thought that formed in his mind felt itself immediately flushed down to the larynx for pronouncement or used as filler during silences. But these were important days even for Caesar. He began to muse.

Life had been plugging away smartly the last few years: All manner of conquest up north, taming that petulant Cleopatra of Egypt, best-selling memoirs (#1 on the non-fiction list 17 weeks and going), pulling off a bold march into Rome and getting charge of things here while everyone else just dithered and argued.

And now, ahead only a few days, the prospect of going off to another grand war. This time the war would be out East, which would be fun. The household and all the city crackled with the expectation that always broke out before a major military campaign, giving extra zing to the day's festival.

"Please, your honorable worthiness, unclench your left cheek a little." Nimbus had begun making measurable headway against a double knot around the torso. "No, please, your other left cheek, sire."

Caesar had been growing tired of all the intrigues and gamesmanship in Rome and could hardly wait to get the march out east started. He was tired of all the lifelong politicians who did nothing but jockey for place and squirm about with their subtleties and schemes.

He grinned as he imagined the hearty military campaign that was to begin soon, where he could get up and give straightforward, stirring talks to his soldiers. And you had enemies who you knew were enemies because they wore different clothes than you (and no formal dress-up, either) and who waved around different looking flags and standards.

He never understood why more people didn't see military campaigns like going on a great big camping trip with lots and lots of friends.

"If you would, my lord," Nimbus said, "see if you can wriggle your shoulders."

"These things are damned impractical," Caesar announced. "Why can't togas have pockets, for one thing? I was planning on bringing the new paperback of Pindar's Word Teaser today. I'm just coming to figure out how Pindar thinks, which of course is the key to it all."

"Caesar may be aware that special folds can be formed in a toga to help convey smaller items," Nimbus suggested as he gave a yank near the coccyx. "However, that may be an option we would best consider exploring at some time in the future."

Caesar decided to focus his attention on the big speech he was to give. He tilted up his head to start to practice it to himself. He was to offer up the speech from his private box during the festivities later in the day.

Mark Antony had written it, and everything was in the works to make this speech a real show stopper. Standing up for the common citizen, advancing the glory of Rome, fighting outside dangers. The speech had it all. But the house-slave interrupted before he could concentrate on his lines.

"Please try to hold still," Nimbus said, before adding – a few seconds late and a register or two too low, Caesar thought – "sire."

Caesar had snapped up Nimbus at a great price through a slave broker a few years earlier, and the man was certainly a bargain as servants went. But he did have that air of directed efficiency that could be off putting.

"You do understand Caesar will have to tinkle soon," Caesar said.

He felt his abdomen resume its accustomed correlation to gravity, a downward flopping that offered another reminder to

Caesar of the need to get out of the lure of Rome and its endless banquets and feasts.

"There seems to be some opposition here," Nimbus said as he yanked near the lumbar region. "Very bothersome opposition at that."

"Mon dieu!" Caesar blurted after a moment. "'Bothersome opposition.' That reminds me. I wanted to try one more time to meet with some of the Opposition from the Senate and see if I can't get them yanked onto my side somehow."

Nimbus, competent in his work, continued working silently. It was like this every day with Caesar; the mind had its own inclinations. Caesar almost let another solemn intonation come on, but it was aborted when a final chest flap flung open and Nimbus announced the project had ended in success.

"Phew," offered Caesar.

"Where shall I put this particular toga, O Caesar? Box it up, perhaps?"

"Hmm," said Caesar. "'Box.' That gives me another thought. It wouldn't be a bad idea to invite one or two fellows from the Opposition to come to the private luxury box I've got set up to watch the Festival today. Get the unstoppable Caesar juggernaut working on them. Yes. Good, isn't it?"

Caesar typically did not await answers to his own questions.

"In fact," he continued, "I'll ask Gaius Cassius Longinus to join me. He can be a real pill, but I'm sure I can push him into being more cooperative. Then we'll really be cooking with gas. As I like to say, if at first you can't beat them, then try, try again. You know, it is fortunate you mentioned 'bothersome opposition' and 'box.' Honestly, if Caesar did not know better, Caesar might think you were planting ideas in himself. But is it too late to send an invite?"

Though he had been taken into the household as personal servant to Caesar, Nimbus once again showed his efficiency in all matters.

"Given the urgency of events these days, almighty one, I believe an IM has been ordered up, in case you had any last-minute communiqués to send. An invitation can probably be gotten through the city quickly enough."

"An IM," Caesar reflected. "Where have I been hearing of these IMs? It that the latest form of instant message delivery I keep hearing about?"

"The younger population of patricians has been utilizing IMs for some time to communicate with each other," Nimbus explained.

"I know I've heard of IMs, but I just can't put my finger on where or why."

"And you are correct, Caesar, the IM is indeed considered the highest speed communication available. An Impelled Maniac should be arriving here shortly on foot. You can give him your invitation to deliver."

"Okay."

"And may I remind Caesar he indeed has a very full day ahead of himself?"

"Okay."

"The Senate sent over a substantial quantity of bills for you to sign, including the budget for next year. These await on your desk."

"Okay."

"There is an hour session with your hair styling team."

"Okay." Caesar's attention had been fixed at the closet, where he'd gone to find something else to wear.

"The Great High Priest has requested five minutes of your time at some point."

"Okay."

"Mark Antony has sent his daily list of detainees whom he has scheduled for advanced truth extraction and/or physical elimination."

This last remark jostled Caesar's concentration.

"I'll say this." Caesar was working to separate three enmeshed hangers. "Mark Antony isn't a bad apple. He does work hard – those lists of his keep getting longer and longer – and he keeps himself really toned. I think he's actually going to be dashing about in that run they do at the end of the festival today. But he can get pushy. Whenever I see M.A. these days, he goes on and on trying to convince me to agree to that big plan of his. The one he says will change everything. I have to have lunch with him later on, don't I?"

Nimbus had been discreetly folding the subdued toga and continued silently doing so as Caesar's mind lurched ahead.

"Mind you, it's not the worst plan. I do agree with giving me all that power to really get a lot done and stop all the bickering. But why does he have to make these things so complicated? This plan even includes giving me a pretend crown somehow. I'll have to get him to explain that bit again."

Caesar took a moment to regret not buying the woolen beret he had seen in a shop window while conquering the Belgae. But what would it go with anyway?

"Of course, Mark Antony won't like hearing I invited the Opposition to my box. He'll go off and warn me for the gabillionith time about his undercover reports on the Opposition. About how they're having another secret session to plot against me. Honestly, this politics get tiresome, doesn't it?"

Nimbus, competent, knew very well which questions were suitable for answering and which not.

"Perhaps Caesar would like to dress himself today in a tasteful but undemanding robe of state."

"Hey," Caesar said, "don't forget to pack me enough razor blades for the campaign this time. You know how much I hate stubble in the middle of a war."

He briefly considered going smart casual or perhaps upscale athletic.

"Wait, that's it!"

"Caesar?"

"I just remembered where I heard of Impelled Maniacs." Caesar reached in for a red velveteen tunic. "They keep showing up on those lists of Antony. Which actually reminds me: That Daily Word Challenger I've been working on. Is the proper term *ex*head or *disen*head*ening*?"

This was one that one would answer.

"Be, O Caesar of grand conquests. I believe the word you are looking for is to 'behead.'"

GO

The old man widened his eyes into punctuations of urgency. "And that is why we must act covertly to achieve our final liberation." The old man glanced cautiously about the room. "Secrecy is the way it must be in our perilous circumstance. Danger envelops us. You understand, young friend, do you not?"

Directly across from the old man, unmoving, sat Paul. Paul had been understanding everything the man was declaring not at all. None of it. Yet he did not like the way it all seemed headed. He initiated a small courteous nod.

"You and I will be in the vanguard." Squinting, the old man leaned over the table to whisper, offering Paul a breath of mysterious intrigue, as well as of glazed meatloaf and pudding. "You do come to apprehend my meaning, do you not?"

Again, Paul did not. He never understood what the man was getting at. He added an equivocal smile to his nod.

What Paul did understand was that he had only seven minutes left on his authorized lunch break. His sole aim at this point was to hastily finish his cheese sandwich and rhomboid of applesauce and get back to his cubicle.

"But we will have to be especially cautious on whom we trust." The man spoke with wary deliberation. "You and I will develop a clandestine code and meet only after midnight."

Paul had paid for his meal four minutes earlier. He'd then scanned the employee lunchroom, eyeing the one empty table in the corner. He serpentined quickly to it, hoping for a few moments alone to wedge the food from his compartmentalized lunch tray into his mouth. Until this point, nothing in Paul's life had prepared him

15

to think he could ever be subjected to good fortune or opportunity. But there was an envelope awaiting him in his cubicle. A tantalizing envelope. Paul was being offered a quiet new job in a far-off corner of the city.

To Paul, that envelope would mean an unexpected end to years of relentless running and scrambling that he had always taken for granted and, more importantly, a finish to the increasing peril of real harm he faced in his current work. Paul's goal at the moment was to get at that envelope.

The old man had slid in across just as Paul had gone for the first bite.

The old man was pleasant enough to work with and had an earnest quality. Paul just did not have time to sit and listen tactfully. The man always talked – on and on – about one topic: Somehow, at some point, getting changes made to the Employee Handbook of The Winged Owl Messaging Service (LLC).

The man had seemingly been Assistant Accountant for The Winged Owl since before the ancient kings were run out of Rome and he knew every word of company policy by heart. When he wasn't sending back purchase order requests for revision or doing inventory in the stockroom, he was seeking out other employees he knew would sit long enough to listen to his latest plans.

"Until we're guaranteed paid leave for the first week of jury duty, which they get at Mercury Fast Couriers, we are no better than barbarian slaves," the old man insisted.

He had had the habit of grasping at his listeners' forearms for rhetorical emphasis. This left Paul only limited opportunities for transporting food mouthwise. After swallowing only the third or fourth time, he started considering a plan to get away and get to that envelope.

A plan, as it happens, at that instant was executed for Paul. It was executed thunderously.

"Paul!"

The room froze. Several lunch specials plopped off suddenly quavering forks.

At the swinging lunchroom door stood the Shift Supervisor of The Winged Owl Messaging Service. The man was as scowling, as bovine, and as holding a half-eaten summer sausage as he had ever been.

The old man scooted his chair instinctively away from Paul.

"Paul, up and center!" The Shift Supervisor, according to his habit, did not speak so much as he performed an aural vivisection.

Paul spiraled out of his chair and darted over. Getting himself firmly positioned in front of the Shift Supervisor, he then began resolutely to not quote from The Winged Owl handbook on guaranteed employee break time.

"Here," he instead quoted, embellishing his oration with an unmistakable warble.

"Job at the estate of Julius Caesar." The Shift Supervisor's voice had the feel of a rope burn along the ears.

A square of metal was pushed into Paul's hand. Paul looked at it blankly.

"What kind of jackhole of a Roman's never seen one of these?" Morsels accompanied the words from the Shift Supervisor's teeth. "A security permit."

Paul continued staring wordlessly into the thing.

"You show it to Caesar's guards. To get in. You think with all the hit men and spies around, you'll just foxtrot right into Julius Caesar's estate? You're picking up a message from Caesar and bringing it the Senator Gaius Cassius Longinus. Is that simple enough to understand?"

Paul forced a nod of assent.

"And don't think of asking me why in the hell you, of all the chowderheads, were chosen for this job."

Paul discreetly transitioned from nod to compliant shrug.

"Go," the Shift Supervisor commanded. "Now. As in right!"

Believing in multiple approaches to staff incentivizing, he buttressed his directive with a progression of curses, threats and growls that would have exfoliated a prefect of the Praetorian Guard.

Calling up all his grit, Paul aimed his body to the lunchroom door, pushed off, and was outside The Winged Owl within roughly 1.5 moments. He bounded four steps. And stopped cold. He found himself flat up against a coagulation of humans yawping, guffawing, besotted people, surrounding him on all sides. He'd forgotten. Today was a holiday.

This, in the seven hundred and second year after the founding of the city, was what it meant to have a job that took one up and down the streets of Rome.

This, then, was what it meant to be Paul.

Paul had never intended to commit his life to running other people's messages through a packed metropolis. Around the time of the six hundred and ninety eighth anniversary of the founding of Rome, some few years earlier, Paul had been gaping at a loaf of marbled rye. It sat in a storefront display, and he had not eaten in a day and a half. The shop proprietor, seeing an open mouth, offered Paul a deal that day. Run a box of finger sandwiches to a garden party across the Tiber within 25 minutes, said the proprietor, and you'll get not only that loaf but an even bigger reward. When he returned 46 minutes later, Paul was handed a note with a recommendation for employment to be given to the Shift Supervisor of The Winged Owl.

Paul turned out to have been made for this kind of thing. His slight physical construction and elastic agility nicely fit with the three duties required of an Impelled Maniac:

1) Run to someone's place and listen to their message.
2) Run to someone else's place, repeat the message and get a response to go back to the first person.
3) Keep doing that.

To accomplish these tasks, Paul had swiftly picked up the skill of leaching. He spent most of the working day leaching, as well as squeezing and eking and wriggling, through the swarming streets of Rome. In his attempts to navigate from As to Bs, he had over time developed the tactics commonly used by steam. He couldn't tell you one fact about the world outside the walls of Rome.

But Paul had come to know the widths, traffic patterns and relative openness of most every street, alleyway, adjoining rooftop and drain system in the city. He may not have been especially dexterous in facing life when it remained stationary, but he knew how to move.

Eyeing the holiday crowd surrounding him, Paul began calculating. From his periphery he noticed a gap in the congestion and made for it. His instincts taking control, he began sidling and bending through clumps of people, looking for breaches; avoiding, scuttling, jumping, and evading.

As he osmosed his way around the margins of the crowded fish market near the temple to Isis, the taunting scent of a freshly oiled trout caught at him. This whiff reminded Paul of one extravagance he had been doing without for some time. Regular meals. While his job did bring a small bag of money at the end of each week, it had not quite kept him swimming in marbled rye. His attempted lunch – lying 7/8th uneaten on a cafeteria tray back in the employee lunchroom – had been his first food since the morning before.

The bouquet of seared garlic wafted off as he capered around a living statue dressed as Bacchus. Paul felt a sort of tap on his shoulder. It was the tap of a thought, which had begun running alongside him. Thoughts had a habit of accompanying his runs like this. This thought, sprinting smartly along, reminded Paul of the empty bins and cupboards back in his little efficiency apartment, as well as of the two-months-overdue rent.

He sped up.

He vaulted over a lump of mule droppings and banked off the cockeyed corner of a florist's, dropping equidistant between a couple who had just shut their eyes and begun working themselves toward an embrace. Neither noticed, as Paul darted ahead, how close to taking part in a little threesome kink they had just been.

For Paul, the flash of this scene brought forward another thought to his side. It was the thought of the night before. He began – while evading a wayward toddler and pivoting into Via Ulpia to avoid the inevitable swarm at the old forum – he began to reverse engineer last night in his mind. Within two blocks, this thought convinced him that his girlfriend might have dumped him.

The first tell had been her use of the phrase "maybe start seeing other people who don't affect my digestion." The goodbye kiss provided some corroboration. She'd pulled her hand up to her lips, then tapped his cheek with her fingertips. In hindsight, it all felt like watching a process server delivering a summons.

Paul would probably know soon enough. The envelope waiting for him in his cubicle came from the household of his girlfriend. Until this unnerving thought hinted to Paul that she might now be his ex-girlfriend, he had been expecting a letter from her father.

It was her father who had lined up Paul's tranquil new job. He had promised to send the details, and the envelope had arrived that morning. It was to be his passport to safety and quietude. But Paul had been racing around all day and had no chance to open it yet. Now he could not be so sure what exactly the letter offered.

By the time he'd considered all this, Paul had begun to slalom down a crowded avenue of jumbled tenements near the Aventine. This might have offered ideal positioning to make a quick stop for some advice. Just down this street lived his mother. But at this, Paul only felt the companionship of a third disconcerting thought.

His mother was the only living relative Paul ever knew. Yet she was a handful. Raising him all by herself in their small apartment, she had always been quirky – dreamy, tending to the absentminded, overprotective. But in the last few years, she'd gotten, honestly, odd.

He sprinted past her rickety building. Glancing up to the window three stories above, he could be sure his mother was up there just then. In addition to growing more peculiar, she was very nearly a recluse. Paul brought her a bag of groceries twice a week whether he could really afford to or not. But it was the only time he ever saw her. And when he did, she would mostly just sit there and offer him a strange series of jumbled tales. His mother occupied her own reality, a reality of outlandish stories with no connective tissue that she gabbled about with far off eyes. He could only imagine what advice she would offer about a possibly dissolving courtship and lost employment prospects.

Emerging from the tenement blocks where his mother lived, Paul compressed himself through a human clotting near the Pantheon, and after getting briefly crosswise with a confused calf, risked three dank alleys that led to the quarter where Julius Caesar lived.

He began slowing himself and letting his thoughts sink away. These thoughts all had been unsupportive noodges; he was relieved to be rid of them. Their great accomplishment on this run had been to unhelpfully remind him of:

- ✓ His poverty
- ✓ The apparent collapse of his relationship and the hope of a tranquil new job attached to it
- ✓ The peculiar ways of his mother

But now he faced one more thought, about the future. And it was probably the most menacing of all. Paul took five or six deep breaths and made up his mind to get in and out as quickly as possible.

These were times in Rome when everyday vocabulary had picked up terminology such as "extrajudicial proceedings," "arrest without warrant" and "are still searching for the head." Paul knew nothing about the powerful except that they were always clashing and bucking. And they did this in ways that ended with lots of souls, certainly including innocuous messengers, being dashed about.

That he held a security medallion just to get inside (hit men and spies, the Shift Supervisor had said) was enough to make Paul blench. This final thought emphasized that there was something very not right about being sent on a job like this.

This was not, by far, a typical assignment. His usual assignments were more of the kind he had been on earlier in the day. Before his attempted lunch, Paul's mission had him facing no more danger than carrying the words of two post-pubescents who lived in fashionable districts on the opposite sides of Rome.

From the first youth that morning, he was given the message: "Hey."

Paul ran this communiqué across the city to announce it to the second youth. He then was obliged to work his way back with the response: "Hey. Bored. You?"

He ran through Rome a third time to deliver, from the originator of the communication, "Me too."

He again ran through Rome.

"Go to the forum or something?"

Run through Rome.

"Dunno."

Run through Rome.

"Come on. Let's do something. I am so bored." (Paul's instruction here had been to significantly elongate the vowel in "so.")

Run through Rome.

"If I can get money from my mom."

Run through Rome. In this last instance, rather than reciting a message, he was made to look at the recipient and to laugh out loud.

Paul was used to helping the children of Rome's parvenu carry on such conversations or to perhaps run a coded communication between a couple of nervous lovers. Now as he braced himself for what lay ahead, he wondered if the Shift Supervisor had decided on somehow doing him in.

A final √ emended itself to the accomplishments of Paul's thoughts:

✓ Realizing he now faced the real peril of becoming entangled in something very treacherous.

He emerged into a neighborhood of festooned facades and burbling fountains. There was openness all around. And opulence. As he collected himself, he could not help noticing, despite the danger of the assignment, a satisfying character to the surroundings. No crowds around, no braying and no shouts.

At the point where Paul stood to catch his breath, one could not help but admire the sumptuous sight up ahead, leading the beholder to gape skyward toward the rich statuary lining Caesar's roof, guiding one's gaze down to the lavish friezes just below, to the florid capitals of the Corinthian columns underneath and the elegant fluting of the colonnade that finally directs the eye lower – in Paul's circumstance at least – to the glare of a gate sentry who is making, with his thumb, the universal signal for You're-Going-to-Want-the-Service-Entrance/Dumbass.

Paul responded by providing the universal Yes-I-Guess-I-Do/Am grin, before moving along.

OPPOSITION

Birds shut up. Half-drunk laborers froze into statues of sobriety. An otherwise stout tavern owner looked down to notice his own feet had begun shuffling uneasily. Several drinks gave up their fizz, and even so-so mothers clasped their hands protectively over their children's eyes.

Gaius Cassius Longinus didn't mean to be frowning so effectually.

We have already seen that there are those in life whose personal characteristics lead them to make progress in a fundamentally circuitous manner. Who don't confront obstacles but find ways around them. Who leach their way through. But there are others in life who possess the personal carriage and deportment – to say nothing of the Tyrian purple garb of a Roman Senator – which force obstacles to clear away in front of them.

We have met Paul. We have seen that Paul tended, as a rule, to leach his way through life. Gaius Cassius Longinus did not leach. Cassius cleared.

As the day's revelers parted in front of him, backing cowcatcherly toward the nearest street gutter when he strode into view, Cassius dimly sensed his demeanor might be spoiling some kind of fun up ahead. Yet despite his reputation as the city's preeminent buzzkill, it was not the endless holidays in Rome that Cassius objected to or even had on his mind at this point. No, he could not care about what the people of Rome may have been up to at the moment.

Another meeting.

Gaius Cassius Longinus was tramping down the center of one of Rome's main avenues, just north of the old forum, going to another meeting.

He did not want to go to another meeting. Cassius fully understood the importance of building consensus among his colleagues in the Opposition. Or at least he tried to understand this. But he did not want to sit through another bloody meeting.

His frown doubled down on itself and those in front of him scampered with even more vigor.

It is not that Gaius Cassius deployed these frowns with intent. Despite what he'd originally put in for, Cassius had been born with a face that frankly attracted, more than anything else, aversion. He wasn't an entirely bad looking individual: His appearance simply did not bring forth feelings of gladness and comfort from its beholders. It was almost as if there had been a shortage of face skin when he had been constructed, so they had to pull what little they still had in store tight over his head, to get it to fit.

The result was to highlight a number of already sharp features. In effect, Cassius protruded: a lean nose, over-ambitious cheekbones, lips of almost no existence, and a humorless pin of a chin. No matter what, Cassius always seemed to be bustling and snappish.

At this moment, he undoubtedly felt he had good reason for utilizing one of the most piquant from his frown collection.

Rome was not merely in trouble: It was moments away from calamity – the kind that empires rise and crumple on. The upcoming war out East was ominous enough. But it signaled more; it signaled great power grabs and shifts.

For years, Caesar and his sycophant Mark Antony had been usurping control, trampling the ancient laws of the Republic. Again and again in his public career, Cassius felt, Caesar had shown himself possessed of a glittering intellect and bombastic ability to direct the people. Yes, Caesar at times offered apparently disjointed and even odd comments and seemed – *seemed* – to act erratically.

But this was quite obviously to throw everyone off from his hidden schemes, to drive his opponents to underestimate him. Now all signs suggested a final plan to take absolute power and end the Republic forever. The Opposition had to discover those plans and then act on them. Or face the worse consequences imaginable.

Yet all his fellow members in the Opposition – the collection of men who had not yet fallen under the thrall of Caesar and Antony – all his fellow senators could think to do was to once more get together. The time for mere talk had long passed; Cassius felt this as strongly as anything. It was time for immediate action.

Nearing the Mulvian Baths and Conference Center, he began

playing through in his mind how the chattering would inevitably halt along at the meeting, which he was nearing.

There'd be the befuddle-faced Flavius Flavian going off on a tangent, and tiresome Livius the Younger with his inane proposal. There'd be the doughy Bilbius Dilbo quoting the rules of order and banging his damned gavel every seven seconds. Of course, Cicero would be asking everyone to turn in their expense reports. Then there would be The Outside Communications Consultant, blathering about some new marketing strategy or whatever it was he went on and on about.

It was all insufferable to consider. And worst of all, no one understood the urgent need to find out exactly what dangerous scheming Caesar was up to.

A pushy dog swaggered toward Cassius, confident of a scratch behind the ear or a scrap of food. Cassius had just then gotten to the mental image of Lucius Crispius Totovus: Last time at the conference table, Lucius Crispius Totovus had eaten his way through three boxes of honeyed dates before yanking out a length of dental floss and running it through his teeth for half an hour.

The dog and Cassius locked eyes, and the dog abruptly began to proceed as if it just remembered a pressing appointment on the other side of town. It wasn't long before the fuel from his fuming began to clear out streets before Cassius even turned the corner to come to them.

Yet ire can be blocked.

In the forward thrust of humanity, there are times when one pebble or a lone peach pit can scuttle the march of the smartest legion. A single soldier in tight formation stomps on something, twists an ankle, and it's an eleven cohort pile up. It is so with fret, too. Fret can be tripped up.

As he breasted the Esquiline Hill, a whiff from below of the first flower market since winter brushed against Cassius, and at that moment, his eye caught the creamy reflection off a sensuous statue of Athena astride a small temple. He did not consciously note this. But the caravan of horribles in his mind faltered just a bit.

The thought floated into his mind: Maybe I am being a little unfair. Perhaps I need to approach this meeting with more charity and grace.

After all, he considered – as the scent of lilacs and lilies pressed deeper into his being – my fellow Senators at least mean well. It isn't easy these days being in opposition to Caesar and Antony; any gathering to even talk about going against the strongest and most dangerous power around is to be admired.

He gazed softly at the Athena's marble breasts, and they seemed to gaze softly back.

Yes, Cassius decided, I must enter this meeting with the right attitude for my brother Senators. We may be a disheveled, unruly group, but at least are trying to do what is right.

After a few slowed steps and six or seven full flaps of the diaphragm, a passable smile fought to make it onto his face.

He considered Livius the Younger, whose cockamamie remarks inevitably bubble up at least once during these meetings. Yet instead of clenching his fists, Cassius gave himself up to open cheerfulness at the image of the man's simplicity and eagerness.

Brutus would be there too, and Brutus very nearly counted as a voice of reason, someone Cassius could count on to at least listen.

"Freshly dried plums," a nearby costermonger called out as the morning sun slanted orangely into the street. The vendor had not noticed Cassius coming along. "Dried plums!"

The position of Senator demands the highest dignity. Yet in his new humor Cassius felt unable to keep from fairly capering toward the cart, to gamely pluck out a packet of fruit and, in one happy little whirl, insouciantly flick over a sesterces with a playful wink and cheerful tap on the man's back.

He spun back around and kept on his trek. A pack of plums would make for a fine little offering of conviviality to bring inside to the meeting. A small symbol of communion. And to provide commerce and encouragement to an honest tradesman is the duty of those blessed with position and power, he considered with some satisfaction, while turning toward the conference center.

The vendor, it might be noted, interpreted this exchange somewhat differently. During the brightening of mood of the past minutes, not a muscle in Cassius had actually jiggered. Nothing of his emotional transformation manifested itself on the surfaces of his body or in his looming deportment. He looked exactly the same before as after his transfiguration.

Later that night, the operator and sole proprietor of the *Veni Vidi Vendi* Green Grocer Wagon told his wife about the day he had. He told her about looking up to see a cross, frowning senator lunge up from nowhere and jostle his cart with an angry yank only to pull out the cheapest item for sale before making him dive humiliatingly for payment and finally glowering with a menacing twitch and shoving him with an act of misdemeanor battery as he turned to leave, the sum of which resulted in the cart slipping from its wheel blocks and lurching down the street to strike a startled schoolgirl, toppling and dislodging its entire inventory onto the sidewalk.

Some people, no matter what, just have that kind of effect on other people.

Putting the packet of plums into a fold of his toga, Cassius pounced over every third stair, and sprung through the atrium and anteroom. He let his sleeves flutter as he glided into the waiting room of the Mulvian Baths and Conference Center. He felt good, and he felt like he would do right.

Looking about at the scene he encountered as he got inside, Cassius stopped; he felt a doubt play in his mind: This might not end well after all.

INVITE

Paul found his way round from the towering façade of the estate of Julius Caesar. He passed the garbage cans and rotting garden sheds along the side wall and got himself to the service entrance.

A looming guard there took his name and security medallion, then frisked him. Alarming events from Paul's perspective. He had now been officially noticed and recorded in the public rolls. From there, he was handed off through a series of retainers and guards and two refriskings. Finally he was brushed into a large red room.

It contained two people.

Near a writing table stood a stiffened, thin-nosed, wisp-haired individual. The man's drooped eyelids and distant gaze suggested that in his line of work he ended up having to repeat a lot of things. This man turned to the other.

"The IM, sire." Nimbus spoke slowly. "You told me you wished for an Impelled Maniac so that you might send a message of invitation to Gaius Cassius Longinus of the Opposition. To ask Cassius to join you in your private box at the end of the Lupercalia Run later today. I believe this young man is he. The IM. Sire."

The other individual held a document in both hands. The paper drew all his attention down. It also drew down an advancing line of forehead sweat. For several minutes, he glared at the paper unblinking. Paul stood still and watched uneasily, glancing from time to time to the house servant who offered back an expression Paul could not quite understand.

When the second, paper-gripping person gradually looked up, he stared straight into Paul's eyes. The effect was unnerving. Paul did not follow politics at all. What's more, the man staring at him did not quite emanate a sublime aura or come off as the demigod he had sometimes been described as. He was perhaps a little smaller than Paul had imagined he would be. Arguably also moister. Yet, for all that, this was still Julius Caesar in person: The most renowned and celebrated figure in all of Rome. Paul caught his breath.

"What," Caesar finally asked in a low voice, "what, in your opinion, is a four-letter word for 'cheeky Frenchman'?"

Paul stood dumbly, blinking and unable to respond. He coughed once, and the sound echoed throughout the large room.

"Sire," Nimbus inserted, "I do believe we are in fact engaged today not in a crossword but in a find-the-word puzzle, is that not so? Sire."

"Wonderful. Of course." Caesar stared at the paper again and then back at Paul. "Now in find-the-word game, the words can be across, down and diagonal, but can they be backwards or up?"

Paul looked over to Nimbus. Years of service to Caesar had allowed his house-slave to convey more meaning with a slight retooling of a chosen facial muscle or two than the average legendary philosopher propounds in a lifetime. For a second, the face of the servant Nimbus seemed to be saying, yesterday it was a misunderstanding over the Junior Jumble.

"Er – the ... uh," Paul opined. "I ... buh. That is –"

No, Nimbus explained, not backward, not in a find-the-word puzzle; nor up. Words can only be formed across, diagonally and down. By then, however, Caesar had lost interest in the project and had dropped the paper onto the writing desk.

"Explain to me, young man, how you IMs operate," he said to Paul.

Paul reiterated, word for word, his most recent riposte (see three paragraphs above).

This left Nimbus to clarify.

"This youth, O Caesar, is an IM, or an Impelled Maniac. He will memorize a message from you. It may be up to 50 words long. He will then run to the place of your intended recipient and orally repeat the message. He will then return again here with any response that is given, and so forth. In other words, he shuttles hither and thither delivering brief messages between people. There are a few other terms and conditions. However, that is the gist."

Caesar had begun making the motorboat sound with his lips. He had apparently been listening to the explanation, however. He asked a series of questions which Nimbus patiently provided answers for, which answers are as follows:

"No, mighty Caesar, punctuation does not count as a word."

"Because Impelled Maniacs are hired for their dexterity and speed, many users find they provide quicker-than-standard communication back and forth."

"Seven."

"A comma does not, no, count as a word."

"No, venerable conqueror, our long-distance messaging is with a different provider."

"I believe, lion of lions, you placed it behind your ear a moment ago. No, your left ear. *Left*. Yes, that ear."

"Correct, because the messages are inside the head of the Impelled Maniac, that would indeed be the only way to permanently delete a communication."

"Seven sesterces per *month*. First month free."

"Yes, with the low wages they make, they are most often cheaper than paper and pen."

"No, sire, seven sesterces is not typically considered to be, in common parlance, 'a lot' of money."

With that, Caesar frowned proudly, as if by marginally understanding the system, he believed he may have invented it.

Paul then watched a remarkable event come to pass.

Caesar's shoulders began to plump; his torso took on a turgid quality, the pupils receded, and all the animation in the man seemed, in an inexplicable way, to almost leak out. For a moment, Paul wondered if some kind of medical condition might be at operation. He had never seen anything like it.

But in that moment of transformation, the man in front of Paul suddenly looked distinctively like the conquering hero Julius Caesar. It was the Caesar of statuary and coins, come to life. It was Caesar preparing himself to offer up a solemn intonation.

"Caesar," Caesar intoned, and even his voice had ossified in some way, "Caesar now shall take this time to compose a missive that shall be sent out beyond his ken, as he works to bring peace among opposing factions in Rome. For this, history herself calls upon Caesar to accomplish."

Just as quickly as the process began, he exhaled. His body immediately folded back into its fleshy self; a middle-aged politician stood once more where the likeness of the stately Julius Caesar had issued forth for a quick moment. If Paul had not seen it himself, he would have sworn there'd just been two different men playing Caesar in front of him, an elocuting one and now a 5/8th scale model stand in.

"Anyhoo," the littler Caesar said, "time to bang this thing out."

He pulled a pencil from behind his left ear, turned to the writing table and for the better part of half an hour mumbled, scribbled, erased, sang to himself, crossed out, re-scribbled, rolled his eyes and cussed.

Paul stood motionless during all this. Waiting, his mind fixed itself on one topic. His mind fixed itself on Tharmex Vindd. Paul had worked with Tharmex Vindd. A cheerful sort, always with an upbeat laugh. A week earlier, the Shift Supervisor had ordered Tharmex Vindd to the residence of Mark Antony.

There were those back at The Winged Owl who later said Tharmex Vindd must have abruptly decided to return north to his home on the Rhine. Others suggested he had fallen into a sinkhole, though this seemed unlikely given his running skills. Paul, though, believed the whispered accounts about why Tharmex Vindd hadn't been seen since: He had been entrusted with a message that turned out to be too hot to be kept circulating. Tharmex Vindd, Paul believed, had been permanently deleted. And there were a lot of other stories of Tharmex Vindds making the rounds among the IMs of Rome.

Finally, Caesar handed Paul a scrap of paper. Paul braced himself before looking into it and reading the contents.

Got a box to watch the fun today. Corner of Fifth and Via Sacra. Hope you can make it. Hey bring Brutus too if he's around. (Insert smiley face.)

"I went back and forth about whether to use an exclamation point or a smiley face at the end," Caesar explained. "Isn't the smiley used as a kind of punctuation sometimes? Plus sometimes the exclamation point can seem kind of swishy, if that's not inappropriate for me to say."

Before Paul could stammer a disjointed response, Caesar was back at the writing table, rooting around for something. Paul read the message two more times to memorize it, as he was trained to do. He handed it to Caesar's servant. Nimbus handed him back a different slip of paper, with the address of the Mulvian Baths and Conference Center and the name Gaius Cassius Longinus.

Paul was almost in and out with having made no impression at all, which had been his goal. But at the doorway, he turned and spoke his first fully formed word of the whole encounter.

"Gaul."

An unthinking grumble of "huh?" came out of Caesar.

"Gaul, sir," Paul said. "A four-letter word for 'cheeky Frenchman'. You asked when I first came in."

Seconds ticked with no response, only the sounds of Caesar

grunting as he tried extricating his hands from a thicket of rubber bands. Paul scuttled out, red faced that he had spoken up and feeling more than a little foolish.

He hurried down the wide corridor, berating himself for not having simply left silently. As he found his way back toward the service entrance, a cannonball of Caesarian laughter grazed along the walls, followed by the distant intonation: "Cheeky Frenchman! Gaul! I get it!"

.

MEET

The senior leadership of the Opposition of the Roman Republic – the guiding force of the resistance against the party of Julius Caesar – seemed quite relaxed. Especially for an assemblage possibly facing imminent extermination.

The Opposition leadership sat on benches lining the back waiting room wall of the Mulvian Baths and Conference Center. The positioning strongly suggested there would be no alertness of any kind breaking out soon. The Opposition leadership indeed seemed very, *very* relaxed.

On the rounded left shoulder of Bilbius Dilbo rested the thin right jowl of Marcus Tullius Cicero. Dilbo's right palm in turn splayed out on the sternum of Livius the Younger, while Lucius Crispius Totovus seemed to have frozen in the middle of an intimate conversation with the fastidious Pompilius Pulcher. There was here a head faced to the ceiling, there one to the floorboards and no fewer than eleven feet snagged together.

At first consideration, this oblique posturing – bodies pressed at angles against each other, limbs and faces in almost studied equipoise – gave off an artful quality. If made of marble, this might have been the statuary group on a temple pediment, representing The Schools of Philosophy in Contemplation or perhaps The Gods Pensive.

Further observation revealed, however, inarticulate sounds emanating from the tableau and splotches of drool forming on several garments.

"Ornkf," Lucius Crispius Totovus asserted. After freeing a less coherent sound from elsewhere, he repeated this comment with

32

more vigor.

Gaius Cassius Longinus surveyed it all. He had been standing before the grouping for some time, agape.

"Gentlemen," Cassius finally said. Though startled at the sight when he had entered the waiting room, still, he spoke with the solicitude that comes mechanically when we first walk upon someone enjoying a nice little nap.

Taking a cue from the earlier and more vibrant communication of Lucius Crispius Totovus, Cassius repeated himself more vigorously.

"Gentlemen!"

He followed this up with an artificial cough.

The jarring effect worked. Except for one of its members, who dropped off the side of the bench, the Opposition's senior leadership blinked and jerked up into bearings of readiness.

After a few throat clearings, Bilbius Dilbo staggered up and mumbled something about "just resting one's eyes."

"We are most heartened at your attendance," he said hoarsely, rubbing his temples. "Though you were no doubt wondering why we are all in the waiting room instead already meeting."

Cassius was.

Typically, the Opposition leadership convened with each member arriving singly at the Mulvian Baths and Conference Center. They then would move nonchalantly to their usual meeting space in the building, which was invariably the Esquiline Conference Room. Although their gatherings were not strictly forbidden in Rome, Cassius had always said it was best not to attract undue attention to themselves.

As members of the Senate, they were all theoretically protected from the detentions and other dangers swirling about, but there was no guarantee that would last. Cassius had always suggested everyone getting there individually and not being seen together. He had expected that they would have already been in the conference room by now.

"This does seem a bit – " he began.

"Unfortunately," said Dilbo, "there was apparently a mix-up with our room reservation, and we are waiting to see if something else opens up."

A willowy figure of a man with a clipboard came in just then.

"Gentlemen," he said wearily, looking down to a chart. "I have confirmed with our management that all our standard conference rooms and meeting halls are fully booked today."

"Poop," said Dilbo, and the Opposition membership looked

around at each other forlornly. "We really need to meet today."

"Of course, if you'd like," the man with the clipboard said, "we did just receive one cancelation for a private bathhouse room that could accommodate you."

"A bathhouse room?" asked Pompilius Pulcher.

"That is all we have available."

Not especially fond of the water, or of any change in routine at all, the Opposition leadership nevertheless gave off a shrug of reluctant acceptance. There did not seem to be much alternative.

"You should count yourselves most lucky," the attendant continued, glancing down his clipboard. "The space was originally booked for the birthday party of an eleven-year-old, but he woke up measled today. Although naturally, I am required to disclose that the rental will cost fifty more denarii per hour than the Esquiline Room."

"And why exactly is that?" asked Cicero, Finance Chair of the Opposition.

"This is by far our most popular room, of course. It is usually booked six to eight months in advance. Indeed, parents have been known to come to fisticuffs over an unexpected vacancy. You would, I think, be grateful to be able to get into The Squirt'n'Shriek Soaknatarium."

As the attendant led the way down a side hall, he laid out the rules of acceptable behavior in the private baths. There were rules regarding running near the pool (not acceptable), horseplay (no), profane language (banned), open sores in the water (disallowed), and the extent of management's right to eject any unruly patrons (utter). The Opposition leadership showed no interest in the swimwear requirement or the location of the changing room, since none knew how to swim. But a grunt of relief followed the attendant's revelation that outside food was in fact permitted in the bathhouse room. It was Lucius Crispius Totovus who grunted this relief.

A few words about Lucius Crispius Totovus at this point would not be amiss.

There may be those not familiar the tradition of "victory names" in Roman history. From its earliest days, the Republic of Rome conferred an added name onto its preeminent warriors, to honor their conquests. The victor is, in effect, awarded with the name of those he has vanquished. This new name is attached at the end of the one he was given at birth.

Thus, Cornelius Scipio becomes Cornelius Scipio *Africanus* following his subjugation of Libya, and the general Marius Calder is known as Marius Calder *Germanicus* after destroying the Teutonic northern tribes.

The bestowal of such victory names is akin to being presented with the fallen battle standard of your enemy, the definitive spoil of war. By attaching your enemy's name to yours, you have captured his identity and have had your triumph grandly avowed.

Until his forty seventh year, Rome knew of a Lucius Crispius. But the name ended there. Then it was that Lucius Crispius noticed a handbill hanging in his favorite delicatessen. Five hundred denarii, the handbill announced, to he who eats, within thirty minutes, all the contents of the red bowl atop the pastry counter. It had never been done.

The planning, sallies and eventual mop-up operations of the campaign can be told in a separate after-action report. It is enough to know that the Zingerman & Zingerman Gut Detonator Challenge was faced that day, and that thence walked in the Republic a man newly christened with the final name Toto Ovus – or, for short, Totovus.

Lucius Crispius *All the Eggs.*

There had been 42 of them in the red bowl, every one of them hard boiled and pickled. The victory was utter; the enemy routed. And it signaled the start of a long and growing relationship between Lucius Crispius Totovus and the eating competition circuit of Rome.

It surprised no one, then, when Totovus had eventually volunteered to chair the Refreshments and Victuals Subcommittee of the Opposition. He made this offer shortly after suggesting such a subcommittee be established. A good selection would class up the meetings, he had said, although it was understood that fundamentally Totovus wanted to keep in training for the next contest.

As a result of his good offices, there always was a bounty of things to eat at all the Opposition meetings. And not just little sandwiches with shiny buns designed to hide the fact that there aren't enough cold cuts inside. Totovus always came with at least a dozen white takeout boxes. They were labeled to indicate dates, figs, mini-éclairs, pita pockets, melon, fried eagle gizzard, geometric cheeses – cheeses cubed, wedged, and wheeled – and a surfeit of cocktail napkins.

Watching Totovus struggle his way down the hall, his top box jiggling precariously higher than his head, Cassius pulled from his pocket the little bag of dried plums he had bought from the street vendor and arced it into the nearest trash can.

For Totovus, balancing the boxes proved difficult. But it was not the only challenge the Opposition leadership would face. On entering the Squirt'n'Shriek Soaknatarium, a number of material differences from the usual Esquiline Room presented themselves. To begin with the Esquiline was a richly appointed space with paneled walls, pitchers full of ice water and lots of side tables to put snacks on.

There was no side table here. Or any flat surfaces at all. Where there would have been a large mahogany conference table in the center of the room, here there was a sunken swimming pool. Where the ergonomic leather conference chairs would have been placed, the swimming pool was instead surrounded by oversized seats of a kind. Each of these had been brightly colored and was shaped like a sea creature of one sort or another.

Some of the seats seemed like the sort you sit on. Others seemed liked seats that you essentially ride upon. They had all been affixed to the floor on columns and rose to varying heights. The taller ones had ladders attached, apparently for mounting. Also unlike the Esquiline Room, festively painted children's slides were interspersed between the seats.

Finally, the walls and floors had an undulate quality to their design and were painted blue and white, making them look like big foamy waves.

"Welcome to the Squirt'n'Shriek Soaknatarium," the attendant said before shutting the door behind him. "I'll go turn everything on. Enjoy."

After listening to quibbling about who should go where, followed by grunts and moans as ladder steps and human joints creaked throughout the space, Cassius ended up inside a clam around halfway toward the ceiling.

He looked around the room. It was filled with bugged eyes, fingers grasping at handles, sweated up faces, and long sighs. This, Cassius thought, is all that stands between Caesar's onrushing despotism and the tradition of a celebrated republic. But he remembered his vow on the way to the conference center. He would try to keep optimistic and patient.

"Let us push ahead with action, gentlemen," Cassius called out, taking advantage of the quiet as everyone tried to accustom themselves to their places. To his left, Cicero grasped the safety railings at the top of a yellow slide and was making an effort not to look down. "I wish to impress on this group that we must discover, immediately, the menacing plans of Julius Caesar. We have seen his ability to manipulate the people of Rome through his inflaming harangues and strident rhetoric. And we must not be fooled when his behavior sometimes seems curious and even incoherent. That is all obviously a shrewd smokescreen to mask his deep intentions. With his minion Mark Antony, I believe he is about to take a momentous step. But what exactly? When? Against whom? I must insist that we focus today on finding answers to these questions, so that we might strike back. To wit, I propose the following action."

These were the only words Cassius would manage during the meeting.

Finally positioned, several senators began to speak up. The meeting, they started to note with consternation, had not been officially convened.

"We must follow proper procedure," agreed Bilbius Dilbo, speaking gravely from atop a polka dot snail. Finding no particularly good place to bring down his gavel, he struck at the top of a snail antennae, which began to twang and metronome back and forth on its big exposed-spring coil.

For the next hours, through points of order and through new business and old business, through flowers of steam that bloomed from the painted volcano domes on the walls, through grumbles and intermittent snores, Cassius sat silent. During most this time, The Outside Communications Consultant had the floor (in an entirely metaphorical sense, since the room essentially hadn't one).

As the room filled heavier with mist, Cassius listened to a soliloquy he could not and did not wish to comprehend – words about "staying on message", and "modern opinion tracking methodology" and "focus grouping."

Cassius did raise his hand at one point, but the chair recognized Pompilius Pulcher instead.

"Let the record reflect that this setting will not do for my toga." Pompilius Pulcher had already complained once about his turtle messing up the creases. "It is dry clean only."

The next time Cassius attempted to speak up, he felt something clunk his head. It turned out to be approximately half a cantaloupe.

To his right, Lucius Crispius Totovus smiled down from a pink narwhal.

"I've got a lot extra here," Totovus whispered, leaning down and waving a fruit wedge in Cassius's face. He gestured to his white takeout boxes, which he had rested on the narwhal fins projecting from his seat. "Or do you want a pancreas puff first?"

Cassius offered a frown that demonstrated no thank you.

"If you don't want any, start passing it around," Totovus whispered.

And so The Outside Communications Consultant continued to

talk and talk – big tents, granular analysis, prebuttals, managing expectations, reverse spinning – while Cassius transferred, from his right hand to left, food.

Cassius had always felt the presence of The Outside Communications Consultant at these gatherings equal parts useless and risky. He had opposed hiring an unknown advisor from the first. But the others felt that this was their best answer to being relentlessly outsmarted. Cicero, after all, had once employed an image coach who did some quality ghostwriting and helped out his law practice.

But Cassius never quite learned where this particular individual emerged from, and he worried about his loyalties – whether, for instance, he possessed them. Now he had to listen to the man's droning once again.

With the room full of vapor, after a time Cassius could no longer see the food he was passing along. But the emptiness of the gathering and the sensation and smell of snacks had begun getting to him. Though normally possessed of a small appetite, he decided to have a little something.

He absently leaned forward to bite into a squishy incoming ovoid from Totovus, an object that felt like a large grape or a modest olive.

An immediately resultant yelp revealed that he had in fact placed, between his teeth, not a piece of fruit but, rather, a dangling big toe attached to Lucius Crispius Totovus.

Cassius twisted backward in perplexed abhorrence. As he did so, his right elbow struck at an unseen lever on the side of his clam. Nearly simultaneous to this movement, a second howl rang out at the other side of the room, followed quickly by a generous splashing. Peering through the haze down into the swimming pool, Cassius thought he could just make out the flailing arms and mostly submerged face of his fellow senator Pompilius Pulcher.

BENCH

L ike many of us, Paul, throughout his life, had been confronted by a fair number of sentences. Phrases, too, and sayings and expressions. Among all of these, there was one series of words that Paul heard spoken far more than any others. It was these:

"Oh, I didn't notice you there."

To start with, wherever he went Paul brought with him an unassertive, scant body. Breezes and particles of light often didn't bother going round him or reflecting, seeing it was just as easy to pass through. He also had about him a quality that felt slightly imperceptible to most people. He did not speak especially often, and when he did it was never up.

Paul's face tended to the color of a cracker, and it did not offer many arresting features, save for a habitual arched puzzlement around his muted blue eyes, which suggested a mind half unsure how the universe, himself inclusive, ended up that way. His hair might have been notable; it hinted at a reddish ash seen mostly in the far provinces. But his mother usually cut it, and she invariably did this while lost telling one of her tales. The resultant fashion might best be termed Roving Cowlick.

As for lips and chin, Paul could not make hair show up on these even if he clenched his jaws and concentrated. He certainly never followed trends in apparel: His clothing in effect merely happened. Nor did Paul insert himself into places. He would just be there for a while before he got noticed. Even a high-strung squirrel might walk over his feet before looking up with some surprise to find a human staring curiously down.

It did not irk Paul, then, when he found himself sitting for a long time in the waiting room of the Mulvian Baths and Conference Center. After working his way there from the estate of Julius Caesar, he approached the center's attendant and told the man that he had a message to deliver to one Gaius Cassius Longinus.

The attendant had responded to this by going about his business, flipping through his clipboard and writing, before finally looking up.

"Oh, I didn't notice you there," he at last said to Paul dully. He explained how very very busy he was but that when he got the chance he would let Cassius know and in the meantime Paul should please have a seat.

That had been an hour 45 minutes ago.

Waiting long after running hard often comprised his workday. He did not so much mind waiting. Except that it gave time for the return of pestering thoughts.

Yes, he decided, his girlfriend probably had been trying to tell him something the night before. He could not understand why she ever stuck with him in the first place, and he would not be sorry to do without the understated jibes about low ambition, dress habits, and tiny apartments. But she was always companionable.

And her father had promised that fine quiet job. It was to be working for a wealthy art collector of some sort far from the center of Rome, mending objects and dusting things off mainly, as far as he understood. Tranquil, solitary, and with no security permits needed.

Paul wondered again if he should talk this all over with his mother. But last time he visited his mother, she spent most the time telling him of wondrous youthful adventures across the Mediterranean she said she had, of an enchanting valley off somewhere, of being made the slave girl to some fabulously rich senator.

Paul began figuring she wove her outlandish fantasies to make up for her dull life growing up in Rome and raising him by herself. Yet it wasn't always all innocent madness. He could swear she once mumbled an allusion to the amorous drive of the historical figure Spartacus. Something about him taking her home with him. Paul had feigned a coughing fit at that point.

A piercing noise broke through his thoughts. In his work, Paul over the years had gotten used to not paying attention to a lot while waiting to deliver messages: Raised voices, flesh squeaking against flesh, unforeseen juices, incongruent odors. These were all experiences of which he tended not to take note. But the industrial grade splash chasing a mincing shriek out of the hallway were hard to ignore. The whooping had about it a polyphonous quality of girlish terror mixed with a melancholic baritone woe. The splash itself which followed implied, by its thunder, the displacing of a very large amount of fluid.

Paul, though puzzled, went back to his thoughts. He began to imagine his life if he could get that job that the father of his girlfriend (ex-?) had promised; relaxed days alone in a hushed room with maybe just a cloth and possibly a dustpan. No dangerous messages, no people to run into or avoid, no city cacophony. And all with solid, regular pay. And all now possibly becoming out of reach.

Another clamor shot out the hallway. This second one began not quite with a shriek but with a stammering bawl. The booming splash, however, sounded identical to the first. A third set of turbulence came some minutes later. Before the yelp and explosion of this third uproar, there was an eerie squeak, like the sound of skin rubbing hard against plastic.

Paul started recalling to mind the message he was to deliver when a fourth distraction emerged. But this disturbance differed markedly from the others. This one had flouncy long hair, thick lips and clear complexion, and it was wrapped tightly in a tunic. This one Paul could not ignore.

She sat on the next bench over from Paul. He could smell her perfume and creams. His heart gave a flutter. Paul, as his girlfriend (ex-?) would have attested, had a way with women. A gawky, sluggish, stuttering way.

Within the first five minutes after the girl on the bench arrived, Paul achieved:

- The slow straightening of his posture
- The imperceptible flexing of what little upper body muscle he had
- Armpit sweat.

Ten minutes after this, he worked up the spirit to glance her way. He did so for one half of one second. He was able to make out that she held a magazine, which he read as "Today's Celery," with a cover showing three especially flowering green stalks. He decided to plunge in and risk it: He decided to strike up a conversation.

He knew for a conversation, if there's any chance of it succeeding, it often helps to express interest in the other person's interests. Facing the woman directly – his heart now speeding – Paul said to her, in clear tones, "They're great with a cheese spread.

Or chopped up in a tuna salad."

Two facts immediately came to Paul's attention as he fretfully looked for a reaction. The first was that the woman had noticed him; she looked up over her magazine and began staring at him quizzically. The second was that, upon further examination, the name of the magazine in her hands was in fact "Today's *Celebrity*" and the cover art presented the image not of any vegetables but of three anemic folk singers with funny green hats.

"Errg," Paul said quietly.

Possibly out of mercy but more likely from disquiet, the woman next ignored Paul and looked back into her magazine.

Paul would have left it all at that. He wanted to leave it at that. He wanted to leave the waiting room and bang his head into a hard substance. But the attendant took that moment to remember Paul. He sauntered over.

"Who are you here to see again?" he asked fussily.

"Gaius Cassius Longinus."

"And who shall I tell him you are from?"

"From Julius Caesar."

The attendant pivoted away.

Paul rarely had the feeling of being stared at. Not being stared at is one of the central daily activities experienced by those who often go unnoticed. But as he went back to his thoughts, something tickled at his mind. He glanced over to the woman. She had lowered her magazine again and had been frozen with wide eyes looking directly at him. She smiled dumbly. Paul felt immediately uncomfortable.

"Julius Caesar?" she asked in a buttery voice. "Did you just say you came from Julius Caesar?

"Rmmm," offered Paul, by way of trying not to offer up something stupider than his original comment to her.

Disturbances wrapped tightly in tunics had a tendency to elicit such utterances from Paul. She nevertheless dropped her magazine and came over to his bench.

"Tell me," she said, "all about him."

"About Caesar?"

"I can't believe I'm sitting next to someone who just came from Julius Caesar. I want to hear all about him. Were you just there?"

"Where?" Paul felt his tongue losing its lubricants and his throat tense.

"His house. Caesar's house."

"Oh. Yes."

"I bet it's such a great house. Where in his house were you just now?" She moved in even closer and put a hand on Paul's arm.

"We were in his dressing room, in the private quarters."

"No! Just you and Caesar?"

"And one of his servants."

"When you're with him, do you sometimes just stare at him in amazement that you're so close to the great Caesar himself?"

"Well. Let's see."

At one level, Paul knew he had been given an opportunity he could start taking advantage of. He had the spellbound attention of an extraordinarily alluring woman, sitting so close to him that if he squinted just right he could probably make out the serial numbers on her mitochondria. He could engage in swagger, or in aplomb, or in puffery. He could put forward any attitude or employ any mannerism.

But addled by both her presence and the larger peril from this job that he knew he faced, Paul felt himself able to do no more than bluntly respond to the questions she volleyed at him.

"What is his voice like in person? As grand as when he's giving a speech?"

Paul thought about this for a while.

"Actually you'd be surprised," he said, clearing his throat, "but it's like there are really almost two Caesars, a public one and a private one. He seems to be able to turn it on and off."

"Wow. You know all about the private Caesar. That is too amazing. Are you helping him with his war plans? What did you two talk about just now?"

"Let's see." Paul remembered the one word he had spoken during his encounter with Caesar, giving him the answer to a crossword clue. "He had a problem figuring out what a cheeky Frenchman meant. I did help him with that. You know, Gaul."

"You advise him on foreign affairs? That is so amazing. And is he as majestic and as magnificent in person?"

Paul had to think again. He recalled that stature-wise, Caesar did not loom.

"Actually, it might be disappointing to hear, but he's really not that big."

The woman sagged a little.

"But is he at least totally intense and energetic when you're with him," she said hopefully.

Paul thought about Caesar fumbling for his pencil and getting his hand stuck in a clump of rubber bands.

"Okay," he said, now convinced that all the moisture in his body had probably been pushed out as sweat. "I'd have to say that at least the Caesar I know may not be as sharp as you might think."

"For someone who's so close to Caesar, you don't have a lot nice to say about him, do you?" The butter in her voice had started to congeal. "Next you're going to tell me he's not all that grand."

"I'm sorry," Paul offered. "I'm just telling the truth. Caesar really is not as big or as imposing as a lot of people think. He just isn't."

The woman's initially eager smile continued working itself down into a glower.

But how about the way his mind works, she asked warily. Surely Caesar's mind must be as supple and nimble as a fresh gladiator. Paul recalled witnessing a distinguishable lack of focus in the man and indicated this as tactfully as he could.

Then how about his mastery of the language?

That sexy swagger he gives off?

His brilliant attiring?

Within another five minutes, the woman had wordlessly slid back toward the bench that she originally chose. After another minute, she looked back at Paul, picked up her magazine and trotted over to the other side of the waiting room.

Paul breathed with relief. At least, he thought, no great harm done. He knew he had just been a botched mess, but it wasn't the first time. The quantity of women who had quietly watched Paul humiliate himself before them had already begun to approach, by this point in Rome's historical development, a plurality.

He went back to his thoughts.

During this encounter, Paul had not noticed that the squeals and cannoning sounds down the hall had stopped awhile earlier. The meeting of the Opposition leadership had ended.

And standing around the corner from him, listening with grave interest to every word that had been said in the waiting room, stood Gaius Cassius Longinus. As Paul's encounter ended, Cassius was frowning with wizened thought and the germination of an idea – a possibly precarious idea, but one perhaps called for in precarious times. The proceedings he had just sat through were aggravating, to say the least, but they may have led to a remarkable opportunity.

In the next room, Cassius thought, may be the savior of the Republic.

MINUTES

We are fortunate in this chronicle to be able to include a number of primary source materials. These are actual word-for-word documents generated at the time and adhered directly onto these scrolls, as you can see.

The official Opposition meeting minutes of this date do not provide a full scope of acoustic detail or descriptiveness. Words such as slosh and yelp rarely appear in meeting minutes. However, an examination of this contemporaneous record will provide the reader a direct look at the workings of the Opposition as Paul sat benched in the waiting room of the Mulvian Baths and Conference Center.

As you will witness, some of this document was damaged at the time. We therefore begin at the point where the senator Pompilius Pulcher, during a temporary recess in the proceedings, has been dredged from the swimming pool of the Squirt'n'Shriek Soaknatarium:

... Regular meeting continued.

Cicero presents Report of the Finance Committee. Review of balance sheet and income/cash flow statements reveal Opposition funding may have begun to plateau. No new monies have been raised since 51 BC when Opposition won the 50/50 raffle at charity auction for Sad Horses Foundation. Ideas for new funding sources are requested. Member Totovus suggests bake sale. Member Cicero also requests members turn in any expense reports asap, although it is noted that reimbursement might be delayed.

Motion. Member Pompilius Pulcher makes motion to respectfully request explanation from conference center management for failure of seating equipment.

> In favor: **14**
> Opposed: **1**
> *Motion carried.*

Flavius Flavian presents Report of the Recruitment Committee. No new members have been added to the Opposition since previous meeting. However, it is noted that eight individuals have filled out the "I Want to Learn More" postcards that were mailed out. Temporary recess called to recover Member Cimbus from swimming pool following monkfish failure. Committee chair Flavian concludes report by urging every member to try to recruit five more members in the next five days. [Three paragraphs illegible.]

Motion. Member Casca moves to authorize Marketing Committee to design new Opposition logo and consider new slogan ideas. The Outside Communications Consultant says he has a "solid guy" who can help, at a "very reasonable" hourly rate. Report truncated as mouth of Member Casca fills with stream of water, which it appears had been emitted from spout of beluga whale on opposite side of pool.

> In favor: **13**
> Opposed: **2**
> *Motion carried.*

Motion. After consideration, member Pompilius Pulcher moves to call for conference center management to compensate for any damaged clothing. [Illegible.] Amends request to also demand that "Silly Soaker" fountain, which has emerged from middle of pool and begun spinning and spraying throughout the room, be turned off.

> In favor: **9**
> Opposed: **6**
> *Motion carried.*

Member Publius Servilius Casca presents Report of Committee on Site Selection. Suggests in future unorthodox accommodations should no longer be accepted for official meetings. Temporary recess called as Member Cicero loses grip and slides into swimming pool. Member Casca remarks, see, that proves my point. As part of Refreshments and Victuals Subcommittee report, Subcommittee Chair Totovus asks if anyone has seen plate of fried roots that should be making its way round. Motion made to never convene in future except in settings of faultless decorum.

In favor: **15**
Opposed: **0**
Motion carried.

[Two missing pages.]

Warning offered. Meeting Chairman Dilbo alerts leadership that he believes he has determined cause of current procedural/sitting difficulties, i.e. small levers and buttons embedded in seats. Speculates that some of these devices have been engineered to allow occupant of one seat to cause a fellow occupant to be quickly deposited into swimming pool or to discharge pressurized jets of water from one seat toward that of another.

It is speculated that these are intended as methods for those in attendance to enjoy levity with each other. Caution is advised. Questions are raised on exact placement of alleged levers and buttons.
Temporary recess follows, as three Members enter pool, including, for second time, Pompilius Pulcher, while one Member is blasted off his manatee by inadvertently fired surge.

Livius the Younger presents Report of Committee on Policy. Member Livius the Younger presents what he terms a "momentous and sweeping" proposal. States that Roman government should undertake responsibility of painting home address numbers on the curbs.

Says this is very important to him. With home addresses painted on curbs, people will know whose house it is for sure. Thinks that black lettering on white background may be most effective approach.

Acknowledges he has not decided on most appropriate font yet, though Times Roman and Sans Humor fonts are not under consideration. Reminds assemblage that he has offered curb painting proposal more than 43 times in previous meetings to no avail. Says he is determined to find way to achieve ambition. Motion made by Livius the Younger. *No second offered.*

Motion. Let's file a lawsuit, proposed by Member Pompilius Pulcher. Against the conference center. Suggestion includes possible amusement park code violations. Also, cause of action for Negligent Infliction of Emotional Distress.

> In favor: **8**
> Opposed: **7**
> *Motion carried.*

Member Lucius Cinna presents Report of Committee on Security. Formal inquiry into possible leaks of confidential information has produced no results. Those potentially leaking information were requested to stop doing so. Member Cinna also expresses regret for mistakenly releasing compendious spurt from mouth of sea cucumber in direction of Member Pompilius Pulcher.

Motion. Member Pulcher, noting that he is now trembling and his garments presumably ruined, moves that special legislation be introduced in Senate condemning conference center building to immediate demolishing, along with bill of attainder declaring conference center management as enemies of state. Deliberative method of execution recommended. Discussion of motion includes many positive comments about conference center's Esquiline Room.

> In favor: **2**
> Opposed: **4**
> Abstaining: **9**
> *Motion failed.*

Report of Recording Secretary. Apology made by Recording Secretary if minutes end up being incomplete, owing to Recording Secretary earlier finding self thrust off his tilapia. He does note that he kept his right hand, which held the meeting minutes, above his head the whole time, leading to only a few water marks and the loss of just a couple pages *in toto*.

Motion. As thunder sound effects commence and large measures of water begin showering from ceiling, Member Cinna moves for indefinite recess and also that everyone should try, as a matter of courtesy, to fish out as many snacks floating in pool.

In favor: **14**
Opposed: **1**
Motion carried.

Meeting recesses ...

COIN

After its final vote, the Opposition leadership took some time to examine itself. It was decided that its condition perhaps did not offer the appropriate stateliness to quit the building just yet.

Shuffling to the changing room of the Squirt'n'Shriek Soaknatarium, the sight of big fleecy towels and freshly lit braziers to hang clammy clothes over brought expressions of great relief to the Opposition leadership.

One of their number, however, was not thinking of dampness.

While sodden garments flopped off shoulders onto the floor and men slapped themselves to warm up, Gaius Cassius Longinus stalked the aisles of the changing room. He was trying to regain some calm. He had tried going into the meeting with a collegial spirit and to see it as an opportunity – the last one, possibly – to drive his fellow Senators into understanding the growing threat of Caesar. But the experience ended up as merely a sopped version of every gathering they had ever had.

Cassius felt at wit's end, unable to find anyone who seemed to grasp the great crisis facing the Republic or willing to take the dramatic steps that he felt sure had to be taken.

Trying to release himself from his funk, he nodded with forced politeness to one of his colleagues — the bashful senator, whose name he could never remember and who was just then socking the left side of his jaw to jiggle pool water from his right ear – and approached Marcus Brutus.

"Good friend Brutus." Cassius spoke with attempted composure. "You were especially silent during the meeting today."

"As were you, Cassius," responded Marcus Brutus. "Of course my silence must not be taken to imply any positioning one way or another on my part, nor any final commitment to or against any principles."

On paper, the words Brutus spoke may seem almost cold and obtuse. But their effect on Cassius was temperate. Marcus Brutus, much unlike Cassius, always had that effect on people. There was something about his comportment and his look. It was as if the factory defaults for his countenance had been left at "open." His winsome eye took in everyone who came across him, and his plush voice could have been used as a timed-release soporific.

Brutus never knew what it felt like to not be liked or how to be unlikable. It was said that even his placental fluids had had a certain charm.

"Understood," Cassius said, wringing his toga. "I know that being part of the Opposition is not easy for you in many ways."

"And I sense that you would have the Opposition move more dramatically these days," said Brutus, amiably. "I sense your frustration at times."

"Having to listen to that so-called The Outside Communications Consultant can be tedious, and Livius the Younger raising his curbs initiative yet again grows tiresome." Cassius spoke in a low tone. "That is true. This is not the time or place, but I am coming to believe that we are reaching a moment beyond the usefulness of meetings; a crisis point, a time to make, if I may term it, a definitive and concluding stroke. And I will need you on my side more than ever. The people know you are honest and will listen to you when the time comes."

"You know I will always at least keep an open mind."

"Caesar grows stronger, and the rumors we hear of his plans are most troubling. We have seen how brilliantly his mind works. I worry as much about Mark Antony, too. Especially after Caesar appointed him Urban Prefect of Rome."

Looking into a sheet of polished copper on the wall, Brutus adjusted his clothes, and he thrust his hands into his hair to fluff it out.

Topping off all his iridescent qualities, Brutus had the most beautiful head of hair on the Italian peninsula. In younger days the hue of gold currency, it now radiated a gloaming starlit quality; at certain times of the day, there were many who believed his hair possessed its own soft bioluminescence. When the winds of the Mediterranean blew into Rome, his bangs would billow like a mainsail, framing a face resplendent with a perfectly straight nose which led to a mouth that housed perfectly straight teeth. His hair never frizzed, even in August. And even wearing it in a feathered fashion nearly to the shoulder, a look that hadn't been seen especially often since around the days of the Second Punic War, Brutus made it work.

"I cannot say but that you may be right," he said, shaking his head like a terrier to get that final, full look into his hair.

They spoke a little longer before Cassius finished his own dressing and shook hands with Brutus.

As he exited down the hallway, he began to wonder if there was any hope left at all. He frowned. Even if this unmanageable grouping could be focused, he thought, it was still unclear exactly what they should focus their resistance on.

Rumors churned everywhere that Caesar and Mark Antony were about to make a major move and grab at ultimate power. But unless it could be known what that move might be, it was all flailing guesswork.

As he approached the waiting room, Cassius's ruminations were interrupted. It was at this moment that he heard the name of Caesar coming from the waiting room. He stopped, pushing himself against the wall to stay unseen.

There was a conversation between a man and a woman going on. The man, it became clear quickly enough, knew Caesar. Rather well. And it also emerged that he did not think highly of Caesar.

"Actually" – Cassius heard the male voice saying – "you'd be surprised, but it's like there are really almost two Caesars, the public one and a private one."

The woman had been asking questions, and Cassius listened with growing wonder. Could it be that a close advisor to Julius Caesar sat there in the open, criticizing the man?

"I'd have to say that at least the Caesar I know may not be as sharp as you might think," the male voice opined. And Cassius had already heard him reveal that he had come from Caesar's private dressing quarters, apparently discussing urgent matters of state.

Cassius was struck. He had never heard anyone so frankly deride the eminence and power of Caesar. Either from trepidation or conditioning, everyone in the civilized world agreed that Caesar ranked as the most august and dangerous figure in Rome.

Yet just in the other room sat a man scoffing at Caesar's glory. And more stupefying, this man, from what he had been revealing, apparently served in an intimate counseling position to Caesar himself.

"For someone who's so close to Caesar, you don't have a lot nice to say about him, do you?" the woman asked, giving voice to Cassius's thoughts. "Next you're going to tell me he's not all that grand."

And that is exactly what the male voice reported.

The conversation lasted like this some time longer. Cassius waited until he was sure the talking had ended. He went into the waiting room to see what remarkable figure could have made such daring comments. Off to the side sat a slight, younger man seeming lost in thought.

A moment later, Paul felt a hand on his shoulder. He turned. Looking over into the closed countenance and senatorial toga of the man standing before him, he froze.

"Young man, forgive my intrusion." Cassius said. "I could not help but overhear your words, your brave and daring words against the mighty Caesar. It is my high honor to meet one such as yourself."

It is said that there are dog breeds that can directly shed almost all their fur when greatly shocked, as if they forget to hold onto their hair in their immediate fear. Paul now lost his mental grip not only on the words he had been saying a moment before but on every memory and thought he had ever experienced just shy of his own name.

"Buh," he offered the glaring face of Gaius Cassius Longinus.

"I wonder if we may meet again in more conducive circumstances," Cassius said.

An intuitive impulse had struck Cassius. This young man was an intimate retainer or especially close companion of Caesar's. That much was clear. Yet he was one who did not think highly of Caesar, to say the least.

The gods may be presenting an opportunity here: The possibility of taking advantage of inside eyes and ears, from right in the middle of Caesar's household. A disgruntled member of the Caesarian inner circle, and one willing to speak so candidly, might be exactly what the Opposition needed if they were to find out Caesar's plans and fight him.

"I have unusually keen instincts about people," he told Paul. "You seem a sensible and strong individual. May I ask what brings you here today?"

Paul got hold of himself and worked up enough saliva to say he had been sent with a message from Caesar to one Gaius Cassius Longinus.

"This is indeed capital," said Cassius. "I am he. And it is an honor that Caesar would send one of his closest personal compatriots with a communication. What word does Caesar offer?"

Paul let his memory take charge of his tongue: "Got a box to watch the fun today. Corner of Fifth and Via Sacra. Hope you can make it. Hey bring Brutus too if he's around."

"I see," Cassius said. "Caesar bids me to watch the Lupercalia with him. Fascinating. And may I ask, young man, what it is you are doing right now?"

"I am smiling," Paul said through bared teeth, trying to keep his lips from moving too much.

"Yes, I suppose you are."

"Caesar called for a smiley to be inserted at the end of his message," Paul explained, beginning to feel his jaw hurt a little.

"Young man," Cassius said, "let us discuss some matters, if you will, very soon. I may have a proposition for you. It could perhaps entail real peril to yourself, but I can already sense that you are an individual of great valor. And I think you may have the answers to some of the crucial questions I am looking for."

"The answers?" Paul said, clenchedly.

"Take this as a token of possible future endeavors together." Cassius handed Paul a metal object. "Given your closeness with Caesar, I suspect we will see you in his private box later today. Till then, adieu. And you can stop smiling now."

As Cassius left, Paul looked at the coin in his hand. It was by far bigger, shinier, and golder than any coin he ever held or had even seen. On its obverse was stamped the image of the goddess Libertas, the patron of freed slaves and personification of personal independence. The coin was so big you could count the points on her crown that shot out like rays of light, and you could see the irises of her clear eyes.

But the symbolism did not touch Paul's spirit as much as did the fact that this one heavy piece of metal, he estimated, would cover at least four month's rent.

ANTONY

"**B**eware the *what* now?"

"I can repeat the message, sir, if you would like."

"Yes, please, do that: Repeat the message."

Julius Caesar had been picking at his bacon-and-cheddar omelet, waiting for Mark Antony to show up. He sat alone at a table in the Senate cafe. This was one of his favorite haunts. Caesar liked showing his fellow Senators and their credentialed guests that he could be an accessible and approachable person. He also really enjoyed the cafe's omelet specials, offered every Thursday. It was the one day Calpurnia would let him leave the house without his lunchbox.

In between bites, he'd stared at the brainteaser on the placemat and half thought about whether to go up and get a side of boiled oxen tonsils when a slightly out-of-breath stranger had approached. The stranger had introduced himself as a messenger from Mercury Fast Couriers. But Caesar had been able to make no sense at all of the message when he first heard it.

"The message, sir, again, is: 'Beware the Ides of March,'" the messenger repeated.

"I thought that's what you said. I just have no idea what it means. Sounds like a laundry detergent or something."

The messenger did not respond.

"Anyway," said Caesar, "thanks. I'm sure it means something. The Ides of March. Interesting. By the way, are you one of those Impelled Maniacs?"

"Yes, sir, I am."

"Ah, I thought so. I had one of your colleagues at my place this morning while I was dressing. Great guy, too. A big fan of word games."

Caesar chuckled, remembering Paul's answer to the clue: "Four letter word for cheeky Frenchman." ... Gaul!

"Say, who sent you here with that message anyway?" he asked.

"Name blocked," announced the messenger, "at request of sender."

"Huh?"

"I can't say who."

"So are you allowed to accept tips?"

"No, sir, we are not. If that will be all, I will be on my way."

As he found himself again waiting, Caesar briefly considered asking Phil the cook to fill up a donut with mayonnaise and put it on the table near where Antony would be sitting. But he remembered his status as Caesar and shook the idea away. Plus, Mark Antony always only pretended to be amused by a good gag anyway.

Antony did not show up for another twenty minutes. It irked Caesar a little that there was no apology offered for being late. Particularly irritating since it was Antony who had called the meeting. And Antony would almost certainly be going on and on again about his convoluted Big Plan. Caesar almost felt a solemn intonation about promptitude coming on but decided to let it pass.

"You look like I could use a drink," he said instead, filling up his wine glass.

"It begins this day," Antony announced flatly, scanning the room before pulling up a chair and setting down a velvet box he had under his arm. "I want to make sure we both understand how this will all roll out. Today is the first step in a plan to bring order and stability to Rome. This will be our dress rehearsal, if you will."

"It is true that Caesar got into the job of governing to get things done here without all the usual infighting and mess," Caesar said, deciding to go along for the time being. "Pass me the dipping sauce, would you?"

Caesar wished he could just start marching east to the new war without having to go through another set of intricate political maneuvers. It had all gotten wearisome. But he knew that would not be possible. Antony would push.

"I'm just still not sure whether this plan of yours is too involved," Caesar said. "And, if you would, the toothpick dispenser there. You not going to join me for a bite?"

"What we do at the Lupercalia Run today is the essential prelude to our final act in the Senate." Antony's voice betrayed a small amount of pleading, a note he almost never allowed to play in it.

"Remember, this is part one of our two-part plan. The people worship you and revere your military conquests. They will follow you anywhere."

Caesar grunted acknowledgement while struggling to dislodge something from between two molars.

This was the trouble with having people like Antony around, he felt. They can be a handful. They may be right about a lot of things, but they press and press and push.

Admittedly, Antony seemed to get it right almost all the time. More or less writing those memoirs for him had been especially cricket, and, as it happened, crossing the Rubicon to take charge of Rome a few years earlier worked out better than Caesar expected. Then back in Rome, volunteering to serve as Urban Prefect gave Antony control over all the troops in the city, a headache Caesar didn't want for himself.

But like most of Antony's plans, this one seemed needlessly complex. As Antony had explained – over and over, he'd explained –they would be acting some "political theater" at the Run today, as he called it.

"Behind you," Antony said, breaking Caesar's thought.

Before Caesar could react, Antony jolted up, reached over the table and had a neck in his grasp. In a continuous motion, he placed the neck, along with the remainder of the human connected above and below, onto a chair at the next table.

"Explain yourself," he said in the chopped way he spoke, staring down into two fully rounded eyes and holding his grip so tight that neither explanation nor air could emerge from his captive. "You do know we have operatives who have never failed in truth extraction for many, many generations."

Caesar saw a pencil and notepad hanging from the fingertips of the frightened creature staring back at Antony, which appeared to be a girl who would not be leaving her teens unless immediate circumstances for her changed soon.

"You can most likely release her," Caesar said. "She came for my autograph. Didn't you, young woman?"

Caesar did have to acknowledge that in addition to his supple mind, Antony had some great reflexes. His tiny, black pupils hadn't dilated during the encounter, nor had any sweat or color come to his skin. The man always kept to a rigid workout program and firm diet, and it showed. Both his mind and body were packed tight. He was thirty-six pounds of air in a twenty-pound tire.

An expression of regret and some frogurt money later, the two men were back at their table talking.

"This should serve as a reminder of the dangers not only of exposing your person unnecessarily," Antony said, "but of the general risks lurking in Rome. It is one of the reasons I have to be as ruthless as I am and why we need a more disciplined approach to governance."

"She was, I think," Caesar conjectured, "thirteen."

Antony took the big picture from there. He outlined the alarming events of the previous years: Civil wars had rent the Republic, senators fought against their own kind, while the common people grabbed for more power. Except those times when a single strong figure took coldblooded control, the state was falling apart. Chaos had hovered for years, and even the most rigid methods of authority were proving ineffective.

"The people and other senators have full faith in your abilities, and you already hold the supreme position of consul," Antony said. "May I offer Caesar an historical analog to help illustrate my point about our plan? It is commonly believed that during the Punic wars, our general Flaminius Nepos was ultimately defeated by the Carthaginian general Hannibal. I maintain it is more accurate to say that Flaminius Nepos was in fact defeated by pusillanimity."

"Not Lake Trasimene?"

"Caesar?"

"I thought Flaminius was defeated up north, by Lake Trasimene."

"I see. Yes, he was that, too. The battle did take place *near* Lake Trasimene. But the thrust of my metaphor is that I believe the cause of the defeat ultimately came from pusillanimity."

"The town?"

"What town?"

"Isn't that the name of the town," said Caesar, "by the lake?"

"Pusillanimity?"

"Yes."

"No, pusillanimity. Cowardice. It's –"

"Then what's the town by the lake, near where they held the battle? I'm sure I've been."

"When I say this, Caesar, what I mean is that if it were not for our general being paralyzed with pusillanimity prior to the battle, Rome would not have been vanquished." Antony was almost never seen to drink. Exception was occasionally made during conferences with Caesar. He grabbed at the bottle of wine.

"Yes, Caesar sees your point now," said Caesar. "Before going up against the Nervii, there was a moment when I thought I'd have to call the whole day off if the swelling from my thrombosis didn't go down."

"No, Caesar, the word pusillanimity means –" Antony continued the pour. "Caesar, let's leave history aside for now and focus on the plan."

Glancing around to make sure no one was near, he picked up the felt box he had brought. He carefully swung open its hinged cover.

"For you."

On a blue felt bed there rested a delicately plaited ribbon, embellished with a string of yellow diamonds, jade and other gemstones.

"A headband?" asked Caesar. It seemed a little fruity as a gift from one man to another, but he did not mention this point. "Thanks, I suppose."

"The diadem, Caesar. This is the prop I have been talking about. For our political theater."

"Ah," Caesar said. "The widget you're going to try to give me at the end of the Run. The pretend crown."

"The diadem, Caesar, yes. I designed it to look somewhat like a royal crown but kept it slightly indistinct to give its meaning some ambiguity. I will be offering this to you in front of the people today. In doing so, we shall be putting the idea in the public mind of you being crowned King of Rome. But, remember, you will refuse it. This will give the people the impression that you do not seek more power. Then our real move to increase your authority will look modest by comparison. Three times I will place this apparent symbol of power upon your brow. Three times you will remove it and make a speech of ostentatious demurral."

"Somewhere around three," Caesar agreed. "Right ho."

"Three times, Caesar."

"And you really sure we need to go through with all this complicated planning and do this all right away."

"Caesar knows that the tide must be taken when it is favorable. We must act when we must. For Caesar understands the number of lives that the gods grant to each of us mortals."

"Of course. Let's see. Number of lives per person. Somewhere between zero and one. Right?"

"There is a paradox," said Antony, who had developed a remarkable facility for plowing ahead regardless of Caesar's commentary. "The people will tolerate great power being vested only in those who seem not to want it. This step is where we make them believe you do not want it. I assure you, Caesar, after we have completed the second step, when you take power for real, you will find this all the best way to calm all the squabbling parties tearing Rome apart. I give you a pretend crown. You refuse it."

Caesar silently twirled his toothpick, a red pepper flake speared at the end.

"Squab," he said, "Parties. You know, I've got to make sure Nimbus provides enough minced pigeon in my box today. It was a big hit at the last gathering, but we ran out before the dwarf ensemble even played. I will say this about Nimbus: He is one of the good ones, even though I do get a hint of impertinence from him at times. You know, I got him for a very reasonable price after the Servile Wars, when everyone was afraid of bringing in new house-slaves. A broker came to me out of the blue one day, and with my honed negotiating skills, I bought the man for a steal. Naturally Caesar knows how to make a bargain. He's a clever chap, too. Nimbus, that is. Very active in that club they have for servants. I actually got him into playing word games too. Or maybe it was the other way around. In any event."

This response would have disheartened most anyone. It did not Antony. He knew such non sequiturs – or almost sequiturs – did not necessarily mean he hadn't gotten through to Caesar. There still was a good chance Caesar would do the right thing in the end and agree to his plan, if for no other reason than to be sociable.

"Minced pigeon," Antony said. "Yes. Very delicious."

"And what about renting some t-shirt cannons for the festival? People love t-shirt cannons."

"Caesar, I'm afraid I am not familiar with such weaponry, but I do ...."

"I should tell you, too," Caesar continued, "that I've invited Cassius and Brutus to my box today. I know you object to my continually trying to reach out to the Opposition, but I think it's worth one more try to push them over to Caesar's side."

"As you wish." Antony's tiny pupils enlarged almost imperceptibly. "I ask you one favor, Caesar. Please be careful about what you say. I know far more of the Opposition's plans then they do of ours, but I hope we can keep it that way. Caesar, I trust, will remember what I have told him about the grave threat the Opposition presents to us."

Gaius Cassius had a birthday coming up. Caesar was about to suggest going halfsies on a name brand kitchen zester, but in light of Antony's mood, he decided it might be best to scotch the idea for now.

"By the way, you should know I am fixing to make a big surprise announcement at the next session of the Senate." Caesar stood to bus his tray to the return conveyer. "Something that might even raise the eyebrows of the imperturbable Mark Antony. Something to bring everyone together after I'm gone."

"Good, I love surprises," Antony said through a jaw that had remained rigid for some time.

Caesar sensed that perhaps Antony's actual enthusiasm on this did not match his words. Which was too bad. Caesar had been looking forward for some time to springing his surprise announcement on Rome.

"Did I understand you're actually taking part today?" he asked. "In the ... the Whatchamajingy Run?"

"The Lupercalia. As one of the leading patricians and Urban Prefect, it is my honor to be among the few to play a formal role in a hallowed ritual that celebrates the gift of fertility. Yes, I shall be running today. In fact, O Caesar, I need to get to the starting place now."

"You always do know how to bring out the best in you," said Caesar, as he put his tray onto the return belt and watched it rumble toward the maw of the dishroom, marveling at the smart march of modern technological advances.

"I bet it's a water wheel," he offered. "Could be a slave underneath the floor somewhere, but personally I would hook it to a pig, I think."

He checked out the dessert menu board on the way out and explained that he did not frankly understand how anyone could eat tapioca.

"But you really should try the Italian ice," he said. "Gooseberry Blast today."

They began to leave the cafe in silence when Caesar turned to Antony.

"One more thing." The inquiring tone of his voice raised in Antony some hope that there might follow a remark related to the political plans he had been trying to coax Caesar into understanding.

"Yes, my Caesar?"

"What's an ide?" asked Caesar.

"What's a what?"

"You know, an ide. I'm supposed to be worried about several of them apparently. The ides of some such something."

"I see," Antony said. "Caesar, in the new calendar system, what we call the Ides is a single day connected with the full moon. For example, next week, March 15th will be the Ides of March, which happens to be the day on which we shall execute the final step of this plan. You might remember, we had this discussion about dates when we came up with the new calendar just a little while back."

Caesar did now remember. Here was another reason to trust Antony's judgment. The man had designed a whole new calendar system that was proving very popular, and he had the consideration to name it for him, for Julius Caesar. The Julian Calendar.

"That's what it was. The Ides of *March*. That's what that messenger said. Part of me thought that if it wasn't a cleanser, maybe he was talking about a new miniseries. But yes, a day in the calendar. That makes more sense."

Antony's steely patience seemed almost to buckle. He nodded a farewell and departed.

FIGURING

Employees of The Winged Owl Messaging Service were expected to spend their days scampering. They had no assigned work spaces back at headquarters. But most of them rigged up little spots in the backroom, where they could await the next assignment or work though the invariable paperwork that came from the Assistant Accountant.

In one of these makeshift cubicles there featured, at the moment:

- A floor comprised of mismatched tiles
- A small footlocker holding:
  - A spare tunic
  - Five working sandals (though an old reliable pair of rope sandals is all anyone actually needs)
- Owing to its improvised nature and almost perfect lack of light and cross-ventilation:
  - The sensation less of a workspace and more of a medium-size cistern to be crawled down into and out from
  - Several unidentified varieties of mold spore
  - Odors
- An unsteady three-legged writing table that gave halfhearted purchase to:
  - A desk calendar printed before the Julian system had been adopted
  - After-action reports from the Assistant Accountant to be revised
  - A framed engraving of a fairly attractive girl, of

whom the evidence that she was most likely dumping her boyfriend had been mounting, partly in the form of the next object over on the table:

- An opened packet containing a low-priced finger ring, which the boyfriend had given to her for their one-month dating anniversary and which she had just sent back to him, along with:
  - A note saying, in effect, she was most likely dumping him
- o An orange that looked like it understood it should rot but could not quite get the timing right
- o A large coin, with the goddess Libertas stamped on the obverse, the one object that should unquestionably have given its owner comfort except that to the coin was attached:
  - A big problem.
- A ramshackle stool that unexpectedly seemed able to withstand the weight of:
  - o A recently enriched employee of The Winged Owl, who breathed slowly and possessed, it will be emphasized:
    - A large coin.
    - A big problem.
  - o Itself

Paul rarely indulged in self-pity. He hardly even realized it might be one of the options. When he noticed himself running down the street sporting a bucketful of offal, for example, it wasn't the fault of a thoughtless second floor apartment dweller emptying the trash the instant before, nor was it generally part of life's conspiracies. Not in Paul's mind. Paul would more or less figure it was just his turn to wear garbage.

He did from time to time, however, allow himself the luxury of freezing into a state of hushed alarm.

Paul could think of no fix to his big problem, and he had thought about it a lot. The coin had become warm with his fiddling embrace, picking it up and putting it down; this was the only motion his body had been visibly making as he sat in his cubicle. The way he analyzed matters, he had gone in a few hours from being one of millions of unrecognizable ciphers in Rome to becoming some kind of object of official attention. A whole lot of attention. He had been suddenly sent to face two of the world's powerful men. One of them, Gaius Cassius Longinus, expected some kind of information from Paul – "the answers," he'd said – and already started paying him for it. Paul could not imagine what this meant, but it was obviously dangerous and big. And apparently Paul was expected to know these answers from the other of them, the mighty Julius Caesar.

It all made Paul's head squeeze up and feel steamy.

That was the big problem. He faced another dilemma.

He put the coin down and picked up the letter that had been waiting for him in his cubicle. He began reading it for a fourth time.

"My dearest, sweet Paul ..." The letter began with some hopeful indicia of affection, or so had Paul thought three reads earlier.

The letter continued, ":"

This following his name – instead of Olivia's customary♡ , or even a disinterested comma – had given Paul his first chill after he realized the letter was not actually from her father as he had expected.

"Last night you may not have totally gotten what I was trying to tell you," the letter went on. "You are a great listener but sometimes you seem to pick things up not so fast. Paul, it might be time for us to move on, separately.

"I've been talking with the Major, and we agree that honestly maybe you don't have the drive that I was hoping for. I need someone with energy and life. And the Major feels that's what's needed for the new job he wanted to get for you. Plus we've been hearing things about you and your situation that seem weird.

"You and I need to take a break, at least. You have been saying you want to spend more time with your mother and she is such a dear sweet lady with all her crazy fun stories (ha! ha!). And as you know I want to devote myself to the great things in life, like the theater and macramé. I'm planning to take classes next month at the adult learning annex!

"If you can show me and the Major some drive, maybe we can patch things up. But let's see till then. Oh, here's that little ring you gave me."

And, the letter concluded: "Bye!"

It was enough for Paul to almost pick up the coin again. Instead, he scanned back to the lines about "the Major," which he hadn't paid much attention to before.

The Major was Olivia's father. She always referred to him by title, even though he did not strictly speaking hold a military rank. He was, rather, the majordomo for one of the wealthy households in the city. He butled. He also served as president of the Junior Zeus Club, an association for valets and other domestics. It was at this club that he had gotten the job lined up for Paul.

What made her lines especially strange was that in the past few weeks, the Major had seemed to be taking a liking to Paul. And what to make of her comment about hearing weird things?

So here he was, chucked aside by his girlfriend apparently at her father's suggestion, which also would mean no more promise of a solid, safe job from him.

Paul did have to acknowledge that from the first he never understood very much of his relationship with Olivia. They met while he was delivering messages to her father concerning the biennial Conference of Menials, Vassalage and Stewards. Her attentions to him – flitting yet protective – rarely differed substantively from those she offered to most objects that came off a little vulnerable.

More than once, he felt she had positioned him on her fluffy daybed so he would lay like one more of her decorative animal-face throw pillows. As to the possible new job, he hadn't sought it out, yet she announced one day she had arranged the position for him with her father.

He never quite communicated with her on the same level in any way, either. His mother's stories, for example. He could have used someone's thoughts on how to handle a parent who is apparently losing hold on reality. Olivia just thought his mother told awfully adorable tales about faraway places, hidden treasure, famous people in history and the like. Quite simply, Paul figured, it was all impossible to figure out.

He eyed the orange. Apparently it had found the right moment to rot.

Paul now felt that perhaps he should consider engaging in some self-examination, if not self-pity.

For as long as he could remember, Paul asked little of life, hoping only that it would go its way and let him go his. He had an almost ideological attachment to finding himself not involved with as much as possible.

When things had middles, Paul avoided getting in them. Until this day, he had done a pretty good job of it. As a child, Paul had no father to give him guidance. But he always listened to his mother when she warned him to walk away from fights or confrontations.

Neighborhood bullies funded their higher education savings accounts with the lunch money he turned over. For a couple years, the elderly seamstress next door wet her beak, threatening Paul with a weekly umbrella thrashing if he didn't cough up enough protection money. As he grew older, he stayed out of pool halls and never made eye contact with the local syndicate. After he landed his job as an IM, he took the taunts and upbraiding of the Shift Supervisor to be able to earn his small bag of money. But he never complained of any of this.

If he could afford counseling, a psychologist would probably tell Paul he became an IM out of a metaphoric compulsion to run from entanglements, obstacles and most people generally.

As he reflected more, it occurred to him that his problems actually were impossibly bound together. They were not a big and a little problem. They were one mush of quandary. How could he plausibly convince his girlfriend and her father of his drive or respond to anything they were hearing when his current circumstance had become a profound chaos?

He looked at the coin again and exhaled.

"You!"

The gong of the Shift Supervisor's voice nearly took down the sides of the cubicle. Lost in thought, Paul hadn't heard the man coming. Instinctively he sprang from his stool and dove, in shock, straight into the middle of the table.

"Are you deaf!" The Shift Supervisor overlooked the fact that two writing table halves had just been formed, with one of his employees sprawled on the floor between them.

"Been calling for you for five minutes," he growled through his teeth (which were as mismatched, color-wise, as the tile floor). "To Caesar's box at the Forum Vinarium. Go. Go!"

Paul, in his disorientation, took another security medallion from the Shift Supervisor's hand as he darted between the Shift Supervisor's legs, aiming himself, for the second time that day, out the door.

JOGGING

As Paul pushed away from the building, plotting the speediest way to Caesar's private box, an improbable sight faced him.

Pavement.

The streets, so full up in the morning, lay almost emptied. Paul looked round in surprise before starting off. He managed to get in several minutes of direct, luxurious, straight sprinting before coming to the Via Sacra. And even this, the main road in Rome, was abnormally empty. If luck held, he calculated he would be at Caesar's box very shortly.

As he hotfootedly sped up, one thought vexed him: a niggling notion that he was being thrust to the last place in the lands he wanted to be. Still, with his steadfast rope sandals holding out, he was making very good time getting there.

Luck reverted to form.

As he eased around the road's bend, Paul came to the reason for the remarkably good traffic conditions up till then. There squirmed ahead a pile up of people. A full-throated crowd. It seemed the entire city population had squished itself down into the upcoming street. It was a baying and incited population he approached, a population whose slurred howl immediately suggested that a field sobriety test would likely not go well for anyone.

As he neared, Paul felt some other discordant aspects to the scene ahead. This looked to be no ordinary crowd. For one, Paul had the feeling of being watched. The throng was looking his way, as if anticipating him. And as he closed in, his presence began effecting what it had done to the writing table back at The Winged Owl; the crowd began splitting in two, parting just a little to create a corridor down the middle. There was one last oddity. The collective voice did not sound quite right. It lacked something. Paul began to feel the impression you might get from watching broth vibrate, or from falling down a shaft that mines the world's supply of soft, rounded vowels.

The cause became clear as he came upon the first person. She reached out and touched her fingers up to his face as he went by, brushing his check and sort of giggling. This person – as the pronoun in the previous sentence has already stoutly indicated – was a woman.

They were all women. (Or almost all, as a few falsettos and veiny arms revealed.) And as he pushed deeper through the crowd, every one of them began reaching out and hooting for him, as if he were a top seeded gladiator or the Today Only sale at Viblio's Discount Outlet.

Paul did not understand in the smallest way what was going on, but he knew he better start ducking and weaving.

His training as an Impelled Maniac served him well. With a number of timed tucks and slides, he wended down the gap and avoided at least some of the flapping fingers directed his way. But the experience only got more startling. He found himself jogging in lock step astride the only other demonstrable human male around.

"Honored comrade," his new companion said, glancing at Paul while they made through the narrow breach, both of them being touched at and admired by the spectators. "I salute thee in the name of the Great She-Wolf and wish thee the providence of Mercury."

The outstretched arms and waggling fingers kept outstretching and waggling and Paul kept trying to squirm his way between them. The most helpful analogy might be to imagine an appetizer being steered through the pulsing *villi intestinali* tentacles of an inflamed GI tract.

Trying to stabilize his mind in some way, Paul dropped back a couple paces.

He began to feel like he must have been knocked cold by the writing table and was still in his cubicle in a state of comatose hallucination. No other explanation made sense. He knew his legs continued to move and his other senses seemed in working order, but his mind swam.

The problem fundamentally was that Paul had never paid much attention in history class. In addition, he never had the time or funding to take part in the countless holidays and rituals of Rome. But Paul had put himself directly into the middle of the sacred and ancient Lupercalia Run, a yearly and purportedly holy practice that went back hundreds of years.

No one knew the original purpose behind the Lupercalia. But it was understood that if you were a woman you were to stand by the side of the road, and if you were one of the select patrician men honored to take part, you were to run through the women as they reached out and touched you all over. It was said to have some relation to primeval rites of fertility and bravery or some such tradition.

There was a vague understanding at one time in the far past that by touching a hallowed male the woman would receive some kind of luck of the gods. Possibly she would become impregnated. By this era in Rome's development, the Run had become mostly a carnival of gropes. Rich men ran down the street getting felt up by lots of women.

Paul's companion seemed to be performing his part well. He jogged with a graceful rhythm while letting himself be pawed all over. Paul, after another minute or two of being handled himself, decided to ask his new friend what exactly was going on. With a burst of energy, and avoiding a new set of outstretched hands, he got himself up closer.

He reached out to tap the man on the shoulder.

Unfortunately the timing of his touch had the effect only of distracting his companion. It distracted the man just enough to force him to miss a step. As it happened, this step was a vital step, one not to be missed.

Thrown off, the man pitched over the foot of sturdy matron near the curb and became propelled gymnastically skyward. The force of his momentum continued his course neatly. He very nearly alighted onto the smart new hats atop a grouping of middle-aged homemakers before, during his parabolic descent, he was brought to a stop by a box of kohlrabi cabbage.

The operator and sole proprietor of the *Veni Vidi Vendi* Green Grocer Wagon had, that morning, gathered his spilled merchandise from the sidewalk after an earlier difficult customer encounter. Thinking to appeal to health conscious women (actually this was his wife's idea), he had moved his cart to the site of the Lupercalia Run. To his relief, despite some close calls, he had experienced no damage or upset from the raucous festival tumult.

Now he watched as the great majority of his vendibles became very suddenly displaced by a Lupercalia participant who was suffering from an obviously decaying orbit. One moment the cart offered a fine assortment of colorful fruits, vegetables, figs and spice jars; the next an incoming patrician began sliding across. Along with the cart's produce, a ribbony and jeweled object shot from the runner's pocket, and all of this mix skittered and bounced toward a gaping drainpipe.

What struck Paul most during this entire development was that, all the time while airborne and then as he was coming in hot, his companion had managed remarkably to gyrate his body so that he kept his eyes – suddenly rather vengeful eyes, despite their black pupils barely enlarging – focused entirely on him. Focused entirely on Paul, that is.

Paul, reacting quickly as ever, picked up his pace a bit.

JAZZ

For its privileged guests, Caesar's private luxury box at the finish of the Lupercalia Run offered more than the adequate comforts. The box had it all. In addition to allocated parking and a private tunneled entrance out back, there were the rows and rows of steamed-up chafing dishes inside, half a dozen rolling beverage carts, and green seat cushions that oozed air when you sat on them.

Off to the left, a three-piece jam band – bass, vocalist, trumpet – modestly kept the energy level just so. And affixed to the front of the box, a retractable glass panel let you watch the action beyond but with a satisfactory level of remove from the tumult and smells of the forum.

Caesar was paying attention to none of this.

"Acrostics are kind of fun too. You know, where you use the first letter of a word to say something else."

Paul nodded.

"For example, take Caesar," Caesar said. "I'm thinking of having this chiseled into my front room wall. The name goes vertical – you know, up and down – in big capital letters, and the sentences go across. C is for 'Cleaned up the silt in the port.' The A is for 'Always tries to eat healthy." E would be 'Astute use of military tactics."

An ovation from the other side of the glass panel broke his thought at S. The Lupercalia Run ended at one of Rome's largest forums, letting a large portion of the city's population gather to watch. Another runner had started coming into view, and the crowd was responding robustly.

"If you don't mind me saying," Caesar told Paul, "I was a little surprised to see you coming up through the forum as one of our festival runners yourself. No offense, I hope."

Caesar's surprise at this matched Paul's. After the encounter that had lifted his fellow runner momentarily aloft, Paul had worked his way through increasing thickets of women. It took all his ability to filter through the streets and make it to the forum. He entered the space to a thunder of applause and sought out Caesar's box. Looking down, Caesar had motioned for Paul to be brought in.

It was Caesar's habit to majestically congratulate all the Lupercalia runners as they finished and hand them a tin of thin mints, packaged specially for the occasion, and then see them ushered away. But he recognized Paul as the IM who had been at the house earlier in the morning; he had bade him come in and sit down.

"You're very good at word games and clearly a fellow who loves figuring out puzzles," Caesar continued, "but frankly I didn't think someone of your occupation would be asked to run today. Usually it's the really rich and powerful who get the honor. Though not necessarily in that order, of course. I'd be out there myself if I were a couple years younger."

"As a matter of fact, sir," Paul said, wriggling in his comfortable chair, "I understand you wish to send another message?"

Paul wanted only to be on his way as quickly as possible. The runner he had inadvertently tripped up would probably be coming in at any moment. Plus there was the matter of everyone in the box and tens of thousands outside the box possibly finding out he himself had been part of the Run only by mistake.

"Do I?" Caesar said preoccupiededly. "A message? Well, that may be, I don't know. I do wonder what's keeping Antony. He had this all planned out so precisely."

"So no message then?" Paul glanced toward the exit.

"Anyway, let's take advantage of the time," Caesar said, motioning for his servant.

"Did you remember to bring my Mega-Crossword?" he asked Nimbus. "The one I was working on this morning?"

From a valise, a dog eared and beaten up paperback was fetched.

"Crosswords obviously are your first love," Caesar, flipping through, said to Paul. "Of course, the key to solving these is getting into the mind of the writer, as you know. I've got most these solved, but there are a few hard ones I've been trying to get all day. It's all I can do to not to peek at the answer key. Ah, here we go. First one. 'Paid for the most expensive triumphal march in history.' First two letters are L-I, and it ends with an S. Eight letters. Any idea who that might be?"

Seeing that Caesar apparently didn't remember wanting to send a message, Paul had been discreetly eyeing obstacles between himself and the exit to the back tunnel, trying to figure out his escape.

"Er," he began. Paul knew not one usable fact from history. But he thought he should go along with Caesar until an opportunity to get away arose. He dimly remembered the names of a few historical figures his mother had mentioned during her cryptic pratings. "Could it be ... uh ... Licinius?"

Caesar stared off into the distance for a good half minute.

"Yes," he whispered. "Yes, yes, a thousand times: Yes. Nimbus, bring Caesar a pencil!"

Nimbus pointed to Caesar's left ear.

"Fully brilliant," Caesar uttered. "Licinius Crassus. Wealthiest man in history. Won the Servile War as general, of course, but he was so distrustful and hoarding, he brought half his riches with him during the campaign, and it all disappeared. It was the most expensive triumph ever. Yes! Truly, young man, you have a great mind."

He grinned at Paul and leaned back.

"But I'm sure Antony was supposed to be here by now," Caesar mused aloud, possibly to himself, possibly not. "Still, let's get back to business. This next one's bugging me, too. The clue is 'Fake fur.' Four letters. Ending in an X. What could that possibly be?"

Before Paul could stammer an irrational response, Nimbus came over with a tray of little foods. Feeling nauseous already, Paul offered a no-thank-you grin. But Nimbus pushed the tray under his nose and nodded purposefully for Paul to look. It was mostly colorful seafood on toast points, along with some greasy wieners.

Yet in the middle, he noticed, stood a square of pâté. And drawn clearly into the gray paste was a word. A four-letter word.

"Surely you will get this, my bright young friend." Caesar turned to Paul as Nimbus backed away. "'Fake fur.'"

"Um," Paul put forward by way of preface. "Erm. Maybe. 'Faux'?"

Again, Caesar stared off for half a minute. Again, he followed this with a whisper of affirmation.

"Brilliant! I should have known. I think Calpurnia's been hinting for weeks she wants an imitation otter scarf for our anniversary. Okay, last one. The clue is 'Use those assets.' Nine. Also starting L-I."

While Caesar stared into the book, Paul watched Nimbus begin to visibly point into a carafe and then write a number in the air. When, after Nimbus repeated these gestures enough times to lead Paul into carefully enunciating the words "liquid ... eight," Caesar about had a fit of joy.

"My young friend, you must be the best crossworder this side of the Tiber," he declared. "To use your assets is to liquidate them. People sell their stuff and get cash. Makes perfect sense when you hear it. Wow, am I impressed. Nimbus, I want you always to use our new companion here for all our future messages."

Caesar smiled broadly at Paul.

"As you wish, sire," said Nimbus. "Right now, I do believe the last runner of the festival is approaching for your good wishes."

"Boo hiss," Caesar said, disappointed at the interruption, but willing to perform his duty.

He rose, swelling himself to offer an earnest intonation and monogrammed tin, and here Paul saw his opportunity. He moved fast.

It almost worked, too.

He sidled from the chair. Keeping his eyes to the floor, he slipped past four or five huddles of patricians, several highboy cocktail tables and some sheet music, and started his way down the short staircase out of the box. He made it into the canvas entrance tunnel and had three more steps to take before he would be free outside.

A hand grasped his shoulder. A familiar hand.

Paul stopped, inhaled and turned around.

"Most impressive." Gaius Cassius Longinus released his grip and offered Paul a smile; his version of a smile, at least. Behind him stood Marcus Brutus, with an authentic smile.

"My intuition about you was right, young man," Cassius said. "You confirm it. I had expected you to be here, but I am surprised you did not you tell me you were actually a participant in the festival Run. A truly distinguished credit to you. And I saw you talking confidentially just now with Caesar."

Before Paul could fully comprehend what had begun happening, Cassius directed him off to the side. He suggested Brutus return to the box to keep an eye out.

"We cannot talk freely here, of course," Cassius whispered. "Come see me at my villa when a discreet opportunity arises. In the meantime, tell me, is there any critical information the Opposition needs to know right now? We face such a myriad of questions. Did you get any answers from Caesar that could be helpful?"

"Answers?" Paul began, clearing his throat. "Yes. Urm ..."

It seemed odd that one senator would show such fervent interest in another's crossword hobby. But Paul did not know the ways of the great. Maybe they had some kind of wager going about who can solve the most puzzles, and Cassius was looking for an edge.

"Please," said Cassius. "I assure you, you can trust me."

From the direction of the forum, a cheer cannoned through the canvas tunnel.

"Licinus Crassus." Paul blurted.

"You need to speak in code?" Cassius said. "I understand. And I think I know what you mean. It is most disturbing. Go on. Quickly now."

"Faux?" Paul next offered.

Cassius's face clouded over for half a minute while Paul eyed the exit.

"So Caesar has his eyes on those he considers his enemies," Cassius said. "The Opposition is truly in grave danger. We are indeed the foes of Caesar."

"Actually," said Paul, "I think it was referring to..."

"Anything more?" Cassius asked darkly. "This is sounding most troubling."

"Yes. Uh. I did get one more answer."

"Please do not hold back now. The daunting truth must be confronted, must be faced directly."

"Liquidate," said Paul. "When you are looking to –"

Given its natural state, this was not easy to notice, but Cassius's face fell into an expression of great solemnity.

"Such dread," he exclaimed, pulling Paul in closer and clasping his hand. "The Opposition is to be liquidated. Friend, you have performed a great service to the Republic. Yet it is too dangerous here for you. You must leave now, until we can talk again. What is the best way for me to contact you?"

Paul told Cassius he could be reached through The Winged Owl Messaging Service.

"Very smart," Cassius said in a low voice. "We can communicate through the use of Impelled Maniacs to help ensure confidentiality. I have heard of these IMs and am most glad you have, too. I will simply ask to be put in contact with Caesar's special envoy, no? That too will be our sort of code. Now you best be off. Godspeed, dear friend."

A second exploding cheer from the forum shot through. Its exit speed out the mouth of the tunnel only just exceeded Paul's.

Brutus came back down to find Cassius alone, nodding in thought.

"It is far worse than we imagined," Cassius said. "As Caesar's foes, we are facing nothing less than a liquidation. Just as in the days of Licinius Crassus."

"You better come back and see what is going on up there," Brutus told him. "I'm not sure what to make of it all, but it must mean something."

Paul already had gotten a quarter mile away from the whole place when he realized he carried, in his left fist, two more Libertas coins.

DEMURRAL

A t the same time that Paul had been making his escape from Caesar's box, Caesar was running through Antony's plan in his mind one more time.

The plan was: Antony sprints vibrantly into the forum amid great applause. The mid-afternoon sun is slanting perfectly into Caesar's box, just when the people are at their pitch of excitement. Caesar greets Antony. Antony shows Caesar the fancy headband. (What did Antony call it? The diadem?) Three times, Antony places the thing on Caesar's brow. Each time Caesar takes it off, saying the words Antony wrote for him about having no wish to become King of Rome. Eventually somehow in the long run this makes Caesar some kind of dictator, with Antony as his deputy.

That was the plan. Antony had arranged and timed it with precision.

But the plan hadn't been unfolding quite right. Runner after runner came into the forum without any sign of Antony, and the day got longer and longer.

In fact it was almost half an hour after sunset before Nimbus finally called Caesar up to greet the final runner. Coming into the forum, the man looked to be hobbling. He certainly was not sprinting, vibrantly or otherwise.

Already packing their lunch baskets and puzzled that any runner might have still been out, the crowd nevertheless began to offer some claps. Antony waved gamely as he pushed himself through the forum. He shuffled up to Caesar's box, trying to hide a limp he had recently acquired and holding his tunic closed in front, where a hat pin had rent it.

Caesar knew this to be his cue. Get up, go congratulate Antony. Three diadem offers, three demurrings.

He grasped a tin, gamely bound from his seat and strode up.

There was a loud bonk.

Caesar had forgotten to order the glass panel in front of the box retracted. Caesar did not see it in the twilight.

The first roar heard by Cassius and Paul in the canvas entrance tunnel some moments earlier had been the crowd's cry of bemusement in response to this scene.

Caesar staggered backward into the arms of an elderly senator as a drizzle of thin mints pattered onto the first two rows of seating; two slaves hastily cranked down the glass panel.

Caesar blinked half a dozen times and rubbed his nose before offering an "I'm okay" wave to the crowd. To this, the crowd responded with a second cheer of sorts; its curiosity had been awakened.

The forum stared as Caesar inched himself carefully to the edge of the box, reaching ahead of himself to make sure the glass had indeed been lowered. From below, Antony bowed. Caesar leaned down.

"I'm sorry," Caesar murmured.

"We best just continue." Antony turned so both men faced the crowd while clasping hands. The crowd watched back with cocked-head expectation at what would come next.

"It's just, that was the last tin of mints." Caesar tried keeping his voice low. "I don't have another one for you."

Both men had begun speaking from the sides of their mouths, outwardly smiling and trying not to move their lips; the way you talk when you find yourself being loomed at by large predators one pounce away.

Gazing ahead into the throng, Antony pulled an object from his tunic and raised it above his head. A silence had spread through the forum.

"What's that?" Caesar glanced over. "What happened to that diadem gadget you showed me a couple days ago? That looks like – like a bunch of collards."

"Swiss chard," Antony said with some edge. "The diadem was sabotaged. I'll explain later. This will work. I shaped it like a laurel wreath. Please, Caesar, lean down a little more."

Cautiously Caesar crouched; Antony worked the object onto his head.

Back at the vegetable wagon, Antony had done the best he could after watching his diadem slide into the sewers. Several broad green leaves had been compressed as tightly as possible, and a dozen Bing cherries and assorted nuts were affixed with chicken wire along their red and yellow stems. It was all tied off fairly neatly in back. While a competent makeshift, though, the effect was not fully what Antony had been originally going for with the diadem.

Caesar stood to full height, puffing himself before the forum. As he took a moment to prepare for a somber intonation, one of the leaves wilted over his right ear, suggestive of a basset hound becoming disappointed, and he had to begin tilting his head left when the whole apparatus threatened to slip off.

"I know not the meaning of this, O Antony," he began to intone in full theatric volume, as two or three of the other, fresher stalks started blossoming to their natural firmness. "Yet I tell you, Caesar has no ambitions. I seek not for power except to protect and aid the people of Rome. So if this be the gleam of a royal crown you would, on behalf of the people, bestow upon Caesar" – gesturing to the growing greens atop his head – "I must tell you, it is not for Caesar's brow. Caesar wants neither the splendor nor the burden of such an extravagant crown. Caesar in his humility shall not be King of Rome."

In the distance, the top scoop of a Freez-Em-Up™ cone flopped to the ground while farther off someone cleared his throat. Shortly after, two macadamias ejected from Caesar's headwear. These comprised, as Caesar held his pose, the most stirring activities within the forum.

He silently counted to ten, for dramatic purposes, before slowly removing the object. Crouching to hand it back to Antony, he asked how the program seemed to be clipping along.

"Change in plans," Antony said under his breath. "You best just deliver the post-Run speech. Let's just move on."

"No more with the fake crown?" Caesar whispered, loud enough for several hundred nearby Romans to hear. "I thought we were going to do this three times."

"No more with the crown."

"Okay, your call."

Caesar re-inflated himself. He then went on to give a rather good speech. He spoke of the magnificence of the upcoming wars, he called himself the people's guardian and talked of reviving the grandeur of Rome, free grain for the poor, thwarting all the dangerous agitators and malcontents. He paused here and there and modulated his voice at the right points, and he knew not to speak too long. By the time he got to the and-let-me-conclude part of the speech, the forum had started to liven up nicely.

"Caesar wishes you the best of... of ..." – he couldn't remember the name of the festival – "... of a very fun night, and I commend your health and happiness to the eternal gods."

The crowd gave Caesar a third hurrah as Antony came round to enter the box. Though so often having to induce Caesar to action and then hope that Caesar wouldn't bollix what he'd been induced into, Antony felt relieved. In all the years he had known Caesar and put up with Caesar, Antony continued to be startled that someone so puzzling in day-to-day life could project such a striking public image.

"A very well delivered speech," he told Caesar as the applause died away.

"Of course you wrote the thing. But, yes. I think this day has gone off really well."

"Caesar, we are yet to make our crucial maneuver. We must not forget that the Opposition will check us at every turn." Antony motioned to Cassius and Brutus, who had just returned to the box from the tunnel entrance, after their encounter with Paul. "I ask you again to please remember such men are enormously dangerous."

Caesar looked over to the two and nodded.

"Yond Cassius has a lean and hungry look," he agreed thoughtfully. "I should probably go offer him a nice slice of carrot cake."

Antony clenched his fists.

"I hope you don't mind me saying." Caesar waved for Nimbus to come over with the wine. "But you look quite bedraggled, and you did come in a lot later than I thought you said you would."

"Caesar will be shocked to hear this." Antony brushed at his lacerated tunic. "A saboteur assailed me during the Run, forcing the diadem from me and delaying my appearance. I suspect he was a planted operative doing the bidding of the Opposition. And I shall make him pay, dearly, when I find him. As Caesar knows, I never forget a face."

BEFORE

Rome spent the next days in a state of earnest calm. A major festival had just ended and a war was coming up. At street sides lay heaps of drained jugs, punctured beach balls, broken folding chairs, and uneaten side salads.

Soldiers stayed indoors packing and repacking their gear and talking sullenly with girlfriends and life insurance agents. From smithies and wheelwrights, a rhythmic clangor gave to the city the impression of a foretelling clock, counting down to a momentous point.

Time, to Gaius Cassius Longinus, was nearly out. He had determined to find a way to work on Brutus. If he could arouse Brutus, he'd decided there might still a chance the rest of the Opposition would come to life.

"We are coming to the fulcrum point where we shall have no choice if we wish to maintain our ancient Republic."

"It is all doubtlessly troubling," said Brutus with his nondescript affability. "I have to say, this business of closing the Senate House just now certainly is strange in and of itself."

"Yes, most."

Cassius had asked Brutus to meet him at the Senate's offices. When they had arrived, though, a sign on the front of the Senate building announced, "Closed for Renovation. Sorry." A chamberlain informed them that sessions were going to be held nearby for the time being in the Theater of Pompey.

"They might have at least sponged off the floors," Brutus said, trying to lift his sandals against the suction of congealed butter and other presumed juices.

"I am afraid, dear Brutus, if we don't take rigorous action at the next session, whether it is here in a theater or anywhere, we will have to get used to the Senate having entirely no place to meet. The Senate will be closed forever."

"You may not be wrong," Brutus offered genially. "Did you see the new proposal from The Outside Communications Consultant? He's thinking we go with sandwich boards, followed by a high-level sponsorship package at the next major festival. I do like the slogan he's suggesting. 'Rome's Opposition: Steady. Ready. Let's Be Friends.'"

Except for some cleaning crew that looked to be on indefinite break, the theater was empty. Cassius gazed down to the bare stage. He pondered that the final scene of Rome's ancient government could soon be played there – even if he had to act the part alone.

"It seems the Fates might have some notion of providing us assistance, even when we think they are being obtuse." Cassius leaned into Brutus for emphasis. "I don't know who was responsible for our unfortunate meeting at the Mulvian Baths and Conference Center, but the result did allow me to meet Caesar's young confidant and coax him onto our side. And you know the answers to all our questions about Caesar that he revealed. Caesar plans to go back to the days of Licinius Crassus. He is going to order a proscription, declaring us enemies of the state. Then he is going to liquidate the Senate. That's the word Caesar used, liquidate. Our liberties and very lives are in danger if this is allowed. We must act now. We have seen, as the world has seen, how quick-witted and ingenious Caesar is."

"Could be, could be," Brutus said. "I'll think it all over for sure. But, listen, I have an appointment for highlights and a scalp toning in 20 minutes. Let's consider a little more about our options, shall we? Keep me posted on any more word you hear from our young friend. His sharp mind and courage, from what you told me, are most admirable."

Not very far away at that moment, as he was being discussed by two members of the Roman Senate, Paul lay in the bed of his little efficiency unit. He was fully awake and fully inert. He had been driven hard by the Shift Supervisor since the Lupercalia Festival. This accounted for part of the reason he clung wearily to a frayed blanket, face ceilingward.

With an upcoming war, there were opportunities for profit, which always kept IMs darting throughout Rome. And the Shift Supervisor had put Paul on the most disdained duty that any Impelled Maniac could be made to perform: Spontaneous Private

Appeal Messaging.

"Hello [insert name]," Paul would say to the soldier whose house address he had been given. "It's me! Why haven't I heard from you? Remember you told me I'm sexy? I will show you a very good time. A deep massage is just what you need right now. Please let me hear from you, stud. Love, Tiana Bangkok."

Paul would conclude by making a kissy face, as instructed. If lucky, Paul would then merely watch a door slamming in his direction. A few times he had to elude a hairy fist. Only occasionally, the recipient would send him back with a response, always a variant of, "You sound hot. What size breasts, and do you have a face woodcut I can see?"

It was all enough to make steam come off one's rope sandals and to assume a position of immobility during the rare time one had off from work. The main cause of Paul staying in bed, however, did not relate to physical exhaustion. He was at a loss.

Paul's problems had been blossoming, branching and further tangling themselves up, he realized. Inadvertently in a very short time:

A. He had become the messenger of choice for Julius Caesar. And might have made friends with the man.
B. The Opposition of Rome had begun paying him as a vital informant against Julius Caesar. And had doubled his salary.
C. A man of seeming consequence had tripped pretty badly. And seemed very unhappy with Paul about it.

This was a list not favorable for convincing increasingly ex-girlfriends and their fathers of one's drive or that weird things were not happening.

He turned to his side to see three gleaming coins on the upside down orange crate that acted as his nightstand. The odor of some kind of braised meat worked its way into Paul's room. As a converted basement room at the back end of a back alley at the bottom of a crowded hill, Paul's living space acted as a retention basin for half the noises and a quarter of the odors generated by Rome.

His stomach insisted that he use the money to feed itself, but the major centers of fret in his brain pointed out the dangers of bandying about such coins. The stomach was overridden.

The scent at least did not linger long. As a basement apartment, Paul's room had once been the end point for garbage from the wealthy tenants above. On one of his walls, a veneer of wood partially covered the discharging end of a now-defunct refuse chute. In the winter, the chute sucked up any warmth that came from his little stove, but now it thankfully took up the taunting odor of food quickly enough.

But that was a very small bright spot in an otherwise very black big picture for Paul.

If he had known right then that back at The Winged Owl headquarters the Shift Supervisor was bellowing for him to make another run to Caesar's house, Paul more than likely would have continued turning over and begun eating his pillow.

"Yes, Caesar," Nimbus, on the other side of the city, was explaining at this same moment. "I called for him to come from the IM service more than an hour ago, but he is not available."

"More's the pity," Caesar said. "I rather like the young man. Reminds me of the son I never knew I didn't have, in a strange way. We're very different, but this doesn't stop people from feeling a natural kinship, of course. He spends his days zipping around the city, while I am as constant and unmoving as the north star. That is what I'm as constantly unmoving as, isn't it? The north star?"

He turned to Antony, who he had been seated with for some time. "He's a very brilliant fellow: one of these Impelled Maniacs you hear about. I hope you two run into each other someday. He loves wordplay almost as much as I do. He's got a real talent for listening, too, the kind of person who really hears you and feels what you're saying. I was chatting with him in my box just before you finished your sprint through Rome. Of which speaking – that sprint – I just figured out what it looks like."

"Caesar? What *what* looks like?"

"Macedonia."

"I'm not sure I follow, Caesar."

Antony and Caesar had been meeting for several hours. Antony during this time had been struggling to steer the conversation with Caesar but found himself relentlessly and with great effort having to work against Caesar's drifting thoughts. Antony felt not unlike a done in coxswain being lobbed about in the center of a Mediterranean gale.

"You know, the province," Caesar said. "Macedonia. Your hematoma, from when you tripped during that run. It looks just like Macedonia. It's even got the yellow sections to indicate mountains. Go on, lift up your tunic, and tell me it doesn't."

"Please, Caesar, may we return to the purpose of our discussion? I must tell you again, that the time has at last come for you to accept the position of dictator. Have you had the chance to read the speech I sent you, the one I would like you to give in the Senate?"

"Oh that," said Caesar. "Yes. Absolutely. Excellent. Really excellent."

"Good. I am pleased that Caesar found favor with my humble attempt. Did my choice of words fit with your speaking style?"

"Words?"

"In reading the speech, did you have any concerns or questions?" Caesar raised his goblet, motioning Nimbus to top it up.

"Oh, no," he told Antony. "I haven't looked at that speech at all."

"But. But I just asked if you had a chance to read it, and you said you did."

"Exactamundo. And it was an excellent and ideal chance," said Caesar, "One of the finest chances I've ever had. But I didn't actually get around to reading the thing, sorry."

Antony briefly clenched onto the sides of his chair with both hands.

"I do have to say," Caesar continued, "from what you've told me about everything, this seems like one of those deceptively simple plans you always enjoy working out. I bet you were really burning the midnight owl to come up with that headband scheme. So you're saying to get this done tomorrow, are you?"

"I will have the votes lined up just as soon as you finish proposing the new position. It will be accomplished before anyone even fully realizes what has happened, and you shall be off to the glory of another war and we back here can look after everything on your behalf. This is one of the reasons I had the Senate Building closed."

"Did you? Closed the Senate Building?" Caesar's first thought went to the Senate cafe. Tomorrow was Chili Day. "The Senate is closed? All that inconvenience just for this?"

"I believe control of setting and surroundings can be very advantageous," Antony explained. "You get great benefit from exerting power over where your opponents go and are positioned. I've explained this before. One might, for instance, pressure the management of a conference center and baths to incommode one's opponents in their attempts at meeting. As an example."

"Oh? Might one?"

"By moving tomorrow's session to the Theater of Pompey instead of the routine Senate chamber, you will be able to announce our plan in grand style. We will confound the Opposition, too. And, if I may raise an uncomfortable topic, the theater will be far more safe."

"Safe? Safe for what?" Caesar spoke tonelessly; his concentration was directed mostly toward the living room wall, where he had begun wondering if maybe he should just have a "JC!" carved in, instead of going with an acrostic.

"I know Caesar does not want to hear this." Antony paused. "But many of our friends agree with me that the Opposition is ruthless in its cunning. They will stop at nothing to thwart you. Nothing. And Rome cannot afford to not have Caesar. You are too important to us. Your personal safety must be pro-tect-ed."

"Or is it deceptively complex?"

"Excuse me, Caesar?"

"It's always confusing. If something seems to be one thing but it's really the opposite thing, do you say it's deceptively what-it-really-is? Or deceptively what-it-seems-to-be? Are your plans deceptively simple, or deceptively complex?"

"Caesar. Let me assure you that the Opposition has been unyielding in their dangerous conspiring against you. Have no doubt on the matter. As you know, I have my pulse on everything going on in this city."

Indeed, Antony had been closely tracking the activities of the Opposition leadership through his network of agents, although he did not think to report the details of their movements to Caesar. Since the conclusion of the Lupercalia Festival, these had been the most notable doings in relation to the Opposition leadership:

1) Pompilius Pulcher bought two new togas – his wife told him he needed only one, but the second was thirty percent off – and visited his attorney five times.
2) Cicero had a mole removed.
3) "Several neighbors complained of suspicious activity. It was determined that suspect Livius the Younger lacks criminal record. No charges were filed. Suspect however was asked to refrain in future from illicit measuring of curbs." (Police blotter, Precinct 54, District 8, 3-12-44BC)
4) The name of Lucius Crispius Totovus was entered in the 5th Annual Uncle Arnold's Finer Foods Ham Eating Invitational.

"Your plan does make some sense to Caesar," Caesar said. "But I still just don't know. Giving me dictator powers here while I'm away at war? I'm just not sure how that helps me. If I'm fully understanding what it is I'm saying, I guess I got the feeling at the Run that people are just not interested in anything like this."

Antony pushed.

"Remember, our performance ended up taking place much later

in the day with a less-than-ideal wreath, owing to the Opposition saboteur who assaulted me during the Run. The masses had been drinking all day and were not in the right frame of mind. It is true that the first part of the plan did not operate ideally. But let us remember that we learn only through hardships."

"See I always really felt we learn only through about sophomore year high school. Then it all starts getting hazy."

"This plan will work, Caesar. As I've explained, by voting to give you dictator powers before you go on campaign, we will be able to keep a lid on Rome while you are gone. As your deputy here, I will ensure the powers are used wisely."

Antony went on, as he always seemed to do. Just before going off to the new wars out East, Caesar would announce that it was too risky to leave so much unattended to back home. As a result, he, Caesar, would accept the position of temporary dictator. That way, he would be able to send orders back to Rome if chaos threatened. And Mark Antony would remain in the capital as his representative, keeping a watchful eye on the city and acting when necessary.

"Rome needs you stepping up now more than ever," Antony said. "With you taking undisputed power while off with the troops and my humble assistance back here, we can – "

He sensed a Caesarian drift.

"I hope," Antony said with new emphasis, "you will take this in the spirit it is meant, but I must tell you that myself and your other friends are very much counting on you tomorrow. Very much."

"You have said that before," said Caesar, and the solemnly intoning version of Caesar almost inflated. "It sounds almost threatening, if I didn't know better."

"No, not at all, my Caesar." Antony nodded to Nimbus for a glass of wine. "But the time has come for a decision."

IDES

B ad dreams rarely troubled Julius Caesar. When most of us lay down to leave the waking world each night, our minds continue to pitch about. Our bodies may be at rest, but our spirits are awake and bounding uneasily through an ethereal dream world, stumbling amid the "palace of King Sleep and his son Morpheus" (Ovid, *Complete Works*, Book XI).

Caesar's spirit, on the other hand, slept there. Most every night, he slid with ease into the peaceful slumber of a hatchling and remained in luxuriant rest till morning.

This was the case on the night before the Ides of March, 44 BC. He woke up next morning feeling refreshed and ready to face a brand new day.

"Nimbus!" he called, midpoint in a yawning wake-up stretch. "Where's my toga? I got a really good feeling about today."

Caesar's servant had Caesar's toga waiting, sitting atop the dressing bench.

At twelve feet by fifteen feet, worsted and folded over on its semicircular self, the toga could have passed for a pile of resting field dogs that might be better left alone.

Caesar, however, rose and strode to it; Nimbus stepped back three paces and poised himself.

It took time. It took all of thirty minutes. It was by no means a pretty feat.

At three points Caesar waved an anxious Nimbus back. Seeing Caesar stuck at one silent juncture, Nimbus had to discreetly supply a reminder lyric from the toga-tying song. ("The commuter gets in the bus, and takes it toward Uranus"[1] – Caesar always laughed at

---

[1] An understanding of Late Roman Republican ethnomusicology, as well as

this one.) But in the end, Caesar had successfully put on his toga entirely by himself. Owing to some confused knots at the midriff, he could not bend over for a full view. But he looked down at himself as best as possible with some satisfaction.

"Caesar is as Caesar does," said Caesar softly.

Nimbus allowed a small smile, too.

Caesar had even managed to form a special fold in his toga around his right hip to act as a kind of pouch, just as Nimbus had taught him. Reverentially, he unlocked a small bronze-plated coffer atop his dresser and raised the lid. Its only content was a folded up sheet of foolscap folio tied with braided red cord.

"This will knock their tunics off." Caesar picked up the parchment. "Did I tell you about my secret document?"

For weeks, Caesar had talked about his secret document more than anything. Nimbus did not remind Caesar of this. Nor did he remind him that it was he, Nimbus, who first brought the document to Caesar's attention and whose questions about it led Caesar to decide to publicly share its contents.

"I'm finally going to read it out at the Senate session today," Caesar said, as if revealing something new to his house servant. "Antony is all focused on that big plan of his, but I don't have any doubt that people will remember today's Ides of March because of this."

He slid the parchment into his toga fold.

Downstairs, Caesar found his wife at the breakfast table. He ate a good, full spread and took his time with the morning coffee. Calpurnia talked for some length about her own inability to sleep through the night, but Caesar mostly just nodded mechanically and grunted an assent from time to time. There was, on the back side of the cereal box, an especially challenging Little Socrates and Friends cryptogram. It seemed absolutely unscramblable, no matter how many attempts at it. Between spoonfuls, Caesar mumbled, scribbled, erased, cussed, stuck out his tongue and rapped his head with a pencil. Yet he was stumped.

"Almighty Caesar," said Nimbus finally, standing at the door jamb. "Your escort party awaits at the front portico."

"Five more minutes," Caesar said, squinting and still quarreling with the box, though he stood to let himself be led outside to his courtyard.

---

contextual analysis, strongly suggests the toga-tying song sounded much like the refrain to Deep in the Heart of Texas. The reader may wish to perform the song as such for confirmation.

Collectively, Rome had long been in the habit of bouncing back quickly from the effects of one holiday to ready itself for the promise of the next. There was almost a rote professionalism to its merriment. Though not officially a day off, this Ides of March took on the air of another festival. The dense streets again began to reverberate with every class of sound. Red bunting had been hung along the route where the next day Caesar and his soldiers would parade on their way east. Street performers had started setting up near the Theater of Pompey, where the Senate was to meet; there, curious Romans congregated amid rumors of big changes coming.

"Good morning, O subjugator," Antony said. He gestured to nine or ten other senators gathered in Caesar's courtyard. "May we have the honor of accompanying you to today's session of our august Senate?"

Caesar announced he would lead the way himself. Two miles lay between his house and the theater. Yet he waved off his litter bearers. He walked the entire length to the theater with an imposing carriage, erect and deliberate, as if leading a slow and majestic procession. His train of followers walked solemnly behind, while startled citizens pointed with wonder. Antony tried getting a word to him, to confirm that Caesar had decided to go through with the plan and understood it. But Caesar did not turn to respond. He kept his head pitched up and his back arced in such a stately way that those seeing him might have marked him a son of Jupiter, or the incarnation of virility. He was in truth awfully uncomfortable and wished he done a better job tying his toga. It just didn't have much give.

"It's Caesar!" a child cried out as the escort party came into view in front of the Theater of Pompey. "Isn't it?"

A stimulated cheer spiked through the crowd. People cleared the way and waved their caps and lifted their flagons.

"Yup," said Caesar, waving back and smiling. "A good day."

The Senate had already been called officially into session. The senators inside seemed not to mind the unusual theater setting. They chattered and lined up at the concession stand in the lobby for free snacks, provided courtesy of – as a notice on the counter clearly stated – Mark Antony, then went to find their name cards on the seats.

The Opposition leadership had been placed by Antony's instruction down in the orchestra pit. The Opposition leadership seemed content there. It was an opportunity for senators to catch up on each other's latest trips and favorite new places to eat and shop. It had become almost a show and tell for them. The only one not taking part was Cassius, who had stationed himself just off stage and could be seen glancing furtively around.

"Tropical wool blend," said Pompilius Pulcher, encouraging those near him to run their fingers up and down his new toga and feel it themselves. "Sixty count thread. I have to have a single house-slave whose sole duty is keeping it ironed, but I am a fan."

Bilbius Dilbo and Casca debated whether the new unguent store down the street was worth it, while the bandage on Cicero's right cheek lost its adhesion as he lifted it again to show off the scar where his mole used to be.

"That's rather revolting," Lucius Totovus told Cicero, as he pulled a hunk of back bacon protectively closer to himself.

"As I was saying." Totovus turned away from Cicero and faced Flavian. "Despite common perception, these contests are about more than how much you can eat. There is a strategy involved. The winner of this next one, for example, is the person who can eat the most slices. So the first task is learning to make the slivers as thin as possible. Less meat per slice means bigger numbers, which means victory."

Totovus had brought a hamper filled with supplies and food in preparation for Uncle Arnold's Finer Foods 5th Annual Ham Eating Invitational. Spread in front of him lay a complete, 36-piece cutting board set along with every variety of pig-based meat he had been able to obtain from Zingerman & Zingerman Delicatessen, as well as some helpful snacks he had picked up outside off the *Veni Vidi Vendi* Green Grocer Wagon.

"Training and the best equipment are essential." Carefully lifting a slender serving, he held it in front of his eyes and offered skeptically, "Brine cured may be the way to go. Maybe. I can almost see through it but not quite. It just may not be thin enough."

Above the orchestra pit, up on the stage, a line-up of senators waited to give speeches. These were perfunctory pieces which virtually no one listened to, least of all those talking. Mainly they were offered only to be entered into the official record, allowing this or that senator to say he did his part on this or that issue or that he had paid tribute to a local constituency.

It was Livius the Younger's turn next. He may have been the only one to actually take reverence in his speech. He reviewed his notes and walked carefully to the center of the stage. In preparation of Caesar's major announcement, Antony had lines of lamps and polished glass positioned at the forestage to pour light onto the speakers. Livius the Younger blinked and squinted to see the audience beyond the brightness and called to mind the words he had planned.

Years earlier, Livius the Younger had been told about the senator Marcus Cato. In the old days, Cato would always conclude every oration he gave, no matter what his original topic had been, with the striking words: "Furthermore, Carthage must be destroyed." The man could be discussing roads or shipping or education, but he ended with that same sentence, driving home what he believed to be the crucial issue that overrode every other one – the final annihilation of Rome's constant enemy. "Furthermore, Carthage must be destroyed."

This notion had impressed itself on Livius the Younger. He decided to adopt the rhetorical device for himself. It is not clear that anyone realized he had done so, since he always gave the exact same speech over and over, and everything he said was on the exact same subject anyway from beginning to end. But Livius the Younger was indulged in this, or at least respectfully disregarded. He was, after all, very old. His father, Livius the Elder, had been gone for 97 years. For longer than anyone could remember, Livius the Younger woke up every day just one day from death.

He worked his way through his speech, which lasted four and half minutes, then paused for the dramatic finish.

"Furthermore," he admonished with a tremulous voice, pausing again before his last words: "Furthermore, addresses on the curbs must be painted by the government."

Typically after his perorations, Livius the Younger would trundle in silence from the rostrum, or, if he forgot to leave, he would be shuffled off by the next senator in line. This time, he experienced a sensation new to him. A clapping sound.

For the first time in years, Livius the Younger grinned, and his feet barely scuffed the floor as he went off feeling very good about himself. He did not notice that the body of the Senate had as usual not paid a bit of attention to what he had said and had actually turned around to give their recognition to the Caesarean party coming in.

"A very good reception for you, Caesar," Antony said, pointing up ahead. "We'll let a couple more of these speeches go on and then I'll make a motion to give you the floor."

"Where is my section?" Caesar asked.

Antony directed Caesar to the empty row near the front. As they went to sit, he tapped Caesar's arm and motioned for him to look to the left.

"Yes?" asked Caesar. "What?"

"Take a careful look at Cassius there by the stage stairs. He's acting restless, and it seems like he's almost holding something under his toga. I suggest you be very cautious around him, my Caesar."

"Probably just has something from the snack bar," Caesar said. "I don't know why they don't make these togas with pockets. You've got to stuff things into folds, you know."

Two more speeches went by. The first called for more emphasis on indefinite pronouns in the schools. As the second speech concluded, this one singling out the Etruscan Women's League (Perusia Chapter) for its help funding the "very handsome" nasturtium planters recently installed in the roundabout by the city's eastern gate, Antony began to rise from his seat.

Caesar touched his arm and checked his movement. Antony leaned in.

"Caesar?"

It seemed that Caesar, his eyes focused in the distance, had a solemnity in his thoughts, as if he had made a historic resolution.

"My Caesar has come to a decision?"

Caesar nodded with a kind of measured gravity.

"Bed socks," intoned Caesar.

Mark Antony, a man not given often to twitching, twitched.

"Caesar?"

"Bed socks."

"Caesar?"

"The cryptogram," said Caesar. "At breakfast this morning. 'Bed socks.' That's the answer. It's a matter, you see, of realizing that the vowels and consonants have been transposed, and then if you shift every letter over three, it has to be 'bed socks.' Simple, especially after I remembered hearing the writer of these cryptograms has been laid up with the gout for the past two months."

If Caesar didn't know better, he might have believed that Antony's reaction to this news, for reasons only Antony could have explained, fell something short of enthrallment. Yes, Antony said blankly, bed socks. By all means, bed socks. He then asked Caesar if it would be appropriate for the Senate proceedings to resume their usual pattern.

"Oh, sure," Caesar insisted. "Please, as you will. Do your stuff."

Antony, his pupils having shown a hint of dilation, rose.

"And now, my fellow senators!" He called out, turning to the seats behind and quickly closing off the buzz of conversation klatches throughout. "I move that we give the floor to he who has brought to Rome uncounted victories and vigorous government, he who shall march tomorrow to defeat our Eastern enemies, he who, it will be agreed, is the hope for restoring our Republic. I move to recognize Gaius Julius Caesar!"

Caesar managed to lift himself with some struggle. He leaned into Antony's ear once more.

"Thanks," he said, speaking above the applause. "By the way, I decided not to go with your dictator idea, sorry. Not today. Let's do it when I get back from the war. I just don't want to overshadow my surprise. Which I have here. Somewhere."

Caesar began carefully working his way into the aisle, stepping slowly, keeping his head up. The Roman Senate watched with admiration Caesar's serene and deliberate mounting of the stage. Although, it might be noted that this measured movement had less to do with theatrics than with his inability to bend his knees or back.

"My friends," he murmured while trying to steady himself at the X taped on stage, a little thrown by the dazzling lights in his eyes. He remembered to puff himself up and shift up into oration mode. "My friends! Tomorrow, in the morn, Dawn's rose-red fingers will reach out over Rome and tickle us all awake. And then shall the city arise to see off its soldiers, marching out to a majestic new campaign."

The Senate clapped. Caesar went on in the same vein. He spoke of Rome's duty to the world, of barbarians needing to be kept in their place, of the honor of soldiery and burden of command. The speech clipped along smartly; he noticed only one senator seemingly not impressed.

Cassius, a few feet off stage to his right, frowned with that constant frown of his. This did not startle Caesar, though he did stop a half second in puzzlement at the sight of Cassius continuing to fiddle around for something.

"But before Caesar marches on the morrow," he continued, "Caesar offers a surprise for the city. I have in my possession a document. You shall find it to be a resource of very great interest to all. It is a document that I believe shall fuse everyone together in Caesar's absence – and it shall be shared by every Roman citizen. Put another way, what is mine shall be yours. And I believe the true value of this shall become real when it has been intermixed."

He watched as the Senate edged itself forward on its seats in anticipation, before proclaiming, "My friends, now it is just a question ..."

He slid his hand into a fold of his toga near his right hip. Very soon, however, the smile he'd put on his face leaked away. A puzzled grimace took its place. He tried his hand in the fold above, and the one below. He began rooting around nearby folds. After a few moments, he began working his left hand into some of the slots on the other side of his body. Soon Caesar could be seen running his hands into and out of gaps and up and down his body.

"Where the hell is that thing?" Caesar said to himself. "Damned togas."

Silently, the Roman Senate watched, staring with not a little degree of curiosity. Caesar's jerking actions and pawing had begun to appear to be the kind expected of a man with a classroom of insects who had just started to practice a suggestive new rumba step somewhere in his clothes.

He began twisting his torso right and left and feeling his backside, running his hands over himself with increasing vigor. The contortions had the effect only of screwing the toga even tighter and tighter. At the same time, distracted by his own searching, Caesar started imperceptibly roving off his mark and heading down center.

"My friends, it's just a question of" – Caesar grumbled, his intonating voice having entirely fallen away again – "of digging deep down enough in the right place."

In the focus on his efforts, he still had not sensed that he had begun to locomote. And he had begun doing so at a relatively steady velocity. Twirling and grabbing himself with more violence, staring down into his clothes, jamming his hands into fold after fold, his unconscious ambulation became almost a trot. But he still was too engrossed in his search to feel himself going forward.

By the time he did apprehend his movement, both inertia and the clenching of the toga made any voluntary course correction almost impossible. It was not entirely too late. He probably could have stopped himself even now. But immediately he saw Cassius leap toward him with a lunge. Trying to throw himself into reverse, Caesar only caused his body to make a spinning gyration directly to the edge.

Seeing his immediate fate, Caesar intoned, with some disappointment, "Then fall, Caesar" – before letting out a gentle eep and pitching off the stage.

His head made a clopping sound as it hit the orchestra pit railing.

During all of this activity, those in the pit below did not know what was taking place. They had no way of seeing onto the stage. They'd had a hard enough time hearing any speeches and had been keeping mostly to themselves. Lucius Totovus, for one, had moved from his experiments with the cutting quality of brine cured and had been pulling out other utensils for testing. At present, he held one of these near his face, examining what he felt to be a passably thin slice it had cut, when he heard a peculiar thump above his head.

And so it happened that the end of the most expensive prosciutto knife on the market held, at one moment, a ham, and, at the next, Gaius Julius Caesar, senator, ruler, warrior.

The Second Scroll

COMMOTION

Mother –

I hope you take the three coins you see there next to this note. They're one of the reasons I asked you over here to my apartment today. They're worth a lot, I think. You always tell lots of stories about different exotic places, over the Alps and down south. Maybe a trip to see them would be good for you?

There's an all-inclusive near Mount Vesuvius I once heard about, with a midnight buffet and 24-hour canasta tables ... It's good you decided to see my place, but I have to go to work now. I'm sorry there's nothing to eat around here. If you wait, I'll see you when I get back home, hopefully with a meat pie or two in my hands.

- Me

Paul finished writing, and he propped his note onto the orange crate where his mother would see it. Then he pulled the Libertas coins from under his mattress and dropped them next to it.

As he tied his rope sandals, Paul briefly considered simply not showing up at The Winged Owl and instead waiting for his mother to come by. But that would almost certainly mean getting fired.

He had brought his mother a bag of apples three days earlier and asked her to come visit him. He had asked her this countless times before. To his surprise, she agreed this time. She had never seen his place, and though it was only one small room, he thought getting out of her own tenement for a while might do her some good. His mother left her own apartment for any length of time maybe once or twice a year. It was as if she had decided to imprison herself.

If Paul didn't bring her food and take out the garbage, he could only imagine what condition she might be in.

But if he had thought her acceptance of his invitation might be a sign of returning lucidity, he was quickly disabused. She did not bring up her favorite recent topic, the thrill of life in a long-gone camp of rebels. But after thanking him for the apples, she had gone on to talk again about her alleged childhood as a frightened orphan.

He reminded his mother that she grew up quietly in a two-bedroom split level in Rome and that her father was a successful door-to-door raincoat salesman. To this she had only laughed and commented about how we tell tales to protect those we care for. He had no idea what this meant. She then went on to speak of her supposedly cruel master who counted his hordes of money like the greedy character in a fairytale.

Finally as he left, she mumbled about the pity that Paul never knew his own father, a man she said many considered the finest human ever.

As he placed the three coins he'd gotten from the senator Cassius next to the note, Paul frowned. On recent runs, he had thought hard about what to do with them. He knew giving them to his mother wouldn't get him out of his problems. But they were after all freely given to him.

And while he could not imagine spending them and possibly calling more attention to himself, he saw no reason why his mother shouldn't benefit.

As he approached his door, an upsetting sound outside stopped him in mid-step.

Paul lived a few blocks from the Theater of Pompey. Since sunrise, a mounting energy had vibrated down the alley which led to his tiny room. Laughter, shouts and boozy song had bubbled into a casserole of resonance all around. Only one noise could have startled the mind at this point. It was that one noise that Paul listened to at this moment – the harsh presence of silence.

It felt like every creature in the city, from teething babies to caged chickens to puzzled inebriates, had all paused simultaneously to try to remember where they'd left their keys.

The stillness outside began to lift almost as quickly as it came, but it did not rise back into the higher pitches of festival when it returned. Instead, a portentous murmur began to echo down the alley. The cadence of horses and boots clomping briefly broke through.

Paul glided up the two steps of his room into the alley, thinking as he did if there was any way to get his life back on track. Could he somehow find his way to that simple new job that once awaited him, that plain life of minimal quietude?

Other than the warped pressed board that served as best as possible as the front door to Paul's little apartment and, at its other end, a narrow opening to the street, the alley was entirely walled up. Observed from left to right, the alley went: Paul's warped board, walls walls walls walls, street.

When he got to the street, Paul noted clumps of people gesturing and eagerly talking over each other. Some pointed toward the theater. Two soldiers on horseback galloped past.

Paul approached the nearest gathering, six or seven people shaking their heads and chattering.

"What's going on?" he asked.

In life, as we all know, there are few greater satisfactions than being the one to tell someone else some really terrible news you've just heard. They all turned to Paul with keen grimaces.

THEATER

As he made his way to the headquarters of The Winged Owl, Paul tried to let the news sink in. But the news wouldn't quite sink; it instead let out a succession of plosive muck bubbles as it mired and foundered in his mind.

Julius Caesar assassinated?

A few days earlier, such a report would have been startling, no doubt, in a distant way. But now Paul needed to figure out how it would affect his own life, whether it would help him rise out from or get more pulled into the menaces facing him.

He did also feel an unexpected little wrench at the notion that the man had been snuffed out. Though he had spoken not more than a full sentence or two to him, Paul had found Caesar, despite being a patrician and a politician, kind of decent.

Paul was not alone in showing an interest at the news.

Every citizen of Rome seemed in fact headed in the direction opposite of Paul: all of them going toward the theater, the site of the assassination. Paul had never been to the beach many times in his life, but the streets suggested to him what he imagined fighting against an incoming tide must feel like.

While he pushed upstream using a choice shoulder-and-sidestep technique, he began considering that this development might eventually work out okay. He did not understand or care about politics (which felt much the same about him), but he understood that this all would probably mean chaos.

And chaos is a great big place to get lost inside. After all this, why would anyone care about what some ordinary IM said, thought or might have been paid in the past? A reset button had been pushed.

For the first time in a long time he felt a burden lifting. The senator Cassius and his friends would be too preoccupied to reach out to him, and whoever he had tripped during the Lupercalia Run would surely be busy. For all he knew, they had all been killed, too, or would be. That kind of thing seemed to happen a lot to powerful Romans. Maybe, Paul thought, the gods were rewarding him for something he had done right.

Pushing open the door of The Winged Owl headquarters, he strode in. His nose met up with the sternal notch of the Shift Supervisor.

Paul stopped.

"To the Theater of Pompey," the Shift Supervisor suggested. (If you want a sense of the exact manner in which this suggestion came off, however, try saying it yourself with your teeth locked, plus put a full stop between each syllable.) "Immediately."

"But that's where ..." Paul stumbled back into the doorway.

"Find the senator Cassius to take a message from him" – still with teeth and the stops, as initially – "Now."

If he had time just then, Paul might have ruminated on the vicissitudes of life. The look of the Shift Supervisor suggested he not ruminate. He clenched the security permit that had just been pressed into his hand, turned around and started heading back.

Paul had never bothered to imagine what it might feel like to be carried helplessly away by the force of a swirling undercurrent at the beach, rather than pushing against an incoming surge. But with a riptide of humanity, he felt himself beginning to issue back hastily in the direction he had come, passing very soon the narrow entrance to his alley and continuing on to the throngs outside theater.

Had he chosen, he could have made the migration as easily without once putting foot to ground, and probably facing backwards, and upside down.

He did need to deploy some of his permeation skills to make it to the entrance doors of the theater itself. It was getting even more crowded. The populace of Rome had been compressing itself tighter and tighter against the building, buzzing and murmuring.

On the spectrum of general temperaments, the disposition of the crowd came off somewhere between that manifested by the attendees at a retail trade show and forest animals that had begun feeling decidedly peckish. There was a stirred curiosity.

"I just heard it from my second cousin," he overheard one loudmouth telling a nearby cluster of onlookers. "Mark Antony is saying that it was that Opposition group that killed Caesar. They thought he was doing too much for us plebeians, so they stabbed him during his speech, just when he was about to make a huge announcement."

"Anyone know who runs things now?" a voice from the crowd called out.

Paul wanted only to get done with his assignment and then figure out how to hide.

"I am here to see Cassius and Brutus," he told a droop-eyed guard at the door, handing over the permit. Except for the complete legionary uniform, boots and helmet he wore, the soldier was stark naked. He nodded and took down Paul's name.

The condition of the theater hall inside suggested intermission during a matinee: Half finished snacks on the floor, drinks still in cup holders, outer garments draped on seats. The guard led Paul backstage and down through a series of doorways into the orchestra pit. The general mood there, as he walked in, was anything but stirred or stimulated.

The leaders of the Opposition sat here and there slumped and silent, none talking or making eye contact with each other. The most animation came from Lucius Crispius Totovus, who rocked back and forth on a chair, mindlessly hugging a jerked pork.

"Ah, young man," Cassius said with forced brightness. "I am most grateful that you would follow my summons. I wonder if you would be good enough to wait a moment while we complete our discussions here. We have a mission of vital importance for you."

Paul found his way to an empty chair, as far removed as possible from the others. There, he initiated the process, as best as he could, of hoping for Earth to blow up, and for it to do so sooner rather than later.

"Fellow senators," Cassius enunciated. His fellow senators shifted in their chairs and escalated their lack of eye contact with each other.

"Senators," he repeated more warmly, "I know we are all in distress and at a loss. But I tell you again, we have to seize this occasion, whether we wanted it or not."

From a far corner came a muttered question.

"Are you sure you didn't do it?" It was from Bilbius Dilbo.

Ignoring the question, Cassius continued: "The people need to hear from us, and we have a duty now to the Republic. If we brood and only wish this had not happened, not only are we sunk, but our hopes and dreams will be lost. In a little while, Brutus will get up outside the theater and address the people of Rome on our behalf about what has happened. Let us focus on that, I beg of you."

"Just tell us," said Dilbo, with higher volume but a lower tone.

"I think we have all agreed we must soothe the anxiety of the people and the rest of the Senate," Cassius said, facing directly to this senator, then that, then another. But none would look up at him. "It sounds outrageous to the ears, but we must accept it. Caesar is dead. Let us take this time now to stand up for liberty and the old ways of the Republic."

"Did you?" Dilbo spoke at full voice, at once standing and looking directly at Cassius.

"For the last time," Cassius said, staring back, "no, I did not attack or push him. This is what I had in my toga."

Cassius reached into one of his folds; the Opposition leadership flinched. What he pulled out was a scroll. He waved it into the startled faces closest him.

"It's a motion to call for a vote of no confidence. That's all. That was the weapon I was planning to use on Caesar. Since no one here could make up their minds on what to do, I drew up this motion. I was standing onstage waiting for the moment when Caesar was going to declare his proscription and liquidation of the Senate, and then I was going to make a point of order. I was going to call for a procedural move to try to stop the proposal. I didn't push or stab Caesar. The truth is, I actually jumped forward to grab him before he fell off the stage."

He stalked away with a now-don't-you-all-feel-foolish stride and approached Paul. Paul during this time had been growing increasingly convinced of the planet's regrettable structural dependability. Cassius leaned down and put a hand on his shoulder.

"Here is what we need from you," he said, mustering up as much amiability as he could. "You are in a unique position, my good young man. It occurred to me you are the one and only person in Rome who was very close to Caesar but also has our trust too. We need you to act as a kind of mediator between ourselves and Mark Antony. Only you can do this, for us and for the future of the Republic of Rome. Only you can be our liaison with Antony. We need you."

The color drained from Paul's face.

"I see by your reaction that you understand the grave danger to the Republic should a serious political breach open between Antony and the Opposition. I knew you would apprehend immediately. Unfortunately, Antony and almost every other senator fled here after the ... the incident. But you will help us mend our break, won't you."

Though less noticeable, the color drained from Paul's inner organs.

"Let me finish speaking with my fellow senators here, and then you and I will decide on an exact message for you to bring to Antony." Cassius turned back toward his colleagues but not before telling Paul: "You may be the only hope of our sacred Republic."

Satisfied that global hyper-combustion could not be relied on to offer adequate relief, Paul realized he had only one choice. As Cassius began speaking to the Opposition leadership again, Paul leisurely raised himself and sidled away from the chair. He had noticed a door behind him, and he began backing toward it. He estimated it to be only seven or eight easy steps away.

It was not to be.

In his line of work, Paul rarely tripped. But he had as much experience in sneaking away from orchestra pits as he had with the beach. Paul tripped.

He felt something catch his sandal and his weight gave way. Panicked, he managed to convert his backward fall into a tucked crouch and at least avoided a conspicuous splat. Heart racing, he peered between two chairs from his new, hunched position. To his relief, nobody had noticed his stumble.

They nearly, however, heard the muffled cry he let out after looking down to see what it was that he had faltered over.

The body of Julius Caesar appeared slumberous. His arms lay at his sides, legs stretched, eyes and mouth closed almost contentedly. The only feature incongruent with the posture of a catnap was the object that obtruded from his chest. It was a carved mahogany handle stamped with the words "Proudly made in Sicily" and the emblem of the International Brotherhood of Cutlery Manufacturers.

Paul felt a chill through his body. Not so long ago, this was a living person, and one who bandied the greatest power known to humanity. And he truthfully did seem like he could have been a fairly decent person.

"I think," Paul quietly said, despite his anxiety, "you were almost certainly a good man, Caesar."

There was no time for more sentiment for the dead. That was all the eulogy Paul could give. He needed to make his shift; he glanced around to make sure his movements still hadn't been observed. Just as he braced himself to run, he looked down one more time.

"Thanks!" Caesar mumbled, before rolling onto his side, putting his hands under his ears to use as a pillow and smacking his lips a couple times.

EARS

A s we try to understand firsthand the dangerous energy of these days, we are fortunate once again to present a primary source. Let us experience what the people of Rome themselves experienced then.

Below is the front page, above-the-fold article of *The Viminal Hill Sun-Picayune and Shopper*, March 15, 44 BC (evening edition), which reported on the public activities on the Ides of March.

———

Senators call for calm, anger after Caesar killing

Local residents 'totally thrilled' to be near theater during eventful episode

Rome, Italy – Promising a thorough investigation of today's events, senators late this afternoon spoke outside the site of Julius Caesar's unexpected passing to crowds that would not let an unusually muggy spring day dampen their spirits.

"It was like watching history being made," said Gloria Rodundus, of suburban Viminal Heights. "I planned to just spend time checking out the holiday sale prices at some shops with my sister and my girlfriend Eveyln, but we ended up hearing these amazing speeches."

Rodundus said she rarely visits central Rome because of the crowds and higher sales taxes, instead preferring to patronize local stores, so she counted herself "very lucky" to be able to watch events unfold there.

Sen. Marcus Junius Brutus [Oppo - District 14] spoke first.

"At times, firm if regrettable action is necessary to uphold the dignity and integrity of the Republic," Brutus said. "We must look for peaceful solutions and remember this was not about any single individual. It was about preserving traditional Roman notions of liberty and rule of law."

Senators gave their speeches in front of the Theater of Pompey, site of the incident. Theater management announced that in light of today's occurrences, the Sunshine Company's performance of its existentialist tragedy "Accidentally Sitting on Other People's Hats" (see our review in "Rome Around Town" section, page 19) will be cancelled for the remainder of the week. Ticketholders should visit the box office for exchanges. No refunds will be offered.

Following Brutus's brief remarks, Sen. Mark Antony [Caesarean - At Large] addressed the audience. He said he wished to direct his words especially to "friends, Romans" and others. Rather than praise Caesar, who authorities announced had succumbed to wounds sustained earlier in the afternoon, Antony asserted that he intended instead to "bury" him.

"Just at the moment that he was tragically brought down, our revered Caesar was preparing to insure the full protection of us all by taking on the role of supreme leader," Antony said. "He was just about to accept the burden of providing for each and every Roman through his generous and caring strength."

The crowd responded with sustained applause.

"Imagine, my fellow Romans, Caesar would have been our provider for years to come," Antony said. "This was the most unkindest [sic] cut of all."

Antony also referred to a secret document that Caesar planned to reveal during the session. The senator suggested this could be Caesar's last will and testament and that it might include significant bequests to every citizen.

During the speeches, the body of Caesar lay covered on a makeshift platform at the theater doors. Antony indicated he might show Caesar's wounds to the public but did not do so in the end.

"I hope those responsible for this tragic day will tell us why they did it," Antony said. "I share your strong passion against this act and could understand if there are feelings of outrage."

Afterward, those who heard the speeches offered their reactions.

"Brutus made some good points," said Varus Pindar, a neighborhood businessman who manages a small chain of popular steakhouses in the greater Viminal area (See restaurant review in our special "Yea Food!" insert, page 31). "But I like how Antony talked about our real needs, and I definitely like his energy level. My wife really wants to know what's in Caesar's will, too."

As for Rodundus – the shopper who went for the bargains and stayed for a memorable day – she says she'll keep close to home for the foreseeable future.

"I just wish these politicians would stop bickering," she said, "and just do what's right for the people. I mean, how hard is that?"

Filed with staff reports. To comment on this article, visit us in person @ our building, 324 Morning Glory Lane, Viminal Hill Business Park.

EATS

As might be expected, a good deal of the activity unfolding on the Ides of March took place behind the public scenes and did not make it into any news accounts at all. A whirl of convulsions, calculating, agitation and positioning erupted from the start.

In the first moments after Caesar had been introduced into a kitchen utensil owned by the senator Lucius Crispius Totovus, a kind of controlled pandemonium had broken out in the theater.

It was pandemonium in the sense that Totovus and most of the rest of the Opposition emitted sounds with pitch levels unlike any they had offered since their unorthodox meeting at the Mulvian Baths and Conference Center. It was controlled in that Mark Antony, rising from his seat and looking into the orchestra pit, quickly assessed the situation and led the rest of the Roman Senate decorously out of the theater.

Cassius, as we have seen, immediately determined that the Opposition needed to act with decisive resolve from these very first moments. The Opposition, as we have seen, did not.

After calming Lucius Totovus and the more agitated Opposition members, Cassius had tried to take charge.

It was clear that the public outside had to be told something as soon as possible. During the ensuing hours, it was Cassius who had worked out an agreement with Mark Antony on how this was to be done. Both Antony and Brutus would give speeches, although Cassius insisted that exact responsibility for Caesar's death not be mentioned. Antony agreed, on condition that the body of Caesar be present during the speeches. Cassius had taken it on himself to write the Opposition's speech and convinced Brutus to deliver it.

"You are the best man to offer the eulogy for Caesar, but you will be too conciliatory if left on your own," he told Brutus frankly. "We need to clearly set forth our position. I will write the words."

Cassius also wanted to block The Outside Communications Consultant from getting his hands on the speech. The man had shown up when he heard the news and started buttonholing senators in the orchestra pit about possible courses of action.

"I've got a friend in advertising who could have billboards up by tomorrow morning," he told Pompilius Pulcher. "To be honest, we need to downplay the violence theme that's been created. I'm thinking a tight group shot of all of you, your arms draped over each other's shoulders, all showing off non-threatening smiles, and definitely warm background colors. Something along the lines of indigo and a lemon chiffon."

There was one other noteworthy aspect of the day that did not get publicly reported at the time but that should perhaps be recorded here.

The Opposition had the responsibility of handling the body, including bringing it out to the front of the theater, where it was to be displayed. Paul's earlier discovery of Caesar's true condition had made it necessary for the Opposition to put some expedients in place. It had turned out, after all, that there was no body.

A substantial white shroud was obtained, with weighted corners. Opposition members acted as pallbearers, bringing the slab out to a makeshift bier that had been set up near the theater entrance. The men had all agreed they would remain close to the bier at all times and bring the slab back in as soon as the speeches ended, not ever letting anyone near it.

But as he had reached the part in his declamation referring to Caesar's secret document, Antony moved toward them and the bier. They looked at each other nervously, knowing they could do nothing to stop him in front of the crowd. The last thing they expected was that Antony would lift up the shroud to the crowd. But it looked like he intended to do exactly that.

"If you have tears, prepare to shed them now," Antony had called out, taking another step toward the catafalque. "This will be a shock for you, but we must confront this reality."

The Opposition senators, to a man, glanced around for escape routes. Antony grasped a corner of the shroud and slowly raised it. At this angle, only he and the senators near could examine what lay underneath.

A fetid stench blew out; Antony struggled not to drop the sheets back in repulsion. Where, by the customs of anatomy, the head of Julius Caesar should be expected, there instead rested a perfectly spherical camembert. Toothpicked into this cheese, at the position of an anticipated nose, sat a pimento olive.

Antony could not get a clear view much farther down, but beyond the camembert, he believed he could just make out a torso-sized spiced York ham flanked by two generous salamis.

CONTROL

It did not take long for the Opposition leadership to understand that events might not go well in the long term.

As soon as the speeches in front of the theater had ended, Antony raised a hand, signaling to an underling commander nearby. From both sides of the theater, files of neatly uniformed soldiers stomped toward the portico. They closed in and formed a line between the public and those at the entrance.

"We need to talk," Antony said. The Opposition leadership stood on the portico with him, surrounded by his soldiers. "And the first thing we're going to talk about is the Caesar salad you put under that shroud."

"'Caesar salad,'" Bilbius Dilbo said with an obsequious chuckle. "Funny. Very amusing, Mark Antony."

Antony was not laughing. He pointed to the entrance door.

The Opposition pallbearers carried the covered slab into the theater, balancing it carefully to make sure no condiments rolled off. Antony gestured the remaining senators to follow suit.

The office of the theater manager fit his purposes well. He positioned himself onto a billowy leather chair in the corner and lifted his feet onto the desk. If there had been a humidor nearby, he might have let the senators wait while he methodically lit an outsized cigar. Instead, he clasped his hands behind his neck and began to stare them down.

He'd had the office cleared of other seating. The Opposition leadership was forced to stand on the other side of the desk. To a man, they would have benefitted from hats with which to have in hand.

"I am going to put all my cards on the table." Antony finally spoke. "And the reason I'm going to do that is because I'm the one who has all the cards. You do not have any cards. I have the cards."

"Listen, Antony," said Cassius. "I know we have not seen many things eye-to-eye, but we are all equals in the Senate, and in honor of Caesar ..."

"The speeches are over."

Antony removed his feet from the desktop and stood. Having been a grownup for many years, Mark Antony had probably not gotten five or six inches taller during, say, the past twenty minutes; to the Opposition, it seemed like he could have.

"You see, while you spent the last few hours holed up here worried about arranging those meaningless speeches and doing the-gods-know-what-else, I've been active. Very active, as you are about to find out. I went and explained to the Praetorian Guard and the legion commanders that you all killed their magnificent Caesar. I told the rest of the Senate that you had plans next to off as many of them as possible. And I have dispatched messages to the city police letting them know that I am taking charge under martial law."

"Damn," said Brutus, though it came out in a fairly sociable way.

"I do not know how you all eliminated Caesar as you did," Antony continued. "You may be surprised to know how much I know about your activities, and frankly, I never thought you were all capable of planning an assassination. But the reality does not matter. Perception does. That's why I am going to make sure Rome increasingly perceives that you offed Caesar with great malice and have even more sinister plans in the works."

A soldier grasping his scabbard appeared at the doorway.

"Pardon me, sire," he addressed Antony. "We are ready to commence."

"Good. Proceed."

The soldier saluted and about faced.

"The first order of business now, my fellow senators, is getting me Caesar's body and the document he had with him." Antony sat again.

Several of the Opposition leadership scooched gradually away from several others.

"I will not, of course, let you get your hands on any wealth Caesar may have in his will. And I will have the body for the funeral pyre. When I light the flames, the era of Caesar ends and the era of Antony begins."

"I think I speak on behalf of all of us," Cicero offered in mid-squirm, "when I say we would like to thank you for not showing everyone what was under the shroud when we were out there."

"Don't be an idiot," Antony sniffed. "Although maybe that's

asking too much of all of you."

Dilbo offered up another soft, fawning cackle.

"If they saw your little buffet under there," Antony continued, "the people and soldiers would have had an unhelpful fit. I will not have my plans upset. I want that document and that body. I give you 72 hours to turn over the body and the paper. That is, if I don't find them first. I've given the order for the guards to start searching this theater."

This announcement had the effect he wanted.

"Very telling." He leaned in. "I can see by your facial expressions that what I'm looking for is most likely still in this building. Thank you for your help."

He called for another soldier.

"Double the search teams here in the theater, and make absolutely sure no one gets out."

"Nerts," offered Brutus, genially.

"Gentlemen." Antony switched to a warmer tone, though one not sloshing with the earnestness associated with actual warmth. "You will find I do things differently than Caesar. With more directness, you might find. Still, if you are cooperative, there is no reason we can't get along. I have no desire to decimate the Roman Senate or appear spiteful right from the start."

It was not lost on the Opposition leadership that among his other duties, Antony had personally taken charge of the Truth Extraction unit of the army and that the Truth Extraction unit had a very good success rate for the past two or three hundred years. The Opposition leadership looked at its feet.

"And there is a larger point," Antony said. "I realize that I do owe you all a big debt of gratitude. You have actually been very helpful to me in the past, and I must thank you."

"Well isn't that sweet!" Flavius Flavian exclaimed. (Flavius Flavian lacked the small but valuable component of the brain that detects the onset of irony.) "What are you thanking us for?"

"You see, whenever Caesar seemed about to go a little wobbly of purpose, I could always get him back on track with the specter of the Opposition's immense, relentless, ruthless power striking him down. You all helped me keep him on the straight and narrow."

"Oh," Flavian said morosely. The approach of irony he didn't get; pulverizing sarcasm he got.

Antony nodded to a third soldier asking permission to enter.

"Senator," the soldier stated, "we continue working through every part of the theater. One search team did report hearing unusual noises in the basement and tried to follow them."

"And?"

"Sire," the solider said warily, "unfortunately the noise could not be tracked, and the sound of a door closing was heard shortly after. But if anyone got away, they should be stopped at the cordon around the theater."

Cassius and Brutus, noted Antony, glanced apprehensively at each other.

BASEMENT

It will interest the student of history to learn the circumstances that led Gaius Julius Caesar – a respected conqueror who had recently earned the reputation of celebrated assassination victim – to wake up one afternoon sporting a flipped-bob blonde wig with a plastic tiara while eying two upside down fruit crates, one of these crates supporting a nice looking woman with a caring, friendly smile.

Narratively, we must again move back a bit. The circumstances begin here:

Before any speeches had been given, faux bodies paraded or threats by Mark Antony offered, Paul, it will be remembered, had begun an attempt to quit himself from the orchestra pit of the Theater of Pompey. He had been called there to act as a liaison between the Opposition and Antony.

It will also be recalled that during his effort to quietly leave the orchestra pit, Paul had stumbled over a motionless body. He had made a remark to this body, and this remark had initiated, to Paul's astonishment, a conversation.

When Caesar had spoken back to him ("Thanks!"), Paul froze. For that matter, everyone in the orchestra pit froze. Though the voice sounded distinctly weakened, the Opposition leadership had heard it and could not mistake its timbre. Silently the Opposition leadership came over and encircled the being at Paul's feet. They stared down as Caesar fetally scrunched himself and burbled one or two inaudible comments.

Breaking the lull, Flavius Flavian offered an observation to be mulled by the others of the encircled Opposition leadership.

"Caesar's not," Flavian noted, "dead."

The Opposition stood in relatively stunned stillness. If you have ever witnessed an adolescent group examining a shattered vase with a baseball lying close by, one of their number limply holding a bat, you are prepared to understand the sentiment of the Opposition leadership at this time. Dread and disbelief rarely mix well together, especially in larger numbers of people.

"I once had an uncle," one senator finally said, "who survived half the night after having his lower intestines ripped out by a panther."

"Yes, yes, oh, yes," another agreed readily. "The human body lingers."

They all kept their eyes on Caesar, most particularly on the handle protruding from his chest.

"Look," said Cicero. "There. Isn't that blood around the knife? Leaking through the toga."

"No," Pompilius Pulcher offered. "No. Just a coffee stain. I noticed it when he came in. Caesar never really was careful enough about his personal appearance."

Not collectively apt as a rule to pick up on practical realities, the Opposition leadership nevertheless understood the awkwardness of its position. They had all heard the truism that stressed the importance of aiming, if one is going to try to take out the grand caliph, straight. Or as Totovus had once advised, to make a good sponge cake, you're going to want to use the right sized whisk.

If Caesar survived, it was understood, the Opposition would not look merely harebrained. No one would believe it was all just an accident. All the retribution that comes with unsuccessfully trying to eliminate an opponent would be theirs. And the consequence for that would be more than paying for a broken vase. Julius Caesar still living, it was silently understood, would be very bad.

The Opposition leadership stared down and watched, quietly.

"Look," said Cassius, calling up as much sympathetic form to his face as nature allowed. "This is agonizing, but we all know the grave decision we need to take with Caesar, do we not?"

"Yes, we do," Bilbius Dilbo declared after some time. He looked solemnly around the circle, expectant and deliberate. "Who among us" – he broke off to let the enormity of the moment take hold, and the men there all did seem to show, with stiffened backs and raised heads, a grudging understanding of their duty – "who among us shall make a motion to open up the floor to debate?"

As the recording secretary of the Opposition did not have a pen with him, there are no minutes or other primary sources to offer the reader here. It may be just as well. The deliberations lasted long; various formal propositions related to the new circumstances were made, were withdrawn, were amended, were re-withdrawn, while points of order were raised, emergency suspension of the rules rejected (by a vote of 2-13-1) and temporary recess twice called on account of lack of quorum when Totovus said he felt nauseous.

At one point, Caesar started snuffling.

"Death rattle?" one senator suggested. "I wonder if we should pull out the knife."

It was bruited about that Caesar had made reference to a secret document – probably it was his will – and if he happened to briefly regain consciousness, maybe he could be persuaded to reveal or change it. Or perhaps a living Caesar could somehow be used as a bargaining chip at some point. This all struck Cassius as close to fanciful, but he could sense it was group rationalizing for where the decision had been headed. Nowhere.

"Do we all yet fear this man Caesar as he lies prostrate before us, at the maw of Hades?" Cassius asked. No one responded. "Is no one willing to do what must be done?"

After forty five more minutes of discussion, consensus was formally reached.

"Having declared cloture on the matter," Bilbius Dilbo announced, "final motion is as follows. 'Resolved, that the Opposition of the Republic of Rome shall not act at this point, or cause to be acted through active agency, in such a manner that reasonably may be expected to proximately tend to the physical impairment, depredation, or discomfiture of any member of the Senate of Rome.'"

Flavian, after a minute: "That means we're *not* going to kill him, right?"

The motion carried with one dissenting vote. An amendatory motion affirmed that the knife was probably not to be removed, since this could be deemed as hurtful.

"Fine, as you all wish," Cassius said astringently. "But let's at least get him moved away from here for the time being. The last thing we need is someone coming in and finding this scene."

Here, Paul saw an opportunity. He very much did not like the idea of facing Mark Antony, as Cassius had proposed he do, nor did he want to get any more involved in Roman politics. Under normal circumstances, Paul would never consider speaking up in front of a gathering of Roman senators. But Paul increasingly accepted that the needle would not be pointing to normal for some time to come.

"Excuse my interrupting," he uttered, "but moving Caesar could get – uh – messy, couldn't it? If he starts bleeding or something. You all may not want to risk signs of what happened to be seen on yourselves, I would think. If you'd like, I can take care of moving him."

He looked around with his eyebrows arched in positions of supplication.

Cicero and the others talked it over a bit before offering that they thought this was a good idea.

"I did hope we could make use of our young friend's keen political background to parley with Antony on our behalf," Cassius said with some reluctance. "But perhaps we could instead hire one of those IMs to run messages back and forth."

He grudgingly agreed that Paul should help with the body instead of with negotiations. It was pointed out, though, that moving Caesar would be a two-person job.

"I have a litter bearer out back who can help," Brutus said. "A big man. And he is a mute, so we don't have to worry about him speaking out at any point."

For a time, all went as smoothly as could have been hoped. Brutus's litter bearer proved to be not only big but cooperative, and Caesar settled deep into an unmoving state that – as the Opposition senators furtively wished, watching him taken off – looked to be a perfect coma.

In the basement of the theater, a deeply isolated room was found. Likely not conducive to convalescence but good for hiding, it smelled of mothballs, turpentine, and mildew, and the exposed pipes along the ceiling dripped and clanged. Boxes lay throughout the room and lined the walls. Affixed to these were yellowed cards with the titles of theatrical productions that had closed long ago. The room appeared to be a kind of sepulchral for failed performances.

Paul and the mute put the board holding Caesar onto a trunk labeled "Good Morning, Nefertiti! (The Musical)." The mute signaled that he would now stand guard outside. He indicated that Paul should sit by Caesar. Paul would have personally preferred sneaking out a back exit and never being seen again.

Three Pauls, however, could have been poured into the mute, with plenty of space left over for a breakfast nook and guest suite. He was a big mute. He also had disturbingly large cobalt eyes and a flattop cut to his flaxen hair, all suggesting a kind of Nordic menace.

Paul nodded. The mute left, closing the door behind him.

Paul pulled up a fake boulder and sat next to the board. Caesar hadn't shifted since he was carried downstairs. The bulk of his twisted toga made it difficult to discern any movement of the diaphragm, and only an irregular wheezing and slight fluttering of the eyes indicated any life remained.

Paul found himself with time to take stock of his situation. He thought of Olivia, of her father, the Major, and his promise of an easy new job. The possibility of living in settled ease was undoubtedly becoming more and more distant.

Even a day earlier, Paul had not thought his circumstances could have bleakened. Yet here he was. The back exit to the theater was just down the hall, but a large silent man stood in the way. Where Paul could eventually escape to remained problematic anyway. The hope of somehow fading back into obscurity itself had faded. Every solution Paul could think of ended up wrapped with new problems. He could confide in nobody either, nor could he figure out who to trust.

As he noodled and renoodled possible scenarios for himself, the door to the room swung opened.

"Is he still ...?" Cassius, standing at the threshold, waited for his sentence to be completed.

"Yes," Paul said. He stood, his reverie broken. "Still alive. But not by much, I'd guess."

Cassius looked around and up and down, scanning the whole place. He finally strode in, shut the door and made his way to one of the boxes labeled with the name of a play on it.

"I would have preferred you helping me handle negotiations with Antony." He lifted a lid and gazed inside. "But I am almost as glad to have you here. I know I can trust your discretion."

Cassius leaned over. He began to jerk objects out of the box and toss them rhythmically into the air. Paul could not see the label on the box, but the props and costumes coming down and piling around Cassius indicated a lighthearted domestic comedy: Vases with flowers glued in them, a pretend box of chocolates, candlesticks, sly gowns and garish tunics.

The process of removal, Paul observed, might be most accurately likened to a seven-year-old rummaging through his toy chest frantic to find his cloth bear Nuzzles. Paul could not imagine what Cassius was looking for or up to.

"Your value in helping bring about what has unfolded already cannot be overstated," Cassius continued, moving to a second box and lifting its lid. "With your intelligence reports, I have convinced the Opposition we must stand now for the Republic."

Paul froze for half a second as a round gray ball with a stumpy cord flew over Cassius's head. On its surface, in very large red letters, it read "Bomb!" The ball bounced on the floor and rolled off toward door. Following it flew out two extra-large prison costumes, half a dozen plastic breastplates and greaves, a bag with a giant dollar sign on it, hollowed out prison yard weight-lifting equipment and fake handcuffs.

Paul decided the best place to watch this performance would be at the farthest end of the room as possible. He inched toward the corner.

"And these will be the decisive hours," Cassius said, moving to a third box. "It has been agreed that Antony and Brutus will address the crowd outside the theater very shortly. Unfortunately, Antony insists that Caesar's body be displayed publicly, and we can hardly find a reason to refuse." Here Cassius paused. "Do you get what I'm getting at?"

It next rained, from the third box, a historical period drama, one most likely set in the royal court of a distant kingdom, a production whose props and costumes suggested it featured a fetching princess on her wedding day, an evil griffin (or some breed of beaked character) and a bedroom scene.

Cassius, his bent body halfway into the nearly emptied box, abruptly stopped. He raised himself, emerging from the box, and in both hands he held a pillow.

"You understand necessity." Cassius pivoted to Paul. For the first time, Paul thought he denoted a twitch of indisputable emotion on the man facing him – a hint of regret, but regret blended with resolve.

Cassius slowly turned toward Caesar and began walking over. He inhaled deeply as he did so. Cassius, his back now to Paul, positioned the pillow in his hands and steadied himself above Caesar's face. Finally, with one last deep exhaling, he bent down.

Life, over the years, had gone through a good deal of trouble to teach Paul that there lay only one sensible course of action when bigger things started happening. Life had stayed on message for Paul on these matters, and the message was: Scamper. Away. Yet Paul – despite how hard life had worked on him, schooling him, tutoring him, testing and retesting him – Paul, for reasons he could not explain then, crouched into a starting block position, aimed his person at Cassius and took a deep breath of his own.

HANDCART

(Much later, at a time in his life when he had grown a little introspective, Paul would take some effort to think about his motivations for the course of activity to which he had stooped himself at that second. There were myriad reasons. In retrospect, he would come to feel he had been compelled partly by a desire not to see another human get finished off. He did sense some responsibility for the particular condition of Caesar, and Caesar did seem like the type who probably didn't deserve the destiny. Not that he had any objection to Cassius. Yet Paul would later concede to himself that a major catalyst for this stoop had been a frenetic compulsion to be speedily somewhere else: After addressing the immediate Caesar issue on the other side of the room, he had a chance of using his inertia to dash out the door, past the mute and to some kind of freedom beyond the Theater of Pompey. But, as we say, these were all thoughts for another point, later in Paul's emotional development.)

Four to seven inches separated the undefended face of Julius Caesar from a slowly descending stage pillow. At the same time, the vulnerable backside of the operator of the stage pillow presented itself at eleven to thirteen paces, assuming a stretched gait, from the leaning figure of Paul.

Paul found his footing and gained his speed.

And after he bound five and a half steps, beginning to angle his shoulder square at the upper spine of Gaius Cassius, the door of the room burst open. Instantly Paul flung both his feet in front of himself; his sandals took on the urgent function of brakes.

Three agitated senators had whirled into the room.

"He's here!" The news came as a harmonic clamor from Cicero, Flavian and the bashful senator whose name Cassius could never remember. "Upstairs! He's upstairs!"

It was Mark Antony. He had come to the theater early, and he wanted to get the speeches started. Brutus had been doing all he could to stall – talking about the damp air outside, sports scores, hair care products – but Antony could not be put off much longer.

"I should have expected him to try to throw us off," Cassius said. "As you can plainly see, I had been preparing just now to prop this pillow under the poor, dying Caesar's head to make his last minutes more comfortable. Consequently we do not, at this point, have a body for public viewing."

"On that point, fret not," Cicero said. "We thought quickly and found what we need, right inside Lucius Totovus's picnic basket."

At the time Cassius did not understand what this meant, but he had been long used to not following the thoughts of his colleagues. The words washed over him.

"Young man." He turned to Paul, who had steadied himself reasonably well, "I ask you again to keep watch here, and I will ask specially that no one be allowed to get hold of Caesar's person. I shall advise the litter bearer of Brutus of the same. Caesar must be – let us say – protected."

Paul was again alone. He stepped over the objects that Cassius had scattered on the floor and went to resume his vigil atop the Styrofoam boulder. He had begun getting tired of trying to figure ways out of rooms and from larger conundrums; he deposited his chin into his hands and sat silently to wait for the next event to occur.

A few times, Caesar's eyes fluttered again, and parts of his body twitched, once making the knife quiver. Far above Paul, senators had began their orations in front of the theater, but nothing of this could be heard deep in the theater basement. He heard only the clanging and drip of pipes and his own breathing.

After some time, the mute burst in. He looked anxious. He motioned Paul to come into the hallway. Quickly. From the far side of the basement, clattering and officious voices could be heard. The mute pointed into the room at Caesar, then to the theater exit, then back at Caesar.

"Soldiers or guards, I assume," Paul said. "That's probably what Cassius was warning about. Coming this way, I'd guess, going through all the rooms they can find. But what can we do? We can't take Caesar outside. How could we possibly ..."

To carry Caesar out openly into public would be unthinkable, and none of the crates in the room could fit a human person even if they wanted to box him up.

The mute performed an additional pantomime, this time picking items up off the floor and waving them around. He had to repeat himself twice before Paul understood what exactly the man was proposing. By this time, the approaching noises had grown markedly louder. Every minute or two a bashing would ring out down the hall, seemingly the sound of another door being smashed in to be searched.

"It could never work, not in a million years," Paul said at last, understanding the mute's proposal. He turned his face up into the much larger face aside him. The much larger face had a glower about it, one that suggested a determined willpower. "But you know what, let's give it a try."

Up against limited choices and even less time, it must be said that the plan was executed fairly creditably. It at least took advantage of the materials at hand.

Paul worked from the bottom up, while the mute started at the head. After they met in the middle, they stepped back to look at the result. Remarkably, the spangled crimson slippers, striped leggings and girdle, and the flaxen wig with jeweled headband had all been slid on snugly and seemed a decent enough fit.

But there was still a very recognizable face and a masculine contour to deal with, as well as a knife sticking out. Glancing around, Paul snapped up a tear-away wedding gown with lace veil, then grabbed up a prop dumbbell (brightly marked "5 lbs"). He placed the dumbbell atop the chest at nipple level, just astride the knife, as the mute snapped on the gown and veil over it all.

Within a minute and a half of their starting, an extraordinarily bosomy if fairly husky bride had been constructed. There was at least a reasonable chance that Julius Caesar would not be recognized.

The last problem was getting him or her out of the theater. As the sounds down the hall resolved themselves into discernible words and individuated footsteps, Paul eyed a handcart along one of the walls. He wheeled it near the newly dressed figure; the mute understood. He slid his arms under Caesar's form, lifting him effortlessly. Carefully, he maneuvered Caesar's limp form vertically onto the footplate of the handcart, letting the body flop against the frame.

It occurred to Paul that Caesar might not be the only one who could find a disguise valuable at some point, assuming they all made it very far. On an impulse, he grabbed up handfuls of the articles off the floor and shoved them hurriedly into a bag.

They all made it out the theater exit just as the soldiers began turning the corner into their corridor.

As the door banged shut and eyes adjusted to the sunlight, though, it became clear that any escape had only just begun.

IMPASSE

The senator's speeches had already ended as Paul and the mute rose up to street level outside the Theater of Pompey, an occupied handcart between them. They confronted a boulevard filled tightly with people and wagons. Intermingled above the heads of the civilian populace, the scarlet horse hair crests of Antony's legionnaires could be seen bobbing and advancing.

"This way," Paul said.

For stability, Caesar had been tied at the abdominal to the frame of the handcart. The mute walked with his right arm clamped around Caesar's shoulders, while Caesar's limp head rested against the mute's broad torso. With a wedding dress draped entirely over the cart and dragging along the ground, its wheels and frame were fully hidden.

A bride seemed to be walking with the help of her jumbo groom in a floating manner – a manner consistent with a woman who had been markedly overserved at her wedding feast and who had presumably passed out shortly after the first toasts.

Paul concentrated on applying a detached look to his face and a carefree walk to his legs, as if he were out for an amble with a couple newly married friends. There had been no time to form a plan on what to do once outside, much less to consider how onlookers might react to their appearance. Paul soon felt his nonchalance might be failing. He felt eyes turning their way.

The reaction of most onlookers to the trio went down the following checklist:

- ☐ Stop.
- ☐ Gape.
- ☐ Elbow nearest person.
- ☐ Point.
- ☐ Discuss theories amongst selves.

Nor was an especially creative mind needed for theory development on the sight. The appearance explained itself with a clear promptitude to most of those beholding it.

An especially large representative of an already big-boned northern tribe who had an additional tendency to growth hormone difficulties would likely find himself with narrow marriage options in Rome. The big chap must have been lonely. A similar frustration would face an unsightly middle-age woman with hormone issues of her own – facial stubble that even a veil couldn't entirely hide, for example, yet remarkably generous yabos. Yet love will out. Or if not love, alcohol.

The consensus among gapers was that, in short, a giant had married a buxom old gnome.

Still, the reaction of bystanders may have ended almost as soon as it began, after some gawking and fleeting commentary. The enormous groom and his unpleasant new wife may have become simply a topic of bemused remembrance later in the day.

It was their companion who attracted even more attention. Or, it might be said, who completed the package of incongruity.

Paul carried the bag he'd quickly filled over his shoulder; it rested on his back. In his haste to leave the theater, he did not realize that this was the bag that had on it an absurdly outsized dollar symbol. To the onlookers, it seemed that Rome must somewhere be possessed of a number of extraordinarily generous wedding guests. As they walked, Paul looked back. He noticed that the onlookers had gone beyond mere ogling. While the three continued to make their way down the street, he glanced back a couple more times to confirm his concern: The onlookers had added another item to their To-Do list.

- ☐ Follow along, see what this might all be about.

The mute noticed the gathering train, too. But he could not move much faster while still maintaining control of the wheels of the cart, and the bag slowed Paul from his own customary agility. They tried walking more briskly nevertheless. They tried quick turns; they tried an alley. All this only enflamed the curiosity of the hangers-on and expanded their numbers. There was no shaking them.

As they bounded along, Caesar's arms flailed lifelessly while his head flopped back and forth, giving weight to a murmuring belief that the bride either drank far too much or perhaps had been doused with chloroform and kidnapped. In any event, it was great entertainment.

A carnival atmosphere began to brew, as more and more Romans started getting behind the triumvirate. By the old forum, they picked up a jury pool on supper break. Passing a sidewalk sale, they acquired two dozen husbands, of whom all had been bored out of their minds. A spry outing of seniors tried to catch up shortly after. And as they neared the Tiber River, an outdoor meeting of the League of Central Rome Curtain Wholesalers became pasted on. By this time, the question could be heard coming from the rearguard: "Anyone know what we're following anyway?"

It was at the Milvian Bridge that the parade straight away came to its terminus.

A centurion coming west had just begun ordering his detachment over the Tiber. From the opposite direction on the bridge, he saw, strode what surely was one of the most perplexing wedding parties ever assembled.

A rendezvous took place in the middle. The standoff could not have been more complete, the west deck of the bridge glutted with geometrically spaced Roman soldiers, the east deck crammed with a heavily breathing demographic representation of the population of Rome.

Stupefied by the couple standing in front of him – the Caesarian head now faced fully up with mouth agape, snorts rising from it – and their astonishing number of accompanying friends in back, the centurion needed some time to scratch his chin and remind himself of his authority.

"Out of our way," he pronounced at last. "In the name of Emergency Leader Mark Antony, I command you."

Circumstances looked honestly bleak. His heart thumping, Paul surprised himself at his own desperate cheek as he spoke.

"Thank the gods we came across you," he said to the centurion. "My friends here just got married, and we are finding ourselves pursued by this crowd of strangers for some reason. It doesn't seem right or fair. I know they may look odd, but my friends only want to be left alone to enjoy their honeymoon."

The centurion during this discourse had his gaze on the generous upper body of the apparent bride. Hearing Paul's story, he turned his eyes, frowning, onto the crowd. The crowd returned a look of hangdog unease. An instant of decisive silence – no stirring from soldiers, onlookers, husband and wife – fell on the scene. It was a standoff.

Hope sprung.

But silence on the bridge, when it broke, did not break with the pack of onlookers succumbing to a phalanx of soldiers.

It broke with a tinking.

It was at this moment that an object lesson in consumer awareness was offered. And this was bad timing. When he had been searching for the finest cutlery available to cut hams, Lucius Crispius Totovus had insisted on buying the most expensive equipment he could find. But the fact is that price does not always buy value.

On the top of Milvian Bridge deck, very near a pair of gleaming crimson slippers, there dropped a prosciutto knife. This knife was completely bent back on itself. Further, the clean blade of the knife indicated it had never penetrated human skin but had merely gotten smushed by, say, a tangled up toga. A thud followed this tinking, and from under the wedding gown rolled out a fake five pound dumbbell.

The centurion, Paul, the mute, one hundred soldiers and many more citizens of Rome watched while the only really eye catching quality of the new bride slowly deflated onto itself. It was the wheeze of the air being let out of hope.

"I think," said the centurion (centurions, as a rule, disdain being made public fools of), "some questioning might be in order."

Instinct suggested to Paul he jump over the side of the bridge. But glimpsing down, he could see the water level of the Tiber at almost zero, leaving mostly gooey mud below. This time, there could be no escape in any direction. It looked beyond hopeless at the present.

Yet – a notion – a notion tickled at Paul's mind.

It is true that he had not noticed the dollar sign on the bag he had taken from the theater, and very little he had done recently called for conscious thought. But in this moment of crisis, his brain benevolently reminded Paul of something he had tossed into the bag in the basement of the theater.

"Yes, sir." He put down the bag and leaned slowly over toward it. "We will come with you, of course. I have my official papers right in here, sir."

Paul did not retrieve official papers from the bag. Both the crowd and the soldiery read aloud the identifying label of the object he did pull out. They performed their reading in exclamatory unison as he lobbed it softly into the air.

"Bomb!"

That almost no water flowed in the Tiber did not impede the great majority of those gathered on the Milvian Bridge. They jumped. Placidly, the marshy riverbed accepted an offering from above, and the banks of the Tiber shook with the thudding sploof of Romans at once adhering deep into its welcoming sludge. As the bridge quickly cleared, Paul and the mute shot back down the way they came, with Caesar pulled behind, still unconscious, in the handcart.

Before they got off the bridge, a soldier could be heard shouting down into the riverbed, "Sir, a fake! It's a fake!"

Paul pointed to the right and took the lead. Looking behind, beyond the mute and his trailing handcart, he could see a handful of soldiers and citizens starting to give chase. Only one reasonable option presented itself. There could be no more running, so it would have to be hiding. With the rumble of the cart at his back, Paul began to hightail it home.

DEEP

"**I** especially don't like the tone of the open-ended comments." The Outside Communications Consultant had been talking in clucking way. "These focus groups are reflecting a pointedly negative strategic climate for our messaging."

The Opposition leadership let out an apprehensive breath.

"Of course, we will need to go into the field for some wider sample polling to confirm these results," The Outside Communications Consultant said. "I'd like to see how this all breaks down along gender lines and with the 18-to-26 year old demographic. This is concerning, to be honest, but if we get some accurate data, I know we can find the right communications approach."

At this, the Opposition leadership inhaled and felt a little better.

It was three days since the news of Caesar's death had been announced. The Opposition leadership was gathered at its first formal meeting since the Ides of March. Little of comfort had been found in the last three days and some reassurance was badly wished for. The Outside Communications Consultant seemed to know to provide this with his latest report.

He went on to quote more focus group respondents, all, he said, demonstrating that the speech Brutus had given at the theater failed to touch the public. A whole new strategic public outreach plan would be needed. Less "liberty and the Republic," he said, more "getting marsupial sausage and potato chips on the platters of real people."

The senators turned to look at each other with studious and grave expressions, as if to share among themselves a dawning comprehension that their entire course of action needed to be corrected. Although, in actuality, everyone turned only to where they earnestly guessed someone else might be.

It was pitch black where they were, and they could see neither each other nor any object at all.

It would not be figurative to say that Mark Antony had driven the Opposition underground. Indeed, he had proven himself very effective at taking advantage of a crisis opportunity. Before the Ides of March ended, Romans had started seeing notices go up on walls throughout the city. Curfews were being declared, meetings banned, rewards offered. All under the authority of the new Emergency Leader Mark Antony. Throughout the city, troops of soldiers drilled and clomped about, and neighbors would be found to have gone missing without warning.

The Opposition leadership in these early days after the Ides of March found itself quickly squeezed and under threat. It was in this atmosphere that the Opposition leadership had managed to sneak from their homes late at night and make contact deep inside an abandoned aqueduct tunnel near the outer walls of the city.

"By the way," The Outside Communications Consultant said, "this is in my contract, of course, but I should offer a reminder that given the added difficulties, my public opinion projects are invoiced at triple rate during any martial law."

Cassius had had enough.

"Listen," he said, and his voice echoed up the clammy tunnel, "we need to focus on the real issues here."

Every other senator thought the same thing: They were all glad they could not see the frown on Cassius's face. Even imagining it made them sad.

"The first thing we would do if we had any money," Cassius continued, "is to pay any soldiers who are inclined to support our cause. That is, *if* we had any money. Which we do not."

If setback let off an aroma, its distinctive odor would be wafting over from wherever The Outside Communications Consultant stood.

"It is true that our funds are nearing depletion," offered Cicero. "If the torches hadn't all gone out, I could give you our exact balance. I was going to actually suggest we might need to reduce our official mileage reimbursement, although such an extreme measure would be, so to speak, down the road."

"The problem of funds leads to our immediate dilemma," said Cassius, his voice steadied but still stern. "But it is a dilemma that perhaps could provide our best opportunity. I think I might have found the solution to what we are facing. I have come to realize that perhaps there is a hidden answer to our problem. Our circumstance, if my assumptions are correct, may not be as bleak as it seems."

The sound of hair being combed, which had been heard for the past minutes, momentarily stopped.

"How exactly do you mean, Cassius?" asked Brutus. "It is not like you to speak in riddles."

"It is no riddle, my dear Brutus. Let us take stock of our situation. Antony has seized control. We are facing danger overall. And we still face Antony's ultimatum. We know we are running out of time to turn the body of Caesar over to him. But what if I told you Caesar may in fact possess something that can immensely help us out."

"Hmmm," said Bilbius Dilbo. Or maybe it was Flavian who said this. It was hard to tell which.

Cassius continued. "We have all heard the speculation about the secret document, the one Caesar was just about to reveal. None of you saw Caesar before he ... before he ..." – Cassius knew that direct reference to the stage fall and prosciutto knife would risk hearing Totovus throw up – "before he had his experience back in the theater. But I did see him. I saw the entire incident from my vantage point on the stage. In those last moments, I believe Caesar began experiencing a TIA mini-stroke. His sudden gyrations and jerking around on stage point clearly to this. But I have come also to believe that he actually had on his person a momentous and, it should be added, extremely valuable document."

The sound of pomade stopped.

"Go on," said Brutus.

"Antony and most others believe that when he spoke of his secret document, Caesar had been referring to his last will and testament. They key off his reference to its value coming after he is gone and his saying that 'what is mine is yours.' This is one of the reasons Antony insists on Caesar's body, so there is no doubt that the will can be executed. I have reasoned out, however, that Caesar had something even more precious. I am fully convinced that Caesar had with him, in fact, the ownership of a vast store of an exceptionally valuable natural asset, with a worth possibly in the billions."

Someone – it was impossible to figure out who – let out a whistle that said, in effect, now *that's* a lot of spaghetti.

"Follow me if you will," Cassius said. "Caesar spoke his last words low, possibly owing to the early onset of his stroke symptoms. But being nearby on stage, I distinctly heard him say, 'It's just a question of digging deep down enough in the right place.' What is more, he earlier made reference to a 'resource' of his. He also gave us a sly hint when he talked of this 'resource' being something of 'mine.'"

Cassius made air quotes as he spoke; this was lost on everyone.

"Lastly, he referred to this object being something that can 'fuse' us together. Another cunning insinuation on his part. Caesar must have been referring to a precious metal. Think this through. Think how artfully Caesar's mind works. Which precious metal requires careful searching out for the exact 'right place'? And calls for particularly 'deep' mining?" And also becomes an alloy, one used for 'fusing' together? It is none other than that almost rarest of naturally occurring ores. It must be – "

A sneeze emitted from one of the senators who had caught the sniffles in the swimming pool at the Mulvian Baths and Conference Center.

" – tin." Cassius chose to ignore the opportunity to offer a friendly gesundheit. "The document must be nothing other than the map to a hitherto unknown tin mine. I am sure of it. And as we all know, when tin is discovered, it is found in enormous quantities. It has to be a wealth of tin."

He had intended some quiet after his declaration, to let his fellow senators fully absorb the import of his words. It would be best, he felt, to give his sublime news some momentous time to sink fully in. But just as this silence took shape, an announcement ran through the tunnel.

The announcement was: "A spider."

Stressing the urgency of the announcement, its broadcaster repeated it six times rapidly and in high pitch. The entire succession came off as nearly a monosyllable. It came out, in less than three seconds, as: Aspideraspideraspideraspideraspider!

The content of the news was troubling. More so, however, was the fact that it came from a wholly unrecognizable voice.

"Fellow senators, those closer to the tunnel entrance," Cassius said with immediate grimness, "lock arms now, and do not let anyone leave."

There was a bustling, but whether arms locked could not be determined.

"Gentlemen, the reason I asked you to block anyone from leaving is I believe we have captured a spy in our midst," Cassius said firmly. "And just who are you? You might as well tell us now."

The earlier silence Cassius had intended now emerged. For nearly a minute, there was no movement or words. Finally, the unrecognizable voice spoke up again.

"I'm sorry," it said, very, very softly. "I didn't mean to be a bother."

"Who are you?" Cassius demanded. "An infiltrator?"

"It's just me."

"Me? Me who?"

"I'm really very sorry."

"You are going to be sorry, I can assure you of that."

"I am."

"Now tell us who you are."

"Very."

"You're only making it worse for yourself."

"Sorry."

The tenor of the exchange continued like this for a bit longer, making considerable progress nowhere. Eventually, though, Cassius managed to deduce the identity of the mysterious voice. He felt a little ashamed of himself as it dawned on him: This was no spy or other kind of outside intruder. It must have been the bashful senator of the Opposition, the one who had never spoken up once in a meeting.

"Well," Cassius said, clearing his throat. To save his own life, he could not remember the man's name. "Well, my good friend. I shouldn't worry too much about it. Apology accepted. Spiders, after all, can be unnerving. No harm done, I suppose. Just a misunderstanding. But I do believe that this serves as a warning. I tell you all somberly that I believe that our plans have been finding their way suspiciously to Antony. I do not want to say we have a traitor or mole in our midst. But I just ask everyone to be especially careful."

A final apology came out from the bashful senator, spoken at a level reaching near to inaudibility.

"In any event." Cassius coughed again. "Let us return to our real concern. You may all be wondering what I've been leading up to, and how all this information about Caesar and his secret map to the tin mine affects us. Time is short for us. Antony is moving quickly, and so we must also. We will need to work fast. Young man? Are you here?"

Given the total darkness of the tunnel, the reader until just now understandably may not have been aware that during these discussions, Paul had been standing silently off to the side. He was not standing there comfortably, but he was there in the tunnel.

Since his narrow escape from the Milvian Bridge with the mute-cum-handcart days earlier, Paul's life had continued to not lack for eventfulness.

His old rope sandals had performed their offices well after the bridge incident. The trio had lost their pursuers half a mile from the Tiber. At a speed that would have prevented any but the most athletic onlookers from following, Paul had led the mute up and down the less traveled streets of the city, Caesar bouncing along luggagely on the lagging cart.

The mouth of Paul's alley was fortunately dispopulated when they got there. They had made it back into Paul's room, dragging Caesar's handcart down the stairs.

Returned to his small efficiency, though, it was no time for futzing. It was time for lavish and robust hiding. This task Paul accomplished skillfully. After sunset, the mute ducked off to seek out his master Brutus for instruction. Paul then stayed holed up in his room by Caesar's side for the next three days.

Caesar had gamely contributed his share to the effort, slowly pulling out of his stupor and coming to life. When the mute had finally come back, Caesar was more than half conscious, able to mumble a few words, and tied securely to the bed. The mute had motioned Paul to follow him, and they wended, under a moonless sky, to a site Paul vaguely remembered hearing had some old tunnels from a broken down aqueduct.

"Yes, Senator," Paul said. "I am here."

"Gentlemen," said Cassius, "if the Republic had a hundred more heroes like this young man, we would not be here today. He it is who may have preserved our future hopes. Do you still have Caesar at your estate, young man?

"Yes, Senator. He's still there."

"Still fully unconscious, I trust. And barely clinging to life."

Paul was not given the chance to answer.

"And, let me ask, did you see a parchment or document on his person?" Cassius asked.

Paul hesitated before offering, "I did see a paper, but ..."

"Good. What I now ask you to do is to retrieve that document and bring it to me. It is, I am sure, the secret map to the tin mines that will be ours in due time. Brutus's litter bearer can assist you once more in case you encounter any difficulties on the way. Then we will rendezvous and you can hand me the document."

A beet glow had begun seeping in from the tunnel entrance, bringing a shimmer of light to the meeting.

"With dawn coming," Cassius announced, "We best disperse for now."

A motion was made, seconded and voted upon. The Opposition leadership felt its way out of the tunnel and blinked.

As he moved from the darkness, Paul wondered whether he should have gone against type and spoken up more.

FOUND

T aking in a first whiff of red sunshine, Nature looked lazily about, inhaled slowly and stretched a lazy yawn. Starlings, terns and doves shook the dew from their wings, and harvest mice and city cats alike awakened to feel only the ambient rhythm of their own contented hearts; and for every living thing whose spirit bid a knowing welcome to the new light, a thousand thousand more inexpressibly sensed – out of the awakening of day – that the gods had made life with care, and they had made it good.

Paul looked to the sky; he squinted and felt a headache coming on. With his size 15½ sandals, meanwhile, the mute unknowingly crushed, in one step, an ant colony and an extended family of tiger beetles.

But perhaps most conspicuously was this: The dawn rang in with a sound that had already begun to feel familiar in Rome since the Ides of March – the sound of soldiering. The entrance of the rotted aqueduct tunnel disgorged its meeting participants not far from one of the plains where several cohorts had taken to doing their morning drill.

"Over there," Paul said. He pointed to a cobblestone street that would be the long way back – but the more prudent way. By circumnavigating along the city's inner walls, they had a chance of skirting the armed checkpoints set up by Antony throughout Rome and getting back to his Caesar-filled apartment.

Their progression, as it happened, ended up taking even longer than expected.

At several points, Paul looked ahead to find a grouping of

soldiers patrolling or checking papers. More than once he and the mute had to duck quickly behind a pillar or into a niche. Given the mute's size, only vast pillars and generous niches proved effective. For one perilous moment, the two had no choice but to stand stock still in front of a thrift store in the posture of mannequins. One of the troopers who passed by glanced their way and presumably decided the shop had a big-and-tall sale going on that day.

Nor was Paul's comrade engineered for the kind of urban slither that had become natural to Paul. Several backstreets narrowed too much. Clefts between buildings were found to be inadequately clefted. At one point, it would have required disassembling the mute and passing him sectionally through a fence chink. But in time, the street that would lead to Paul's apartment room came into view.

By then, the sun had already risen far into the sky, and the city had long gotten to work, or to whatever else it felt like doing that day. The mute lumbered methodically down the road.

Yet something about the atmosphere concerned Paul. He slowed. Something, he sensed, didn't feel quite right.

He yanked the mute's tunic from behind.

"It's a little too quiet around here for late morning," he said softly, looking up and down the empty street. "We better hold back a little and see if something's going on."

There was an abandoned noodle shop a little farther down, where they could secret themselves for a time and get a lay of the land. They went inside and ducked behind a derelict condiment station, peering over the top to keep an eye out.

Paul's instincts turned out before long to be sound. Something not right was unquestionably going on. Very shortly, a contingent of a dozen or so soldiers passed the shop entrance, going in the same direction that Paul and the mute had been. They were soon joined by more garishly festooned colleagues, presumably officers. Paul strained to listen as they talked with each other.

A mingle of coarse voices made it impossible for him to make out any words. But when a final figure passed, everyone could be heard snapping to frigid attention.

"You've cleared the streets?" The question came out less as a query than a demand. It undoubtedly came from the final figure, the apparent leader of the gathering. "I want these streets fully swept of everyone, do you understand?"

Crisp affirmation was offered.

"And we are sure where we are going, and that there is no chance of escape for anyone in there?"

More crispness.

"There better be no snafus." The rigor behind these words indicated that they likely were not meant to be taken ironically.

It seemed clear enough that some kind of military or official maneuver was afoot. There was nothing to do for Paul and the mute but to wait and listen. There was little distance between themselves and the place where Julius Caesar lay. But for all his skills, Paul had never learned a way to skirt round a very somber Roman cohort standing in the middle of the street.

After a time – during which Paul glanced disapprovingly twice at the mute's rumbling stomach – another trooper ran past the store toward the gathered party.

"Sire! The battering team will be here within the half hour."

"Very good," said the authoritative voice. "Now find me a place where I can get some privacy to speak with the commander."

Paul and the mute looked at each other with an oh-yes-it-can-(get-worse) look. The trooper did find a place with some privacy: An abandoned noodle shop nearby.

From his crouched position, Paul could see two men come into the store. Or, at the very least, the lovely pluming atop two helmets came inside. Two humans underneath these helmets, it stood to reason, captained them forward.

While both crests stood erectly impressive, one had more numinous growth protruding. It was from under this first, more grand helmet that the initial words came.

"You were one of my primary supporters, and you are my most loyal member of the high command. That is why I want you to share in the acclaim here."

"Thank you, Lord Antony," responded the less gorgeously embellished helmet. "As Lord Antony wishes, so I shall follow, as I have done."

"Very good. I have personally studied the floor plan of the building we are targeting. There is a long and entirely enclosed alleyway leading up to the building, and there is no egress except through the door we're going to ram, and the door does not look to be more than a warped board of some kind. It leads into a very small room that we will attack. This should all be fairly simple."

"Yes, sire," the not-as-pretty covering said.

"And now you wonder about the object of this exercise, do you not?"

"If you will, my lord."

"This may surprise you somewhat. We are going on a rescue mission of sorts. I have learned that the body of Julius Caesar is actually inside that apartment room."

"Indeed, sire?"

"I have not announced this publicly, but the body was spirited away after the Ides of March by leaders of the Opposition. For what reason, we shall find out soon enough. But we need to retrieve it now. Although there is one possible complication, I am told."

"Sire?"

"Caesar, it appears, may not be fully dead yet. He has perhaps been in some kind of comatose state."

"I see."

"That is why you and I will go in alone after the door is rammed and broken down. And, Commander, we will make sure a body comes out of that place, no matter what. Do you understand? A *body* body. The coroner has a form printed up. It uses the term 'exsanguination.' Let's not disappoint the coroner, shall we?"

"Sire."

"You will be rewarded for your loyalty and your discretion, Commander. When the body of Caesar is lifted tomorrow morning onto the pyre, you will be by my side as I raise the torch."

"By your leave, Lord Antony."

"I want men like you near me, Commander. We are about to begin a new order in Rome, one that will brook no hesitation or weakness. We are entering an era that will be much more vigorous and decisive. Things are about to change in Rome. This must not be said publicly, but Caesar was frankly rather feeble, in the end. You may be surprised to know that he proved to be a rather unreliable tool for me. Do you know, he told me just before his last speech that he had decided not to accept the dictator position, even after I had gotten it all arranged."

Antony's voice took on a bit of an edge, a tint of irritation.

"Soon I will take that position myself. Dictator of Rome. Frankly, if the Opposition hadn't conveniently done Caesar in on the Ides of March – or appeared to do him in – I had my own plans to do the job myself. Caesar's time was at an end no matter what. He was too thick to realize it, but I wanted to create that position not for him but ultimately for me to use when he was gone to war. Then I'd get rid of him forever."

"I see," said the modest helmet.

"He could give a decent speech and somehow knew how to work a battle when it came down to it, but that's all. Caesar. There really was nothing to the man. He had a lot of the common people and soldiers bamboozled, but up close, he was a bumbling blockhead. To say the least."

"Is that right, sire?"

"Somehow when he got up to give a speech, he filled up, and when he opened his mouth, he came across as a strong capable leader of humanity. But if only people saw the real Caesar! I sometimes wonder why I ever pushed him into politics in the first place."

"Fascinating, sire."

Paul, throughout his life, had been commended many times by those who knew him for being a great listener. You're such a great listener, people would tell Paul. They would say this while in the middle of a soliloquy about themselves.

When someone told Paul he was such a great listener, nine times out of ten they meant that they liked the fact that he would sit there agreeably while they prattled on about intimate or troubled aspects of their lives that he never wanted to hear, but he was too accommodating or felt too trapped to slow them down.

Invariably at such times, the voice of the talker changes. As they disburden themselves with more and more verve, the voice elevates half an octave while it hollows a bit, and words get squashed tighter as a flood of feeling jets out. Then Paul would prepare to sit back and just listen, interjecting every so often an empathetic word or rhetorical question. That is what is meant by a great listener.

If the man Paul heard talking at present were not the most dominant figure now in Rome, a man of distinct swagger and drive – Lord Antony himself – Paul would have thought he detected such rising vexation starting to surface in his voice, and he would have suspected the person under the shorter helmet was often told what a great listener he was.

"Do you know that Caesar didn't even know where the Rubicon was," Antony snapped. "Can you believe that? I had to show it to him on a map, and even then, I had to explain it all to him seven times why he had to cross the damned thing."

"Oh?" asked the lesser hat rhetorically.

"I'm the one who wrote his so-called autobiography, by the way. And most of it is made-up crap to make Caesar look good."

"Is that right, sire?"

"Did you also know after the war in Britannia that he never actually said the words, 'Veni, vidi, vici.'" Antony's voice nearly squeaked. "It's the most famous line in his book, but I made it up afterward. To make him sound pithy and clever. And he wanted to take it out, too. He told me 'I came, I saw, I conquered' didn't come off quite right. Can you imagine that? He thought it would sound better if we had him saying, 'Caesar got it started for ya, oh yeah.' The man was really a pill. Finally, I figured out he liked word puzzles for some bizarre reason, who knows why, even though he could never spell for shit, so I would buy him all kinds of word play books – usually for ages 8 to 11 – to keep him occupied and out of my hair."

"I was not aware, my lord."

"I stopped the man from making a fool of himself over and over, too. It got very tiring, listening to that twaddle and trying to prevent him from stepping in his own shit. But fortunately he started becoming less and less useful recently, especially as I got my grip on the urban troops and realized more and more that I could rely on men like you. Honestly, if it weren't for me, Caesar would have probably died years ago in a gardening mishap or some other idiotic screw-up of his."

"Truly, sire, I did not realize this."

"My only regret is not asking him about that secret document. Who would have thought the dinglebell was planning to announce his last will and testament? What an insufferable ass. And he's still causing me headaches. I'll have to put out now that he somehow was the victim of a gloriously brutal martyrdom. Some fanciful story about how many times he got stabbed by the Opposition."

"Twenty three perhaps?"

"In any event." Antony paused, as if in dawning self-awareness that he had gotten off track. A tickle of compunction often comes upon one who has been making use of a great listener for some time. He exhaled and let his voice drop down and the rate of his word flow ebb. "In any event, Caesar may need to be handled in there. If so, I shall handle him myself. There is also the matter of getting the paper. I have no doubt it is indeed his last will and testament, and that it is still with him. I must be the one to announce its contents. I believe doing so shall fully complete my close association with the publicly known Caesar – who the people think of now as some kind of martyr – and cement the new order in Rome."

"Very good, sire."

"Our goal then is simple. Get the body and get the document. When this is done, we will need to mop up some remaining issues." Antony had returned fully to his deliberate tone. "There's some snotty young relative of Caesar's who's coming up to Rome to try to force his way into everything. Calls himself Octavian Caesar or some such, but he shouldn't be a big problem. I do not want the Opposition being bothersome any more, either. But I am more concerned about the fact that there are clearly subversive elements in the city. There is a seditious grouping of some kind, I fear, seeking to upset our plans."

"My Lord Antony saw the report from one of my centurions about the failed bombing of the Milvian Bridge? A description of the bomber has been sent to all cohorts."

"And I was personally the victim of a guerrilla assault during the Lupercalia Run. Frankly, I worry about these underground insurgents more than any political threat. When I catch their leader, I promise you it will be his head."

"Pardon me, sire, but what was that?" Helmet Two asked after a moment.

"Commander?"

"I thought I heard the sound of – it was almost like a –" after another pause, the helmet plumage rotated left and right, indicating that its occupant had begun looking around the room "–like a gulp."

"Please, Commander," Antony said starchly. "Try to stay focused on our task at hand."

At that moment, a trooper stomped in to report that the battering team had begun positioning itself.

"Let us prepare the attack, Commander," Antony said with grimness. And the two helmets disappeared.

Most anyone in Paul's position at this point – let's be honest – would have stayed bent behind a protective old condiment station for as long as possible and then followed a plan that might include walking in the direction of the nearest coast and, upon arrival, continuing to walk. Paul had no desire to stay involved with any of this.

But unfortunately he had an important reason to continue to do so.

"They're going to attack my place," he whispered to the mute. "You don't have to come with, but I have to try to get there before they do. I don't think it would be good for me if Caesar was found where I live. But there's another reason."

The mute cocked his head in uncertainty.

"My mother," Paul said. "She is in there too, with Caesar. I need to get her out."

The mute raised his eyebrows in surprise but quickly nodded in a gesture of understanding: He would be going along.

Paul motioned to a tattered curtain that led to the backroom of the building and out to a narrow passageway behind.

KNOTS

As he and the mute bolted down the alley behind the noodle shop, Paul swiftly drew a map in his mind that might get them somehow back to his apartment room without being seen. He had run along most of the places on his imagined route many times. They had at least a slender chance of getting there, he thought. Very slender, but a chance at least.

He even took into account his companion's unusually spacious volume in formulating their course. Even so, it looked grim. The fundamental question was not even getting there. The fundamental question was whether they could get into his room and then extract Caesar and his mother before Antony's troops attacked.

That particularity of the plan seemed beyond implausible.

"We're going to have to take the high and the long way around," Paul said, leaping up at the raised ladder of a fire escape in the alley. After three or four jumps, he managed to grasp at the bottom rung. But his slight mass didn't provide enough weight to pull the thing down. He dangled for half a minute before the mute reached up and grabbed the rung, feet still flat on the ground. The ladder creaked and unfolded itself to the ground, bringing Paul back with it.

They zigzagged up four flights. The rivets holding the framework into the building complained some little bit, but they did not give out.

Seven roofs later, down a series of back porches (passing a startled bring-a-dish party on the third floor of one building), through a garden courtyard, up a rear stairwell, behind a penthouse condominium, along a servant's hall, and over seven more roofs, they stopped.

They had almost made it. The roof of the building Paul lived in stood not more than a dozen feet away. But there was an enormous obstacle blocking the way. Terror. Or, to frame the matter more dispassionately: Approximately four hundred thousand cubic yards of nothing, all of it gaping in between the wall of the building on which Paul and the mute stood and the wall of the building on which they wished to stand. They would have to jump for it.

"There used to be a scaffolding here," Paul said with disappointment. "There's been a scaffolding here for years. I wonder what happened to the scaffolding."

He and the mute looked over the edge, down four stories to the hard ground below. Paul had jumped over many wide gaps many times without a thought before. But this one looked different. This gap looked more businesslike than most. It appeared confident in itself. At annual gap conventions, it was probably one of the gaps that was asked to give a presentation at breakout sessions on successful gapping strategies, and it would not be surprising if, after a few belts at the hotel bar later on, it bullied the more feeble holes and undersized voids with derisive nicknames.

It was a very, very big gap.

Paul gulped. But the mute shrugged. The mute next backed up a few steps, gave himself a push from his feet and leapt over with ease. Easy for someone with legs the height of flagpoles, Paul thought anxiously.

He looked across to the mute, now successfully across the gap, then looked into the gap again. Despite the mute's success, the gap seemed to have chuckled.

Briefly Paul considered that his mother might actually be just fine on her own. Better than fine, really. In fact, she might be more than a match for Antony and the Roman army. After a few hours of questioning and trying to make sense of her stories, Antony might be the one dragged away, babbling and twitching a bit.

Paul shook the notion from his mind.

He did as the mute did, backing up a few steps. He counted to three. He counted to three several times. On the fifth three, he sprang forward. The edge opened up below; he closed his eyes and, feeling air under his feet halfway over the gap, started to weep.

Paul more or less lost track of time during the operation and, if asked, would probably have told you he opened his eyes again on the following Thursday. When he did so, he still felt air under his feet, but he saw to his full astonishment the mute's hands clamped to both his own wrists and felt himself being dragged up and forward.

"Thank ..." – Paul, panting for breath and his muscles jellied, spoke with the all of the articulatory clarity of a problem drinker in the middle of a three-day bender – "you."

They stood atop the apartment building in which, far below, Paul lived. Also below, they could hear the shouting of orders and scuffling of boots from the alley that led directly to Paul's room.

The challenge now was to get into Paul's basement room and out again, unseen, bringing along two other people on the return trip. Soon.

A hatch-and-submarine-ladder entry led from the roof down to the fourth floor of Paul's building. This floor contained only tenant storage cages, and no one appeared to be around when they got there. So far, so good. A brick core in the center of the floor housed the building's venting and smokeshafts – and, Paul calculated, the uppermost opening to the defunct garbage chute that went straight down to his small living quarters.

Just where he thought the opening should be, he found a distorted sheet of metal tentatively affixed to the wall with three nails, all of them looking tired and about to give up. That would explain why his meager heat in the winter raced up from his room out the chute.

One yank at the most bulging corner of the metal sheet had the thing pulled out.

"Can you find something that could help lift us out of there?" Paul asked. "There has to be some rope somewhere around. And be ready to do some heavy lifting to get us out."

The mute trotted off.

With a second yank Paul pulled himself up to where the sheet of metal had been, balancing himself on the edge of the chute. He looked down to a new gaping emptiness. What this space lacked in girth it compensated for in darkness. Squeezing and maneuvering of this type was not what Paul usually did on the job. But he took a deep breath and decided the principles of motion could not be too much different.

He leaned forward to let his hands press against the opposite wall of the chute and brought his feet behind, pressed against the closer wall. Fortunately the surface was of a rough brick, giving him traction.

It did not look to be a comfortable walk. He had positioned himself facing downward. He pushed his hands hard against the opposite side of the chute, while his feet pressed with equal strength at the near side. The only force keeping him from falling was the pressure he exerted on the walls. He would have to keep pushing his hands and feet hard against the sides, his body suspended in between, and inch his way down. One slip and he would be going the speed of countless bags of trash that followed the course earlier.

Paul decided he would start counting aloud to keep his mind off the dangerous folly of it all. With each number he said, he would try to move a hand or a foot down a little.

"One," he announced to begin with, and his left foot responded after a fashion by shifting itself about seven inches toward the Earth.

"Two," he proclaimed. Nothing happened at two.

"Two," he again commanded. His right hand truculently followed the example set by the left foot. This proceeded sequentially, and the light above faded slowly away.

It would be an exaggeration to say that Paul got a rhythm going or at any point felt good about his position. But he was able after a fashion to track some progress.

By the time he stated 11, he had a good idea of how many inches per shift he was able to make.

At 19, he had jiggled his right sandal back on as it began to come loose.

Around 27, he felt his hands begin burn from the pressure.

At 44, he tried to remember if the Roman pantheon included a god of levitation.

Nearing 63, his mouth had dried out and he had to count silently.

Closing in on 77, he decided he hated the Senate of Rome.

At 103, he remembered an article he had once read on coping with claustrophobia.

At 116, his right sandal slid off entirely and rattled down the chute.

Reaching 128, he began thinking of individual Roman senators he hated.

At 134, he knew it was all over.

No amount of adrenaline or determination could hold him up in the air any longer. At this, a calmness came upon Paul. It was strange. Yet he understood intuitively then what he had been told, that many people in hopeless battle or at the finish of a mortal disease actually find a last moment of ecstasy as they accept their fate.

Paul released his muscles and let the air below encompass him.

He learned, an instant later, the deepness count of the chute: Approximately 136.

"Ouch," Paul said as he met the floor. But this was a perfunctory ouch. It didn't really hurt that much.

He luxuriated about half a minute in the feeling of bottom, while his legs and arms worked to reconstitute themselves into functioning limbs and he groped for his errant sandal. He knew there was no time to lose.

Feeling with his feet, he located the backside of the board that covered the chute opening in his efficiency. It took just one kick to open up a flood of light. It took a minute to adjust to the light and discern the figure in front of him.

"Hello, dear." Paul's mother spoke as if he had just ambled in the front door. "We were starting to wonder where you were. Are you hungry? I can fix you a snack."

She sat on the banana crate where she had perched for most of the past days. She looked exactly like she might on a dull day back in her apartment: Jet hair a little frayed and down to her shoulders, olive face and jet eyes giving off a distant smirk.

Chuffing and trying to swallow, Paul struggled out of the chute and onto his legs.

"Or maybe a glass of water?" she suggested, going to a pitcher next to the stove.

Outside was ominously silent; Paul focused himself on the task at hand. Two tasks, in fact: Julius Caesar and his mother.

Days back, after racing around Rome, Paul had breathed a little easier when he'd gotten to his small room with Caesar and the mute. Then he saw his mother sitting there. He had forgotten about inviting her over that day. He gasped but she'd seemed not at all surprised at the sight of a giant and his mannish newlywed coming in with Paul.

Even when she realized the identity of the bride, far from showing astonishment, his mother treated Julius Caesar as if she had known him for decades. She ended up being a helpful nursemaid since then. She had gotten Caesar laid out and put a wet rag on his forehead. She fed Caesar broth, talked with him whenever he came to and otherwise took care of his needs. For his part, Caesar – possibly owing to his injuries – seemed also to share an unaccountable familiarity with her.

Caesar lay now on the bed, stretched out. His costumery and toga had been removed, and he wore an old tunic of Paul's. He was staring at Paul but it was impossible to tell his level of conscious awareness.

Paul grabbed the tall glass of water his mother held.

"We have to get out of here," he said hoarsely, after quickly downing the drink.

"Of course, dear."

Paul called up the chute.

"Did you have any luck?" His voice reverberated before losing itself in the darkness above. "Send something down if you have anything."

As he stepped back and stared into the opening, Paul realized there was as good a chance as any that the mute was still rooting around upstairs. Or had decided to run off. But then there appeared, without sound or warning, the end of a sturdy fire hose. It even featured a neat fire-escape loop knot. Paul briefly closed his eyes in silent thanks and relief.

"Can you put that around your body, mother? Get the loop under your arms, and you'll be lifted up."

She amiably complied, smiling as if getting onto an amusement park ride.

"Now!" Paul called up.

Just as muffled shouts made their way from down the alley, his mother disappeared up from the room.

Paul went and untied Caesar from the bed and found, to his relief, Caesar weak enough and bewildered enough to be led. He shuffled him over toward the chute as the hose came back down. Paul fixed the loop under Caesar's arms and shouted up again. And up rattled Caesar.

The unambiguous sound of advancing boots echoed down the alley as the hose came back down a third time.

As Paul struggled to slide the loop under his own arms a roaring crash echoed through his little room and splinters of pressed board exploded out in his direction.

CAUGHT

"I'll start with the whipping and beating while you two stir up the heated coals. Let me know when they're glowing red. I want to hear a sizzle this time when we get started."

From his confinement, Paul heard the pitiless voices below so distinctly he could imagine they were taunting him. As he had a hundred times already, Paul scanned the dank garret for any way out. But he knew there was none. Only a small casement window let a meager streak of light into the small space. Sitting on the bare floor, he could not imagine any getaway.

"Don't forget to have the rack ready to go," came a second calloused voice from the floorboards underneath. "Let's have no scalding marks on this one. I don't want to see any unnecessary breakage either. And remember the last one, all that needless oozing that we had to clean up."

Paul had never studied philosophy. He did not know of the School of the Stoics or the wisdom of the classical Greeks who spoke of the acceptance of our fate. But he did know he had no free will at this point. Just when you think you have found a chance for freedom, life traps you, and you have no choice. He knew he would have to await his destiny; that was the only choice he had.

There was just this one hope, this one possibility for the future: In time, it seemed likely, the owners of the The Artsy Tartsy Baked Tum-Yums would have to close shop and go home.

"Where'd you put the jelly roll pan anyway?" asked a third voice below. "We've got to make this batch the best ever."

Paul had barely made it out of his apartment two days earlier. He still could not believe his luck in getting away from Antony and his troopers or that he and his party still had not been captured.

Escapes are not built much narrower. His body had begun

rattling up the sides of the trash chute at the same moment he heard the soldiers crashing in. And even as the fugitives (Paul, mute, a befuddled Caesar and Paul's mother) made their way from the echo of Antony's curses coming up the shaft, Paul began to think through a quick plan to keep escaping.

After it became clear the troopers had left the apartment building empty handed, his mother agreed to go with the mute to the estate of Brutus, where there might be some safety. That left Paul to think of a new place to quickly hide Caesar. Caesar fortunately had shown all the characteristics we want in a kidnap victim who needs to be transported. Ambulatory but with a compliant stupefaction. He went along.

Caesar was coaxed down a number of back streets and a maze of sewer channels. The only moment of agitation came when he saw a strange object floating down a drainpipe. It was ribbony and had glimmering jewels attached, like an expensive headband of some kind. Caesar raised his hands in a gesture not so much of astonishment but of, Paul thought, demurral.

Paul had remembered having delivered messages to the Artsy Tarsty. He had once overheard the owners say they never used the attic of their shop. He'd immediately decided this would make as good a place to hide as any and pointed Caesar in direction of the Bread District.

Once ensconced, he found a disused pantry in one of the attic walls that provided an ideal spot to house Caesar. The previous night Paul was even able to clamber down to grab some buns and a couple day-old crullers.

Before they had all separated, he had told the mute where he would be hiding and asked him to somehow get word over. But no word had come.

And so he sat, waited and listened.

He went to the pantry and pulled open the door.

Caesar lay on his stomach, hands in his chin and lower legs scissoring in the air, staring down at the floor as if at an open crossword book, though he had no pencil and there was nothing under him. He looked up at Paul with a sort of weaning look.

Caesar's condition had been strange, to say the least. Paul had little experience with head trauma victims, but based on Caesar's behavior, he presumed a clomp to the skull must have the effect of randomizing the cells of the brain.

Back at his apartment room, Caesar had showed some signs of clarity, even mumbling questions and asking for water or food. But since letting himself be led to the bakery, he seemed to have notched down into one of the stages of late infancy. There was gurgling and burping, giggling and tactile grasping. He had apparently entered into an imprinting phase of development and looked at Paul with an expression of childlike expectation. Paul felt very much like a benevolent drake.

"I don't know what to do," Paul said, with some gentleness, speaking mostly to himself while looking at Caesar.

Smiling, Caesar lifted a hand and pointed with apparent mindlessness behind Paul.

"Yes we should get away." Paul said. "But where?"

Caesar let out a demanding grunt and pointed with more urgency.

"I am sorry," Paul said. "But I don't know where we can gurf."

Paul, when he had embarked on the previous sentence, had not intended to close it so immediately, nor with a gurf. He had uttered this final thought (gurf) not so much to convey meaning as to indicate emotion. It was a rock that had made Paul's words go haywire: A rock which, a half second earlier, had smote Paul in his nape. Caesar, presumably, had been trying to warn Paul of its approach.

"Gurf." Rubbing the back of his neck, Paul repeated the comment but with a little less ginger the second time. The rock's clunking near his head had startled as much as it hurt. He turned round to see it rolling along the floor.

Going over to look out the window, Paul thought he caught the backside of the mute scurrying away. He returned to the rock. Its objective was suggested by a sheet of paper tied to it. He unknotted and unfolded it.

My dear young man –

I trust this stone finds you well.

Such happy hopes I cannot express for our cherished Republic. She is in greater peril than even you may have feared, my boy. But let us not despair. More than ever, I am certain that Caesar's final document must be the priceless secret map to invaluable tin mines. The crafty clues he provided for those of keen mind (those such as you and I) make this fact incontrovertible. As you know, Caesar found exactly such mines in Brittany during his recent conquest of Gaul.

... Paul had not the slightest idea what any of this meant. He continued ...

Quo vadis? What next? You must join us, good comrade. The Opposition leadership has resolved to journey to those mines and take possession of them. Make haste, oh make haste, and bring us that precious document. With the wealth of the tin mines under our control, we can find our way back to power and opportunity.

We shall lodge in Capua five days hence. Come, and bring, my youthful compatriot, the map. We shall proceed through Greece, birthplace of liberty and a land where I hope we will be welcomed.

We all understand the great risk we face, that Mark Antony certainly will not let us move on in peace. But this is now our only hope.

Know in the meantime that your mother is out of danger. I enjoyed the pleasure of conversing with your mother while at the estate of Brutus, and from her wise words, I came to understand whence you received your radiant intelligence.

One final word. If Julius Caesar has passed on, he is in the hands of the gods. If not – you witnessed the dreadful but necessary action I attempted in the theater. (Never has a single pillow been so nearly critical to the future of a Republic.) I believe you were one hundred percent behind me there. If you see fit to complete what I could not, then you will have done one more service for the Republic. If, however, Caesar still lives, that is another matter. I leave the decision in your capable hands.

May the gods speed our triumph. Your fellow Roman in liberty –

- Gaius Cassius Longinus

P.S. Your mother made you a nice care package. Look for it.

Fully befuddled, Paul ambled to the casement window. He noticed a satchel had been tossed up onto the sill where the rock had come through. He reached out and pulled it in. It was a bag of his mother's. Inattentively, he slid it over his shoulder.

He turned back to Caesar, and Caesar smiled back with bright innocence.

Offing such a creature was unthinkable. And leaving him here alone to be captured would be too harsh, too.

"We will go together," Paul told him, knowing the words were being half understood at best. "We will leave here and maybe we can get you someplace safe. And maybe I can somehow find my way to a calm life again."

The noises below, Paul noticed, had stopped. The bakery had apparently shut for lunchtime. With a little effort, Paul got Caesar onto his legs and began leading him down the stairs and through the kitchen. Caesar seemed perfectly willing to go along. It was thankfully like leading a domesticated mammal.

"There is a temple to Ceres next door," Paul said, again speaking more to himself than his insensate companion. "I'll slip in and grab a monk's robe to put over you, and then we will be on our way."

Paul opened the shop entrance door, poking his head out to make sure no one was around. He waved behind for Caesar to follow. And then Paul felt, at his throat, the icy blade of a knife.

He froze.

"Caesar," Caesar intoned – and it was the resonant Caesar intoning of the past – "Caesar is not as dumb as some may think."

EXPLANATIONS

Having gurfed twice already that day, a third gurf seemed to be pushing it. Paul remained still and silent.

"Caesar," Caesar announced from behind, "knows when to wait and when to act. And I am taking action now."

Caesar's recovery had unmistakably been full – full, and fully concealed. In addition to holding a knife to Paul's neck from behind, he twisted Paul's left arm behind his back, causing not inconsiderable shoulder pain.

"Pretty clever of me biding my time there, wasn't it?" Caesar asked, dropping back to his non-intoning, everyday voice. "Actually been pretty okay for a few days now. I saw the knife back there in the kitchen and, boom. Done and done."

So that was it. After all his escapes, running, hiding and dodging, Paul was going to be carted off now by Julius Caesar, a man he had tried inexplicably to save on more than one occasion. Presumably he would be taken to an execution or, at best, a lifetime in prison. Or maybe Caesar would show mercy and finish him off right here.

Paul closed his eyes. There flickered in his mind a notion he had long suspected: Life may generally be quite unfair, possibly rottenly so. But after the adrenaline draining last days, he felt too exhausted to feel much at all, much less to attempt to struggle.

"Okay," he offered. He spoke in the same way that a person might accept, after some argument, that the returns desk absolutely will make no exceptions to the store's receipt-required policy. "I just hope you're not too surprised in the end."

Paul waited, his eyes still shut tight. He sensed only the knife blade in front and Caesar's breath behind. He waited more. But the knife did not move, and Caesar's breathing slowed a little.

"Huh?" said Caesar.

"What?" said Paul.

"Your comment about being surprised. What did you mean by that?"

In his defeated pique, Paul hardly even realized what he had said. He thought a second.

"I just think you may want to know about some things that've happened."

The knife relaxed a bit.

"Maybe we should discuss matters a little," Caesar said.

Paul opened his eyes. It was an activity he had not expected to ever complete again.

For their conference, Paul was taken to the backroom, seated against a pile of flour bags and told to put his hands behind his head. From there he got a close look at Caesar's knife, which now hovered a few inches from his face. It was big and sharp.

"I liked you." Caesar opened the meeting. "But I can't quite figure out what you've been up to. Tying me up, dressing me up, pulling me up chutes and keeping me locked up. Caesar isn't used to such treatment."

Paul decided to give it a go. He had to do a good deal of explaining. There were many blanks in Caesar's memory, especially over the earlier incidents he had been through. But Paul told him about the fall from the stage in the Theater of Pompey, of Caesar's assumed demise therewith which turned out to be a concussion, of the theater basement, of the chase through Rome and the escape to Paul's apartment room.

Caesar pursed his lips and nodded during much of the explanation. The knife, by the time Paul finished talking, had been pulled back an inch.

"It's all rather fanciful," Caesar said. "But I am remembering much of what you tell me now, and I do know you to be a candid young man. Your mother is a wonderfully sweet woman, too. I'm sorry if I came on a little strong just now, but you can't be too careful these days."

"Yes," agreed Paul. "Thank you."

"So you say I had an accidental fall?"

"Yes, Caesar."

"And you say you were dragooned into stashing me in your apartment?"

"Yes, Caesar."

"So it wasn't just a dream that I was a bride?"

"No, Caesar."

"And you and your mother – a delightful woman, she, I must say – you say you and your mother nursed me back to health?

"That's right."

"I still have a few questions about all this, but – "

Caesar leaned back in thought.

"I am sure Mark Antony will have some good ideas on how we should proceed from here," he said. "I think I know what to do. Let's you and I go have a word with Antony together."

Paul did not think himself qualified to offer political advice. Yet it occurred to him that he ought to tell Caesar political circumstances had possibly changed fairly dramatically recently. But before he could speak, the cadence of footsteps and chattering came from the alley outside. Caesar turned to the door.

"Let's get some assistance from whoever this may be and find our way to Antony's house. What say you?"

Paul glanced around. Just as the door opened, he grabbed one of the flour bags. Giving a heave, he arced it carefully up. Before long, the bag landed perfectly atop Caesar's head and exploded with a puffing sigh.

The woman and two men who entered a half second later stopped cold and stared ahead. On a chair in the middle of the room, a fully dredged and perfectly whitened Julius Caesar sat in stunned silence. Paul looked back and forth. The only motion of the three bakery workers was a gaping of their mouths, followed by a further gaping.

Caesar merely blinked, letting a few flour grains flutter from his whitened eyelashes. This unspeaking, blinking, gaping continued for a good full minute.

Finally, the woman spoke up.

"Great Caesar's ghost!"

Rapidly, the three spun back and ran out.

The woman's shout seemed to break Caesar from his shock. His wits and eyesight recovering, he whirled round and had the knife hard up against Paul's throat once again.

"You ought not to have done that," Caesar said. Despite the powdery film fully covering his head and tunic, the sonority of his words lent as much command to his appearance as Paul had ever experienced. He pushed the knife at Paul's skin. "Perhaps my original plan for you was right. I'm afraid you will need to be dispatched."

The earlier confab had ended rather fruitlessly, Paul realized.

"Maybe I shouldn't have ever saved your life," he blurted. "But

Mark Antony will take care of you, I'm sorry to say."

The knife against his throat did not relax.

"A very good try," Caesar said through clenched teeth. "But you will not fool Caesar again. This time you won't talk your way out of the fate that Caesar has in store for ... Wait, what? – What do you mean, Antony will take care of me?"

Paul glanced down at the knife, then up into Caesar's pasty face. It was impossible to tell underneath the staple food covering him, but there seemed to be an expression of puzzlement on the man.

"It's what I was about to explain to you." Paul spoke with some force and speed. "I heard Mark Antony talking about you. I heard it all. He said he wrote your autobiography for you, and that he came up with all the good ideas himself and he got tired of handling you and getting you in line. And he said you told him, right before your speech on the Ides of March, that you didn't want to be dictator even though he had it all planned for you. He said he decided to kill you himself at that point. I heard him say it all, right before we took you from my apartment."

The knife pulled back half an inch.

"I see," Caesar said with all the intonation leaked out. "Antony is the only person I ever told that to, about not wanting that new dictator position for myself. You say you overheard him say that?"

"And when we took you up the chute from my room, the troops you heard were Antony's. He was coming to kill you."

"Come to think of it." Caesar leaned back again. "I always thought Antony had been getting pretty uppity."

The sound of a knife could be heard clattering on the floor.

"Caesar," said Caesar slowly, "Caesar could use a towel."

BUHBYE

They would pass out of Rome separately and meet again in the Field of Mars, before moving on together to Capua. That was the plan.

Caesar needed a little more convincing, but he did come round. Antony clearly was no friend, and his loyal troops had the city in lockdown. The only option for Caesar would be to go with Paul and meet up with the Opposition. There he would see if he could get his political footing back or otherwise show the world he still lived. He did not love the idea, seeing as the Opposition had been set up mainly to Oppose him, but they did now have a common enemy to fight in Antony.

To seal the deal, Paul told Caesar about the Opposition's formal vote when he was comatose in the theater, specifically committing to not offing him when they had the chance. (Having been learning recently the basics of being politic, Paul left unsaid that that vote was driven by indecision and that the Opposition in fact badly hoped Caesar would stop living on his own.)

Paul had nothing with him for the journey but the worn tunic on his shoulders, his rope sandals and the satchel care package his mother had sent over. Caesar had even less. After they left the bakery, Paul swiped a monk's robe with a cowl hood for him to wear, but Caesar too was otherwise empty handed. They parted company after agreeing to connect again in one hour outside the city walls.

Fortunately twilight gave good cover as Paul worked his way toward the Capena Gate at the south wall of the city. He utilized every remembered alley, rooftop, and drainpipe, skirting away from any clumps of people (the streets were far emptier than usual since Antony had declared a sunset curfew) and from the sight of helmet plumage.

At last, he eyed the towering gate columns. His chest seized up. After a life inside the walls of Rome, running countless thousands of miles in its cramped space, Paul was about to venture beyond. Almost certainly forever. But first he would have to get past the sentries.

Stalling until he could work up his spirit, he pushed himself against a wall and unclasped the satchel. Inside were two packets and a scrap of parchment. He unfolded the scrap.

Dearest Paul –

I know you must leave tonight, far off. Here's that document I found in Caesar's toga. You'll need it more than I will. I also packed you something for when you might need to be a little uplifted. Be safe, little one.

Mother

Once again, and with just a few sentences, Paul's mother did not fail to confound.

One of the last concerns on Paul's blistering mind recently had been the secret document of Caesar's, the paper that meant so much to so many others.

Back in his efficiency apartment, it was actually Paul's mother who had first come across it. This had been the day after Caesar was brought in. She'd been preparing to give him a sponge bath and was removing his toga when the paper fell out of a fold. When she opened it, her eyes lit and she pushed it to her breast. Her inscrutable mind then clamped onto the thing like an odd scrap of a story or the image of a historical figure.

"I had never even hoped I would ever see this," she had told Paul. "And to have found he was carrying it in his toga makes it even more dear to me. There is nothing more valuable to me than this."

It made no sense, but the paper (whatever it was) had precious meaning to his mother, and she had been carrying it with her ever since. And yet now there it was in Paul's satchel, tied up in an oilcloth, along with a mystifying reference about him needing it more than she.

He touched at the larger packet in the satchel and could feel it held several blocks of indestructible toffee that his mother often cooked up. For a future uplift, apparently.

He put the articles back, clasped the satchel and stepped forward. On both sides of the gate stood sentries. They were stopping every person and cart coming in and out, looking at papers and questioning. With curfew fast approaching, the gates would be closed for the night.

Paul began walking as calmly as possible toward an unoccupied guard. He knew all the sentries had his name and description, and certainly no one was being allowed through without documentation. He tried to steady his breathing and talk himself into not running the other direction.

Caesar had told him about what he said was a "sure fire" way to make it by any guard. There was a tradition, Caesar said, to give special treatment to the illegitimate children of the officer corps. You just have to know the magic words, and you can come and go as you please anywhere. So Caesar said.

By an unwritten rule, all you simply had to do was to quietly inform any guard or sentinel that you are a member of the "Legion of the Slick Dagger." You will then get a wink, a nod and a wave through. At least, that's what Caesar said.

"I am a member of the Legion," Paul said to himself, practicing his line as he approached, "of the Slick Dagger."

Since his mother had never given Paul much more than an unreliable hint as to the identity of his own paternity, assuming the role of fatherlessness in itself would not require the employment of method acting. Keeping one's wits while trying to bluff a large fellow with a large sword would require, however, steadied nerves.

He strode up to one of the glowering figures by the gatehouse.

"I." Paul's first word eked out in a squeal from his lips. He cleared his throat.

Before he could speak again, he heard his name called. He knew immediately he should have ignored this, but instincts are instincts. He looked over to see, coming into the city from the opposite direction, Olivia. His girlfriend (ex- ?).

"It really is you!" Olivia called, striding up. She was wearing a tight fitting stola with glimmering gold clasps and seemed authentically happy to see him.

"Paul, we need to talk." she put her hands into his. "I need to explain some things."

Paul looked over to the guard, who looked back and turned up his attention to the next setting of glower.

"Yes, hello, Olivia," Paul awkwardly said. "That's great. But I am really in a rush. Curfew and all, you know."

"Paul, how lucky we ran into each other. Dear, sweet Paul."

For the moment, Paul wished only she would not call him Paul.

"I've been learning so many things about you these past couple days," she said, as Paul watched a line form behind him and the sentry move in closer. "Paul, you've been leading such a terribly fascinating life. The Major heard all sorts of things at the Junior Zeus Club. Why didn't you ever tell me? Father said for me to tell you the job he lined up for you is still open, so you can have your happy life whenever you want it. I just can't believe all the crazy, wild, amazing things I've been learning about you."

Paul had no idea what she was talking about and furthermore did not care at the moment. He grinned up at the sentry and started moving away from Olivia.

"Just amazing," she said. "Let's talk as soon as possible, okay!"

"Yes, soon," he promised her, waving. "I have to run now."

She blew a kiss as she walked off backward, staring at him. Rattled, he turned back to the sentry.

"Papers." The guard spoke with exactly the gravel voice that Paul had expected he would.

"Oh, yes," Paul said. He stood on tiptoe to get near the man's ears and whispered: "You see, I'm – I'm with the Legion of the Slick Dagger."

The sentry's expression did not soften.

"She," Paul said, thumbing back toward his former girlfriend. "Her father – she calls him the Major. But he's not really a major, he's a butler. Not in the military at all. He found out about my – my status, that I didn't have a father. Never did. Well, not never. He's a snob of a civilian, you see, and he didn't want his daughter dating someone with my background. The Major, that is. Didn't."

At this, the sentry's expression did soften.

"Oh, yeah?" He leaned to whisper to Paul. "Yes, I hear that. My in-laws are the exact same way. We special legionnaires need to stick together, don't we? We might not have fathers, but we have each other."

The guard stood erect and announced, for central Italy to hear, "Your documents are in order, sir. Enjoy your trip."

Paul swallowed hard. He looked at the road extending far beyond. And he took his first step ever outside the boundaries of the city of Rome.

The Third Scroll

AWAY

With the unfolding of the centuries, the Romans assembled an imposing web of roadways that reached far out from the capital, laid for endurance and most especially speed: Galloping the gravel-and-block Appian Way with a relay of fresh horses and enough resolve in one's stomach, the city of Capua can be easily reached from Rome in a matter of hours.

The journey can, however, take longer while bouncing on the tailboards of a series of dilapidated vegetable wagons, pretending to be the guide for a blind but surprisingly talkative hermit.

After getting through the gates of Rome, Paul had found Caesar in the field where they agreed to meet. They had quickly come up with a plan to get moving toward the Opposition leadership. Paul would stand at the side of the road and flag down a passing farm cart. Courteously he would ask the hack if it would not be too bothersome to provide a ride for himself and his ascetic companion – nodding to the hooded monastic by his side.

Mostly they were rejected.

When given a wave of assent, Paul would guide Caesar to the back of the wagon, and as they jounced along, watching the hard

Roman road fall away, Caesar would talk. Caesar would go on and on. Caesar talked about the humidity, about which condiments go the best with which foods, how strange it is not everyone appreciates a good prank, popular children's names, what happens when you put a drinking straw in upside down, how to make your vacation dollar stretch, his list of rashes, whether cheese is really fattening.

Caesar turned out to be nothing but a chatterbox the whole way. He never stopped talking.

"I have a theory that if you try your hand at word games you can break any code," Caesar explained as they jostled along with a carriage full of zucchini just north of Casilinum. "The secret obviously is trying to get inside the mind of the person who wrote the game. You know, I bet your mother is good at word games. From what I remember of her in my condition back then, she seems like a very smart, warm person. Being raised by wet nurses, of course, I never had the chance to truly feel my own mother's emotional distance."

He didn't wait for a response before moving onto the topic of oboes.

Caesar did not stop talking while Paul flagged down wagons, and he kept talking as Paul thanked the drivers afterward. He commented, he spoke, he kibitzed. He would botch the punch line of every joke he attempted and tell each joke several times over.

Caesar slowed his talking just once during the expedition, when he lost his balance and tumbled off backward into a bushel of prickly pears. Paul, plucking at one after another tiny spine, spent the next two hours hearing only the word "oook" (exclaimed 147 times in succession).

"Say," said Caesar in an artichoke wagon near the town of Thrumbum, "isn't this where Licinius Crassus had Spartacus and all those slaves offed? Ugly business, honestly. I didn't take part in the Servile War, you know. That was around the time I got abducted by pirates in the Mediterranean. They told me they were going to demand 20 talents of silver as ransom. I countered by suggesting that they actually demand 50. Somehow I had it all backward on who was supposed to pay who, and I thought I was doing a great job dickering. Anyhow, that's how the legend started that I suggested a higher ransom because I thought so highly of myself. Funny, that. I'll tell you, my feeling is that the one thing a person should never be falsely modest about is his humility."

It was as if Caesar felt compelled to make up for any unaccomplished chats he missed throughout his coma and captivity.

"Of course, I've grown quite fond of Calpurnia," Caesar offered during a jarring ride in an eggplant lorry. "As a wife, she's been a grand old bean, especially when you consider that we patricians don't get married up for love and so forth. Sometimes I think my marriage will last only as long as it seems like it's already been. But I wonder what that all feels like. Love. The real thing."

Paul blocked out most of it. For days, he was effectively too stunned to listen. His nervous system felt like the chew toy for one of the heads of Cerberus. His mind whirred at the glut of green scents all around and at the uncanny way spaces didn't stop at a wall or a crowd but seemed to wander off in every direction till they couldn't be heard from any more.

The world was evidently big.

There was also the reality pressing on him that he had no idea how he would live and no reason to believe he was moving toward anything like safety. These last days, starting with that initial jaunt to Caesar's residence, seemed to have blurred faster than the horses that hurtled past the lumbering vehicles he rode on. How and why he had been driven to this point seemed unfathomable; the strange remarks Olivia had made at the city gate only added to the mystery.

The trek offered two or three moments of real peril and scrambling too.

On the second day, Paul noticed they were being driven into a military outpost. He interrupted Caesar's monologue on phlebitis in time to suggest they both clamber into the cucumber barrels at their backs. Later that night the two were able to creep from the camp, but not before Caesar had to swim his way out of a brining vat and slot himself for several hours in a grease trap.

On the fifth day of their odyssey, the jerking cart of cabbages on which they sat breasted a hill.

"End of the road," the driver called back. "Capua."

Caesar, as they neared the town where the Opposition had ensconced itself, let out a sigh. He had been feeling some new doubt about leaving Rome and approaching the Opposition for help.

"Gaius Cassius is particularly a hard nut to crack. I think he really doesn't like me."

"Oh, no," Paul tried assuring. "He does. When you were out cold in the theater basement, Cassius came down to visit and check on you. He even insisted on finding something for your head."

"Is that right?" Caesar brightened a bit.

Uncovering the lodgings of the Opposition leadership did not prove difficult. An inquiry at the Greater Capuan Convention and Visitor's Bureau revealed that an assemblage of senators from Rome had checked into a bed and breakfast on the city outskirts. Directions were obtained.

Approaching the veranda of The Sluggish Goose Inn, Paul almost told Julius Caesar to shut up – he didn't care just then about the foolproof way to fix a misaligned cabinet door – but instead suggested Caesar wait on the porch swing. Caesar thought it a fine idea and plopped himself down.

Paul went in. A matronly hostess sat at an ornate writing table, going over papers. She immediately paid no heed to Paul. He coughed. He coughed again.

"Oh," she said, half glancing up. "Oh, I didn't notice you there. The service door is on the east side of the inn."

Paul, self-consciously brushing a kale leaf off his tunic, said he was there to see the new visitors from Rome.

"I see." She looked Paul up and down. "If they are expecting you, you can find our Roman guests in the smokehouse out back."

"The smokehouse." Paul repeated. He was not sure what the word meant.

"They told me that they wanted as much privacy as possible. You'll find it past the ornamental swale just beyond our butterfly garden."

Paul decided it would be best to simply wander back and see if he could find anything. There were a number of out buildings behind the inn. He walked about a bit before hearing, emanating from one of them, some familiar voices. They were letting out familiar phrases: "All opposed?" – "Point of order" – "The motion fails"– "Has anyone seen my hair pick?" The voices came from a gabled structure in the distance, which he directed himself to.

A knock at the door stopped the talk inside. After a minute, the door slowly squeaked and a set of frowning eyes could be discerned through a narrow crack. Quickly, though, it swung fully open.

"My dear young man!" Gaius Cassius Longinus looked over the threshold, and his face seemed to indicate gladness.

Paul stood motionless. He still felt diffident before a collection of Roman senators, in addition to which a blast of charcoal and saline odors had stormed his nostrils.

"I never doubted you," said Cassius. He grabbed Paul's elbow, pulling him in and shutting the door. "I knew you would join us. We have waited anxiously for your momentous arrival."

At first, there seemed to be more senators standing around than could be compressed into the small structure. The space seemed to be no larger than the buckboard full of arugula that Paul and Caesar had trembled atop while passing the outskirts of Antium. As his eyes adjusted, Paul realized that many of the shapes that initially looked to be senatorial heads were in fact not. They were plucked turkeys hanging from the rafter beams. He coughed again.

"Senators," announced Cassius, "I suggest that we put our regular agenda into abeyance and formally turn our attention to our young compatriot here."

This was moved. Seconded. Motion carried.

Paul was not quite sure what to say. He cleared his throat one more time and decided it might be best to begin generally. He spoke of Antony's martial law, the city streets filled with soldiers and the other conditions in Rome as he had left.

"And what of Caesar's funerary ritual?" Cassius asked. "How did Antony manage to conduct a proper ceremony of public cremation without a body in attendance?"

Paul did not know the answer to this.

"We ourselves all had begun our journey beforehand," Cassius said. "Antony must have substituted a different corpse. He probably bribed and bullied the coroner. Antony remains a looming threat to us, until we can get our bearings back. But, at least we are finally done with the problem of what to do with Caesar, correct?"

Paul began forming a word, intending to disabuse Cassius of this last notion, when the smokehouse door opened. A tall goat walked in.

More accurately – Paul squinted to make sense of the image – a little, badly hunched man toddled in hauling, upright on his stooped shoulders, the front portion of a slaughtered goat, from its ears down to its forelegs. He made his way between the senators, muttering as he did, "Sorry, this couldn't wait, fellers. Hope you don't mind the smells, neither."

With its black eyes wide open, head cocked and source of mobility almost buried beneath, the goat's face passed directly in front of Paul, giving the impression that the animal itself had offered this apology. Cassius raised his hands to indicate to the others that they should watch their words until the man left. (This did not stop Pompilius Pulcher, holding his nose, from asserting a stern hope that the inn laundry would turn out to be at least halfway capable.)

The man did not leave for some time. As the Opposition leadership fidgeted and looked away, they heard, from the far end of the smokehouse, sawing, hacking, cursing, spitting and long wheezes. Their noses then began tickling; several sneezed.

"That'll be the pepper there you're smelling," the man said. He spoke gradually and evidently without the assistance of teeth. "Gives the mutton its flavor and keeps the bugs away. What you need to do is to boil up some sugar and salt and pepper and brush it over the whole carcass."

"Is that so?" asked Lucius Crispius Totovus. He licked his lips.

"Oh sure, sure, sure, and pert near the perfect mix, too, this mix is. If you all want, step on around here, and I'll show you just the right way to sweep it on. It's a matter of using the right strokes and putting on the right number of –"

"Thank you," Cassius said, in his clipped manner, "but no. We are rather busy at the moment."

"Fine, fine. You're the chiefs."

The bent little man left the smokehouse. As he did, he was heard to mutter something along the lines of: Buncha gasbags from Rome.

"Young man." Cassius turned to Paul. "Given the constraints of time and space we are facing here, let me cut through the anticipation and ask you the question on the mind of all of us. May we see now the map to the tin mines? You have it on your person, do you not?"

Between hearing out Julius Caesar and experiencing life outside Rome for the first time, Paul had almost entirely forgotten about the parchment his mother had given him, the one she had found in Caesar's toga. He reached into his satchel and pulled out the oilcloth she had wrapped it in.

"A most momentous moment," offered Cinna as Cassius unwrapped the packet. "Our map to safety."

"And even," said another, "to real power."

Cassius asked Paul to open the door halfway to let some more light in. The Opposition stared at Cassius while Cassius glared into the paper. Slowly they watched as the organic grimace of his face began to sink. It sank passed scowl, passed sneer, passed distortion. His face sank to a frown variant that had not been seen since the time Flavius Flavian reported signing up the Opposition to sponsor a bowling team, including the upsell to custom retro shirts and silk jackets. Cassius let out a moan.

"What is it?" asked Brutus.

"I think." Cassius generated his voice from the bottom of his stomach, "I think. It says ... It says it's a – a – a word game."

Just then, the scent of hickory and chili pepper began filling the room. Smoke began gushing up from the floorboards. The building's inhabitants started immediately to cough and lose each other in an aromatic murk.

"Intolerable," said Pompilius Pulcher, feeling his way toward the door. "Such odors as these are impossible on high-count camel's hair fabric. I shall speak with mine hostess about this."

Paul had darted out right away, but as the room rapidly fogged, the others who were left compressed inside struggled to find their exit, hacking and burbling as they jostled themselves, clonking into swinging meats, tripping into walls. Seen from the outside, the entire structure looked as if it had begun twitching and mumbling to itself.

The Opposition leadership after a time did get free, staggering out amid gouts of dark, flavorful smog. As they bent doubled, panting and struggling to fill their lungs with fresh air, Cassius stood in silence on the front doorstep, clutching the paper at his side. He stood unconcerned that he might have just passed away in a food processing mishap.

The old hunched man doddered up to him.

"Guess I forgot to tell you all I was turning the smoke on," he said with a compressed chortle. As he turned away, he mumbled some more words about the big city of Rome. None of this registered with Cassius.

"What could it all mean?" he asked numbly. "What could Caesar have meant with this? It's not a map to a tin mine at all. But what could it be?"

He handed the paper dazedly to Brutus. Like the others of the Opposition leadership, Brutus had just been deeply cured and gave off the bouquet of fresh fatback and brisket. Cassius did not notice this either.

Brutus straightened out the sheet. He read it aloud, between blinks and coughs.

Crossword Puzzler

A game for the whole city to take part! Starting from the middle square, go eleven up and five right. Last clue: What is a four-letter word for "something priceless"? If you solve this, that is what you will get.

"Hmmm," Brutus reflected. "Interesting. Almost sounds like an advertising campaign or something. Remember when that goober company had all Rome looking for the golden peanut in their snack bags?"

The Outside Communications Consultant, Paul noticed, averted his eyes at this comment and shuffled into the background.

"But what could it mean?" Cassius spoke haltingly. "This is the great secret document Caesar planned to announce? Could it be?"

Cassius had evidently addressed his questions to the world at large, in the same way a derelict might ask abstractedly where his life had gone wrong. But Paul felt it would only be courteous to answer.

"If you like, you can ask him yourself," Paul said.

"What's that? Ask? Ask who?"

"Caesar. You can go around and talk with him yourself. He's sitting on the porch up front."

It took a moment for this to register with Cassius. But through his mystification, an image began to push into Cassius's mind. It was the image of a great big stage pillow.

CARRIAGE

For Paul, the journey heading away from Capua progressed in much more comfort than the trip getting there had been; markedly, it was much more hushed.

The Opposition leadership struck out early the next morning.

Paul and Caesar accompanied Cassius and Brutus in the lead carriage. For most the day, the only sounds to be heard were the springs of the coach and, for one leg of the journey, the baying of three or four spaniels running alongside licking their jowls; no amount of bathing and scouring the night before had purged the savory vapor coming off the Opposition leadership.

Paul and Caesar accompanied Cassius and Brutus in the lead carriage. For most the day, the only sounds to be heard were the springs of the coach and, for one leg of the journey, the baying of three or four spaniels running alongside licking their jowls; no amount of bathing and scouring the night before had purged the savory vapor coming off the Opposition leadership.

Cassius and Caesar were not on speaking terms.

The day before, Cassius had stomped up to the porch of the Sluggish Goose Inn, waving a sheet of paper in Caesar's face. For half the night, he questioned Caesar.

No, Caesar explained, there never was a tin mine map. Or a will, for that matter. Yes, that's right, it's a fun puzzler he thought the people of Rome would get a kick out of trying to solve; nothing more. It says it's for the whole city to enjoy, after all.

Where did it come from? His house servant Nimbus had brought it to him one day, saying it had been tied to an arrow stuck in a tree. Sure, by all means, go apply a series of acids and bases to see if it contains invisible ink, but you won't find any. It's all meant purely for fun. And maybe it's not about crosswords, maybe it's actually a scavenger hunt or something along those lines, who's to say?

By the time the carriages had pulled out that morning, Cassius had tired of asking questions and Caesar had gotten pouty at being interrogated. They both mostly looked glumly out at the scenery of southern Italy passing by.

A few miles outside their first night's destination, Cassius finally spoke up.

"What think you, Brutus?" he asked.

Swaying to wagon's rhythm, his head ensconced in an inflatable travel neck pillow, Brutus had spent the trip undulating in and out of naps. His first response to Cassius's question did not contain vowels.

"Mrllmph," he asserted. "Gnnqb."

While Brutus worked his way back to consciousness, lazily asking for a mirror, a robin alighted onto the sill of the carriage window. It got a whiff of the passengers and, to the extent this is possible, plugged its nose before flying off.

"I was wondering," Cassius repeated, after giving his companion time for a quick revamping, "what your thoughts are on this matter. Of the document."

"It is an interesting piece of paper," offered Brutus. "But perhaps we should be directing our attention to what next steps need to be taken. Overall."

"Next steps. How do you mean?"

"We should perhaps all take stock of our situation and think through a new plan, now that there is no tin mine. We can be sure that Antony will be coming after us, most certainly with countless legions. And now we know we will have no funds coming. I hate to sound too down, but I'm afraid we are all in fairly grave trouble at this point."

Caesar had been following the conversation. He liked where it was headed – away from puzzlers.

"Very true," he inserted. "Very true. I'm honestly a little disappointed that Antony turns out to be a jerk. On the other hand, maybe he always deserved to be one. By the way, Brutus, I've always meant to ask, what do you use to keep your hair firm without it looking too treated?"

"My hair? I have a special mix." Brutus said with some pride, "consisting of three raw eggs, flat beer and half a lemon slice."

"You too, Brutus? That's exactly what I use." This was not strictly true. Caesar had no idea what the stylists put in his hair. But he didn't want to risk the topic of word games coming up again. "I guess it's true what they say, similar minds think alike."

Brutus returned to his original thought.

"If it comes down to it, for example," he said, "do we know how many legions will be loyal to our cause and how many will be loyal to Antony? We're already heading out east. Maybe that is fortunate. The troops farther from Rome may be less under Antony's thrall and more likely to follow us. And what about the latest suggestion of The Outside Communications Consultant? Shouldn't we consider that?"

"What suggestion is that?" Cassius asked tartly.

"Umbrellas."

"Umbrellas?"

"The Outside Communications Consultant thinks we need a memorable campaign with strong visuals. To recapture the public's attention. He proposes that on a perfectly sunny day, our supporters are seen suddenly carrying black umbrellas all around Rome. Fully open, over their heads, mind you. It would become a symbol of silent protest, highlighting the darkness that Antony has brought to the Republic."

"Hey, that's really good," Caesar offered.

"Frankly," said Brutus, "We're lucky The Outside Communications Consultant decided to stay with us after we told him we're postponing his retainer payments."

The carriage began slowing, and the tumult of a city could be heard up ahead. The train of wagons was approaching Venusia, site of their first's night's stop.

"Or what about this idea for a visual," Caesar said. "How about we make lapel buttons with the letters WIN? 'Whip Imperialism Now.'"

Cassius ostentatiously ignored this proposal.

"I am awed that I am about to make this suggestion," he said. "But I think you are right, Brutus, and that we need to call another – as much as I hate this word – meeting. Tonight. Frankly, I think we might need to consider it a council of war. We are going to need to brace ourselves."

Brutus nodded.

"There will be one particular topic added to the agenda," Cassius said. He had to speak louder, over the blubbing and whine as Brutus squeezed the air out his travel pillow. "What exactly should been done about ..."

He glanced over to Julius Caesar.

"Yes, Caesar understands," Caesar said, and he looked out the carriage window again. "It must be decided what, exactly, is to be done about me."

GREECE

The Opposition leadership did hold another meeting in Venusia that evening. It lasted long into the night. It had to be held in the backroom office of a cut-rate dental clinic.

It required three separate runs for takeout (not including the narrowly passed resolution that led to the dromedary dumplings being sent back as overcooked). But something singular emerged from the meeting that night.

Achievement.

At least a little of it.

Partly the senators felt far out of their element and did not squabble as energetically as usual. Partly the reality of their perilous circumstances weighed on them, as rumors churned of Antony preparing to march his legions out against the Opposition.

Yet one of the reasons for coming to any accomplished decision had to do with the presence of Julius Caesar.

He did not speak a word at the conference table. But for those present, Caesar appeared as majestic as ever. He had put on a fresh tunic, and his eyes looked off in a far, museful way. The Opposition senators instinctively felt the need to impress the man with some show of seriousness and resolve. For them, this was still, after all, great Caesar sitting amid them, suffusing the room with his legend, his command.

In truth, Caesar simply still felt petulant over Cassius's churlish questioning about the puzzler. He had decided to keep his chin raised and his chest flared to present Cassius an impression of hurt aloofness, hoping to get an apology from him. (This was unlikely to happen, as Cassius had no idea he had caused any offense in the first place.)

It was decided that the Opposition would make for Macedonia, just north of Greece. The few senators with any military experience had heard the place could offer some strong defensive positions and that it would be a serviceable gathering ground for any legions loyal to their cause. Word was to be sent forth.

Meanwhile news had been brought that a young distant relative of Caesar's, by the name of Octavian Caesar, had shown up in Rome. This Octavian had started making noise like he was the true heir to Caesar, and he seemed to be getting along smartly with Antony. Questions were raised about whether he should be taken as a serious threat.

Yet hints that Caesar's opinion on the matter could be helpful went unheeded at the table. Caesar merely stared over toward Cassius, who squinted in mystification at the look he was getting. But Caesar's stoic reticence again only further impressed the Opposition.

The one topic not discussed during the whole night was Caesar himself. With the great man sitting gravely in their midst, the gathered senators could not think about what his role might or might not end up being. They skirted the issue.

But in the end, a full package of action was otherwise agreed to. Provisions, communication lines, reconnaissance, chains of command, contingencies: The Opposition leadership actually had a strategy, even if it was admittedly rickety and raw.

"Meeting adjourned," Bilbius Dilbo announced at 3:34 am, and those around the table – all except Caesar – found themselves applauding themselves. "Nice work, everyone. Can a couple senators stay back awhile, and we'll clean up all the food containers?"

In the coming weeks, the plan performed in an odd way, a manner that the Opposition leadership had not ever experienced with any of its previous plans. It did not immediately fall apart. It was, for a long time, followed.

The Opposition leadership left Venusia next afternoon. The Italian coast was reached according to schedule and a trireme secured for passage to Greece. Only seven Opposition members threw up into the Aegean Sea on the voyage over. A modest Macedonian town by the name of Philippi was chosen for the final destination and the rendezvous of any loyal legions.

In Cassius's opinion, his colleagues may have spent a little too much energy during all this time talking of lawsuits, curb painting, points of order and subcommittees. There was a little too much time spent thinking about Caesar's puzzler, too.

"It's strange that the sheet with the clues didn't have an actual crossword puzzle," Bilbius Dilbo pointed out one day. "Maybe it got lost."

One faction speculated that the crossword itself would appear in one of the daily papers soon. A minority speculated the clues had been put out by a candy company to generate buzz, and the puzzle would show up on the inside wrapper of a chocolate bar. Totovus keyed off the part about a four-letter word for "something priceless" and insisted it must be related to the reservations for a fashionable restaurant with limited seating.

Yet despite small quarrels and diversions, most everyone felt like the plan was indeed behaving itself well. Philippi, just north of Greece, was reached after not too long and camp began to be set up.

"I think it all might work," Brutus said to Cassius one day, while they watched from a newly erected Command Tent as the first Roman troops came over nearby Mt. Orbelos and in ships from the Aegean.

"That it might," Cassius said over the clang and rattle of a camp under fervid constructing. He was beginning to feel some real confidence for the first time since they had left Italy. "Yes, that it just might."

The person who enjoyed these days more than anyone turned out to be Julius Caesar. He quickly enough overcame his earlier irritability and took to his new lifestyle. Paul suggested he should probably disguise himself more effectively than slipping on a monk's robe every morning. Caesar accepted the suggestion happily. He began to grow a sporty beard, got himself darkly tanned and let his hair grow into a bush.

It happened that Caesar was not naturally bald nor did he have naturally straight hair. Antony had suggested the shaved-head-and-straight-cut-fringe look years earlier as an affect. The amount of styling required to achieve the image invariably had taken a whole lot of time, which Caesar always hated having to sit through. He had also always been encouraged to show himself as slim.

Part of his pique about togas was that he had been expected to use them for corseting as much as for fashion. Now Caesar let his jaunty gut hang down, and he often wore not much more than a fluffy loincloth.

Cassius asked Paul to keep an eye on Caesar.

"I don't feel for some reason he is entirely cordial with me," Cassius said. "But he seems to like you. Spend time with Caesar and try to get inside his mind. I can't seem to figure out his cagey thoughts sometimes."

Cassius could not figure out, for example, why Caesar did not spend time plotting with the Opposition but instead almost seemed to like doing physical jobs with the rest of the soldiers. Caesar took to the exercise and labor of the camp. He got up early every morning and could be seen shoveling slop, chopping firewood, digging trenches or doing anything else needing doing around the camp.

One day, just after dawn, Paul found himself holding a tent stake to the ground at arms' length. He looked up from the ground warily to see the dark, hairy figure of Julius Caesar, tongue protruding a little, about to bring a mallet down. Paul closed his eyes. When he opened them again and saw – instead of his hand flattened to a ping pong paddle, as he expected – the tent stake half in the ground, he and Caesar smiled at each other.

One reason Caesar had not been recognized at all occurred to Paul then. After he had stopped wearing his monk's robe, for a couple weeks Caesar applied some borrowed makeup to mask his features. But since that, he had been seen by untold numbers of citizens and soldiers. He had even taken to sleeping in troop quarters most nights. Yet nobody so much as paused for a second look.

The physical transformation of the man had been remarkable. But even more, Caesar had not, for a very long time, either puffed himself up or intoned a comment. Paul remembered when he first met Caesar. He had the impression then of two men alternating in one body: The turgid public Caesar of speeches and pronouncements on the one hand, and, on the other, a guy. Since leaving Italy, the public Caesar had been neither seen nor heard.

In addition to not intoning at all, he didn't talk as much generally, or at least as much as he had during the start of the journey from Rome.

Which is not to say that he had become demure.

"You got any ideas about the puzzler yourself, Paul?" Caesar asked before spitting in his hands and rubbing them together. "Ready?"

"Ready." Paul closed his eyes, clasped onto the next tent stake and tried to determine once again how far he could distance his head from his fingers without snapping any sinew. A moment later, his right hand tingled with the vibration of a mallet striking the stake.

"Maybe it isn't referring to an actual crossword puzzle," Caesar said. "I'm still working my shifted alphabet theory. It might be a code that tells you where to turn it in for a big prize. Or it could be a letter-to-number cryptogram. What do you think, my boy?"

"I've read the lines a few times," confessed Paul, who had ended up with the paper back in his satchel after it was universally dismissed as valueless. "But I'm stumped."

"You have such a great memory. Repeat the game to me, and let's see if we can figure it out together."

Paul called up the words of Caesar's document in his mind. "A game for the whole cit – "

Clong.

Without any warning, Caesar brought down the mallet on the next stake. Paul had been focused on the word game and didn't see it coming. He looked up to Caesar with a stunned expression, but Caesar, busy spitting into his hands, didn't notice. He kept hammering as Paul got the words out.

"Starting from the middle square – *clong* – go eleven up and five right. Last – *clong* – clue: What is a four letter word for 'some – *clong* – thing priceless'? If you solve this, that is – *clong* – what you will get."

Caesar clearly did not listen during all this, despite the fact that he had asked Paul to say it. Paul, however, found the recital gave him an opportunity to try to forget that at any moment his hand might turn spatulate.

Caesar and Paul soon found a voiceless cadence to their work. For some time, only three sounds were to be heard:

- Mallet against iron
- Spitting and hand rubbing
- Eyes shutting tightly

This became the new rhythm, and it suited Paul fine. He did not need Caesar distracted at this time.

"I heard something funny in the mess hall the other day," Caesar said at last. Paul had known it wouldn't be long before a new observation or arbitrary remark would excrete. "The talk in Rome is that the ghost of Julius Caesar is being seen all over the place. Everyone seems to be reporting that my spirit is haunting the city. I guess your work with the bag of flour back in the bakery really did the trick. I just hope I live long enough to someday see myself not dead."

Paul kept himself focused on hoping Caesar would stay focused.

"I wonder," Caesar said seven or eight stakes later, "how I would be as a ship's captain. Or a school crossing guard. I bet they must have a jobs counselor somewhere at the camp."

The clong/spit-and-rub/shut/clong pattern resumed for a few

more rounds.

"Here's an interesting fact." Caesar stopped in mid-swing, mallet hung over his head. "My bunkmate – you know the one I was telling you about, who I'm teaching the foolproof way of shortsheeting a bed – anyway, it turns out he's from around where the leader of the Servile War was born. Not far west from here. Supposedly was a nice little village in a valley, until that sourpuss Licinius Crassus had the whole town leveled. The really funny thing about my bunkmate is –"

Caesar quieted up; Paul shut his eyes. He tensed for another mallet strike. But when he felt no crash against the stake in his hand, he glanced up to see Caesar staring in the distance, mallet still high in the air.

"What is it man?" Caesar called out to an approaching figure who was waving his arms. "Speak up, speak up! We can't hear you!"

Paul recognized the gangle of the mute. He was coming from the direction of the Opposition Command Tent. As the mute strode nearer, it became clear he was pointing at Paul, gesturing for him to please get up and come over as quickly as possible.

ENEMY

"We have a mission for you – but it could hold some danger."

On hearing such words, Paul just weeks earlier would likely have performed in much the same way he did the first time he gazed up to a dark, hairy Julius Caesar readying a tent stake mallet. More probably, after hearing such a menacing sentence, Paul in the past would have not merely closed his eyes. He would have identified the nearest open manhole or pneumatic tube in which to discreetly deposit himself. He would have been forever gone.

But Paul in this case stood still and listened.

"Mark Antony has come." Cassius was speaking with grim resolve – grim resolve even on the register of the Cassius scale. "He is here. The forces of Antony are on the other side of the ridge. The ultimate battle is nearly upon us. We have no choice. We will have to fight, and it will be a fight to the end."

Paul looked at the faces around the Command Tent. Aside from Lucius Totovus, who was staring down a buttercream frosted torte, they all looked as grim and pale as Cassius. The mute had ushered Paul into the tent a few minutes earlier. The structure perhaps did not offer the eye a robust expression of martial verve.

Strapped for funds, the Opposition had been forced to rent a second-hand yurt from a traveling clothing consignment shop south of Thebes. As a result, conferences took place in a construction that had been formed to look like a massive felt homburg. The setting did nothing to put Paul at ease.

"It may wrong to ask you into service again for the Republic,"

Cassius said. "But ask we shall."

Paul nodded just a bit.

"The plain difficulty we face is this," Cassius said. "Antony outnumbers us quite significantly. His troops have trained and fought together under his steely direction. He is powerful. Our own legions, on the other hand, are just meeting each other now and have never been under a single command. And our own military experience collectively is a little bit, let us say, shallow. In normal circumstances, prudence would dictate we avoid a confrontation at this point."

Totovus went for the buttercream frosted torte. Everyone else stared at Paul.

"But," Cassius continued, "we have reason to believe that we will not be able to hold our legions together for very long. Our troops come here with mixed motivations. And – I shall be honest with you – we cannot pay them."

"Which reminds me," inserted a senator. "I got a note yesterday from the union steward of the Seventh Legion. He says the men voted to initiate a work slowdown unless they have a signed guarantee that they will be paid in full by the end of the week. I think that could perhaps be problematic to any plans we might form. They really want their money."

Others began to recount similar tales from throughout the camp – grumblings about delayed pay, threats of a strike, protest meetings being called.

"The Outside Communications Consultant," Brutus interjected, "believes we should make our assault as soon as possible. Weren't you saying that even if we don't win outright, a spunky showing could get us some positive news coverage back in Rome?"

At the far end of the table, The Outside Communications Consultant rose to speak. He seemed just at the point of saying, "To be honest ..."

"More to the point," Cassius cut him off, "our best and only chance may be to attack Antony while he is still setting up camp and getting himself positioned."

"But I've never fought in a battle," Paul said. "I don't even own a sword."

"You have something more valuable," said Cassius. "We do not know exactly what power Antony possesses or how his forces are positioned. We need a fully trustworthy individual to scout out his strength. We need someone who is nimble, intelligent and resourceful. Young man, we need you. Will you do this? Will you be our scout and discover for us the nature of our enemy?"

There are those who lack the courage of their cowardice. For some, even pushing out an immediate No can be more challenging than facing the long-term consequences of being companionable in the moment.

It is unfair to say that Paul entirely lacked gut. But as he stared back at a tableload of solicitous senators, he could not envision a sound path to refuse the request. He had been getting itchy lately, too. As the reality of war approached, he had been feeling a curious compulsion to seek out a Realtor who specialized in remote continental landmasses. Getting out of camp for a bit and exploring potential escape routes for himself had a certain appeal.

There was perhaps one other factor in his mind as he looked around the expectant room. Paul did not, as a habit, blurt. He almost never let an impulse drag him forward, and he constitutionally suspected any rising urge or instinct. Yet he had spent a whole lot of time around Julius Caesar. Without his fully feeling any change, imperceptibly, the strangely liberating power of blurt, urge and instinct had surely seeped into his fundamentally careful spirit.

Paul, before he could stop himself, overheard himself saying the single word he would have never expected from himself in the past in reply to such a question.

"Yes," said Paul.

He did not utter the word with resonant conviction or very much pitch. And keen misgivings attended even before his lips closed on the sibilance of his answer. But say the word he did. Cassius nodded somberly and the rest of the Opposition leadership looked pleased.

Before he fully grasped what was happening to him, or what he had gotten himself into, Paul was taken out of the tent. He was swiftly brought to another structure, where he found himself facing an especially warted and short centurion.

"This is the young hero," Cassius announced, "who will be going on the reconnaissance mission over the ridge. As we need his report quickly as possible, I ask that you have him on his way within the hour. Can you get him ready?"

Paul experienced the kind of doubtful scrutiny that had often induced him in the past to go round in search of service entrances. The officer looked him up and down with pursed lips and a barely concealed shake of the head.

"I'll try what I can," he told Cassius soberly, "and then hope for the best."

This seemed to be, in any event, what the officer told Cassius soberly. He may possibly instead have said, "He'll dry wood in a cannon when holes afford a vest." Paul could not be sure. The man spoke either with a relatively pronounced accent or another language.

Cassius offered Paul a shoulder pat and farewell.

As far as Paul could discern, the centurion then started offering him the vital instruction one needs to complete a reconnaissance assignment. Paul was shown maps, and he watched gestures being made by the man. Special vocal emphasis seemed placed on several subjects. Paul could make out, at best, every seventh word the man said.

In the midst of this talk, others approached. One disrobed Paul and lowered a thin light colored tunic over him; another rubbed him with some kind of yellowish oil; a third pried off his old rope sandals and shod him with a tall pair of new boots; the last person handed him a stack of blank paper and three pencils.

After a time, the centurion grunted several apparently last syllables, turned and walked off. Paul looked about. There was no one else around. Though not certain, he decided his instructions and accoutering must have ended. He found himself not only fully by himself but dressed in fully new clothes and almost fully with no notion as to what to do next.

Based on the few distinct words he had picked up and some pointing he had watched, he guessed the direction of the targeted ridge he was to go to might be southwest. He picked up his old clothes, and began to trek in that direction.

As he wandered off, Paul passed the grounds where he had been holding stakes far from his head. All the tents had already been raised and no one was about. He decided to detour toward the sleeping quarters where he had been boarding. He wanted to pick up his small satchel to put the papers into, surmising that he was to write his observations of Antony's camp onto them.

Inside his tent, Paul found only a few invalids and a couple cats. He started to undo the stiff new GI boots that had been clamped onto his feet. It took a while. The leather – Paul had never felt leather against his body, and he did not like the chafe – wended halfway up his calves.

He let the things clunk one by one to the floor and slid back on his old rope sandals. If he was going to go on some sort of mission, he figured he would at least be carried on something familiar. He grabbed his satchel and headed out.

As he nodded to the sentry at the camp palisade and looked out to what he guessed could be a ridge, Paul did not know what to think or feel. So he merely walked.

After an hour or more transporting himself from the camp, he began to realize something. He started realizing he had never been really and entirely alone in his life. There had always been people around. Sometimes he only heard them through thin walls and the reverberation down city streets, and even when they couldn't be heard directly, the sounds of their carts at night and scuffling shoes told you they were always around.

Now Paul listened only to the vibration of tree and grasses imbued with wind, and the bark and chirrup of hidden animals. No human voice or human implement could be heard.

Paul did not know whether he should be creeped out by it all or not.

As he trudged, a thought joined up with him, in the way thoughts used to do during IM runs back in Rome: Paul realized one of the reasons he might have returned to his tent before leaving on the mission was to tell Caesar about it. Spending time with Caesar had been taxing. The man certainly did talk an awful lot. And yet, there was something. He had an energy about him and an infecting earnestness. It would have been nice to tell him so long.

Thinking back on what he could comprehend from the soldier back in camp, he believed he would soon crest the ridge that he believed he was climbing, and from there he would look down and behold the army of Mark Antony.

Paul had often run past bas reliefs and triumphal arches festooned with the carvings of army scenes. Considering those, he figured he would be able to look down from the ridge and count the number and size of the tents below. Or something along those lines.

He remembered while waiting in the sunroom of a wealthy client once he had spent some time gazing at a mural of a battle or a skirmish. It showed rivers and forests and elevations surrounding the two sets of neatly assembled troops. He guessed he could sketch a rough map including any rivers, forests and elevations he might see.

But what else had that centurion tried to convey? He had highlighted one point in particular with his head gestures and pointing. One special instruction. Paul could not make out what he meant.

But Paul's main concern for the time being was that the ridge kept coming not any closer. He had been keeping his eyes on the highest point of a high line of ground that extended away from him in both directions. From the slight strain on his legs, he knew he was ascending. But the space between himself and the high point refused to budge. As he walked and walked, he came to an epiphany almost as meaningful as his realization about aloneness. He realized nature was damnably big.

It got knobby, too. The brush he had been stepping over gave way to taller weeds and quickly to savannah. The ground started cleaving down into cavities and fissures and spiking up in flinty jolts.

Between lifting himself up and down all the new obstacles, Paul tried to figure out the officer's special instruction.

A hiss off to his left froze him in place. He listened stock still for a few moments. It seemed at first there might be a snake or other hostile animal nearby. Yet as he stood unmoving, he noted that the strange buzzing did not have an entirely lifelike tone, and it kept up at a regular level. Slowly, Paul turned in the direction of the hiss. He could just make out the source, half a dozen feet away.

It was the sound of water moving in its natural surroundings – an entirely new experience to his ears. He made his way over to a burbling rivulet. He realized how thirsty he had become. Bending down, Paul took a whiff. The water smelled odd (not at all metallic or greasy) and looked too clear for water.

But it tasted like that stuff the gods might drink. He scooped handful after handful into his mouth.

Satisfied, he continued making his way through the thickening growth. And only as he felt that the strain of his leg muscles had shifted did he understand he had gotten over the ridge. He was going down. There was no army to look at, though. Based on the artwork he had seen and common sense, he had fully expected to be on something like the top of a building looking down at an army far below.

Instead he found himself facing only more branches and dirt and leaves. He stopped to think things through.

Finally, as he stood in thought, Paul began to piece together the centurion's special instruction. The man had shaded his eyes with his hand and looked to the left and right and behind himself, in some kind of charade that might have been meant to indicate the need to search or probe around. Something tickled at Paul's mind and made him feel the officer had also been trying to tell him something on the topic of aloneness.

It might have been something about ... about – about turning around from time to time to see if you're being followed?

STUDENT

During his life's work, Paul had learned a number of ways that headway can be effectively made to get from one point to the next. We have seen many examples of this back in Rome. Darting, dodging, jumping, sprinting. One of these common methods of progression, however, did not include being towed down a steep ridge wearing a blindfold.

Paul never saw his captors. They'd worked fast.

One moment he had been peering through growth trying to remember a warning he had been given; the next he had a cloth over his eyes, arms bound. There seemed to be two men moving him along: one up ahead pulling at a rope attached to his wrists, and a second alongside.

The one at his side sporadically hoisted Paul a few inches off the ground by the torso, presumably to carry him over an obstacle. While doing so, he invariably made a crack about wiry frames, little squirts and dangling feet. Paul had once seen a couple walking their blind miniature Pomeranian along a patchy Roman street in such a fashion.

He went along as he was led and lifted and shoved.

As the terrain began leveling, a mush of recognizable noises started seeping into Paul's ears. They formed themselves soon into the clinking, grunts, braying, shouts and hammering of an army encampment. The ground became fully flattened, and he began to notice that, while familiar, these sounds had a different quality from those he had heard while in the Opposition camp. These sounds had a sort of rounded depth to them.

The grunts had no underlying squeak as in the Opposition camp, the shouts lasted a little longer, and even the shoveling had a more ineffably sonorous character to it. The Opposition camp signalman always featured a subtly dulcet quaver in the pitch of his pleasing horn; the man here apparently just used his lips to give the thing a blat. The neighs of the steeds in this camp came off a little self-satisfied, and even the animals that would soon be supper had a tendency to bleat with a certain off-putting swagger.

This, Paul decided, was an army encampment that knew what it was doing.

The cacophony enveloped Paul before long. He no longer felt grass brushing at his calves, and the perfumes of nature were displaced with the presence of three-day sweat. He was halted. Then told to wait.

After some time, the blindfold was pulled off. Paul's eyes began adjusting. He was inside a thickly walled tent lit with oil lamps. Two figures stood in front of him. One he did not recognize at all: A bony, compact creature, more lean even than Paul himself and with all the blemishes of a teenager.

The other figure Paul regrettably recognized right away.

"So this is the special operative of the Opposition?" Mark Antony said, looking Paul up and down dubiously. "Their go-to man for crisis."

His wrists still bound, Paul had only one thing to do: Pray that the facial recognition region of Antony's brain did not work as effectively as his own. Not that he wasn't in enough trouble as it was.

"Catching him was not hard, of course." Antony turned to the pimply youth by his side. "I had my scouts positioned in the fields outside the Opposition camp, waiting for word. Our friend inside the Opposition leadership – the collaborator I was telling you about, who's working for us – simply got a message out to my scouts, saying that this young man would be coming our way on a reconnaissance mission to spy on our camp. By the way, I'm sure you won't be too disappointed to hear we confirmed Julius Caesar is in the camp. We'll be offing him for good when we make our attack, which our friend is also helping us with."

The small teen next to Antony held a yellow legal pad in one hand and was writing this all down. He pushed up at a pair of thick eyeglasses as they started sliding down his thin nose.

Antony turned back to Paul and squinted. He held his gaze for a minute longer than Paul wanted him to.

"And what do you do with spies like this?" The teenager's voice cracked at "spies," which brought a flash of bright red to his face.

"All of this is very interesting to me."

"Bring us refreshments!" Antony called out. "I've got some thinking to do."

Paul recognized the figure approaching with a tray. The man had been Caesar's house servant. By the name of Nimbus, if memory served, and seemed like a helpful fellow, too. He bowed to Antony and handed over a goblet of wine. To the teenager he passed a glass of milk. As the servant backed away, he flashed a pointed look to Paul that could have meant anything or nothing at all. Paul, though, had his mind focused elsewhere.

"A very good question," Antony said to the youth, "from a very perceptive lad. I am still amazed you are related at all to Caesar. So what indeed will I do with our spy? This could be a good teaching moment for you, to learn about dealing with enemies of the state. Do you remember what I ordered done to the quartermaster? The one who tried skimming from the officer's payroll?"

The teenager downed his milk and hastily flipped through his notepad, paging back and forth. Paul stopped breathing and watched.

"Yes, here it is," the teen announced, wiping a white mustache from his hairless upper lip. "My notes reflect that the quartermaster immediately confessed and agreed to be cooperative, so you offered him a full pardon."

Paul let out a single careful exhalation.

Antony: "Yes, I am very forgiving to those who cooperate. I wonder if that will be the case here. I have a feeling this young man can be very useful to us. I am sure he also understands that we have experts who know every technique possible to pry the truth out if necessary."

A pause followed. Paul guessed it was now his turn to speak up with an indication of his own tendency toward cooperativeness. The teenager, however, had continued paging through the notepad before Paul could say or do anything.

"No, just a moment," the youth said worriedly, tapping his pen at the pad. "The case of the quartermaster was not the skimming affair. Your adjutant was the one who committed the skimming. The case of the quartermaster involved kickbacks from a substandard vegetable vendor. I had it written down wrong in my notes."

Antony's eyes slowly lit up, and a dark smile came to his face.

"Thank you, Octavian Caesar." Antony said this with a heavy tone. This might have been a tone of sarcasm. It might have been the tone of a harried mentor who has finally grown tired of being questioned and prodded by an overeager pupil. Such would have been a best-case scenario for Paul.

Such, however, wasn't.

Something else had come to Antony's mind. His tone did not indicate scorn but a slowly emerging remembrance.

"'Vegetable vendor,'" he repeated. "Yes. That jogs my memory. In fact, jog. The word 'jog' jogs my memory. You were there at the Run, weren't you? You're the one, aren't you?"

Antony was now addressing Paul directly.

"The one?" Paul asked politely.

"The saboteur. You're the one who attacked me while I was running the Lupercalia, just before the Ides of March. Who shoved me into the vendor's cart."

It seemed to Paul like the time to reference his own obliging nature had begun passing.

"You'll want to write this down, too." Antony glanced to his side. "This could be a memorable lesson on how to handle personal threats, my good Octavian. You do remember what I had done to that adjutant who skimmed off me. I think our friend here just may be deserving of the same."

"I understand perfectly." Octavian Caesar went to a blank page and started writing. "Let me just get this down. 'Note, spy captured today will get same fate as skimming adjutant, to wit – '"

He stopped.

"A problem?" asked Antony. "You do not grow weary of my lessons, I trust."

"On the contrary. I'm just trying to remember. There's only two Ts in torture, right?"

Antony thought this over briefly before answering.

"And two Ls," he said, "in guillotine."

As Paul found himself being led away, he felt only numbness. The sun fell dully on the camp and its sounds seemed to have receded a hundred miles. He felt giant hands under both his elbows and realized he was half walking and half being dragged somewhere.

A hand shoved his head and he was pushed into a tiny room, or, at best, a large box. He was locked in. The space was more narrow than his arms span, and the ceiling could not have been more than three feet from the floor. He was beyond the point of exhaustion, both physically and mentally. He instinctively pushed at the sides, but even if the walls had been papier-mâché, Paul would not have had the strength to free himself.

He closed his eyes and grabbed the sides of the small space in order to stop the rotating sensation he began feeling.

At such moments, a mind gone so gooey often surrenders control to the body. He did not feel at all like eating. He in fact felt more like throwing up. But his body knew it had to get something inside it. His body remembered the word "toffee." Mechanically, Paul fumbled for his satchel and reached in. From the bottom, he pulled out the package his mother had given him back in Rome, an object he had forgotten about in the succeeding weeks.

He laid the package on the floor and untied the oilcloth and paper wrapping. He began weakly snapping off pieces from the cracked brown ingot inside – nearly as impenetrable as her stories – sliding them habitually one by one into his mouth. And as he began to feel a little strength return, he glanced down at the half-eaten hunk and noticed, on the paper underneath it, writing.

Even in dim light, he recognized the careful, crimped penmanship. Using all his remaining power, Paul lifted up the paper.

LETTER

Dearest son –

There is so very little I need to tell you, for I am sure you already have come to understand everything I will write here. But I must say these words.

These last weeks, my son, you have proven yourself to be unimaginably intelligent and brave in ways I never thought possible. Can it be that that you have been acting out a deeply thought out plan far beyond my ability to understand? I think you have.

Your courageous kidnapping of the great Julius Caesar, simply to bring him to me, was all the proof of your new ability that I needed. I never knew you had it in you.

As I have seen you act lately with such grit and skill, I have come to realize it is the moment for me to tell you directly about all those things I have been cautiously revealing to you over time.

I know that I tried too hard to protect you while you were growing up. Granted, you started out fragile and never built up much from there. (I remember at the parent-teacher conference in sixth grade being told you were the only student to eat lunch under your desk.) But I should not have hidden the truth from you.

As you grew up, I lied to you about our past, to try to protect you. But then I struggled about how to eventually tell you the truth. I am so cheered that you listened to me so attentively these past months and years as I unraveled it all for you. Now I'll complete that course of revelation.

My father did not sell water-resistant outerwear, and I was not born in Rome. Those were two of the stories I invented. I grew up in a village not far from the site of Carthage, across the Mediterranean Sea. We had a happy life, until the Roman army came. That is how one day at age 14, I became an orphan and a slave.

I was taken to Rome in bondage. The terrible man who snatched me was the very same general who'd raided our village. I became one of his serving girls, forced for years to wait on him day and night and on his wealthy and powerful friends. He was a cruel man who got very rich in very bad ways. And I'm not talking just debentures and time share developments. It was while working for this man that I first saw the great and mighty Julius Caesar, though I'm sure he did not notice me that initial time.

Always always, I dreamt of breaking free from that awful master.

When the Servile War of rebel slaves broke out, my master bribed his way to become Commander of the Roman forces in southern Italy. I was sent with him as he marched the Roman legions against the slave army.

Licinius Crassus (that was the name of this master, but you obviously know that) was the one I always told you of, the one who sat up all night counting his piles of gold. He ordered a constant stream of baggage trains to come into his military camp, day after day. These carts brought all his luxurious clothes and riches and furnishings to him.

I saw my chance then. One night, I sneaked into one of the wagons after it was emptied. When it left to return to Rome, I jumped out and found my way to the rebel army camp.

The rebel camp was like nothing I ever experienced. Everyone lived as equals and all fought for the same cause. I'd forgotten what it was like not to be ordered about, not to be forced to serve the desires of rich and controlling Romans. In Rome, I had no choice, no way to stand up for myself and make choices for myself.

And that, Paul, brings us to you. I'm sure you realize what I have been leading to.

You know by this point the question I am about to answer for you. And *about* you. The biggest of all questions. You certainly have long figured out the very answer by yourself. But I must tell you directly who it was who gave you life. You must hear from me the name of your father.

The name of your father, my beloved son, is, of course, the great and mighty –

> – the reader by this stage in our chronicle will be aware that Paul had never, not for a very long time, surmised anything from his mother's words, nor had he understood any of her stray comments over the years except as the evidently disjointed mumblings of a mind that had been jarred, and that every word he was reading now was breaking news to him; so it will not surprise the reader that Paul, gazing wide-eyed at the letter in his hand, had not guessed his mother was leading up to anything at all and was almost frozen in anxious fear for the words he would read next –

– Spartacus, leader of the rebel slaves. Yes, Spartacus was your father.

When I got into their camp, the other rebels learned that my master was Licinius Crassus, the general opposing them. So they took me to see their own leader. Spartacus. All my fears and dreadful memories of the powerful men of Rome fell away the instant I first beheld Spartacus.

I fell in love from the first moment. That is not a surprise. Everyone adored Spartacus. What surprises me is that he would tell me, before very long, that he felt the same about me. How a man so strong and brilliant could find a way to love an absentminded fluffhead like me, I cannot understand.

We had such a short time together in that camp. Yet they were the happy days of my life. We lived freely and in love while we prepared to fight for ourselves and everyone around us.

Spartacus knew the Romans would win that war in the end and that the two of us would be forever separated. Our army was trapped with only some rusted farm tools to fight the full weight of Rome. The night before the final battle, he made me leave his side. He told me simply that I was to find my way back to Rome. His last words to me were to wait for his final message, when he would call me home. I didn't know what this meant and am still not sure. But he begged me to complete this mission for him. I know he also wanted to protect the unborn child who I carried. I agreed, in tears.

That was a quarter century ago.

The Romans, as you know, did win. (Wait, maybe you didn't know that. History was never your subject.) The slave rebellion was destroyed.

Why did I hide all this from you when you were younger? I knew it was dangerous to have any connection with the rebellion, and I did not know whether you were strong enough to handle the truth. (I also remember having to pull you from high school gym when you became worried about being bucked by the pommel horse.) When we have something big to tell, we often do it in a roundabout and tentative way, hoping that clues and hints will be taken up.

This is all why for the past years, I began to reveal these things only slowly and carefully. During your visits, I offered you small bits of the truth over time. I knew with your sly mind, you were piecing it all together in your own way, the way I wanted you to come to understand. Where others may have thought I was a rambling fool, you knew I was cautiously guiding you to the truth, prodding you and enticing you to it. You must even have understood why I had to stay at home all this time, even though I never told you the exact reason – to wait for your father's final message.

If I ever had any doubt whether you were understanding me all along these past years, that uncertainty disappeared the moment you brought Julius Caesar to me. I did not at first realize why you captured him.

How did you know Caesar had that precious document in his toga? How did you know I would find it on him? And how did you know that it was written by your father Spartacus? I recognized his handwriting as soon as I pulled the paper from Caesar's toga.

My son, you astonish me.

No doubt you did the math on all this long ago, my child. (Then again, arithmetic was never your subject, either. Do you still break out in hives whenever you see a multiplication table?) You were born nine months after the end of the Servile War.

One other thing. While I appreciate the gumption behind what you did, please try not to abduct too many more people. It's dangerous for you and for the person you have to clonk. And anyway, Caesar is a nice man. He always was one of the pretty good ones.

I wish I could tell you what all this means – his final message, calling me home, thinking big, the crosswords puzzler. But it was long ago. Plus I've always been a bit of a space case, let's face it. It may be up to you to solve the final questions. I am guessing perhaps you already have done so, and you sit now triumphant in your knowledge and skill.

There is much more to say, but from what your friend Cassius told me, you will be coming here soon to tell me you must leave Rome at any minute. I must close. Anyway, the toffee's almost ready.

Kindest regards,

Mom

SQUIRT

T he letter, by the time Paul had read to its last line, felt like a thousand pounds of iron that had just emerged from a kiln. It fell from his hands.

"Spartacus?" He pronounced the name with the same astonished inflection that a barmaid might use in repeating the order of a shift supervisor who's just asked for a lemon berry spritzer and watercress salad instead of a scotch. Paul was dumbfounded. Not one syllable of the letter made any sense at all. "Licinius Crassus? Spartacus? ... Mom? Spartacus?"

His head swam like it had never so much as waded before. He blinked and tried to let his thoughts clear.

The door to the small room could have opened then to reveal that the entire world had been rotated upside down, the sky turned tartan and the pantheon of gods doing a conga line in the middle of the camp, and Paul would have looked at all this as more banal than what he just read.

"Sp." He couldn't get the name fully out again.

As it happened, the door did open. The sky was blue and in the right place, nor were any gods to be seen, dancing or no. The very large forearm of a very large soldier reached in. Paul shoved the letter back into his satchel before being dragged into the light.

"Die time, little squirt." The soldier yanking him spoke in a very unsoothing manner as he lifted Paul to his feet. It was the voice of one of those who had captured him at the top of the ridge.

Three more guards surrounded Paul; there were two on both sides and two in front. Taking one step for every two of his, they began to march him down a wide roadway. Paul still felt as if his world had been turned upside down, but he had enough presence of mind to know that if he didn't act fast, his world would be ending soon. It would be ending, incidentally, in bewilderment.

As they all moved forward, Paul stooped and bobbed. He was penned inside a very large and fleshy cage, one that was moving him quickly. Squinting, he could see very little in any direction other than close-up torsos and hairy legs that kept him driving forward with them.

But he began calculating something as he tried peering through his guards: While Roman soldiers are trained for much, they are not trained for dealing Impelled Maniacs. He knew the chance of getting clean away had to be next to nil, but those odds gave him about the only chance he had.

And he had this: The frustrations of these past weeks – of the past years – of shift supervisors and senators, of going unnoticed, of food scraps and listening only to others, all to end in this way – these frustrations discharged throughout Paul's being as a burst of resentful force he'd never felt before. With a mix of this and forced daring, and with a slight molasses rush from the toffee, he gauged the small gaps between the soldiers. He counted to three. And he bolted.

Tumbling between the scissoring legs of the soldier on his left, he sprung himself up, gyred around and made for an alley between two tent rows. The immediate response from behind was the sound of eight clown-shoe-sized sandals peeling against gravel. Shouts followed, and these multiplied themselves. Before long, the camp would fill with the blare of horns.

Paul moved fast and kept calculating, his heart racing and the little satchel banging against his side.

He guessed Roman camps might be set up alike. He tried to remember how the Opposition camp was set up. Assuming himself to be running along the officer's quarters, a line of enlisted men's tents would come next, then the stables would be down the way over a short expanse, and just behind this would be one of two possible objects.

At the edge of the camp, he would come up against either an insuperable wall and impassable ditch or, since the army had just arrived, the empty spot where an insuperable wall and impassable ditch were about to be placed.

As he sprinted, Paul recognized a number of familiar sites. The thicker woolen walls of the officer's tents gave way to the flimsy sides of the enlisted men's quarters. He ran past the expected arrangement of auxiliary troop housing, pyramids of spears, a mess hall, hearths with bellows and anvils, and a number of other recognizable objects. The only meaningful difference between this camp and the Opposition camp – and it was a big difference – was bigness.

Paul had to do a lot of running.

When he had been dragooned and blindfolded, he heard what sounded like a more vigorous site than the Opposition's. Now as he darted along, he saw the disparity firsthand. The rows of tents seemed to have no end, and there were dozens of additional mounds of shields and helmets and extra row after row of siege engines. Where the Opposition camp might have featured a forlorn hen in a crate, this camp held a conclave of poultry, and in the place of a single latrine, Paul sprinted past a virtual suite of port-a-johns.

Finally, he emerged into the expected ground that signaled an end to the men's quarters. He saw the anticipated stables beyond, which he knew were placed at the very edge of a military fort. And behind the stables, he could just make out the most glorious vision he ever beheld: He saw the absence of a wall and ditch.

As Paul raced beyond the stables, a few soldiers working nearby looked up. He waved his satchel and pointed toward the ridge, giving them to think he was simply a tiresome messenger on his way out for another tiresome mission somewhere. They went back to their work as he hopped over the taut strings and stakes that indicated the future site of the wall and ditch.

In the opposite direction of the ridge he made out a grove, not too far from the edge of the camp. Paul ran toward it in a crouch that kept him just above grass level.

Before he could imagine it possible, he reached the grove and shot himself into it. He turned back around just in time to see the first cavalry coming out from the camp. The soldiers he had passed were pointing toward the ridge, the direction where he had indicated he would be going, and that is where most the horses headed.

Paul reached behind himself, expecting to feel arrows sticking out of his back. Yet he was just fine. The last thing he wanted to do at that moment was to keep running. The rushes of adrenaline he had been feeling since being taken captive had turned his muscles into porridge. But he started moving again as quickly as he could, deeper into the trees.

That he might have actually escaped still seemed unfathomable. He could not believe his luck (or, he admitted quietly to himself, his pluck).

"Spartacus," he said once more. When he said it this time, he said it only half as a dubious question and half like an assertion of fact.

As he loped ahead, the sounds of horses and horns grew more distant. In the still of the thicket, he heard only the sing-song of his own feet against the ground. It was a cadence that took his mind back to running the streets of Rome. At present, instead of wall and cart and citizen, he shimmied round trunk and scrub and rock.

But as in those urban days, he began to pick up his pace and feel his mind whirring faster.

PUZZLING

Using criteria provided by a professionally certified Stress Measurement Scale (or SMS), offer a weighted numeric rating to the following "life tension events" [100 being extremely stressful, 0 indicating not stressful at all]. Please complete with a No. II pencil and print legibly:

_____ Seeking moderate loan or mortgage

_____ Change in church activities

_____ Narrowly escape beheading

_____ Business-related adjustment

_____ Being told Spartacus was your father

_____ Revision of vacation plans

_____ Hunted by a legion

_____ Alteration in usual number of social get-togethers

_____ Happening upon central role in imperial politics

_____ Seasonal allergies

P aul understood he had little time for fruitful emotional processing, but he did realize he had been provided a lot more to consider than usual. Should he try to return to the Opposition camp? Hide out in the thickets for a time? Look for some kind of help?

He kept running while his mind whirred. It was not the type of movement he had been used to. There is, he saw, a measurable difference between dashing along while trying to remember the message "Does your cook use all-spice seasoning or thyme for his turkey tacos recipe?" and running for your life. In the latter case, for example, there was no clear destination.

Continuing along the footpath, he emerged to a modest creek in a gully that provided a small bit of cover. Though it would do no practical good, he instinctively crouched every time he heard a braying steed in the distance.

He kept along the creek, hopping over fallen trees and skirting large rocks but always moving. Still unsure about how nature operates when on its own, he continued to think he heard the clang of hooves and bang of armor mixed with the wind and scurrying creatures. He tried to recount all his knowledge of ecosystems. All he could come up with was something about poisonous berries, and he had a feeling that creeks tended to run toward big bodies of water, often stopping by towns on the way.

Fully flummoxed about what he should do or how much danger he continued to face, he knew he had to focus only on his present crisis. But like on his jobs back in Rome, thoughts began accompanying his run. The words of his mother's letter jostled around, mixing in with Caesar's puzzler (which actually, it was occurring to Paul, was written by Spartacus? His father?).

If his mother's letter were not one more of her fantasies, then she had once been taken captive by Lucius Crassus, one of the most powerful senators in Rome? Escaped from him? Hooked up with the rebel leader Spartacus? They fooled around? And Paul resulted? And she's been waiting in her apartment since then for something?

Abruptly he remembered a throwaway comment Caesar had made while they were working at the tent stakes. He mentioned that the leader of the Servile War had been born not far away to the west, in a place that was later destroyed. The leader of the Servile War, Paul thought. That must have been a reference to –

"Dad?"

As far as he could remember, this marked the first time Paul ever launched that word off his lips. It did not come out quite right.

"Dad," he said again, to make it sound more natural to his ears, repeating it every ten or fifteen steps. "Dad ... Dad ... Dad ... Dad."

As he moved as quickly as possible, an absence started becoming noticeable to Paul. In Rome, criers could regularly be heard calling out the time. Here, he noticed, nobody shouted when it was. But he understood enough about the sun to know that hours were beginning to pass and that he was moving in a westerly direction.

Lost in his thoughts, Paul did not notice that the creek at some point had decided it wouldn't be going alongside anymore and he had been running along a vacant plain for some time. But a flash came when he could not miss seeing that immediately in front of him, the earth itself suddenly dropped away.

He jerked himself to a stop. The land plunged. It fell down into a great round basin or valley. A jolt of vertigo struck at Paul. He half crouched to steady himself. The space down there looked almost as big as the entire city of Rome but entirely made of an opulent greenness gilded by the mid-afternoon sun, with a few white lines of some kind glinting in the middle. Paul had no idea the planet pounded out such powerful sublime workmanship. He might have stared in wonder for some time.

The echo of a human bellow far back in the distance suggested he continue moving.

FLAT

A large valley basin seemed like a good place in which to go missing. Nearby, a slender bed of low weeds indicated a path down that had gone to seed years earlier.

Gravity did most the work. Paul let out vibrato yawps as his sandals slid and skirted and he windmilled his arms to keep from tumbling into a somersault.

In a minute or less, the basin floor caught him as swiftly as the bluff had thrown him down. He looked back up the sharp crag, chiefly to make sure his skeleton hadn't rattled out from under him during the ride, before turning to the center, where he had noticed a glimmering whiteness.

One special distinction between this space and Rome came to him. Whereas Rome offered a rage of smells – clumps of odors rising from alleys, cookware, body parts, market pens, oiling, tanneries, troughs – this big open place offered one's *Nervus olfactorius* only the impression of a lone, monstrous boutonnicre. He breathed in deeply.

Annoyingly, the words of the puzzler kept tickling at his mind, jostling oddly against one of the countless theories of life that Caesar had rattled off on occasion. He pushed these away to concentrate.

He could begin to make out that the area of whiteness in the valley center was no construction of nature. He was in fact coming upon the outlines of the walls of houses and shops and public buildings. Row after row of them. He had never seen anything like it.

It was as if one of the tenants of Olympus had taken a scythe to the place, or organized a god-sized bocce tournament, sweeping out and squashing down everything – every dimension – except a flat, full-scale representation of a town. Only a lushness of weeds pushing through some cracks gave proof that this must have happened a long time ago.

Entranced, Paul started walking down what looked to have once been the main street of the village. He felt almost as if he were entering the laid out lines of a town about to be built up, rather than one once there. In the windless valley, there was a spectral calm to it all. He passed slowly down city blocks, taking in the geometry that once must have held buildings of every kind. For the first time since his capture, he felt a sense of quiet. The strangeness of the tranquil place began taking his mind from the mash of sensations that had been coming at him.

Just as Paul found himself becoming lost in marvel, a blast of high laughter shot through the emptiness.

Paul instinctively did a yelping dive. He flew into a channel along the road, ejecting his sandals as he blasted off and belly flopping onto a clay surface. The Romans had made it there already? He waited for his ribs to spring back into place, hugging the clay, listening. Feeling his heart thump against the ground, he didn't want to move, but he knew he had to keep going.

Silence returned.

He carefully began to lift himself back up, readying his muscles for what might be out there. But as he rose, Paul began becoming aware of something. He realized the place he'd lunged into possessed the chief characteristic we typically avoid in a hiding hole.

It housed another human.

Three feet away sat a woman. A round face with inset gray eyes stared, though with no great emotion in them, at Paul.

By all rights, Paul should have shot ten feet into the air and shrieked. But by this point, Paul had not a single bounce or yike left inside. He stared back.

"Hello," he offered absently.

"Hell," the woman responded. "It took you much longer getting here than I expect. Did Donkey give you a fry?"

Two or three times in a lifetime, a person may come to that crux, an instant when the thrust of emotions lock up, when he or she must allow that logic has stopped functioning, that Hope has legged it and the only chance of retaining one's sanity in the long run is by peacefully acceding to an inexorable surrounding madness. You go along with the program.

"Yes," Paul agreed coolly. "Donkey gave me a fry."

The woman sat up onto the ground on the side of the channel, and indicated Paul do the same next to her. Mechanically, he did this.

"We will talk now and I will ask you some quest," she told him.

"Yes." Paul continued to speak without tone, nor had he for some time blinked. "We really should chat."

Deep within, a small piece of his centers of reason continued churning and with these, he found a way to begin making sense of his environment. The woman brushed off her yellowed frock. A babushka partially covered her face.

It dawned on Paul that she spoke with a kind of drawling brogue that snapped off the very last part of her sentences. The final syllables apparently got caught in her mouth. Which means, his brain reasoned, she might have been telling him she had a pack animal nearby and had asked if its whinny had scared him.

"You own a donkey," he informed her. "Yes, your donkey gave me a fright."

"He was warning me that you were come. He's tied up outside the vill."

She faced him. Her smile suggested curiosity as much as warmth or humor. Paul did not dine out often, but he had the impression of a sandwich counter waitress watching to take his order.

"I wonder why you didn't come soon," she said.

Paul took some time to look around and continue letting the stabilizers in his mind work. It seemed he was facing the remains of a squared-off city forum, once bordered by shops.

"What do you mean, why didn't I come sooner? Where am I? What is this place? Was this village –" A chill tingled Paul's spine, despite the heat of the late afternoon sun. "Was this the village that I think it is? Is this –"

The woman chuckled, a round laugh that strangely pleased Paul.

"I thought I was going to be asking the quest," she said. "You surely know you are in the village of Spartac."

Paul grabbed the sides of the trench to stop the spinning he felt.

"But you knew all this when you came here, sure?" she said.

She pointed around the forum and told Paul, there's the spot where there used to be the speaker's rostrum, and the little library with its fountain, city hall, and the town's tiny parking garage.

They sat silently.

"So nobe," she finally pronounced. "Such a noble man, who everyone love."

Paul understood he should still be running in fear. But he sat unmoving.

"You knew him?" he asked cautiously.

The woman seemed oldish but not antiquated. True, if she tried returning her face for a full refund, she would probably be told that accepting worn merchandise is against policy. Yet her runnels and blemishes suggested weariness as much as age. She put a liver-spotted hand on his knee and explained that yes of course she knew him. They had played together. They had grown together.

"This is the central forum, where we laughed away all our summer day. Every morning when we were young, Spartacus would gather us to meet here in the mid." In the *middle*. She spoke as if she were telling Paul a story he had heard a hundred times before. And there was indeed a strange familiarity to it all.

Like everyone else in the village, she told Paul, she watched as Spartacus grew into a man of great strength and even greater spirit. She watched him join the Thracian Liberation Militia, and she heard the miserable account of his capture by the Romans. And then she heard his grand exploits: building an army of freedom to fight Rome. Paul listened to it all, entranced by the chronicle and by the aura of the woman.

"And this village," he said, as she finished talking. "I once heard that a Roman general destroyed it."

"Licinius Crassus brought so much destruct," she said with a tint of controlled anger. "Yes, he was looking for something here he thought was hid. His soldiers were told to leave no object untouched larger than a paving brick or piece of firewuh." *Firewood,* Paul guessed.

As his brain continued getting its footing, he remembered his mother talked much of Spartacus's childhood. Everything the woman had been saying he'd heard in some way from his mother. She had said that Spartacus told no one in the rebel camp except her of the stories of his upbringing here, because they were too painful for him to remember.

"You still live here?" he asked.

She again laughed. No, she lived in a small farmhouse down the road, but she came here every chance she could. Resting and waiting, sometimes near the old house of Spartacus, or, on hot days, in the coolness of the clay channel. Always waiting and thinking of those days.

"He would have wanted me to wait here as long as necessary, knowing that you would be come."

"That sounds like something my mother was trying to tell me, about Spartacus and waiting," Paul admitted warily. "But. Who are you? What do you mean saying it was me you were waiting for and knowing I'd be – ?"

His wits had recovered enough to let a thought enter. It occurred to him if this woman of the trench had really known Spartacus so well, she should be able to recognize his writing and possibly even make sense of the puzzler, if indeed Spartacus had written it. He reached into his satchel for the paper.

As she began mouthing the words, she only squinted. But when she had finished, she beamed, exactly as his mother had when finding the sheet from out of Caesar's toga. The woman looked into it a good long time, cherishing the words.

"You know, don't you," Paul said expectantly. "You know who wrote it and what secret it's holding. Tell me, what does it mean?"

She read it three or four more times, mumbling some of its phrases – whole city, four letters, eleven, boxes – before handing it back, her checks now ruddy and her eyes bright. She nodded and let out another laugh.

"No idea what it mean," she announced. "But it sure sounds amuse. Some kind of promotional giveaway, maybe for a lifetime supply of so?"

No, Paul said, feeling an ebb of desolation. No. It is true "soap" is four letters long, and winning a shipment of soap would mean getting lots of boxes and would arguably be a priceless gift. But he did not think that's what the puzzler was getting at.

His shoulders slumped. He felt how hungry he had gotten again. And frustrated. There seemed to be no meaning in anything, none he could find. Maybe there was some little bit of logic connecting what he had been experiencing. Maybe there were some answers somewhere, but he was in no condition to look.

What was he doing here, and where could he possibly go? With no money, no map, no idea how he could keep alive. There were entire cohorts under orders to find him with the objective of shaving his trachea. Yet here he sat with an inscrutable woman he had just met in a ditch inside a smushed out town.

His head ached.

Maybe the letter from his mother was simply her grandest fantasy of all. Possibly Paul, at his moment of great danger, had just fallen into her daydream world. At this instant, he would have been happy to feel the spittle of The Winged Owl's Shift Supervisor shellacking his face with the order for another message delivery. Or even listen to Julius Caesar talk more about how many malted milk balls he could fit into his mouth at one time.

"He never was able to come back home," the woman said, seemingly to herself, "to the place where he start. Our dear Spartac."

In his growing gloom, Paul only partly heard this. For a minute, these last words from the woman swam absently through his mind.

They jostled quietly against the words of the puzzler and words from Caesar that had already been floating there. Paul felt too spent to devote much attention to this hushed mingling of memories and thoughts in his head. But they all worked on each other during this minute, as if they felt they belonged with one another in some way, sidling and brushing against each other, testing how they could make a good fit, finding just the right spot to come together as a group.

When they did, they did something to Paul.

A convulsion arced through his body. It was a mighty convulsion. It jolted more than any molasses rush from his mother's toffee could, or any bellow from a Shift Supervisor. His lungs squeezed up, before he caught a load of air into them and burst it out with one word.

"Home!" he called out, with a billowing strength he had never employed before, and he rose to position himself for a sprint.

THOUGHTS

Today is the 23rd of Quintillus, and it is a bright and beautiful day. At least I think it is. I'm almost sure today is the 23rd of something. Did we actually decide to make Quintillus a month or didn't we? Which reminds me, I always felt we should have named at least one month after my Auntie Zazu. I brought this up a couple times. But somehow Antony convinced me not to, so the year ended up with October. And to think, the whole calendar has my name on it. But I couldn't do anything for Auntie Z.

We put up more tents this morning. For lunch we got chicken broiled with some kind of French ~~beshamul~~ ~~betchamel~~ ~~becha~~ gravy, with flan for dessert and look at that, I just noticed I'm left handed. Or, at least, I'm writing this with my left hand right now. No, wait, hold off a second. No, no that's my right.

Not sure where my little comrade Paul went. He must be doing just fine right now, being the bright sort he is. If he were around at this point I'd probably be telling him all this instead of writing it here. But anyway, Calpurnia once had a therapist who said starting a journal is good.

Paul loves hearing my thoughts more than anyone I've ever met. Sometimes I don't feel like talking, but I know how interested he is in what I have to say, and I always like to be ~~acomodating~~ ~~accomi~~ nice. I've also come to get a kick out of that colossal fellow here who doesn't speak up much, Paul's big quiet friend.

These last few weeks have certainly gotten me thinking. For the longest time in Rome I figured I had to work hard in order to keep pushing myself.

John Hoffman

I was always good at giving a speech and I've got a knack for war. But do I really like doing those things? Hmmm.

I might have come to rely too much on others too, and not just Antony. My chief house servant Nimbus was a good solid man who I knew I could trust 100 percent. I must offer myself a back pat for bringing him into my service, and getting him at a really low low cost too. But the point is now that I know I can do more on my own than I ever realized. I was wrong back then. No, hang on, yes, I was right. I really am left handed. (Haha, I said I was right, but I am left. Ha ha ha.) And which is worse – a tornado warning or a tornado watch?

Hey, got to run. There's the signal for role call (that bugle blower is so talented, he should be in an ~~orchastr~~ ~~simphon~~ band) and I still haven't found my pants from when I napped.

THERE

B are feet, when given options, invariably recommend prudence. They tend to be conscientious. Bare feet know better than any of us the consequences of the leaf that's concealing a pointed stone, the thoughtless picnicker who didn't care where he threw his twist-off bottle cap, or the movement of bowels. Bare feet will always advise vigilance over enthusiasm.

Paul, however, was enthusiastic. His feet were provided no choice.

As a result, some three minutes after he darted from the channel in a flattened village forum, Paul offered, with stridency and fullness, this declaration:

"Ow."

Paul, in his enthusiasm, had tripped. It was a full stumble, including a lurch of several additional steps.

He had been running to a spot that had detonated in his mind back at the channel, a place he had suddenly realized he had to find. He ended up in a furrow, a spot that looked like it might have once have been in a public park or a preserve.

He now accentuated his proclamation, several times: "Ow ... Ow-ow-ow-ow-ow."

It seemed a little late to offer an atoning gesture to the second through fifth toes of his right foot. But Paul grabbed them in empathy and hopped around on his spare. After tripping, especially when painfully and absent of footwear, human nature also demands that we go back and glare angrily at the source of the stagger. To further make amends to his dented foot, Paul went back to find its assailant. It took a little while to triangulate exactly on the object and push away a snarl of growth, but at last he found the attacker.

It was an E.

Put more broadly, Paul found that he had tripped over a small brown brick sticking half an inch from the ground. If he'd had his sandals on, he probably would have walked harmlessly over it. As he cleared away the grasses and weeds to examine it more closely, he saw that the letter "E" had been chiseled on top of the brick.

He stared and thought, crouched and squinting. He might have kept staring at the letter E for some time longer, but a voice startled him.

"Ointmen?"

He twisted around and looked up. The woman was standing directly over him, looking attentively down. She held a large burlap bag in one hand and, lifted up toward him, a small yellow amphora in the other. Paul felt himself in a kind of stupor and could not think straight enough to respond to her offer of salve. He looked at her blankly.

"Did you know," she said, "that you are almost certainly bat?"

Paul vaguely agreed that the odds favored his being batty, but that matter would have to wait for the time being. The solution, he said, had come to him back at the channel. The puzzler made sense now.

"There's something here, I know it."

Dimly Paul smelled an odor, a scent not unlike that of a maladjusted tuna casserole. In accompaniment with the smell, Paul's toes began feeling soothed. Looking down the length of his body, he indistinctly noted the woman crouched down, slathering some kind of goo onto his left foot.

"Home," he said, as he had before sprinting off. "His last words to my mother were to wait for him to call her home."

Still deep in calculation, he remained largely unaware his body had begun undergoing treatment.

"That's what that puzzler was supposed to do. When she saw the paper, she would know he was telling her to go to the home of his village. When you said 'home,' it all struck me. He wrote that puzzler as a series of clues for my mother to figure out. But it was so long ago."

The woman nodded with pretend understanding and globbed on another handful.

"It says to start from the middle square," Paul said. "Everyone thought that meant the little box in the center of a crossword game on piece of paper. But you said something about Spartacus gathering you all in the village square, in the middle of town. What he must have meant was to start in the central forum of his childhood home. That's what he was getting at when he said the puzzler was for a whole city, too. He didn't want all the people of some town to try to solve it as a group. He meant you have to picture an entire city to figure it out. He was thinking big. He turned this village into a giant crossword game, don't you see?"

He glanced again at the E.

"It said to go eleven up and five to the right," Paul said. "But that doesn't refer to words in a crossword puzzle but to streets. He meant to go here. We're eleven blocks up from the forum and five over. Whatever he wanted us to find is on this spot, and it must have something to do with – "

He looked back at the E.

"What is a four letter word for 'something priceless'?" Paul quoted the last lines of the puzzler. "'If you solve this, that is what you will get.'"

Everything fell into place.

"I think I just solved it." He spoke slowly, in a low voice, in the kind of wonder-filled tone we associate with choirs trilling off stage in upper register hosannas of revelation.

In reality off in the distance there was no radiant choir but rather the sort of activity that actually tends to break off the joy of such a seraphic harmony. As it happens, the woman and Paul had chosen an opportune time to be crouched in a sunken furrow.

Coming up, from the direction of the village forum, marched 27 Roman soldiers.

One of them carried Paul's sandals.

MEMORANDUM

To: **Opposition Leadership**

From: **Marcus Tullius Cicero**, Registered Actuary Practitioner

Re: **Petty Cash Fund**

Strictly Confidential

Opposition expense outlays continue to modestly surpass our revenue, leading to an increasing deficit position. See below. This discrepancy has accelerated, due to costs associated with adding "Civil war: Try coming in first" to official Goals and Objectives.

As a result, please be aware that Petty Cash fund use does not contemplate the following recently submitted items and similar expenditures: Souvenir ashtrays and mustache cups, puppet repair, current year edition of local restaurant guides, ear plugs "because the army can get so loud," and Martinizing.

Summary of Current Balance:

Operational outlays: 9,345,223.31
Net Revenue: N/A
Closing balance, quarterly: (123,003,323.18)*

Note: As explained in the past, understand that parentheses indicate "what we owe."

WHACKED

Still caught in the pomp of his epiphany, Paul began raising himself slowly from the ground, as a purified spirit might be lifted up by the welcoming hymns of the heavens. It had come together, the pieces now made sense.

He got himself halfway stood up when he glanced right; immediately, the chorus caroling inside his head broke off in mid-High C and hightailed it out of there.

He dropped back onto the ground, shaken fully back into the world around.

"Roman soldiers headed this way," he whispered. "They don't see us yet."

They advanced in an extended line, each three shoulder lengths from the next. Pressed down against the dirt and looking through a lattice of grasses, Paul could see only the crests of their helmets but distinctly heard their methodical surge pushing uniformly, measured – a portentous wave moving unavoidably closer.

Their faces came into view. These were not, even flattered with the glow of a buttery twilight and framed by fetchingly embossed headwear, pleasant faces to look at.

"And just how do you know they're his sandals anyway?" snarled one of the soldiers, whose trajectory would probably lead him very soon straight into an E.

"Trust me," snapped the soldier next over. "I know what the squirt was wearing. These are his. Size Zero-and-a-Half, probably."

"That's right, I forgot," offered the first one. "You're the brainiac who let the little squirt escape from you in the first place."

Full uniforms could be seen now, their breastplates reflecting the declining light. Paul confirmed, too, that it was his sandals being carried. They dangled off fingers with dimensions seen less often in human anatomy books than in the pages of an industrial plumbing code manual. They were very thick fingers that made Paul's sandals seem very mousy.

"I'm telling all you whoresons," cried out Paul's sandal bearer, "you let me get my hands on him first! The squirt is mine."

Paul's gut told him to get up and run. But that would leave the woman alone. And there was no reason to believe he could escape anyway. Applying the principle of object permanence known to most infants (i.e., an entity disappearing from one's vision has ceased to exist) he decided to instead stash his face as deeply as possible into the ground and wait for the end. With all the neck energy he could muster, he buried his head's facade as best as he could.

Though Paul could no longer see, the sound of the human wave could not be blocked, a thumping forward gush with each collective step. He braced himself. Any second, either a howl of discovery would ring out or a hand would reach down and wring his neck.

It all stopped.

Paul did not want to look up. Nor did he.

He heard a new rhythm: The heavy, close breathing of 27 able-bodied men. As soon as he lifted his face, he would be staring into the grimace of a line of giants, he knew.

But one can't respire through soil forever. Slowly, Paul lifted his face out of the dirt mold of his face that he had stamped into the ground with his face.

Exactly as he feared. The entire phalanx stood on the lip of the furrow, not more than a dozen feet away. The soldier with Paul's sandals stood closest. Yet there was one new, odd and possibly central alteration about their appearance since the moment Paul had stowed his face.

Paul stared up not into a glowering grimace but into a row of skirted buttock. The soldiers were all, to a man, facing in the opposite direction.

Slowly, he raised himself up a little off the ground. He began to make out a voice in the distance, beyond the line of legionnaires. It was a voice of command.

"Next time I say halt," the voice bellowed from afar, "you simians halt right away. And do I need to send you back to boot camp? That was the sorriest about face I've ever seen."

The line of soldiers hung its head a little.

"Now, new orders! The Lord Antony is recalling all search

parties, effective immediately. We are returning to camp. Tomorrow morning, it is a full scale attack on the enemy. We got ourselves a war!"

A thunder of cheers rolled down the line. With another command, the human wave began receding with its rhythmic thrust, none of the soldiers giving the inconsequential gully behind them a second look.

Paul took a long, full breath before returning his face, for an exhausted moment, back into his earthen face form.

Silence would return quickly enough to the basin. Paul and the woman waited in the ditch and listened to the sound of soldiery as it is marched off, marched up and marched away. When they seemed to be alone again and he felt normal operation returning to his pulmonary system, Paul crawled cautiously up out of the furrow. There, he came face-to-face with his sandals.

After a great fright, our minds often find comfort in the vision of something familiar. The sandals were shabbier than ever – fraying, with a number outsole tacks gone, aglitter with dirt and sand and clover. They had arguably just betrayed him to the Roman army. But Paul liked these sandals. Suddenly safe from doom for the moment and eyeing two old friends, Paul wanted nothing more than the consoling familiarity of those sandals.

He reached out to grab them and, at that instant, his head began aching. Considerably. The pain started aft and moved swiftly forward. At the same time, it seemed that the seats vacated earlier by the annunciating chorus in his head got straight away filled by a community ensemble of strident ineptness.

Paul, not for the first time that day, said Ow.

He had been thwacked, hard – very hard – from behind. His head throbbed and his ears rang.

He rolled over half in shock. His dazed eyes worked their way up, starting from the sight of a swaying burlap sack that led to a hand that preceded an arm which ended at an astonishingly spiteful glare on the woman.

"Why?" Paul asked numbly, as he rubbed the back of his head and lifted himself to his elbows, in a state of half-wince if she should go at him again. "Why did you – ?"

He briefly considered calling for protection from the Roman army.

"Now you give me answer," the woman said coolly, swinging the sack as if about to re-thump him.

"Answers?" he asked.

She swung the bag back and forth, giving him time to do some figuring. As he looked up at her scowl, he began to consider that maybe the wallop was not entirely undeserved. After all, during their chat, Paul had clean forgotten to mention a few things. One, for instance: that he had an imperial legion chasing him. Watching the bag, he owned to himself that this could certainly be a reasonable cause of irritation to most anyone.

"Yes," he said with a docile grin. "You do deserve some answers, for sure."

"All of the answer."

"Yes, all of them. Where do you want me start?"

"You tell me what you think you found here, but first you start by telling me why you brought the army of Rome again to this vill."

CONNECTING

T he burlap sack pendulumed.

"I can't explain it all, not until we find out what's hidden here," Paul began, looking up with his best supplication eyes to the woman. "And we're very close to finding it."

The bag kept time with fair precision and rhythm.

"Make a deal?" he asked. "We're running out of daylight. I can tell you what I know now. I know that Licinius Crassus was looking for something when he destroyed this village. Something that was put in the ground."

It was probably swinging at an *allegro vivace*.

"Please. Just help me look for a little while, and then I can tell you everything. And I'm very sorry about the Romans. I should have told you. But as you saw, I'm not a friend of theirs either. They want me as leveled as this town."

Paul silently counted out eleven more sack cadences.

"It was – what we're looking for – it was put in the ground by Spartacus."

The bag seemed possibly to *largo* just a little.

"You know something," he said. "I don't know even know your name. I should have asked."

Inertia slowed the bag from a swing to a sway.

"Ten minute," the woman said. "Work quick."

Paul fought back a smile, which might have been taken as victory gloating.

"And it's Annette, if it matter."

"Annette," Paul repeated. "Yes, your name matters for sure. I'm Paul."

They shook hands as if about to face off for a set of tennis.

"We're looking for letters," Paul said as he lifted himself cautiously. "The title of the game is 'Crossword Puzzler.' But it doesn't mean a crossword puzzle. It must mean words that cross. Do you get it?"

The woman had put down the bag but was offering him a look that might have indicated either "what in the hell are you talking about" or "you now have nine minutes." Or both.

Paul glanced around, squinting to see if he could make out any more letters chiseled into bricks.

"We need to find more bricks like this E. I'm guessing there are a good number of them lined up, and they spell something out, and at some point two lines of these letters must meet up. That's where we need to go. That's where the words will cross."

Five minutes later, another E was found, twenty paces from the one Paul had tripped over. An R showed up further along.

"From the distance of the letters we've already found, we can probably guess at the meaning of at least this one particular word," Paul called out. He had coaxed the woman to look off in the distance while he tried to make sense of the letters already lining up. "But I have to admit with all this growth and the darkness coming, I don't know how we'll find any more of these tiny bricks – "

"Would an F do?" Annette yelled back. (Apparently it's nearly impossible to clip the word "do.")

Paul ran over. She was half a block away. She pointed with a look that bespoke some pride along with ongoing confusion at the purpose of her discovery. Paul looked at it for awhile.

"Free!" he announced.

The woman jumped back.

"A four letter word for priceless," Paul said.

It did not take long from that point. The letters F,R, and E were laid out along one axis. Another set of the same letters followed along a perpendicular course. It had to be, Paul thought, that the two axis lines would intersect exactly at the point where a final E would be. Then it would be solved: The word "free" spelled out twice in bricks and sharing the final E, where they crossed. He grabbed Annette's arm and pulled her after.

"Here. Right here."

Paul pointed to the spot where he was sure the two words would meet at the final, shared E.

But they looked; the ground there was only scrub and grass.

He pushed it all around and dropped onto his hands and knees, looking. No brick or letter was to be found.

"Why would they go through so much trub?" Annette seemed skeptical. "Why not just have a big brick here with a big 'X' to mark the spa?"

Yes, Paul admitted while facing a nonplussed worm a few inches from his face, a good question. Why go through the trouble of having far-off letters that only point to the spot where you've hidden something but don't reveal it directly?

Unless, of course, you didn't want the spot itself to be found by the wrong people. Then you just might, just to be safe, bury the last clue.

"You don't have a shovel, do you?" He looked up to Annette.

As it happens, she did keep a shovel, in her sack. It was arguably the proximate reason for Paul's headache a little while back.

For the next minutes, Paul shoveled like he had never shoveled before. He had, in fact, not. He was very bad at it; he was as poor a shoveler as he could possibly have been. But after a couple dozen piles of dirt and growth had been clumsily upturned, there was a twang – a hard thud that startled the shovel and its bearer into vibrating immobility.

"It must be met." Annette bent down to look. "You hit metal with the shove."

She stepped away as Paul, digging even more hotly, brought down a shower of more mud and sawgrass. There appeared, soon, a metal flatness about 18 inches below ground. He wiped away a final film of dirt. Etched into its center was the letter E. The piece of metal was about three-by-three feet and seemed impenetrable. Paul twanged and twanged at it with the shovel, but it wouldn't give way.

But the vibrations and jostling started to reveal hinges attached to one side of the square. It seemed to be a cover or door of some sort. Paul turned the shovel around and jammed the shaft under the side opposite from the hinges to get some leverage. With a grunt, he shouldered at the blade. The square of metal and the shovel complained together. After a few more grunts and pushes, though, the metal began to surrender.

"Can you see anything?" Paul asked with a groan.

The lid had lifted up about six or seven inches on its apparently rusted hinges. He held it up as high as possible while the woman lay down onto the ground and peered underneath. The last light of the sun slanted directly in.

"Big box," she said, squinting and twisting her head to get a good look down inside. "There are many, many boxes under here, all next to each other, and they are going off in every direct." Every *direction*. "It is very big down there, and on them they all have write."

"What does the writing say?" Paul squeaked out, feeling his grip about to give.

"It says, 'If lost, please return. Sentimental value only, thanks, L. Crass.'"

It was true. What his mother had written in that letter. Everything she had been telling him over the years but that he had dismissed as so much hogwash. Between the weight of the cover and the weight of the reality it revealed, Paul felt his muscles give.

"Look out!" he cried.

Annette moved back just as the shovel handle snapped and the lid smashed back down into place.

She looked up. On her face was the most pure, wide, face-wrinkling smile he had ever seen.

"Amaze," she said breathlessly. "Simply amaze."

Yes, Paul thought, definitely amazing.

Twilight had begun giving itself over to night, and the shovel was broken. There was nothing more to be done that night. They stepped over to a ledge jutting into the furrow.

"Now you talk," Annette said, "and tell Annette what it all mean."

They sat on the grass, now getting wet with evening dew. And Paul talked. Paul went on to unravel the entire account to her – including some of the parts that he did not still quite understand himself. He told her about his job as an IM in Rome; about the apparently nonsensical blathering of his mother that had been very sensical in the end; about Gaius Julius Caesar, a handcart and a trash chute; about the Opposition leadership and Mark Antony; and the letter from his mother (he pulled it out of his satchel, but it was too dark for her to read it).

"I still don't know how, but apparently Julius Caesar ended up with a piece of paper written by Spartacus that was meant to give clues to my mother. About the boxes under there."

As Paul told his account, he knew he must have sounded like his mother, rattling off implausible and seemingly disordered tales. He finished by telling the woman that Spartacus himself just might, in fact, have been his father.

"I can't know for sure whether he was," Paul said. "But I think it's true. I think Spartacus was my dad."

Annette had listened to it all without moving. She stood and went to get her travel sack. Paul winced as she brought it back.

She opened the sack and rooted around, pulling out a big bottle of sea-dark wine and three ham sandwiches.

"Do you know something ... " she interrupted herself in order to dig her teeth into the cork and jerk it out with her mouth – "the moment I saw you coming to the channel, I knew that Spartacus was your fath."

Paul allowed himself a smile.

"Same blue eyes, same red in your hair, even the same spirit in him and in you" – she swigged and passed the bottle over – "and it's not your fault that you're 85 percent smaller and don't have a muscle on your bod."

A blood orange moon had risen over the valley basin.

"What did you mean when you said you were waiting for me?" Paul asked. "When we first met."

"I saw the men Spartacus sent here when he was trapped by Crass. The ones who brought those boxes. All they told us was to wait, that we would be visited by one who would bring freedom if we wait. We didn't know what this meant, but I knew I had to trust to the fate. So every chance I had, I kept coming back to the vill. And when I saw you, I knew you were the one we were to wait for, you are that pers." That *person*.

Paul's face turned the color of the moon, and now it was Paul who laughed. Annette asked why.

"All those years," he said, "you and my mother were both waiting, separated by all these miles, for me to deliver a message."

Annette thought this very funny too.

Maybe the strangest aspect of all, Paul said, was the way the solution came together in the end. From the moment he had met the man, Julius Caesar had churned forth an unending collection of evidently disjointed commentary, sayings, theorems and observations. They filled space like an odorless gas, and Paul would have sworn he had not been paying them any heed. But just at the crucial moment, one of Caesar's half billion remarks had pierced through.

"It came to me that he'd been saying to solve a word game you need to get into the mind of the writer. That's how the answer that Spartacus meant for the crossword puzzler hit me." He finished the last of his sandwich. "I just think it's odd that it was Caesar who led me here. And got me to figure out that my father was talking about coming home to freedom."

"Now we will go to Donkey and lee," Annette declared after finishing off the wine. "We leave now and come back in the morn. You come to my farmhouse tonight and sleep long and dee."

"Long and deep," Paul said. "Yes, that would be nice, although – "

As they walked again through the village forum, a whinny could be heard in the woods beyond.

"Tell me, do you know what is in those box?" Annette asked.

Paul thought silently for a minute.

"A lot of money. At least I'm pretty sure. My mother talked about Licinius Crassus bringing down his riches. And I remember Caesar saying something about Crassus losing a lot of money during the Servile Wars."

Annette said she figured there were four or five dozen chests in the ground. The metal opening was made just big enough to lower them into a much larger cavity – and to eventually take them back up.

"But now what do you do?" Annette asked.

He knew what he wanted to do. He wanted to go find a puffy bed, sleep for fourteen hours and in the afternoon glance through the Want Ads (circling ones saying "No Travel Necessary") before finding a hot tub somewhere. He shook off the feeling.

"I assume there's no way to Philippi before tomorrow morning," he said. "I would have liked to go back to the Opposition camp with the news."

To Annette, this made no sense.

"It's too dangerous for you, and anyway, why would you want to help the Roman?"

"I have a couple of friends there who I don't want to see get hurt," Paul said. "I also have this feeling the other Romans I've been with – they call themselves the Opposition – they might be a little different than most the rest. I don't understand politics. But I think they might not be all bad. They apparently want to do sort of what's right. Although, there is one thing that I have been getting worried about."

"Is that rye?"

"I'm not sure about it," Paul said, "but I think they might all be nitwits."

Annette told Paul there was one good road back to Philippi, though it would almost certainly be filled with soldiers.

"But you let me look at those sandals of your," she said. "I have some tacks and fresh rope in my travel sac. You are a good run?"

"Yes," Paul answered quizzically, "I think I'm a good runner. Why?"

PATHWAY

A t times the best that can be said about a long, long night
is that – judging by the behavior of its predecessors – it
might end.

In the predawn dimness, Paul discerned the silhouette of dozens
of figures out in a field. They were at least half a mile away, all
engaged in some kind of activity. Two figures stood out particularly.

One looked big, to the point of having been probably issued,
when he was born, a building permit rather than a birth certificate;
the other featured a magnificent afro. If Paul had any run left in
him, he would have run in their direction. He didn't. He did
perform a very creditable stagger, however.

It had undeniably been a long, long night getting to the field, and
during those hours, Paul had come to learn the earnest fullness of
the word climb. Also of itchy.

In a donkey cart the night before, Paul had been taken a few
miles from the valley basin. Annette then pointed to an opening in
some thickets. An abandoned smuggler's trail, she said. The locals
had forged it a generation earlier to avoid the harsh Roman tariffs
along the coastal towns. It would arc northward of Antony's camp
and plop out near Philippi, she said.

That is, if the trail were still passable. The Roman governor had
found out about the arrangement years earlier and shut it down. But
the trail was the only way he could possibly make it back to the
Opposition camp if he insisted on getting there.

The first hour going actually seemed just fine, almost pleasing.
Paul set out as the rising light of the moon enameled the terrain in a
limpid platinum. Though scrubby and narrow, the path could be

seen. The land then began giving way. As he tried moving forward, he began to come to ridges, whorls, drop-offs, hogbacks, and streams. All of them skirmished among themselves for dominance of the land. Paul was the collateral damage. He could see the remnants of makeshift bridges and road structures from time to time. But an odd strut or trestle or rotted plank helped not at all. Paul spent more of the night finding purchase and clinging than moving forward. And then his only bit of help left him. The moon dropped away during the final hours of his trek.

But as the world around began to smolder with a dusty new light, he looked down to see his refurbished sandals still in two pieces and still moving, haltingly, along a discernible path, and, more crucially, a path that seemed to be ending into an openness.

Out in the field, Caesar was asking the mute something.

Paul wobbled toward the figures. He could see they were all picking berries or otherwise foraging. Caesar held something high over his head, almost reaching up to the mute's face. Though Paul could not make out his words, the tone of his voice suggested doubt or skepticism.

The mute, looking briefly away from Caesar, rolled his eyes. In doing so, he caught sight of Paul and pointed.

"My dear boy!" Caesar cried out, after following the point. "Paul, old sport, you are alive and – uh. Well ..."

They soon were all three pleased and smiling, and it was a cheerful reunion. The mute spread his arms, and Paul and Caesar found themselves hugged hard and long, their heads pushed toward two respective mute kidneys.

"Tell us of your adventures, my boy," Caesar said when the greetings finished. "It has been all dull here, as you can imagine. But good, honest work. We've been mainly on provisioning duties. I was just asking our friend here what kind of bean or grain this is. See, it's soft as if it has juice inside, and yet it's curved and dimpled with speckled skin. Incidentally, I do have to tell you, now that the issue of speckled skin has been raised, frankly, you do look a bit whiffled yourself. Have you had a bad time of it? Where have you been off to?"

Paul had forgotten about his skin. He started scraping at himself. Knowing nothing about flora and less about fauna, he could not say what leaves and creatures had scuttled over and brushed against him throughout the night. But he wished for some salve or ointment, regardless of its odor.

"I do have news," he said, running his right fingernails up his left arm.

The vibrato of a tuneful yet insistent signalman's horn interrupted. Though easy on the ear, the sound sent forth a message that Caesar and the other soldiers immediately understood.

"Call to quarters," Caesar said. "I'm afraid your news is going to have to wait."

Paul and the mute shrugged.

"We're being ordered to return to camp," Caesar said. "Without delay. It would appear some trouble is coming."

HOPES

The only difference appeared to be with the buttercream frosted torte. It had chopped nuts on it this time.

Other than that, it seemed to Paul that nothing about the war council of the Opposition leadership had changed from the moment he had left the morning before. Everyone sat in exactly the same chairs as when he had gone out on his reconnaissance mission. Everyone wore the exact same outfits, the same facial expressions – grim, it will be recalled – the same achromatic skin.

"We are most happy to see you well," Cassius said to Paul, in a muttering tone, as he slouched at the head of the table.

Paul had been ushered into the hat-shaped Command Tent shortly after getting back to camp. Behind him, positioned alone near the flap and tapping his left foot to an apparent song in his head, stood Caesar.

Since Italy, Caesar had not been spurned by the Opposition as much as he had been gradually overlooked. He had been evolving into a non-entity. His physical transformation had a lot to do with this. His color had toasted, he wore very little clothing and his hair had gone chaotic and big. On a certain level of understanding, even those who saw him every day had begun to believe the reports that Julius Caesar was probably dead.

"Forgive me," Cassius said wanly. It would not have been surprising to learn his head had just been pulled from a commercial-grade fruit dehydrator. He looked bedraggled, to say the least. "I am a little distracted here, as I think we all are. Events have not unfolded especially well recently. And now we have heard that some unusual movement is taking place over the ridge. You have news yourself, do you?"

"Yes, Senator," Paul said. "A report."

He began to recount what he had overheard from the search party the evening before, about Antony's troops being called in from the countryside and about preparations being made for an all-out assault on the Opposition camp that very morning. He also related everything he could remember about the immense size and vigor of Antony's camp, especially his impression that for every one of something in the Opposition site, Antony's fortress seemed to have fifteen or twenty.

As Paul finished, a silence fell in the tent, leaden and oppressive.

"I think there is one crucial question for us at this time," Bilbius Dilbo at last declared, after softly bringing down his gavel. "As meeting chair I should know the answer to this, but I am wondering whether this information should be first presented to our sub-committee on intelligence and then passed to the security task force, or is it the other way around?"

Another silence dropped in.

"This is likely to involve expenditures," Cicero finally suggested. "I think starting it in Ways and Means would be appropriate."

"Fellow senators," Cassius said, beginning to feel a stir of the old dash. "Have you heard what I just heard from our young friend? I think we would be best to order the quartermasters to distribute weaponry and call in our armor bearers, to begin to prepare ourselves for war."

A hand went up.

"The chair recognizes Pompilius Pulcher. Senator, you have the floor"

"I say again that this is all rubbish. Insufferable. I still do not understand why we must all be attired in the same manner simply because we might be going into some kind of battle. You all knew that I specifically had matching baldric and neck scarves embroidered with my name on them, shipped special from Florence."

The buttercream frosted torte with chopped nuts had been eaten by this point. Totovus nodded to the assistant camp prefect to bring in some kind of assortment platter.

"Point of order, Mr. Chairman." Cicero again. "With all due respect, we already had the garmenting vote. That matter is closed. We must respect the process. It was concerning enough that Cassius ordered the call-to-quarters signal without first securing our consensus. I hope we all realize that the bugler charges us 500 denarii per honk."

"Speaking of which," Diblo said, "from what I have seen, I am still not quite sure the men will fight at all unless they have some assurance of pay."

For some long while, quibbling and anecdotes filled the tent, punctuated by numerous gavel bangs.

In time, a centurion broke in. Saluting, he handed Cassius a note.

"Fellow senators." Cassius crumpled the paper after he read it. "Our young friend here was quite right, it seems, and I fear we've now delayed too long instead of listening to his words. Antony's forces are being seen massing all along the ridge, as well as to our north and to our south."

He sagged into his chair. Brutus put a comforting hand on his shoulder.

"How many troops does he have?" he asked tenderly. "Do we know?"

Fifty thousand maybe, Cassius said. Give or take. Possibly as many as seventy.

"Boffo!" Flavius Flavian piped up. "What are we all worried about? That shouldn't be a problem, right? We have twice that number, I'm sure. We'll be more impregnable than the city of Troy itself."

"By the count of our last muster," Cassius said, "and taking into account that we sent the majority of our legions to forage and scout this morning, we probably have in our camp right now a total of a handful."

"Oh," Flavian said. "I thought we had more."

The overtone of a bugle blast shot through: Boots-and-saddles, the signal call for everyone to equip and mount. The call blasted out three times, and none of these blasts possessed any melodic quality. It was all businesslike blare.

"That," Cicero said, pulling out his account book and pencil, "is going to cost us 1500 denarii."

Cassius rose.

"It is all moot anyway," he said. "All of this is moot. Let us be realistic. We now face an overwhelming onslaught, and our own troops will not fight unless they are to be paid. I fear we have no alternative but to wave the white and ask for mercy from Antony. We can expect none. But to do otherwise would be irresponsible and pointless. Without funds to pay our legions, we do not even have a chance."

Paul, until that moment, had not thought about what he would say or do about the buried chests. He coughed audibly and stepped forward.

"Yes, young man?" Cassius said weakly. "Have you more information for us?"

"Actually, yes I do. I figured something out when I was away and found something that might be useful, I think."

CASH

P aul, to the increasingly opened mouths of the Opposition leadership, told everything of the buried chests. He said he did not know how much money might be buried in the abandoned village, but it seemed to be box after box of it. All of it there in the ground, waiting to be taken.

Cassius walked to him and clasped his hands. His eyes glistened, and his mouth had found a way to make itself into an indisputable smile of joy.

"This," he said, turning to his fellow senators, "This, I believe, is the relief for which we have waited. Our young friend once again has proven himself among the great patriots. This is what the gods had in store for us. It has truly been said that to an encumbered army, hope is the reinforcement of a dozen legions. With this revelation, we can fight."

Paul did not know if he had done right. He did not know what Spartacus – his father – would have done. But unlike most other times in his life at such instances, he did not feel a rush of immediate second guessing.

Events moved quickly. Vigor displaced the murky mood of the tent. The flaps were fixed open as assistants and attendants came in and out with armor and livery, bustling along with message bearers who brought in reports of new troop movements. Commitments of pay and lavish bonuses were sent to the legions. And the bugle tootled signal after signal with Cicero not mentioning a word about the cost.

Paul and Caesar found a couple chairs to observe it all.

"There is one other thing I heard Antony say," Paul said. "He's giving orders for you to be eliminated during the attack."

"Oh, I expected that," said Caesar, waving a hand. "Let's just watch the show. Kind of exciting, isn't it? I used to love this type of stuff."

"Oh yes?"

"Gets the blood going. Fun to see again, in its own way. Speaking of fun, it sure is interesting the puzzler turned out to be a map of sorts after all, isn't it? And you applied the old trick I told you about, of getting into the writer's mind to find the solution. Very good, that. But you know, I'll tell you something, Paul. I'm not sure anything can save the day at this point."

Paul looked at Caesar with some surprise.

"Remember what I said back when I had that knife to your throat in the bakery?" Caesar said. "I know I can get a little talkative and go off track at times. But Caesar – that is, I – I may not be totally dull-witted. I know a thing or two about battles. Looking at the numbers and positioning, I hate to say it, but even with a zillion dollars, everyone here is pretty done in."

Paul said he was sorry to hear this.

"I've had some time to do some thinking lately, and this air and exercise have done me good." Caesar spoke breezily. "In the end, the Antonys will win. Of course, I've always liked to believe that if you dream big enough, there is nothing that isn't impossible to accomplish. But frankly, whether it's him or someone after him, the Republic's already pretty kaput. I'm not sure if we deserve a republic anymore anyway."

Paul knew nothing about military tactics or the ends of republics but assumed Caesar might.

"Having a bit of power is terrific fun," Caesar continued, "don't get me wrong. But I'm liking my new life. I hang around with a great group of guys, I'm enjoying the outdoors, I've dropped 15 pounds. Yes, I suppose I do miss my favorite carpet slippers back in Rome, but that's about all. I was talking with my bunkmate and a couple other of his friends. We're thinking of heading out west. Start an avocado ranch when this is all over. Who knows, maybe I'll even find real love out there. You should join us, my boy. I just hope not too many people get hurt today."

The Opposition senators, as Caesar spoke, scurried more quickly and more energetically.

"I'm not sure all this fighting is all that healthy either," Caesar said. "I've come to like my bunkmate and his cronies more. The camping part of it all is good, but the slashing part, once a battle starts, gets pretty ugly."

Cassius came by at this point.

"How are you, my old friend?" Caesar asked. "You look like you might want to take some time off after all this."

Cassius let out a long, steady wheeze of a sigh. It was a sigh, if his mouth had been affixed to a hose, that would have inflated a dirigible.

"Only the gods know how this day shall end," said Cassius. "But I fear for the future, even with the new hope our young friend has delivered."

Behind him, the tumult continued. An oversized situation map was brought in and laid out on the table. A half dozen women reservists followed it in, carrying boxes of scale army figures and long poles to move the pieces around. Flavian yapped when his torso armor got strapped on too tightly, while Pompilius Pulcher cursed about chafing. Off to the side, Totovus could be seen pulling little candles from a box, then going to whisper something into the ears of the guards at the tent entrances.

Oblivious to this, Cassius shook his head.

"I've been thinking lately. We stand and speechify of the ancient Republic, but is it all just fine words? Do we really think of each other as equals? It occurs to me, young man, that I do not even know your name."

"Paul," Paul was about to say, but he didn't get the chance.

"You know something else," Cassius announced, "if you can, young man, I think you should get as far from Rome as possible."

In the background, a box of $1/56^{th}$-size red army figures tumbled off the table. Not noticing, Bilbius Dilbo stepped on a cohort, whooped, and crashed down onto the floor.

A messenger approached Cassius with the latest word: Many of the Opposition troops had returned to the camp but most still remained out in the fields.

"That is one fact that particularly irks me about all this," Cassius told Paul and Caesar. "Antony seemed to know that this was the morning when we were sending out large numbers of skirmishers and foraging parties. He's been one step ahead of us the whole time."

That reminded Paul of something – something he felt a little abashed that he hadn't thought to mention earlier. He had one more piece of news to impart. He told Cassius what else he heard from Antony: Someone in the Opposition leadership had been passing on information. There was a spy in the tent.

The face of Cassius for the past minutes had taken on an unusually soft quality. Now it took on red. He was fully back in the present, and he was fully Cassius again. He stood and turned around.

"Senators!" All the sound in the tent snapped off, and the room turned his way. "I have very troubling information to report. I ask that no one be allowed to leave this place. Our young friend has confirmed that there is in our midst a traitor. And frankly, I believe I know who it is. A man I have suspected from the beginning."

The Outside Communications Consultant had been unusually silent during the meeting. His only comment had been to say he never thought much of the puzzler as an advertising device. Cassius began to point a finger at the man.

Exactly that second, the tent flaps went down and all the oil lamps went out. The space became entirely dark. For a good while, no one moved or spoke. Then a tiny array of flickering appeared off in the back.

From above this new light source came a voice. A singing voice.

"Happy birthday to you! Happy birthday to you! Happy birthday, dear Cassius, hap –"

The voice noted a lack of expected accompaniment. It stopped singing.

"Open up the flaps and relight the lamps," ordered Cassius.

When light had been restored, Totovus was seen at the back of the tent. He was in possession of both a lemon sheet cake and a look of befuddlement.

"It is your birthday today, isn't it?" he asked Cassius.

Everyone looked to the seat where The Outside Communications Consultant had been. And still was. He hadn't moved. It looked like everyone else had remained in place, too.

But then it became apparent that someone was in fact missing. Someone who had been even more silent lately than The Outside Communications Consultant.

"Livius the Younger," Cassius said. "He's gone."

SHINY

Having already recounted the sequence of close calls, narrow escapes and averted disasters that Paul faced since that day he was sent as an IM to the house of Julius Caesar back in Rome, and having spoken of the din of emotion that attended him during these activities, it may be close to anticlimactic to report on a heap of buried boxes nearly stolen and a frightful sword fight with Caesar's former house servant.

In the interest of historical completeness, however, let us see this narrative through:

Soldiers were dispatched immediately from the Command Tent to try to apprehend Livius the Younger. Meanwhile preparations for the coming battle continued apace. The Opposition leadership kept struggling to strap on its fighting gear.

The women reservists placed their small army figures onto the big situation map, using their poles to shift and push the miniatures as reconnaissance information came in. When they ran out of red pieces, they had make do with birthday candles, and paper clips painted red. Most of the boxes filled with all the oatmeal-colored figures remained taped shut, however. (The color assignments for each army – red for Antony, oatmeal for the Opposition – had been decided two days earlier by an 11-4-2 vote.)

"I have a thought," said Caesar.

He and Paul had continued watching all this from off to the side. "Oh?"

Caesar waved for Cassius to come over again. He complimented him on his smart body armor and shiny shoulder plates.

"Thank you, kind Caesar," said Cassius.

"It has occurred to me that the treasure we are all counting on," Caesar said, "may not be safe. Livius the Younger, unless he his caught, is undoubtedly making his way to Antony's camp and will report the find. Antony undoubtedly will send troops to snap it up before you can send anyone there."

Cassius nodded.

"I think our young friend here should be sent back immediately to cover up the hole," Caesar offered, "to keep it hidden until you can spare men to retrieve everything in there. What think you?"

Cassius immediately thought it a good idea.

"I'll need some help, though," Paul said. "Maybe Caesar and the mute can come with?"

Some negotiations were required at this point. Caesar resisted going himself. He said his place was with his new comrades and the soldiery of Rome. But Paul said he would go only if Caesar went. Caesar finally relented. They would go together, with the mute.

"Will you do us one other favor?" Cassius asked Paul. "Do you have a little space in that satchel of yours?"

Cassius called the Opposition to order. After getting their attention, he asked if anyone in the tent had a small memento to be taken away. He had in mind perhaps an ancestral ring, a short message for a loved one or another little remembrance – a token, should the battle go badly. The Opposition leadership, however, did not take the hint and, after a thirty five minute discussion, voted to include Flavian's scrapbooking collection, made up mainly of approved meeting minutes, authorized reports and favorable newspaper clippings.

As the three left the tent – Paul, Caesar, mute – Cassius attempted a maneuver he never had tried in his life with any other human. The hug. He came up with a stiff embrace that managed to perfectly fuse the melancholy with the inept. But the three went along with it and hugged him in return.

When they reached the trailhead of the smuggler's route, they turned round. The gates of the Opposition camp had been opening and a fair number of cohorts marched out. Facing them on three sides of the camp waited a much larger number of legions holding the standards of Antony. It did not look good.

"That was awfully sporting of Cassius," Caesar said to Paul. "I'm sure he agreed to send you back in order to protect you from the battle as much as the treasure. I think he's rather fond of you. I only wish you didn't insist I go, too. That was awfully shifty."

"Two can play at the same game, O Caesar," Paul said. "Remember, you're the one who first suggested I be sent away in the first place."

"And it was beyond decent for you to come back to the camp with all your news. I've known no soldier with more pluck."

The trek back over the smuggler's trail took all day and another night. The mute proved to be agile on crags and gorges, but Caesar needed a little help. More than once, someone had to shoulder his backside up an incline or give him a pull. Paul could not figure out how, but at one point, Caesar got his head stuck inside a cactus. It took the better part of a half hour to extricate it.

Paul had not slept for two days by the time the bluff over the village of Spartacus village came to view. Though tired and aching, he felt a bolt of life.

"Licinius Crassus," Caesar said, as they looked to the white outlines below. "A true nincompoop. I remember back then when he announced he was sending an army to destroy this place. We all thought it was out of spite against Spartacus, but he must have heard his stolen treasure was hidden down there."

"But he came away empty," Paul remarked. "You Romans ..." – understand, Paul had never used a phrase like "you Romans" before, having never really thought of himself as a Roman or as not a Roman but only as himself, and he spoke these words now with no rancor or intent to mark distinctions – "you Romans sometimes go through a lot of trouble and don't see the things you crushed right under foot."

"If it makes you feel better," said Caesar, "just after he did this, Licinius Crassus led another military campaign in the East. He wanted to steal the riches of King Orodes. It did not go well. I remember I was in the Senate the day an express mail package arrived from the Parthian Empire. It had a label on it. 'Anything that fits in box, one flat rate.' The head of Licinius Crassus, as it happened, fit."

As they studied the area more carefully, the early morning sun illumined a shimmering square, like a polished mirror, in the basin below.

"That's got to be the cover of the hole," Paul said. "It's surprising it's reflecting that much, though. It was actually pretty rusted out."

The reason for this became evident after they had worked their way down to the valley basin and over to the furrow.

The hatch had been lifted wide open.

It stood at almost a 90 degree angle. Someone, apparently, had been there. The underside of the covering had not oxidized over the years; it glowed with the radiance of dawn. The contents in the hole below were entirely exposed. The three approached cautiously, silently scanning the area. Paul noticed something else dissonant. A freshly cut tree branch lay a couple feet from the mouth. It was blackened on one end.

"Still warm," Caesar said, tapping at the char. "Someone was using it very recently as a torch. Possibly to look into the hole there."

It was agreed that the Caesar and the mute would start walking in corkscrew courses away from the hole, looking for any more indications of activity. Paul would wait by the hole and keep watch.

"Shout if you see absolutely anything at all," Caesar said to the mute as he started jaunting off.

The mute looked at Paul and shrugged.

Paul stalked up and down the furrow three or four times but saw nothing else unusual. Going back to the opening, he crouched down. Earlier the sun had not bothered to chuck much light into the pit. Now it had risen enough to begin to shine on the contents down below. It was the first time Paul actually had been able to look inside.

Annette had been right. Clearly a very large number of boxes had been stowed underneath. Paul could make out the writing on them, announcing their ownership of Licinius Crassus.

On top of one of them, near the opening, he noticed a narrow bottle lying on its side. It was just within Paul's reach.

Paul reached.

The bottle was of a glazed material; a foot or so long and a few inches wide. Paul dug at the leather strapping that secured the lid. There was a letter inside. It was gray and brittle but still supple enough to be unrolled. Paul recognized the handwriting as soon as he began opening it: It was the same handwriting as the puzzler. He took a deep breath before sitting down.

Good friend (for friend I expect you are) –

I hope that in some way you came to be here from my wife – my cherished wife Ellia, who time and fate let me love only too briefly. But since I do not know who you are or what you know, I will offer you an explanation.

I am Spartacus. I am now a free man living among free people. I write to you from the army camp of fellow ex-slaves fighting for ourselves.

These chests you see here once belonged to the Roman Senator Licinius Crassus. A real wad if ever there was one, from everything I've heard. My dearest Ellia told me of these chests. She escaped from this Crassus, her master, and found her way to our rebel camp. She told me of the cartloads of valuables that Licinius Crassus had been bringing down from Rome to the fortification where he has stationed himself, hard against our army. We organized a raid on the laden trains of his, and struck it lucky. There are enough coins in these chests to build a new empire, I think.

But it is too late for us here and now to use these monies. The power of Rome will be too great. For now. The army of Crassus will almost certainly attack tomorrow, and we do not have the weapons or positioning to fight back. So I am asking four or five of my most trusted countrymen to spirit these treasures out of our camp tonight and to hide them in a safe place until the time is right.

I believe I have an unborn child who is being taken away from our camp in safety right now, in the womb of Ellia. For that child and for all who deserve freedom (that is to say, for all good people) use this treasure and win a victory for liberty.

Paul put the letter gently on the ground. He could not read the last lines clearly, for the wetness in his eyes.

When he looked up, his eyes still glistening and the sun at his face, he could discern a human figure. He blinked repeatedly and squinted. The person there – now approaching – was not, as he first imagined, Julius Caesar.

It was the former house-slave of Julius Caesar, a man who Paul had last seen serving Mark Antony.

When faced by an incongruity our minds often require a few moments to make sense of it. Paul naturally did not expect to find the house-slave Nimbus coming toward him. What is more, on the other occasions when he had seen the man he held something along the lines of a salver with a couple cocktails on it. Not an 18-inch machete.

Nimbus brandished a very large and very sharp weapon, and he was moving very quickly in Paul's direction. This was enough to freeze Paul. Making matters even more alarming, his mind experienced a second convulsion at that exact instance. Far in the distance, he caught sight of the mute also sprinting in his direction.

It almost sounded like the mute was shouting something, and shouting it with great emphasis.

Something about a total defeat.

PHALANX

P aul, faltering at the sights and sounds coming at him, fell on his back. Two or three steps away and closing fast, Nimbus began to raise the machete. The blade shimmered in the sunlight, the man's eyes enlarged. In the last second, instinct took over: Paul rolled away to evade a looming slash. He cycled himself 360 degrees in another second.

Yet when he looked wincingly up again, he did not see a slashing machete.

He instead watched a departing Nimbus.

Caesar's ex-servant had stepped right past him and kept on striding. Paul gyrated himself into a crouch and saw, now three feet beyond, the withdrawing rearward of Nimbus. That in itself was odd. But three feet past this rearward stood an immense Roman soldier facing the frontward of Nimbus.

The two – Nimbus and the soldier – were inches apart from each other staring with weapons raised. Paul, it seems, had been just an object in the middle of the two.

Above his head the soldier held a gladius, the long two-edged tapered sword of the Roman army. Paul recognized the man as the trooper who had first captured him near Antony's camp and had nearly nabbed him again at this very spot two mornings before. The one who had been dangling Paul's sandals on his oversize fingers.

Paul goggled. For half a minute the two adversaries silently sized each other up. As he sized up the confrontation himself, frozen, all Paul could feel certain about was that the little Nimbus would not last long when action commenced. It was David versus Goliath, if David had spent a lifetime folding linen and answering the doorbell.

Paul could not see the expression on Nimbus's face, but the soldier at last beamed hungrily as he stared down into Caesar's former servant. He gave his gladius a swashbuckling swirl up in the air, as if it were a decorative highball toothpick he was fixing to plug into a maraschino cherry.

But just as the soldier went to land his downward thrust, a fully unexpected interruption broke his concentration.

"We shall have no fighting today!"

It was a voice. A voice both very familiar and yet a little alien. It was the voice of Julius Caesar – puffed; and intoning.

"Close ranks, by the order of Caesar!" It was the old Caesar, the Caesar of Rome, of elocution and majestic command, coming up to the furrow.

The soldier froze again. He did so with his eyes forward, as he had been instructed to do reflexively at boot camp. He had come impulsively to attention.

Nimbus saw his opportunity. Having sized the man up, and then continuing up, followed by still more up, and ending up with an addition of up, he had apparently guessed even his machete would probably do little harm. He instead dropped his weapon and at the same time dropped his own self onto the ground, crouching in front of his immensely larger opponent. Firmly hugging the soldier's enormous right calf to his slight self, he gave the most powerful yank he could.

For half a precarious minute, the outcome remained at issue. Trying to keep his balance, the soldier half spun and half kicked. He shimmied, he lindy hopped, he was forced into a brief hokey pokey, all the time trying to steady his left leg while Nimbus pulled and heaved on the right.

In the end, the soldier went tumbling backward. He grunted as his back hit the ground.

He tried to shake it off as quickly as possible, slapping his face and standing himself back up.

By then, circumstances had changed.

The soldier was no longer facing only a little creature. He instead faced an odd and assorted phalanx. It was comprised of the original smallish house servant, but along with him was now a creature that looked strangely like a Julius Caesar that had gone feral, and, even more troublingly, a new participant, one nearly as large as himself.

The mute had come back. He was standing next to Nimbus and Caesar, the three of them staring down the soldier.

The soldier made his decision quickly. He bolted, quickly.

"I think I recognized the blighter," Caesar remarked. Caesar had already deflated himself as the soldier ran into the background, and he offered his commentary mundanely and to no one in particular. "Served at the Battle of Arminium. As I recall, I had to discipline him for pilfering from petty funds. A repulsive sort. I think he might have been caught buggering the legion's mascot, too."

By the time Caesar finished recounting the man's military record, the soldier had gotten half way up the bluff.

"I didn't expect to use that speechifying voice of mine ever again," Caesar said, "but it did come in handy there, didn't it? I figured it might get the attention of even a disreputable veteran like him."

There was a time when such an abrupt series of events would have left Paul's head aswim. These types of things had been getting fairly commonplace, however. He relaxed himself into the grass to let his heart slow down.

Caesar turned to his former servant.

"Nimbus," Caesar said, "where are my manners? It's very nice to see you again."

He spoke as if coming across one's ex-slave wielding a large weapon in the middle of a Thracian valley counted as routine.

Nimbus had been daubing at his forehead with a handkerchief and smoothing out his slightly rumpled tunic.

"I feel quite the same, Caesar," he reported evenly. "I had heard rumors that you had been transformed into pure spirit – the ghost of Caesar, it was said – and other reports of your ongoing survival. I am pleased to find the latter to be more accurate."

"Have you been well since we last saw each other?"

"I have very few complaints. Thank you for asking, mighty Caesar. I was regrettably taken with no choice into the service of Mark Antony after your unfortunate disappearance, but one must accept one's station, I believe. Incidentally, I must thank you deeply for saving my life just now."

"Ah. So Mark Antony got his hands on you. Yes, that could not have been a thrill. I've come more and more to realize Antony is quite an ass and probably always has been."

"Just so, great Caesar. And now, if you will permit me, I suggest we best leave catching up and comment for a later time, though certainly there will be call for much explanation among us all at some point. Perhaps now we might wish to take some immediate action, in light of recent occurrences."

Though not as wrenched with confusion as he might have been in the past, Paul – after he caught his breath – did begin to feel an appreciable curiosity about a number of things. One circumstance in particularly came to mind. It was something that in the first excitement of the encounter he had forgotten.

"Hey." He lifted himself from the ground and went over to the mute, who had also been watching the dialog between Caesar and Nimbus. "Did you just say something?"

The mute looked down at Paul and shrugged.

"There was a lot going on just now," Paul said, "but it just occurred to me that I could swear I heard you saying something."

"Nope," the mute said. "I've just been standing here listening."

"Oh, okay. I guess I must have gotten confused in all the excitement. Sorry about that."

Nimbus stepped over to Paul and nodded an acknowledgement.

"Master Paul, I am sorry we were not able to talk during our earlier encounters over the past weeks. It appears you have acquitted yourself very well and likely never did need the safeguarding that it had once seemed you might. There is perhaps much else we can illuminate to each other, when the time is opportune."

Paul had no idea what the man was getting at.

"I'm guessing we all feel the same," Caesar affirmed, "about the need to figure out what's been going on."

Everyone indeed did. They all had the desire to get and give explanations to each other. It was as if they all needed to figure out how to settle up the tab after an evening in a tavern, when one person had ordered top shelf drinks, another had only a diet soda pop and the third hadn't touched the nacho plate.

"But as I say," Nimbus said, "I do recommend focusing on action right now, with a commitment to full and frank discussion later. We can expect many more soldiers from Antony's camp to be here fairly soon."

"Wait!" Paul exclaimed. He turned back to the mute. "You just said something again. Just now. You really *can* talk."

The mute shrugged again. He didn't say anything for a minute, instead looking around a little absently, letting his eyes fill up and giving off three or four big breaths.

"I'm not sure what hurt more all this time," he finally said, "people thinking because you're a mute that you're either stupid or that you have no feelings. I'm not deaf. And being tall and burly like this brings out even more stereotypes. I'm the big, dumb slave. And I get that the word dumb has more than one meaning. It hasn't been easy keeping my mouth shut all these years. And try finding love in this condition. Impossible, believe me. Who's going to love a giant mute? Honestly, having my arm around a man dressed as a bride is the closest I've come. What could that possibly say about me? You know something, though, it's good to finally start getting this all out."

He spoke with a perfectly round baritone timbre. It indeed seemed a good deal had been piling up on his mind over the years, all of which he had developed an overstuffed urge to talk about. Caesar came over, reached high up and patted him on the back.

"You have a wonderful speaking voice, especially for a mute," Caesar said. "You could have been an orator or a politician, if you were into that type of thing."

The mute thanked Caesar for the kind words. He began to explain that he actually had been once in politics. He was Village Clerk of a medium-sized coastal town up in the northwest. In fact, he had been thinking of running for assemblyman when he was captured by Germanic slave traders. He'd been suffering strep throat that day and decided to just keep rolling with it. He figured playing the part of a mute might be more prudent for a slave, so from then on he just kept his mouth permanently shut. Brutus had bought him shortly after that.

"But what was it that you said?" Paul interrupted. "When you were running down the bluff. You were shouting something."

"Yes, that," said the mute – who, by the way, told everyone he had a name: Frank Littleton, but it was alright to call him Little Frankie, the ironic label he had been given in grade school. "I ran into a couple locals on the road. The battle is over. Antony won completely. The Opposition is entirely wiped out or captured."

"The poor blokes," said Caesar, speaking for everyone. "It's a real shame."

"That's why I decided to start talking again, honestly," Little Frankie offered soberly. "I actually rather liked Brutus, despite everything. But with him unfortunately finished there really is no reason to keep up the act of not being able to talk, is there?"

Caesar offered a sympathetic nod.

"I am sorry if I may be sounding importunate about the value of deeds over conversation just now," Nimbus at last said. "But I think this latest information on the adverse conclusion of the battle only further emphasizes our need for swiftness. If there indeed is large treasure here that could be acquired, perhaps we best focus on that. And then we should probably get on our way very quickly."

In the rush of attacks, unexpected reunions and a mute beginning to tell his story, everyone had quite forgotten about the reason they were all there in the first place.

"The problem is how could we possibly take all that?" Caesar pointed to the open hole. "And where would we go with it and how would we get there?"

Paul gave these questions some thought. They were good questions.

"I might know somebody," he said. "I have a feeling she might be willing to help us out. And then, yes, I'd be interested in getting some questions answered to everything else that's been going on."

YOINK

Annette was pleased to see Paul. And, yes, she would be happy to help out.

"Let me first fix you a raisin bagel with a smear of cream chee," she said. "And how are those sandals holding up – they seem like they're pretty resil." Pretty *resilient*. "You just came all the way here from the vill?"

The run had taken almost an hour. A couple new thoughts had accompanied Paul on the way; about Antony's troops still prowling about, about getting his mother out of Rome if possible.

"You said you might need some equip?" Annette asked as she rooted around the icebox. "We'll go to the barn and get some things, no prob."

Paul had explained to her the situation back in the Spartacus village, about Caesar, Nimbus and the mute and, most pointedly, about the fact that Antony's armies would be almost certainly coming back.

"The other issue is getting away from there even if we get all those boxes out," he said. "We'll need to move fast and far."

Annette came back to the table and set out a spread.

"Where do you want to be go?" she asked.

Well, Paul said: Away. In the opposite direction of Antony's victorious legions. Annette thought about this a minute. There was a trunk road not too far off they could all take, leading farther west. There were some towns that way that might prove helpful.

"I'll just need to get Donkey some water and foo," she said. "A journey like this is going to be work, but it's one you can hand. Who knows, maybe I'll join your little groo." Can *handle* and your little *group.*

When they got back down into the basin of the Spartacus village, Nimbus and the mute – that is, Little Frankie – were sitting on a temple foundation, lost in animated conversation together. They apparently had hit it off nicely. In the distance, Julius Caesar was trying to teach himself how to do the cartwheel.

"Gentlemen," called Paul, "meet Annette. She is going to help get us packed and on our way."

Stepping to the mouth of the hole, Paul looked down with surprise at what he found. Everything inside remained untouched, just as it had been when he left to find Annette's house. No one had done any work at all with the boxes. Or had they opened one up and found it empty? It seemed to him half of them could have been out by this time.

Caesar spun over (doing three nearly complete body rotations and sticking one full tuck jump in the process) and looked expectantly at Paul.

"Well?" said Caesar, with a grin, between deep breaths.

"Uh, well, what?" Paul asked. He was too polite to speak up, but he did wonder why nothing at all had been done.

"We've been dying for you to get back," Caesar said. "We talked about it after you left and decided we didn't have the right to get at the stuff ourselves. Whatever is in those boxes is really yours, Paul. It's all yours. You should be the one to open up the first box and see what's inside."

The others had gathered around, too. They all beamed.

"Know something?" Paul declared. "I think there's been enough saving of each other's lives and helping out – not to mention accidentally getting each other almost killed – to say these don't belong to me, but to *us.*"

The chests were not quite as big as expected nor were there quite as many of them. But they were heavy. And, if the contents of the first one ended up being repeated in the others, they were all jammed to the top with big shiny coins.

"Specially struck," said Nimbus, running his finger over one. "I believe Licinius Crassus received permission to mint these from the captured booty of his Carthage campaign. They are, if I'm not mistaken, 22 to 24 karat gold and considered to be, in monetary parlance, full bodied."

"Except for having the ugly mug of Crassus on them, they're kind of pretty," Caesar remarked, taking hold of it. "I haven't seen one of these since the consulship of Lupus Sentilicus."

Annette, Paul and Little Frankie owed that they had not seen one of them since ever. It was Little Frankie who asked Nimbus how much they might be worth.

"That is not a simple question. Taking into account today's currency debasement and the presumed inflation that generally follows a domestic disturbance" – Nimbus wrote some numbers in the air as he talked, doing a good deal of carrying – "just a single one of these coins, I would estimate conservatively, would buy, to use one example, let us say, dinner in Rome."

"Oh," said Annette, slightly deflated, "one of these will buy someone a din. That's at least better than nothin."

The others shared her disappointment. It seemed to them offhand like it would add up to a lot of money but not necessarily the colossal amount they had expected or secretly hoped for.

"At least it should be enough to last us all awhile," Little Frankie said, "although who knows where we could go at this point."

Nimbus continued air calculating before finishing his sentence: "... dinner in Rome for approximately 62 percent of the city population."

Human beings, it is known, are capable of generating many kinds of silences. There are brooding silences and huffy silences, the silence of a sleeping child and the silence brought on because of overestimating how much sauerkraut you thought you could handle in one sitting. At that instant, a more rare variety of silence issued forth in the furrow of the basin of the village of Spartacus. It was a robust, radiant and sparkling silence. It was a silence that would have left any other silence passing by absolutely speechless. It was the silence of the gobsmacked.

It lingered. Quietly, Nimbus put the coin back on top of the first opened chest. Then soundlessly, everyone went about their work. The only noise to be heard were those of chests being examined (and all found fully gold filled), being heaved up and being stacked. For a good long time, no one spoke. They moved about half zombified.

When they did get to talking again, it was mostly pleasantries. Bandying the banal can often give us time before we need to brave thinking about the sublime. It's a way of stalling big thoughts from emerging. For this reason, we talk about the humidity at funerals and swap recipes before appearing on a game show.

Annette and Paul discussed more of the stories of Spartacus. Little Frankie, who hadn't used his voice in 20 years, opined on children who chatter too much. Nimbus told Caesar his new rustic look suited him well, while Caesar talked about whether the marmoset makes a good house pet or not.

At last, in the late afternoon, using a makeshift block-and-tackle system, the chests had all been pulled from the hole, dragged across the basin and lifted up on to the wagon atop the bluff.

"Now what?" said Caesar.

"There is a westward trunk road in a few mile," Annette said, "The people along the coast can be trusted, I promise you, and with this money, we will be able to get go."

"How long would it take us to arrive thence?" asked Nimbus.

"With the weight on this wagon, we would not get there before the sun set. But I do know a safe lay for us to spend the eve."

Everyone nodded and got to moving again.

They camped that night in a grove, one that Annette pointed them to. It was situated a half day's journey from the village of Spartacus and then a half mile off the trunk road. The donkey and wagon had been pulled out of sight off the road. Kindling was collected and food taken from Annette's travel sack.

Paul had heard the haphazard whirr and beeps and undulating skirl of a few forest insects before; this night he heard a symphonic bug score. The group all sat around a cautious fire.

The expedition had started out successfully but not without anxiety. Paul had sat in the back of the wagon. His task was to keep an eye out for any soldiers that might be coming from behind. But with his lack of sleep and the metronomic rhythm of the pitching wagon, he could barely keep an eye even open. Once or twice he had felt himself oozing into a half sleep and at those moments could not be sure whether he imagined or actually saw mounted soldiers down the road.

Around the fire in the campsite, the struggle to stay awake became even more difficult.

"We will need to go far," he heard, through a sluggish haze, Caesar tell the group. "Antony will try to eliminate all of us, to make sure history tells the whole story of these times the way he wants it to, if for no other reason. And obviously he will want all this gold, too. My only concern is how far we'll need to go to escape the grab of Rome. It's got long fingers now. I'm afraid part of that is my own fault."

Paul faded to sleep briefly, and a rush of images trotted through his mind: The face of the Shift Supervisor, waves of sand, a triumphal arch in Rome, plucked turkeys hanging in a smokehouse, an endless wilderness of trees and grass he did not recognize. He woke up to the sound of voices having suddenly stopped. Everyone had caught their breath as they listened to the clatter of a cohort passing down the trunk road in the distance.

After it went by, Paul felt himself drop into another nap. When he awoke the next time it was to the smell of burnt marshmallows and the voice of Nimbus.

"That is how I made my way to the village today," Nimbus was explaining. "The traitor, this Livius the Younger, showed up bedraggled this morning before Antony. He told the story of the secret treasure. Antony seemed more interested in the battle at hand. I could see, however, the eyes of one particular soldier light up as Livius the Younger spoke. I knew that that soldier had been to the village the day before as part of a search party and that he had found the sandals of our young friend Paul. So when he removed himself quietly out of the camp, I, after procuring a rather unwieldy machete, managed to follow him. I knew then that I was about to find the solution to very long search of my own, one I shall perhaps tell of later. As I arrived at the hole, I saw this soldier lifting his gladius behind our unaware young friend, and that is when I went at him with my machete."

Paul realized he hadn't shown his appreciation to Nimbus for saving his life back in the village. He mumbled a thank you before fading off again.

When he jerked awake once more, there was a turkey kabob under his nose.

"Have some," Little Frankie whispered in his ear. "Then you sleep a lot. And tomorrow, Caesar says, we'll hold a meeting to decide what we do next."

Paul slowly opened his mouth and bit into a cube of meat.

"Yes, meeting," he said in a stupor between chews. "Just promise, no points of order or motions for cloture."

And he closed his eyes again for the rest of the night.

CONVERGE

Every meeting throughout the rest of history on every continent should be held in a murmuring woodland around 9:30 in the morning right after everyone's had a long, long sleep and a breakfast of three farm-fresh fried eggs, a big coffee, back bacon, sliced mango, and icy spring water.

That – at least it seemed to Paul – might be the secret to a successful result.

Sitting on rocks and logs around smoldering ash, in the scope of thirty-five minutes the travelers scoped out the future they intended for themselves.

"If it is not presumptuous," Nimbus said when they finished, "may I summarize what we have decided?"

Heads nodded; Annette passed around a plate of muffins.

"With the complete victory of Mark Antony, we all understand that we cannot – nor is it our wish – to remain in lands controlled by Rome. A few hours travel from now, we shall come upon the coastal town of Thessaki. We will ask for help of the people of Thessaki to convey our newfound wealth far away. Our ersatz mute friend Frank Littleton, aka Little Frankie, as well as Julius Caesar, are familiar with the lands and peoples far north and west, outside the boundaries of current Roman control. We shall aim ourselves there for the time being, working through the details as we go."

Another round of nods indicated consensus. With that, camp was broken, and in a short while, the donkey began pulling west, yanking five people and a whole lot of money.

In the town of Thessaki, seventeen volunteers would sign up for the odyssey almost without asking a single question. Annette rode the wagon straight up to the town, saying its contents would be perfectly safe with the inhabitants. Indeed, everyone there not only greeted her cheerfully but looked like her and talked like her.

Paul had never seen a place like it. The town had been built almost at 90 degrees on a precarious escarpment overlooking the sea, each building virtually stacked on top of the next. It looked insecure, to say the least, as if at any moment it could topple into the Aegean. If someone went to return a book to a neighbor up high, Paul thought, it would be unsurprising if they were required to take a bag of flour back down to avoid upsetting the town's uncertain balance. Paul walked on tiptoe the first night.

In the main tavern that night, a building that hung atop the local novelties shop, Annette laid out the plan to those who came to listen. Nimbus again summarized.

"If you come with us, you will be more than provided for. We will live equally and freely. We will go far away from any Roman governor or legion, and we will have the ability to build our own lives."

After Annette had written down the names of those who said they wanted to join, Paul asked her if she knew of a way he could get a message through to Rome. He wanted to see if he could find any way to get his mother out and meet up with her.

Next morning, Annette led Paul to the pier, leading him down a street that came off less as a road than a ladder. The captain astride a diffident skiff said he would make the arrangements to get a message through over the sea and to his mother in Rome if they could come to an agreeable cost arrangement.

This might have been an obstacle to Paul's plan. One of the bigger problems in those first days of the journey turned out to be making change. Try paying for a packet of razor blade refills with the kind of coin more commonly used to buy Triple AAA sports team franchises, and you'll get the idea. Nimbus had worked discreetly with the local banker on some mutually acceptable exchange rates.

Paul's message itself was short. He thought it would be prudent not to write too much. He simply put down a date in the future, a location and, at the bottom, a single line: "Come meet the son of Spartacus."

Caesar had suggested the location, a secure little lodge in the Alps where he thought Paul and his mother could safely rendezvous. It would be a few week journey from Thessaki and accessible from Rome, assuming the message could be gotten through to her and his mother would be willing and able.

"You know," Paul said to Annette as they ascended back up through town, "that is the first time I actually sent a message myself."

In the tavern that night, Paul got half drunk on Greek wine. Surrounded by cackling of the villagers and his fellow travelers and a warm fire, he looked around and thought, for a minute, he could settle in Thessaki. He sat back and smiled.

Nine or ten Roman soldiers erupted through entrance. Their sudden presence brought with them one of the mainstream sorts of human silence we all experience from time to time: The silence of the buzzkill. They dropped themselves down at a table in the center of the tavern. They then began to speak with obvious voices, having presumably been ordered to be overheard around town.

"Yes," said one in a stilted and overly voluble tone that no amount of acting lessons would have made seem natural. "I am told by the centurion of my unit that there is a large reward for anyone who provides information about that supposed treasure and those who took it."

"Oh?" another vocalized in mock surprise, as if doing a script reading. "That is interesting you would say such a thing. Because I had heard that there will be great punishment for anyone that has information but does not provide it to the Roman command. There is a high price on the heads of those who stole that treasure."

The donkey and his newest companions left Thessaki early the next morning.

The route that had been chosen was not altogether unpleasant, although the troupe did need to avoid main roads and cities near any Roman garrisons, so the travel took longer than it might normally.

They all agreed on a cover story, too, to allay suspicion and offer a way to move the treasure more discreetly. They were, they said, a traveling ensemble, specializing in ragtime and novelty songs. In some burgs and inns, they got strange looks and double takes, especially when it required two roadies to, for example, carry in the clarinet case.

More than once during the voyage, the company spirited itself out of a place in the middle of the night after catching wind of troops or possible Roman spies nearby.

Throughout, there was little time or opportunity for discussion or explanations about the events of the past. Each night, a gathering would be held to talk through plans. Often this took place in the corner of an inn or the snuggery of a pub. In the interest of openness, everyone in the company was invited to take part. At times during these discussions, locals would gather round and urge the group to play a set or two.

"Sorry, but our drummer has laryngitis," Nimbus would explain, "and the manager is going through an ugly divorce."

This information would usually startle away any solicitors. Still, there was always a commotion among the group. And the group, little by little, kept getting bigger and bigger. From town to town, people would decide that there was something appealing about these traveling musicians. Every day, another handful of escaping slaves, pooped housewives and recent grads searching for identity would find a way to join up.

As they reached the foothills near Italy, Paul managed to get some alone time with Caesar. He showed him the message of Spartacus that had been kept with the chests.

"He said someone could start a new empire with this money," Paul said. "That's really something."

"How fun," Caesar said, sliding on a pair of half-moon reading glasses and taking the letter. "So Spartacus was your dad? You know, I'm glad he got all that gold from Licinius Crassus. The guy could be a real pecker. I remember the time he sold me a thousand shares of stock in a company that supposedly had found a cure for the hiccups in farm animals. Never saw a dime from that."

"What do you think? What will we end up doing with all the money?"

Caesar shrugged.

Later that night, Paul talked with Little Frankie about the lands far from Rome.

"There is a giant sea up there unlike anything you could imagine," Little Frankie said. "Remember those knots I tied, to pull everyone up the garbage chute back in Rome? My people are born to take to the sea. Not to be immodest, but I could rig a sail or pilot a boat that would make the Roman trireme look like a dinghy."

Paul wanted particularly to get some time with Nimbus.

But when Little Frankie and Nimbus weren't traveling or talking with the larger group, they spent a good deal of time off in corners, hunched and whispering to each other. Presumably discussing plans for the troupe's future. Finally, a day away from where Paul was to meet his mother, he got a few minutes with Nimbus in a motel bar after one of the group's nightly gatherings.

"Mark Antony purchased me immediately following the Ides of March," Nimbus told him. The man spoke as prosaically as always, never giving off emotion. "He wanted to gain information out of me about Caesar and the secret document. However, I have learned some lessons over the years about discretion and was able to keep my confidences."

Paul mentioned that his former girlfriend Olivia had once said Nimbus knew everyone and everything going on in Rome.

"That is flattering hyperbole," Nimbus said. "But I did have reason to keep my ears open, as the saying goes, and to conduct a search of my own these past years."

"What is your connection to all this, to the treasure and everything?" Paul asked. "You said you had a lot to explain to me."

Just then, someone came up and handed Nimbus a slip of paper requesting a performance of "The Riverport Stomp." Another clutch of people gathered round and started up a drinking game. The night was lost, and Paul didn't get any more explanation from Nimbus then.

On the evening he was to go meet his mother, Paul felt unaccountably nervous. For one thing, he knew he should brace himself for disappointment. There was every reason to believe that his message had not made it through. Or that his mother could not or would not come. And then Caesar gave voice to another worry.

"It could be a set up. If Antony's agent's intercepted the message you sent, the lodge might be crawling with Roman troops. That's why I suggested this particular lodge for you to meet. It has lots and lots of exits, if need be. I had a conference there once with a Gallic viceroy and his seven burly sons. I can tell you, I kept looking over at the fire escape the whole time."

Paul swallowed hard. Caesar told him of a precarious backway path to the lodge that might be difficult to traverse but ultimately more prudent. No sense walking up the front driveway into a waiting ambush, he pointed out.

"May I make a suggestion?" Caesar asked. "Bring Nimbus with you. There were times the man maddened me with his relentless efficiency. But his judgment is nearly never off. And even though he doesn't show these things, I know he's taken a liking to you and would hate seeing you get hurt. By the way, I hope you know I feel the same."

The sentiment warmed Paul. But he demurred. The journey was one he would do on his own.

Summer had melted most of the high mountain ice. As Paul found himself making his way up an alp, the gravel and dirt still were slushy with ooze. More than once during the hike up, he wasn't sure whether his rope sandals would keep him on the narrow trail; one slip would mean his last words being heard, with the Doppler Effect, by a mountain goat. As he saw the roof of the lodge come into view, he struggled to take in a deep breath of the scant air and then gave himself another push.

She was there, alone.

Standing on the back porch, in a light blue dress and her hair down, his mother smiled.

"Paul. My little son. The son of Spartacus."

He had forgotten about the placid lilac essence she always wore. They hugged a very long time.

"I am returning these to you," she finally said to Paul. She held the three Libertas coins he had given her back in his little efficiency apartment on the Ides of March. "I could never spend them. They reminded me too much of you and your spirit."

"Mother." Paul grinned. "I wish you had spent them for yourself. When you find out how much money we found, you are going to ..."

He was going to say "lose your mind" but stopped himself. Instead he grasped her for another long embrace.

She emitted, then, a low sound that sounded a lot like a "huh?" Her arms fell away from him and she pulled back.

"Andre?" She spoke with a doubtful lilt. She was looking directly behind Paul. "Andre Finch? Can it really be?"

The moment brought back to Paul all his fears of his mother's gabbling and apparitional meanderings back in Rome. The thought for a second flashed into him that she really had been unhinged the whole time.

He turned around expecting to find that she had begun addressing air. But there, coming up the path behind Paul, arose Caesar's former servant. He had apparently followed Paul up the path. His presence at this moment surprised Paul almost as much as when he had encountered the man with a machete weeks earlier.

But his activity just now startled him even more than his emergence. Nimbus had initiated a function, as he approached Paul and his mother, that Paul did not think the man capable of. Tears were guttering down his face.

"Yes, it is I," Nimbus said to Paul's mother, touching her fingers with his own. "I have not heard the name of my birth in many, many years. And how long it has been since I have been able to call you by yours, my dear Ellia? I began to fear we would never again actually – "

He pulled out a handkerchief and stiffly wiped away the wet from his cheeks, before putting it to his nose to blow a long resonant honk.

No army signalman ever bugled so melodically.

FAR

They made it. Led by an increasingly bushed donkey, the growing company of refugees made it beyond the borders of the empire of Rome, bribing their way past the last legionary garrison in northwest Germania and then, for safe passage, doling out big presents to the dubious tribal nations they passed through on the way farther up and away.

They built a small city. Their little community rose near the beach not far from where Little Frankie had grown up, within spitting distance of the island of Britannia. Paul, during all this time, finally got all the explanations about everything he had been waiting for. In between urban planning, evading capture and building a hidden new society, they all settled up any outstanding information they had for each other.

The accounts all came together somewhat nicely. Somewhat like – like, thought Paul at one point – like a pretty well bound rope sandal.

Nimbus began telling his own part immediately after getting back down from the lodge with Paul and his mother.

He had been born in the south of Gaul, Nimbus said, with the name Andre Michel Finch. Born into slavery, he had been relatively well taken care of all his life, as far as being a slave went. He was eventually purchased by the owner of a large discount liquor chain in Rome, who eventually made him general manager. But as soon as he heard about the fight for freedom, he knew he had to take part. He walked from the home of his master one night, left Rome and found his way to the rebel army.

That was more than a quarter century ago. Spartacus recognized his talent almost immediately. Nimbus became the right hand of Spartacus during the Servile War – his trusted advisor, CFO, and top deputy.

"I'll be damned," Caesar said as he heard the account. "So my man Nimbus was one of the leaders of the slave rebellion. At least I can say I was as smart as Spartacus to pick you out when I had the chance."

"I'm afraid there is more to it," Nimbus said. "It may be more accurate to say I chose you, mighty Caesar."

He continued his account. As the Roman army led by Licinius Crassus had been closing in on the rebel slaves, Spartacus gave Nimbus two assignments. First, he was to arrange a safe haven apartment for his wife Ellia up in Rome. Ellia would sneak out of the rebel camp. Then Nimbus was to leave himself a short while later.

"What did Spartacus mean doing all that?" asked Caesar. "I'm fully confused."

"Spartacus knew a few things for sure that night. He knew Crassus would defeat his army the next day. He had in the meantime gotten all the treasure taken from Crassus spirited away to be buried in the town of his birth. The problem was how and when to let others know about the treasure in the future, when the time for another rebellion might be ripe. He knew he could not tell any single person everything. Doing so would put such a person in too much danger of the Roman torturers. So he asked Ellia to hide in Rome. Of course, he also wanted her safe from the coming battle. He then had me leave the rebel camp too. I was to wander about Italy for some months or even years, carrying the document he had written. The puzzler. I was to wait until circumstances settled before getting the paper to her. In effect, he had it all in code and kept us both half in the dark. The code would be solved by Ellia, who alone would have known it referred to his childhood back in his hometown."

"Nicely done," Caesar said. "Gosh, I'm sure I would have liked that man."

"I had been trying to find Ellia for many years," Nimbus continued, "Spartacus used to refer to myself as the key and Ellia as the tumbler. I understand now fully why. He had given each of us enough information so that together we could find the treasure."

"But what happened?" Paul asked. "What went wrong? How come you never got the puzzler to my mother back in Rome."

"This is a question that has troubled me for some time. I had arranged for a hiding place for her in an apartment in a removed part of Rome. But when I went to find her, she was not there. So I had to do everything in my powers to otherwise discover her location. I knew your mother. I knew she would be somewhere waiting, in the memory of Spartacus, wherever she was and for as long as she could."

Paul's mother had been half listening to all this. She was busy cutting up toffee and passing it around the table.

"I am sorry about the trouble, my dear Andre," she said. "I can't understand it. For all those years, I waited for you. Roseway Apartments, 346 East Pine Road, Unit 51. Isn't that the address you gave me?"

It could not have been easy for Nimbus to retain his full composure at this point, but he did so.

"No, my sweet Ellia," he told Paul's mother gently. "You were supposed to be waiting for me at the Pine Apartments, 51 East Rose Way, Unit 346."

"Oh dear," Paul's mother said, as she knifed into a square.

Yes, Paul thought, she wasn't mad and incoherent all these years, as he had once thought, but his mother certainly had always been something of a dingbat.

"This explains much," Nimbus acknowledged. "I must confess that the hunt over the past decades did tax my abilities. That is where you came in helpful, O Caesar. I changed my name to Nimbus after leaving the rebel camp. After I learned of the demise of Licinius Crassus in Parthia, I felt Rome might be safe again and worked my way back there. I decided I would try to get myself into your service. The broker who sold me to you as a slave was actually in my employ. I paid the man to approach you and offer me to you, and I arranged for you to feel you had made a great bargain in bringing me in as your house-slave. I knew that such a position would give me access to a good deal of information, to help me locate Ellia so we could fulfill Spartacus's last wish."

"Spot on!" said Caesar. "You truly are a clever chap. I should have used you for more than tying my toga and looking after the household."

"To further enlarge my network of information, I joined the Junior Zeus Club for domestic servants. Our club president was a man who called himself the Major. He told me of his daughter becoming acquainted with a certain young Impelled Maniac. He told me this young man's mother had the habit of mumbling supposedly outlandish stories about Spartacus and Licinius Crassus. I thought quite possibly this could be Ellia. So I am afraid through my manipulation, I interfered with young Paul's love life in a number of attempts to get information. If you wondered why your female companion behaved rather erratically with you, I'm afraid you were feeling the effects of my work on the mind of the Major. I regrettably felt it necessary to use her to try to drive you into being open to more risk and ventures."

"And you're the one who kept calling me to take messages from Caesar," Paul said, "to learn more from me and get me involved."

"Just so. I hoped to shape you into a confident and proud freedom fighter."

Annette, looking out the window, noted that the sun had started rising. It was time to move on.

"Perhaps we best complete telling this tale later," said Nimbus. "There is just a little more to unfold."

When the refugees made it beyond Rome's control, having gone through very few of their gold coins, and decided to build a town, they wanted to name it the City of Spartacus. Much as he liked the idea, Nimbus pointed out this might raise suspicion if Antony found out. Caesar personally lobbied for the place to be named either Cool Town, I Hate Mondays or Steubenville.

"One finds you just have to let him talk sometimes," Nimbus whispered to Paul while Caesar went on. "It will pass."

Nimbus told Paul more than once that he actually always rather liked Caesar, despite the man's foibles. When he had heard rumors that Antony was preparing to turn on Caesar, Nimbus had been the one to send the message to beware the Ides of March.

"I should have known that warning would not take with him," Nimbus confessed. "But I had to try. He never paid heed when I attempted to tell him anything directly, so one always had to find circuitous means. Hints need to be dropped with Caesar over the course of time."

It was Nimbus who had piqued Caesar's interest in word game in the first place and told him about the intriguing puzzler itself. He then put the bug in Caesar's ear about announcing the game publically.

"It was a rather desperate idea," Nimbus said, "but I hoped your mother would hear the words and perhaps search me out through Caesar."

Eventually everyone settled on a suitably unprovocative name for their new community, one not likely to attract much attention. It was Annette's idea. They called their town Donk.

By the time they reached the coast, they had picked up several dozen new followers, and construction went quickly. An architectural firm was hired and laborers brought in from the countryside, all of them making more than they ever had in their lives. In fact, most of them ended up building houses for themselves there.

In time, Donk became a haven for more escaped slaves and expatriates from the civil war. They brought news about Rome and the world beyond.

One year, the former operator of the *Veni Vidi Vendi* Green Grocer Wagon in Rome showed up. He'd been run out of business by a protection racket. He had financed his trip up north using the proceeds from the strange looking gems tied to a ribbon he had found floating in the Tiber one day. The jeweler he'd sold it to used the word "diadem."

The Assistant Accountant of The Winged Owl Messaging Service appeared. He brought with him stories, as well as Paul's official work file. Paul had failed to fill out an exit interview form before leaving his job in Rome.

"The rumors of you and this town are swirling throughout the city," he told Paul.

He told also of a clandestine memorial that had been sculpted in a defunct aqueduct tunnel at the edge of Rome. It had become a covert shrine of sorts to those who wanted to remember the old Republic. With its winsome smile and cheerful eyes, the bust of Cassius looked almost unrecognizable, and an extra large block of marble had been needed to do justice to Brutus's hairdo. That is how they would be remembered.

"They both got at least something of what they always wanted in the end," Little Frankie remarked.

A copy of Antony's first State of the Empire address made it to Donk. There was lavish praise for his lamented good friend Caesar. And among Antony's threats and promises, a single line was noted. The government of Rome, Mark Antony announced, would be painting street addresses on everyone's curbs, for free.

The Outside Communications Consultant, it was learned, had been subsidized all along by Antony to be part of the Opposition. Antony considered the man's ideas entirely imbecilic and wanted him to continue in his advisory role to keep flummoxing everyone up more than they already were on their own.

Following the defeat of the Opposition, The Outside Communications Consultant had landed a consulting contract in Persia. There he engineered an ill-considered publicity campaign that had the newly widowed king taking part in a night of speed dating. The King of Persia had the man's head chopped off the following day.

News eventually came that Mark Antony had started a dalliance with the Egyptian queen Cleopatra.

"Won't be good for him," said Caesar. "Antony had it in for me, and the guy is entirely too serious. Which made it a hoot to see his pupils get big when he figured I didn't know what he was talking about. But still, even those who ought to suffer certain fates probably don't always deserve them."

Finally, word arrived that young Octavian – the eager student to Antony and distant relation of Julius Caesar – had proven himself the best dissembler of all. As Antony got more and more distracted with Cleopatra, Octavian smushed Antony's fleet and all his legions. This took place not far from Philippi. Octavian then gave himself the name Augustus Caesar and paraded around saying the Republic was back in business, with one difference. Augustus Caesar would be calling all the shots. He took on a title the people of Rome were not used to just yet. He called himself the first Emperor of Rome.

Antony reportedly had written an autobiography centering on his relationship with Julius Caesar (working title: "It Was Me All Along") but ended up committing suicide before finalizing with his literary agent.

Augustus Caesar heard about the city of Donk. He began sending threatening envoys. By this time, the city had thousands of inhabitants and was becoming a notable center of nettlesome activity outside the control of Rome. Augustus Caesar made his intentions clear. It would only be a matter of time before he marched troops up and attacked. Like the village of Spartacus, everything they had built up would be torn down, and they would all become hunted fugitives again.

"It's kind of unthinkable," reported Caesar. "After all this. That precocious, astigmatic twerp. Calling himself Augustus now and making himself dictator for life. I met him a couple times at family reunions. My uncle's cousin's son's something-or-other. Someone said he's actually been going around Rome with some kind of document claiming I intended to adopt him. Of course, I never thought much of the child. Always seemed more the towel-boy-holding-the-squirt-bottle sort rather than the quarterback. No offense, my dear Paul. It just goes to show, you can't trust appearances. Still, it's all bad for us. When you think about it, we're all in no better of a place than we were when we squeaked out of Rome. Worse, really. How does the expression go? 'All roads lead away from Rome'? The problem is, we're clean out of the damned things. Out of roads, that is."

Nimbus and Little Frankie, however, did have one final idea.

AT LAST

I t fell to Nimbus to begin unfolding the plan. He spoke at one of the weekly gatherings that tended to take place in a plain just outside Donk.

"The proposal you are about to hear might stretch credulity. Yet it might be that we have all already traversed together beyond the borders of the plausible. Put less poetically, I think there is a way. Our colleague Frank Littleton and I have been spending some time conferring and calculating. I turn now to him to offer the specificities."

"A mythical land," said Little Frankie, addressing the city's populace. "Those of us growing up around here always heard stories of a mythical land, clear on the other side of the great sea. In talking with Nimbus, and consulting maps and myth, I believe it all to be true. It would require some first rate shipwrights and really good piloting, I admit. But there are said to be routes that would take us far north of Britannia, and then, when it gets so cold that you can make crushed ice with your tears, you start heading west, and then you go south, south, south, until you come to a place far away from here. According to ancient legend, it is said to be a big and green land with no emperors, no slaves and very few meetings."

It was exactly the kind of bold enterprise that could be expected to appeal to a city built with the dreams of hope-infused refugees – they who had wagered their lives and renounced family to flee an empire, they whose intrepid spirits had converged to share an inflexible devotion to freedom.

"It is," said the first Donkard to address the proposal, "it is by far the stupidest, most dangerous and squirrel-brained idea in the history of stupidity."

For some time, the rest of the population stared wordlessly at

Little Frankie and Nimbus. With a cricket chirp and the bounce of a tumbleweed, the image would have been complete. The gathering broke apart, and it seemed the idea dissolved with it.

A strange thing then happened. During the growth of Donk, Paul had largely reverted to his old patterns and habits. His experiences getting there had changed the way he regarded a lot about life. But mostly he pitched in quietly here and there and let others take the lead. (Looking at Paul, the only noticeable difference to be found might be an ever so slight bit of surplus weight around the midsection: He had not missed a meal since crossing Rome's borders.)

Yet over the coming weeks, the people of Donk started talking to Paul about the plan. They stopped him in the street or met up with him in the field, coming singly or in small groups. They wanted his opinion. It was a position Paul had never experienced and didn't especially like.

"We know," an old-timer explained. "We know all of what your father did, and what you done, and we know that without you, we wouldn't even of had a chance."

Paul told everyone who asked him that he always figured Nimbus and Little Frankie knew what they were talking about. He said too that it didn't seem to make sense to just give up without a fight. Or a run.

In the end, about two thirds of the people of Donk signed up for the last journey. The rest divided up the remaining gold to spread forth and create new lives elsewhere. Those staying back all vowed to use the money to agitate for freedom one way or another.

The night before the ships set sail from Donk, there was a modest wedding ceremony in one of the nondenominational churches in the city square.

Paul had noticed his mother spending a lot of time with Nimbus after their reunion at the lodge. His father Spartacus had been right: Paul's mother and Nimbus were yin and yang, tumbler and key. So it was not at all surprising when she asked Nimbus to stand up in her wedding. He, of course, agreed, and he was pleased to hear who she would be marrying.

Since the Alps, Paul's mother and Caesar had rekindled the friendship they started in Rome at Paul's efficiency apartment. His mother had grown tired of being alone, and she liked listening to Caesar's stories. For his part, Caesar – though he didn't quite realize at first – had fallen madly in love with Ellia. He gave her a set of steak knives for a wedding present.

Annette presided over the service. One day she had declared

herself high priestess of Donk. The title meant nothing, but the townspeople sat through her sermons every Sunday. She was barely intelligible, but it gave them time to sit and think about what they wanted to do in the upcoming week.

"Naturally, I would have married you myself," Nimbus told Paul's mother at the wedding reception they had on the beach later that night. "If things had been different for me."

Another modest wedding ceremony followed the next morning, with the newlyweds Caesar and Ellia now standing up: During their time together, it became clear, Nimbus and Little Frankie had apparently planned for more than a community escape. Love was in the air of Donk.

Paul's mother and her new husband said they were too set in their ways to travel to a wholly new land. They talked about maybe finding a place to settle out east. Bithynia possibly, or Crete. Caesar heard there might even be nice weather and interesting things popping in a place called Judea. He thought they might go there.

Paul, his mother Ellia and Gaius Julius Caesar did a hand holding circle for a good amount of time before the boson's whistle called final boarding.

"It is something, my Paul," said Caesar pensively, "we both were forced from Rome to look for what we didn't know we weren't seeking. And yet we found it."

Caesar had on the baggy caftan and stretch-waistband slacks of his own design that he had taken to wearing. Paul nodded. To him, Caesar's observation made perfect sense.

"And Caesar," Caesar murmured, "only hopes everyone can feel as smiling as I do right now."

Before they separated, Paul confessed to his mother that during all the years she had been trying to tell him the truth about herself and his father and everything else, he had thought her quite mad. She found this touching.

"You mean you spent all that time sitting there, thinking you were just soothing your screwy mother? I can't think of a better way for a son to show how much he cares."

So they all left behind the city of Donk that they had built. The crossing to the new lands took the fleet three seasons, and five of the ships turned back at various points. But everyone who made it found the lands to be verdant and welcoming. On an island in a harbor near where the refugees of Rome eventually settled, Paul buried the three Libertas coins he had gotten from Cassius. He pushed dirt over them with his sandals and patted it all down.

"A symbol of our hope," he told a curious local resident who watched him doing this from afar. "Someday someone can put up a bigger monument to freedom here. We'll see."

Her name – the name of the curious local in the new lands who asked Paul why he had buried those coins with his rope sandals – was a hard-to-pronounce word. In her local dialect, her name meant Striped Towel. She smiled at him cockeyed when he offered his explanation. Paul smiled back.

She asked Paul how he and his friends had gotten there. He told her as best he could that they built great ships to escape an ominous empire and used these ships to cross perilously over the great sea between their two lands.

"Oh, you mean that big wet thing out there?" Striped Towel said. "Here we call it 'the ocean.' But, either way works."

The following spring, Paul asked permission of her clan chief, a nice man called Standing Water, to marry her. The chief nodded. The chief always nodded. Everyone in the new lands turned out to be very agreeable. No one there even knew what a helmet was, either.

Striped Towel took to referring to Paul as my Little Fet-Fet. Paul could not be sure if this was to be taken as a term of endearment or a speech impediment, but he went with it, and in time it is what most everyone called him.

They had many children together. To their first child they gave the first name Tin.

Whenever her classmates poked fun of this, her parents told her she must explain to them the story behind her entire name, the whole train, front to back. Anyone hearing it will be too awed or too puzzled to keep making a bother, they promised her.

Tin Spartaca Ellia Caesarea Brut-Cassia agreed.

"We make a pretty good alloy, don't we?" Paul told Striped Towel and Tin one night at the dinner table in their little home. "We all seem to work well together."

There's not much more to say about any of this, I guess.

The travelers brought with them a good deal of writing supplies, which helped pass the time as we got ourselves situated. I managed to gather a lot of the letters and various writings others picked up along the way, too. Plus there's everything I learned through my information networks over the years.

When I finish covering these rolls with ink and pasting in the last of these documents, in a couple minutes, I'll roll everything up and squeeze it all into one of the amphorae we used to bring some foodstuffs over here. Maybe like the treasure of Spartacus, these will be found one day. Although, I have no reason to believe anyone would take much interest in them. As for myself, I will say there are certainly things – and certainly people – that I miss about the place I came from. But it had its downsides. For one, I always hated having to help Julius Caesar put on his toga.

Editor's note: Only one artifact connected with the lost scrolls you have completed reading has survived: The olive jar in which they had been allegedly stored. As this book went to print, laboratories at the New Jersey Institute of Technology – near the site where the documents were found – announced the results of recent advanced thermal testing.

The results reveal that the vessel had been formed with a clay mixture found only in Europe circa 100 to 50 BC. A faded inscription inside the jar was also discovered. It reads: "Zingerman & Zingerman Delicatessen, Quality Foods of Rome."

THE END

Glossary of Significant Persons, Places and Etcetera

Antony. *AN-tony* (Mark Antony). Chief supporter of and advisor to Julius Caesar. Talented military commander and administrator. Kept himself in shape.

Caesar. *SEEZ-er*. (Gaius Julius Caesar). Part of established ruling class in Rome. Gained dominant political power largely through military achievements, especially his conquering of the province of Gaul (modern day France). Also advanced his position through popular speeches, well-admired memoirs, and being generally upbeat about things.

Opposition, Roman Senate. Grouping of Senators organized for the primary purpose of thwarting the activities of Julius Caesar and his political party. Chief Opposition leaders:

> **Brutus.** *BROOT-us* (Marcus Junius Brutus). Widely esteemed by all classes and political parties of Rome as fair-minded, kind-hearted, honorable and often tanned.

> **Casca.** *CASK-uh* (Publius Servilius Casca). Regular chairman of Opposition meetings. Hobbies included scuba, making own wine, clog dancing.

> **Cassius.** *CASH-us* (Gaius Cassius Longinus). Primary organizer of Opposition, known for stubborn attachment to traditional principles of Republic. For disambiguation, see also *Cassius (boyband)*.

> **Cicero**. *SIS-er-oh* (Marcus Tullius Cicero). In Late Republican period, renowned orator, barrister-at-law and CPA.

> **Livius the Younger**. LIV-ee-us thuh YUNG-er. (Livius the Younger). Little is known about early life and career, except that he might have once won a Christmas tree in a raffle of some kind.

> **Pompilius Pulcher**. *Pom-PILL-ee-us PULL-cur* (Reginald Pompilius Pulcher). Member of wealthy Pulcher family, self-avowed reader of romance novels and contributing editor to *Natty Hats (and More!)* men's magazine.

> **Totovus**. *Toe-TOE-vus* (Lucius Crispius Totovus). Modestly regarded political figure. Listed in existing Senate rolls as only known member to participate in every frequent-diners

reward program offered in Republic.

Nomenclature. A Roman citizen would be given three names at birth, in the following order: the *praenomen* (one's given name), the *nomen* (indicating gens or clan) and the *cognomen* (name of family line within the gens). This system was confusing to many Romans, who consequently often greeted each other with forced enthusiasm as "Hey Monkey Boy!" or else acted in conversation like they knew the other person's name but found a way to avoid having to say it.

Quince. An oblong fruit common to the Middle East and borne by a small deciduous tree. Rind can get pretty tough at times.

Vomitorium. This is not what you think, really. You can look it up yourself.

ABOUT THE AUTHOR

- ✓ Daily newspaper reporter and columnist.
- ✓ Speechwriter and press secretary to politicians.
- ✓ Lawyer.

As soon as he earns his state certification to become an HMO claims analyst, John Hoffman will have wallowed in all of the most disdained professions available in contemporary society.

John earned his journalism degree at the University of Illinois/Champaign-Urbana. He wrote a humor column for *The Daily Journal* (Wheaton, Illinois) and subsequently stumbled into a law degree and political communications work.

For bonus content – including an exclusive sample of John's five-volume opus on the life of legendary South American liberator Granblaniar – please visit JohnKHoffman.com

COVER ARTIST

Cover design and artwork by © Michael J. Mikottis. To explore more high quality original works, visit MikeMikottisArtworks.com

24205894R00170

Made in the USA
Lexington, KY
17 December 2018